SECRET SIDE

R. A. Jordan

To Terri.

Thank you for your help with the Rally arrangements.

Rajinda.

May 2019

Book five in a series of five books chronicling the lives of Sandra and Sienna Wall during the first decade of the twenty-first century.

PREVIOUS BOOKS BY R.A.JORDAN:

TIME'S UP

ENGLAND'S WALL

LAUNDRY

CRACKS IN THE WALL

The author's web site is: www.rajordan.co.uk

CONTENTS

ACKNOWLEDGMENTS

The author acknowledges the help of numerous people who are known to him, who have provided invaluable assistance or information used in the writing of this book. They may have been unaware of their contribution, provided in conversations but such insights were stored away for future use.

Thank you to everyone who has assisted in writing the whole of this pentalogy.

"There are many experiences and adventures, happy times and sad times, opportunities taken and regrets forgotten in the fulfilment of a full life.

During the experiences of life there are moments, fleeting moments that are banished to the inner recesses.

They are a secret.

They form your 'Secret Side'."

- Robert Jordan, 2018.

PROLOGUE

TIME'S UP

The Walls lose the head of the family – father and husband Peter – on New Year's Day in the year 2000. Suicide, rather than murder, seems the only logical explanation. As Chairman and founder of Wall's Civil Engineers in Chester, he had amassed land and debts. His two daughters Sandra and Sienna, discover just how deep the problems are.

There are valuable insurance policies on Peter's life that should pay out to his business partner, Roger Whiteside and Ann, his widow.

Sandra, a commercial lawyer, takes control of Wall's and Sienna, a chartered surveyor, becomes managing director of Wall's developments, which in the boom of the millennium, become very successful once land ownership is sorted out.

The family's new solicitor, John England, is a tower of strength to Ann Wall. He becomes romantically involved with Sienna. The Police are convinced that Peter's unusual death is suicide, but as they are about to get a decision from the Coroner the situation changes. Who will benefit from the insurance money and how will the Police unravel the death of Peter?

It transpires he was murdered and the murderer was found to be Peter's business partner Roger Whiteside. As the police were breaking the news to the Wall family the news came through that Whiteside had been found – dead in the River Dee.

ENGLAND'S WALL

Casual, drunken sex has consequences, not least of which is an unwanted pregnancy. But how is this connected twenty-five years later with the unusual death of prominent business man Peter Wall, the murder of his employee Fred Appleyard, and then the murder of his business partner Roger Whiteside?

England's Wall relates to how Peter Wall's family, his wife Ann, and daughters Sandra and Sienna, cope with the deaths and pick up the pieces of the business. At the same time they are dealing with an arson attack on some empty houses at Squirrels Chase, a new development site, the plot thickens. Then there is an attempted murder of Sienna's boyfriend, John England and the suspicion that Sienna had been administered Rohypnol during a supposed business meeting but why?

As a result of Peter's death there is a large amount of insurance money at stake. These events seem to indicate that someone outside the family is trying to extract a share, and is prepared to go to any lengths to achieve that end. The result was that a rouge developer was to blame. He was Dafydd Jones. Both Jones and Whiteside as young men after a party at the local working men's club in Wrexham picked up a girl in Dafydd's van and offered her a lift home. They were all drunk. Before arriving in Mold where she lived the boys had illicit sex with the girl. No more was said until the girl, Gwyneth, discovered she was pregnant. She was shipped off to a relative in Wrexham during her confinement. Her father was still furious and determined to discover the identity of the boys responsible. Gwyneth died in childbirth, but first received the forgiveness of her father in hospital. She gave him Whiteside's name as the father.

Young Rhys Williams was raised by his grandparents. He did well at school and university ending up with a job in North Wales Police forensic laboratory.

Rhys was involved with the DNA testing of Whiteside. Eventually John England found him and through the DNA sample was able to declare Rhys was the legal heir to Whiteside and inherited his fortune.

LAUNDRY

A fortune beckons Wayne and Michael into the buy-to-let market. They even find a financier Niall Phelan, open-handed enough to run a charity to save youngsters from drugs too. The pair, using Niall's money, form a strong business relationship with Wall's developments allowing their customers to buy properties constructed by Wall's to maximise their profit.

John England and Sienna Wall were married. Sienna's godfather Frank Stringer gave her away. He had been given a life sentence for killing Roger Whiteside. He was the family doctor. At the wedding he arranged for an envelope to be given to him, which contained poison. He took the pills and died in police custody.

There is little to suspect the horse racing aficionado Niall, when he requires Michael and Wayne to move all profits to Spain on a weekly basis, there is nothing the two boys can do about it. The agreement they signed in the beginning gave Phelan all the power in the business.

They were then forced to work for a man they no longer trusted. Their business was booming with the help of Wall's, but misgivings and mounting evidence that Niall was not the man they thought they knew. Only his PA Sarah, can identify her brother's torso outside the stud Niall used in Tarporley near Chester. The owner of the stables Jo Stafford transported horses from Ireland to England and back again for Niall Phelan. He also was transporting drugs in a secret compartment in the horse box, as well as the torso which he tried to hide in the copse opposite the stables. He was discovered by the police. From jail he agreed to sell the stables to Sandra, as the horses had to be attended to.

If their worst fears are true, they are already framed as money launderers for the international drugs trade. If Niall suspects them of spilling the beans, how long before they too, are found dead? They had a dilemma.

Wayne is murdered in Spain when someone tampers with his Ferrari, and his now girlfriend and PA to Phelan, Sarah Perlaki, was severely injured. She was killed by Phelan whilst in hospital. Once two of the three signatories to the bulging Spanish bank account, Phelan being the remaining signatory, emptied the account to his bank in Ireland.

When Michael Fitzallen discovered this he was furious. He knew there was no chance of recovering the money from Phelan. He was introduced to a shady character called 'Goose'. He had a super yacht 'Wild Goose' tied up in Puerto Banus. He agreed to get Michael's millions back for him in exchange for a significant fee. Goose, by way of a long journey in his motor yacht shipped what Phelan believed to be a large quantity of cocaine. It turned out not to be so, but cement. Phelan in a rage opening every packet himself triggered a pressure switch in a bomb and killed him and two other helpers. Goose fled in his boat.

The money was recovered for the 'false' drugs in cash when the handover took place at sea twenty miles off the Irish coast. Goose placed this money in offshore banks. He tricked Michael when he gave him fake euros, which nearly landed Michael in jail in Switzerland.

Michael's task was now to recover the real money from Goose.

CRACKS IN THE WALL

John and Sienna welcomed young James Peter England into the world on the 17th September 2007. Soon after whilst at the shops in Tarporley young James was kidnapped. The desperation in the England household was at maximum. The police headed by DI Jon Kim did everything they could to recover the child.

At more or less the same time the bank put the boot into Wall's saying all its borrowings were to be paid off by the end of January 2008. This amounted to more than three million pounds. There were substantial assets but the bank would not agree to allow the loans to run further.

Sienna was married to a local solicitor John England, who was also solicitor to Wall's Holdings, found themselves in the centre of a massive hunt for their baby James.

Simultaneously the banking crisis hit the UK and other international finance centres. The mortgage business for the buy-to-let properties the company was building virtually dried up. The banks, very nervous having been bailed out by government themselves, wanted overdrafts paid off. The added pressure on Sandra as CEO of Wall's coupled with her sister's distress at the kidnap of James was almost too much for the family. Eventually due to an error in the police photograph of James, he was found. The money however was still owed to the bank. In desperation Sandra placed adverts to try and sell half of the block in Manchester. To her amazement Michael Fitzallen sitting in Spain reading the Sunday Times responded. He then bought half with the cash Goose had recovered for him.

Wall's were off the hook.

Fitzallen and Goose hatched a plan to look after classic cars, and then secretly sell some cars to a contact in the Middle East. They hired a young mechanic Terry Pritchard, the nephew of John and Sienna's domestic help. Fitzallen used the services of his drug distributor Ali to arrange for the removal of six expensive cars one weekend, and put them into containers, and they were on their way abroad. The premises they used at Sealand in Chester belonged to Ann Wall, previously used as the Wall's headquarters. As soon as the cars had gone Ali, on Fitzallen's instructions, set fire to the premises. Terry, who had a previous conviction when a child for arson, was convicted of the offence and sent to jail

DS Tarrant and DI Jon Kim despite the conviction of Terry, were uneasy that there was another hand in the arson attack.

The problems for the Wall family seem never-ending.

CHAPTER 1

Detective Chief Inspector Jon Kim, now 55, was at retirement age for a Police Officer – retirement was too early for Jon, a prospect he didn't relish.

Jon's life had been one of great contrasts: he was born in Hong Kong to a Chinese mother and father both of whom worked in the hospitality industry – well, when asked in their later lives that is how they explained it. His mother, in fact, was a waitress of a large restaurant in Hong Kong whilst his father was a doorman at the InterContinental hotel. He was exceptionally proud of his uniform and having achieved senior status he was put in charge of training younger members of staff, in the art of hailing taxis, opening doors and carrying bags.

When young Jon was born in 1955 his mother took some time off, but not long. Jon saw more of his grandmother than his own mother and father. He believes he owes his success to the upbringing by his grandmother. A very traditional Chinese lady who kept the house spotlessly clean which having regard to the house and the weather was a feat only she could achieve. She had ambitions for young Jon; education, education, she would repeat over and over. She ensured that Jon never missed a days' schooling, to his ultimate advantage.

Jon couldn't recall his grandfather; by all accounts a strict disciplinarian and a man of upright stature, very smart in his uniform. A member of the Royal Hong Kong police. He only made sergeant – Jon would have loved to have met him – the stories he could have told of the drug dens especially in Kowloon, would have been invaluable now. He never knew the man although those that had known him spoke very highly of him, which gave Jon an inner glow of pride.

Jon was educated in a local school: being an only child - the Chinese authorities not having any control of the birth of children in Hong Kong – nevertheless, their views extended on a psychological basis to the size of families. Many of Jon's friends at school were only children. He hadn't made many friends, it was not easy to ask people back home after school, so he made the most of every day in his own little world, a loner, but a clever one for all that. His academic abilities enabled him to win a scholarship to the Royal Hong Kong Police College where he was one of the top pupils of his year.

Once he graduated in 1977 at the age of 22, with a distinction, he was made a constable on the understanding that he would be fast-tracked through the force, so long as he passed the exams to allow him to progress.

Whilst he was a student, his favourite pastime and relaxation was to spend a Saturday in the Red Devil Bar. He would wear his Manchester United shirt and watch every match he could. Like many people in Hong Kong he was a gambler - not a big one but sufficient to make the matches interesting - yet when he won just a few tens of dollars he was so pleased he generously spent his winnings buying drinks for his friends, well, people he met at the Red Devil Bar, acquaintances really, still preferring his own company, the study of criminology, and the exploits of Manchester United. He would just love to go to the 'Theatre of Dreams' at Old Trafford Manchester just to see a match live for once. One day maybe.

As a constable in the Royal Hong Kong Police he dealt face-to-face at street level with some pretty nasty characters. Whilst he was not tall by western standards, he was tall for a Chinaman. He wore the uniform of the force with pride and cut quite a figure when out on patrol wearing the very familiar uniform of khaki shorts and shirt with brown leather belt and cross belt. The belt held his pistol. His hat was a flat peaked cap with a badge on the front: this badge was polished regularly as were his black shoes which reflected his long socks, which stopped just below the knee.

He loved his time in the force. His grandmother remained alive to see him graduate from Police College, but she had done her bit and passed away a week after he graduated. He was involved in the day to day policing of his neighbourhood in Kowloon, perhaps the rougher part of Hong Kong. The racketeers and drug dens were a daily part of the life of a constable in Hong Kong. Murder and extortion were a regular feature, and he became hardened to these events. Jon's abilities had seen him be promoted to Sergeant, his grandfather's rank, a point referred to by the Chief Constable when he was promoted. He was filled with pride and emotion by this.

He was determined to become a detective, so he worked as hard as he could, and without distractions of girlfriends, he made the rank of Detective Constable. His parents were very proud of Jon, although their lives were still very frugal. They worked every day. Jon never knew where they had contracted the Hong Kong flu which affected fifteen percent of the population. Jon's parents died from the disease quite shortly one after the other. Jon being in a privileged position was required and obtained an inoculation against the virus. His parents were cremated in an effort by the authorities to try and reduce the spread of the disease.

Despite being a loner he now felt more alone than ever. He threw himself more into his work more than ever before. This was at the time Hong Kong was subject to riots by the Chinese Communists who were agitating for the Colony to be handed back to the Chinese. On 30 June 1997, the lease the UK had on the island from China expired. Chris Patten was the Governor of the Colony. He was appointed specifically to negotiate the handover and for negotiating the on-going arrangements known as 'The Basic Law' which he hoped would be honoured by the Chinese after handover. It was the best that could be done.

Some residents, Jon, amongst them, who was now 43 and a senior detective in the force were given the opportunity to apply for and get a British passport. He was so excited at the prospect of going to Britain, so as to be that much closer to the love of his life Manchester United.

HMS Britannia took the Governor and Prince Charles back to Britain. The sight of the Royal Yacht departing the harbour in Hong Kong for good, was a sight that would live with Jon for the rest of his life. The colony, an outpost of Empire at an end, he decided it was time for a change, he had no ties and was good at his job. He had attained the status of Detective Sergeant and, no longer in uniform, he applied to the Metropolitan Police for a job – they were very pleased to see him.

Jon worked as a Detective Constable and then promoted to Detective Sergeant in the Met for three years until an opportunity arose for him to move to the Cheshire Force. They were short of experienced detectives so Jon's arrival was a great help in bolstering the forces ability to detect drug related crimes. Jon retained his rank. The attraction for Jon was to be closer to his beloved Manchester United. He had attended as many matches as he could whilst in London. The London games were always attended by him but Old Trafford, the theatre of dreams, was the place! He hadn't a season ticket but when he moved to Cheshire he promised himself to splash out on a season ticket in the Executive Stand once he arrived. He had never married although had a number of girlfriends in Hong Kong but failed to make a connection in the UK. He loved his job and knew the unsocial hours and the unexpected call in the middle of the night – the late nights would destroy a marriage – he'd seen it too many times with his colleagues.

At 55 he really didn't think he was ready for retirement – no, not yet. The Force's rules required you to retire then. His birthday being in December allowed him to stay until December the following year so he would be 56 when he retired – what to do then was the question!

His musing was brought to an abrupt halt by the phone. "Yes, Kim."

"Sir, we've had a possible murder."

"Wonderful!" he said ironically, "I was just thinking of going home! Where is it?"

"Tarporley, Sir."

"Very well, organise a car and tell me the details on the way."

The details were sketchy but the all too familiar name of 'Wall' was part of the story. The police car and two police constables stood guard over the scene. The SOCO team had arrived and the Home Office Pathologist had been summoned but not yet arrived. It was virtually dark when Kim arrived. The floodlights situated on the back of The Swan brought in a degree of illumination to this far corner of the car park.

Kim walked over to the corner when the body lay. He showed his warrant card to the PC on guard because he was not recognised. He enquired if anyone knew who the victim was and importantly who had found the body.

"No Sir. We have no information on identification. He may have something on his person that might help but we haven't touched the body."

"Who found the body?"

"This lady, Sir."

"Good evening. I'm Detective Superintendent Kim - and you are?"

"I'm Ann Wall, Superintendent. We have, I regret to say, met before."

"Oh yes Mrs Wall, we have. How did you come to discover the body?"

"Well, Superintendent, I live at Church Cottage just the other side of the churchyard. There is a path through the churchyard from this car park over there. I use this a lot as my preferred way home."

"When you left home – what time was that?"

"About 5 o'clock this evening. I needed to get some groceries I'd forgotten and a local paper. I was on my way home when I saw this pile of what looked at first sight like rags."

"Did you investigate the rags?"

"Yes, only to discover it was a body – not a pretty sight!"

"Did you phone the police?"

"No. I asked The Swan to do that. They gave me a small brandy as I was a bit upset."

"That was good of them. What time did you say this was?"

"It must have been about half five."

"Did you see the body on your way out?"

"No. I don't go out this way. For some reason I walk

along the pavement in the village on the way out. It is only on the way back I come this way."

"Mrs Wall, thank you for your assistance. We shall not detain you any longer. If we need to speak to you again I know where to find you."

"Thank you, Superintendent. It's been a bit of a trauma."

Kim understood very well the upset this event could cause a woman whose husband had been murdered. It would bring it all back.

The Home Office Pathologist had arrived. He and Kim exchanged pleasantries.

"No, I can't give you time of death but I will tell you one thing – she wasn't murdered here."

"She? Murder? Are you sure?"

"It isn't normal for a suicide victim to batter themselves to death with a blunt hammer-like object. That method produces a great deal of blood. There is none."

"Female as well - doesn't look like a girl?"

"Take it from me Kim it's female that I can be sure of," he said with a smirk on his face.

"Okay, a body dumped in a car park, that might be a simple matter to prove, I think. Does the Swan have CCTV Tarrant?" enquired Kim of his sergeant assistant.

On enquiry of the manager of The Swan, it was confirmed they did, indeed, have CCTV

"Can I see the readings for the last 24 hours?" demanded Kim, in no mood to be messed about at this hour.

"I'm sorry, Sir, but there are none," bleated the manager, "we've had a problem with the system and we await the engineers to attend to it."

"What is the nature of the problem?"

"Sorry, Sir, I don't know."

"Where is the recording unit?"

The manager took him to the under-stairs cupboard just before the Gents WC. On close inspection Kim held up a wire from the back of the unit which had clearly been cut.

"I guess this is the fault."

"Yes, Sir, I think you are possibly right."

"Who has access to this cupboard?"

"Well anyone really. As you see I keep the vacuum here and various bits of cleaning materials. The hooks hold the outdoor clothes of staff whilst they are working and the recorder is on the shelf above."

"Why don't you lock this door?"

"Why would we do that?"

"To prevent someone sabotaging your security systems!"

Outside in the car park SOCO had taped off the whole area. Anyone wanting to visit The Swan tonight would have to park in the road.

"There isn't much we can do tonight but as you don't have an identification of the body, please let me know if you find anything that might help." said Kim to the pathologist.

It looked like SOCO would be in for a long night.

CHAPTER 2

"Jon, the Chief Constable would like to see you if you are free this morning?"

"Yes, I can come now before the reports on last night's murder hit my desk. Make it in half an hour, please."

"Good morning, Kim," the Chief Constable said in greeting. "Have a seat. Now Kim, this year it is a rule of the Force that you have to retire. If you wish, we can hang on until December."

"I know, Sir, it is not a prospect that I'm looking forward to. I had hoped I could negotiate a new contract until I was 60 at least."

"Good man, most people can't wait to give up."

"Well, not me, Sir, my life is the Force. I'm not married and I believe I still have a lot to offer."

"I'm sure you have but the rules are the rules."

"Isn't there a way we can work something out, Sir?"

"Well, I very much doubt it but I'll take your request to the Police Committee and see what they say."

"Thank you, Sir."

"What's the murder you have at the moment, Kim?"

"Too early to say, Sir. A body in a pub car park."

"Maybe a falling out after a night in the pub?"

"No, I don't think so, Sir. Head smashed with a hammer and a female in men's clothing murdered elsewhere."

"Seems likely you've got your hands full."

"Another job, Sir, but we shall get to the bottom of it."

It was lunchtime by the time Kim returned to his office. A brief initial report with draft stamped all over it was on his desk from SOCO. He opened the front page just as the phone rang.

"Sir, it's uniform. One of our patrol cars has found a white estate car parked illegally at Chester railway station."

"I'm not yet involved in parking offences. You'd best deal with it Sergeant."

"No, Sir, the significance is that there is a lot of blood in the rear of the car. We thought you might be interested."

"Ah, yes I am. I will send the SOCO team to look at it. We need to bring it in."

Turning again to the preliminary SOCO report it confirmed the view of the pathologist that this person had been murdered elsewhere. Apart from a few drops of blood in front of the body they had no evidence at all of anyone else's involvement. The car park was tarmacked so no trace remained of car tracks. The report confirmed that Kim's initial findings that the CCTV recorder had been tampered with by cutting the camera feed wire.

"Umm," Jon mused to himself, "not much to go on here. Maybe the car will turn something up."

"George, it's Jon Kim. Have you done the autopsy yet?"

"No. It will be 2 o'clock today."

"Can I come?"

"Of course, my dear fellow - you are always welcome."

"Thanks. Have you found anything on the deceased that might be of interest to me?"

"Yes. I have a key with a circular disc attached with the number 6 embossed in black on the other side."

"Is that it?"

"It is."

"Ok, see you later."

"Tarrant, I want you to go to The Swan at Tarporley immediately. I want you first to discover how they identify their keys. Then carefully have a look at Room 6. If it is empty and has been empty since the murder, seal it as we may need SOCO to sweep it. Give me a ring on my mobile as soon as you have answers to these questions."

"Okay, Sir, I'm on my way."

As he was putting on his coat, it was raining outside, Jon felt his new front door key and key ring.

"I knew I had something to do, I must chase Michael Fitzallen about the other set of keys that must have been provided with the new locks for the building he rented from Wall's Holdings. It was him, or his company that changed the locks. So there has to be a third set of keys somewhere. I need to find out who had them." Jon left himself a Post-it note to remind him to follow this up.

*

Jon entered the gallery overlooking the dissection table ready for the autopsy of the murder victim. Some orderlies brought the body in on a trolley covered by a green plastic sheet.

When the sheet was removed Jon could see immediately this was a relatively young woman, possibly 25 or so. She had a shapely figure, dark hair but half her skull and facial features had been removed entirely by a severe and ferocious attack with the inevitable blunt instrument.

George, the pathologist, acknowledged Jon in the gallery and he requested an orderly to switch on the sound so that Jon could hear George's commentary as he went about his work. Two hours later the autopsy was still in progress. It had taken nearly an hour to take the detailed photographs of the injuries which were at the front and rear of the head. Jon's phone rang.

"Yes, Tarrant?"

"You were right, Sir."

"Right about what, Tarrant?"

"Room 6, Sir. It was occupied by a young lady but she hasn't been seen for 24 hours. I've sealed the room – it hasn't been let."

"What about the key?"

"Oh that, yes. They have the key to Room 6 – it was left behind at Reception when she went out."

"What does it look like?"

"Well, it is a Yale type but no name on it."

"No, you fool, what's the key fob like?"

"A wooden strip, quite heavy with 'The Swan Hotel' and a number 6 stamped on the opposite side."

"Okay, thanks. I'll come and look at the room."

"George, can you hear me?"

"Yes."

"I have to go. I'll get your report in the morning?"

"You never know! Bye."

Kim drove all the way to Tarporley again and parked at

the rear of The Swan.

"Is my detective here?" he enquired entering the pub hotel. He didn't require an answer as Tarrant appeared as if by magic.

"Have you been in Room 6, Tarrant?"

"No, Sir. All I did was to make sure the key fitted."

"Have you got the key?"

"Yes, it's here, Sir."

Proffering the key to his superior, Jon held the key found on the body which was now in an evidence bag but being clear plastic it was possible to establish that the keys matched.

"Okay, let's have a look in the room."

Kim gingerly used the hotel's key and opened the door. He told everyone, who were now part of the drama including the hotel manager and housekeeper, to keep out. Jon and Tarrant went in. It was a modern room furnished in modern style with en-suite bathroom. The bed was made or hadn't been slept in. There were woman's clothes on a chair and in the wardrobe; cosmetics and hair brushes on the dressing table; some bathing lotions, in addition to the complementary stuff the hotel provided, in a rack in the shower cubicle.

"What are your first impressions, Tarrant?"

Before he could answer, there was a commotion outside. A loud female voice demanded to know who was in the room. Kim opened the door with his right hand raised. He insisted that the lady outside who was remonstrating with the manager could not enter.

"I'm a police officer, you cannot come in. Tarrant, lock the door. Please, madam, come with me."

Turning to the manager Jon enquired, "is there a room I can use to speak with this lady?"

"Use my office - that is private."

"Okay – lead on."

The manager took Kim, Tarrant and the extremely cross lady who was demanding an explanation all the way to the manager's office. Once inside, Kim requested she sit down. Tarrant remained standing. Kim used the manager's chair behind his desk.

"May I ask your name and address please, madam?"

"You can fucking well ask all you like but until I get an explanation of what is going on, you're not getting anything from me."

"Very well. I'm sorry that you are being inconvenienced but we are investigating a murder and there is a link to your room with the murder victim. That is all I can say at the moment."

Then rather more contrite than she was before she gave her name and address. "Gemma Blackshaw is my name – you may know the name."

"Why should I know your name?"

"It's famous, that's why!"

"Oh, famous for what?"

"I am a TV star."

"Oh, I see. Eh, what programme do you appear in?"

"Coronation Street, of course! Don't you police people know anything?"

Kim chose to ignore the barb. "Why are you staying here?"

"That's my business."

"It's mine now, Ms Blackshaw."

"Like hell it is!" she continued in her mixed accent of refined Lancashire.

"Miss Blackshaw, please co-operate. It is possible that there is a perfectly rational explanation for the association with your room but until I have established that we cannot permit you to return to your room."

"I'm here on personal business."

"What sort of personal business?"

"Oh, shit – we are not filming 'til the back end of this week so I came here to meet my lover!"

"I see. Why didn't you want to tell me that before?"

"Because I'm married, you dick!"

"Ms Backshaw, please refrain from using that language or I'll have to ask you to accompany us to the station. That will ensure the matter makes the Press."

It was, of course, exactly what she was trying to avoid.

"Very well, I will tell you exactly what is going on. Can I have anonymity in this? It will destroy my marriage if my husband finds out."

"That all depends on what you have to say."

*

Thursday night was not normally a night he would choose to go out but this was a bit special. Having returned from Marbella especially for the event, Michael Fitzallen put on his dinner jacket ready for the reception at The Grosvenor Hotel, Ballroom Entrance, Park Lane. He was glad he'd ordered a taxi to collect him as it had just started to drizzle. Blast, he thought to himself, I wish I'd brought a mac.

Luckily his taxi driver with 'the knowledge' followed a circuitous route that was probably unknown to anyone other than a London Taxi driver, as he was able to drop him right at the door. Eight pounds for a ten minute taxi ride seemed a bit steep but this was London after all. The event was the 50th Anniversary Dinner of the Institute of Letting Agents – he had been invited by one of the firms he and Sandra had instructed to let the Manchester block of apartments. If he knew anyone at the event at all when he arrived that would, he thought, be a miracle. Everyone, well the men anyway, were dressed in dinner jackets – the uniform for a posh dinner.

"Hello, thanks, for coming," a female voice said, off to the side – it was the manager of the agent's in the Manchester office.

"It's Rachel, isn't it?"

"Nearly, Raquel actually," responded the buxom dark haired lady in a black dress which certainly did complement her ample figure.

"I thought I would find you with the girls," came another female voice.

It was Sandra. "Sandra – how are you?" He gave her a peck on each cheek in typical European fashion.

"I'm just fine now."

"Now? Why what's been the problem? I haven't heard from you for ages."

"You were at perfect liberty to ring me at any time, Michael," she retorted crossly.

"We aren't going to have an argument are we? Not tonight!"

"No, of course not."

"What's been the problem?"

"Another time, Michael. It's a long story and I'm here to

22

enjoy myself this evening."

The MC announced, "dinner is served – please be seated." The two of them each hoped secretly that they would not be sitting together. Round tables in the mirrored ballroom were all beautifully decorated. The seating plan had them both on Table 6. Only time will tell if they are together: they were!

*

"Miss Bradshaw in your own time please let us have all the details. This is not a formal statement, Tarrant will take notes if it is appropriate and may need to ask you for a formal statement later."

"Okay. You're all the same."

"Oh, you've been interviewed by the police before?"

"No, I didn't mean police, I meant men."

"In your own time."

"When filming the last two episodes was over and some OB shots …"

"OB?"

"Outside broadcast. Anyway, it was necessary for some VT – video tape – to be taken to slot into the storyline. I had to come to Chester for that. It took a couple of hours but I had to tell my husband I would be away until Friday."

"Okay – who with?"

"With my lover, a beautiful boy, a researcher on the programme. It's just an infatuation – it's just for sex, you see."

"So where have you been today? Where's your lover?"

"I've been to Chester shopping and Kevin will be here later."

"Shopping? Where are the purchases?"

"In my car. Why?"

"Were they clothes?"

"In a manner of speaking."

"What does that mean?"

"They are personal items for a lady's bedroom. I was going bring them in from the car through the back door but thanks to your lot I've had to park in the street. I certainly wasn't going to walk down a public street with an Ann Summers bag, okay! Sexy stuff. Don't you get out at all? I'm a star – I have to be careful who sees me and with what."

"Okay. So Kevin will be here later?"

"Yes. We have a meal in the room. He stays the night and he slips out unnoticed in the morning whilst I make a presence at breakfast."

"Give Tarrant your address and Kevin's, please. Have you had anyone else in your room?"

"No. How dare you!"

"Please do not misinterpret my questions. I will see if the management can find you an alternative room."

The manager was summoned and he agreed he would move Ms Blackshaw to another room.

"Do you recognise this key?" Kim asked showing the key fob in the plastic evidence bag to the manager.

"Yes. Where did you get that? We've been looking for it for days."

"So it belongs to the hotel then?"

"Yes, yes. Can we have it back?"

"Sorry, no it's evidence. Why is it different from the main hotel key?"

"It is a spare key we have or had one for each room. See, there was insufficient room on the hook for two keys with the main hotel key fob. We keep these in case a guest requests a second key or we need access to a particular room. There are only three master keys."

"I understand. Please make arrangements for Ms Blackshaw and then I will need to hold a discussion with you."

Ms Blackshaw was less than pleased when she was told that absolutely no contents of her room could be moved until SOCO had done their investigation.

"What the hell am I supposed to wear? I can't even clean my teeth."

"Sorry, madam. We are conducting a murder enquiry which I know is inconvenient for everyone but there it is."

Kim sat down with the manager in his office this time allowing the manager to sit in his own chair.

"Tell me who occupied Room 6 say in the last 14 days."

"That's easy, I can show you the registration cards."

Kim was handed three cards.

"Is that it? Only three people?"

"Yes, but one was here for ten days, I think."

Kim looked carefully at the cards which provided the main details of the visitor, their address and nationality, and payment details.

"Why hasn't this one got an address?" handing a card back to the manager.

"I suspect they may have stayed with us before."

"Can you please dig out their address and preferably the earlier completed registration card?"

"That will take a few moments, but please bear with me."

*

Once all the guests were seated, ten to a table, the Master of Ceremonies read the Grace and then dinner was, in fact, served. Michael and Sandra chose to speak with their neighbours.

"I see we are a person missing," observed Sandra of the young man sitting to her left.

"Yes, she was supposed to be here but we had a text message saying that she couldn't make it."

"Would I know her? My property is managed by your Manchester office."

"You might – Denise Ward."

"Oh yes, I know Denise. She is a pretty girl and I think she is the manager - is that right?"

"Nearly, she is the assistant manager. Raquel is the manager," she said pointing across the table.

"Oh, I didn't think I had ever met Raquel. No matter, Denise does a good job for me – pity she isn't here I would have liked to have had a chat with her."

"Yes, something important must have come up. It isn't like her to miss a social event – she likes to party, does Denise."

"Do you know Denise, Michael?" enquired Raquel who had heard Sandra's enquiry.

"No, no I don't, all the management of the block is handled by Sandra."

"Oh I see," retorted Raquel, "how do you know Sandra?"

"Well that is a very long story. I wouldn't want to bore you with it."

"As you are my only neighbour as Denise isn't here, I would love to hear the story."

"Well, going back to the early years of this decade a friend of mine and I decided to set up an organisation for helping people to become landlords for the first time. The buy-to-let boom was about to take off, property prices were growing and mortgages were readily available. We started a company called Inside Property Investments – IPI as I know it, you may have heard of it?"

"Yes I have but it's stopped now hasn't it?"

"Soup sir?" enquired a waiter balancing three bowls of soup. Michael realised it was easier to say yes than try for something else. The prospect of a bowl of soup down his back was ever present.

"Yes, yes, thank you"

The soup was delivered without mishap.

"Yes you are correct Raquel, but it was good whilst it lasted."

"I see, did you buy new properties for your customers?"

"We didn't actually buy any property except for the very first development. We took options off-plan of properties that were to be built and sold the option on to private individuals at a profit and it included a guaranteed rent for the first two years. Many people bought without even seeing the property so keen were they to get on to the buy-to-let bandwagon."

"That is amazing to think people will commit so much money on buying something without ever visiting the area."

"They saw the whole proposition as a win-win situation. There were mortgages of ninety five percent, guaranteed rents so the deposit could be paid with their credit card. Frankly it was so easy it was ridiculous. I am pleased to say we made a lot of money from IPI."

"Why isn't your business partner here?"

"He died in a very bad car crash in Spain."

"Oh I am sorry to hear that, he missed out on all the benefits."

"He did alright whilst he was alive but in fact it transpired that he was murdered. Someone had tampered with the brakes of his car."

"Oh how awful. You must have been upset?"

"Yes I was, but that is all water under the bridge. It caused me some problems securing the cash we had made, but it was sorted in the end."

"That all sounds most intriguing," responded Raquel, who would like to know all the ins and outs of this story. She was convinced there was a great deal more to this than Michael was telling.

"Chicken or beef Sir?"

"Oh beef for me."

Raquel opted for the chicken.

"The food is really good here," continued Raquel, "I bet the two of you ate out all the time when you were running IPI."

"No we didn't much, it was very often a sandwich. You see Wayne was running the Spanish end of the operation. He didn't come back to England very often."

"Ooo, that sounds exciting, were you doing the same thing in Spain as you were doing here?"

"No, it was a financial arrangement Wayne was looking after, we were also developing a villa for our use."

"Gosh you really were in the big time, did you have a

Rolls Royce?"

"No, I didn't." Michael wanted to get this conversation away from him, he was giving far too much information away. "So what do you do other than let property?"

Raquel started off telling Michael all about her holiday in Mallorca with her girlfriends.

Michael just let her prattle on, not really listening. He could see Sandra looking at him with a wry smile on her face realising he had a companion who wouldn't stop taking about something Michael held not the slightest interest for him.

After the dinner there were the inevitable speeches from the top table. Again Michael switched off, at least it had stopped Raquel telling her life story.

"Sandra," said Michael in a break in proceedings, "what would you like to do afterwards?"

Fortunately for Sandra the speeches started again, so was unable to answer. It gave her time to think of an answer. Eventually Sandra retorted that she was going to her room as she had an early appointment. Michael felt dejected but was certainly not going clubbing with Raquel and her friends which was the alternative. He retired to bed.

CHAPTER 3

In another hotel two hundred miles away and ten hours later in Tarporley, DCI Kim was arriving at The Swan Hotel to further their investigations of the murder of the young lady found in the car park.

"Tarrant, you need to make some enquiries about the people who've stayed in Room 6 over the last two weeks. It seems there is only the one key, someone may have gone off with the other key."

"Okay, Sir. I'll get on to it I will be there as soon as I can, I've an interview with the Chief Constable at 9.00 in the morning."

Jon had requested that the manager assemble all the staff at 10.00 the next morning as he wanted to interview everyone.

*

The following morning Tarrant kept his appointment with the Chief Constable.

"Tarrant, you have been a DC for nearly five years. Jon Kim has given a glowing reference. I am pleased to advise you that from this morning you will be a Detective Sergeant," said the CC.

"Thank you, Sir. I'm very grateful."

"No need to be grateful, Tarrant – you've earned it. Are you happy working on the Serious Crime Team?"

"Yes, Sir, I'm very happy. I hope to make a good show of it."

"That's good. You know your superior can't go on forever."

"I understand, Sir."

"Have you and Kim anything on at the moment?"

"Yes, Sir. We have a murder enquiry in Tarporley. I would, if it is all right with you, Sir, like to go now. We are interviewing all the staff at a hotel this morning."

"In that case, off you go."

Tarrant drove to Tarporley arriving only ten minutes late with a wide grin on his face.

"What's cheered you up?"

"I'm now a DS, Sir."

"Congratulations. In that case, you do the interviews – I need to get back to the office."

Tarrant gulped but realised he was now a more senior officer and expected to take on more responsibility.

"Is there any particular aspect you are interested in, Sir?"

"Yes, I want to know who the last person was, other than the deceased, to hold the key to Room 6."

Back at police HQ Kim had received the autopsy report. He poured a cup of coffee from the machine and settled down to read it.

"Phew, my God!" he uttered almost imperceptibly under his breath. 'The Cause of Death' as a sub-heading concluded that the deceased was killed by a mixture of ecstasy and alcohol. 'Physical Damage' was the next sub-heading and explained that the battering of the skull, and in particular the face, rendered a facial identification virtually impossible. Tests had been carried out to see if there was a matched DNA on the database and also for any fingerprint matches but nothing had turned up. It seemed she was dead before the facial mutilation.

"Why would anyone do that?" he asked himself. Finding out who this girl is, or was, is not going to be easy. He thought he had fully understood the report when a further page of information he had missed caught his eye. It's just as well he spotted it – apparently the girl was about two months pregnant.

"So do we have crime of passion – someone who couldn't allow a child to be born - perhaps she wasn't in favour of a termination?" All speculation he knew but lines of enquiry to followed up. "George, it is Jon."

"Read the report, have you?"

"Yes, very interesting. Can you get a DNA trace on the foetus? If so, would it be different from the mother's blood and also would it give a clue to the father?"

"Yes, on all counts – the samples are being analysed now. A bit more complex than a normal DNA sample"

"Let me know when you've got it, George. Thanks."

Jon wrote down on a pad the following: death by alcohol and ecstasy, facial mutilation, pregnant, dead for 24 hours at least before discovery, the Room 6 key. These were the elements he had to consider. He also needed to know a great deal more about the previous occupiers of Room 6.

*

Sandra's mobile rang at about 8.30 just as she was leaving her room for breakfast. "Hello Michael."

"Good night wasn't it?"

"Yes, very enjoyable, thanks."

"What do you want?"

"I don't want anything in particular - just to chat about our business venture and so on."

"Okay. When and where?"

"Shall we say 12.00/12.30 at Carluccio's?"

"That will be fine thank you," she said rather curtly and hung up.

No time for small talk. Sandra puzzled over breakfast about Michael – shall she confront him with her suspicions about the classic car business? She couldn't decide – maybe the conversation will steer that way.

They met at the appointed hour at Carluccio's – not the embrace they once enjoyed.

"Hi, Sandra, have I upset you?"

"Yes, I guess you have. I would have thought you had spotted that," said Sandra.

"I had no cause to upset you. The monthly statement, is great, the investment is doing very well - I'm pleased with the investment," retorted Michael.

"Good, I'm glad. Pity the banks couldn't see that or maybe they could and were hoping by playing hardball they could end up owning the block for a fraction of the value, to their own benefit."

"It wouldn't surprise me. They have been doing some very crazy things," said Michael "however I am delighted that I was able to assist and purchase half the building in Manchester. It is nearly fully let as far as I can tell from the figures?"

"Yes you are right about the lettings. I knew it would work out, it's a great pity the banks couldn't see that."

"I am very glad they didn't otherwise I wouldn't have been able to make the investment."

"Anyway, I'm sure you have not invited me here to discuss the activities of the bank," said Sandra.

"No," said Michael, "firstly I wanted the opportunity face to face to say how sorry I am that the old Wall's head office and warehouse was burnt down."

"You're sorry! How do you think I feel?" retorted Sandra, "my mother's income will be affected."

"Yes, I guess you are pretty cut up about it but you must have had significant pay day from the insurance company as a consequence of the fire."

"We received the sum insured but not until someone had been committed for arson," said Sandra.

"Yes, that's the little shit Terry – oh sorry, they want our order." A waiter stood by with a notepad.

"Would you like a little longer, Sir?"

"No, we can order now." Sandra decided to have spaghetti with pine nuts and bacon; Michael opted for spaghetti carbonara.

"Why was Terry a 'little shit'?" enquired Sandra

"It's surely obvious. He torched the building."

"It surely is not as simple as that. Cars were stolen first. How on earth did Terry organise all that? No Michael the wrong person is in jail, and it upsets me."

"Well who do you think torched the building?"

"I wish I knew, but I am certain it wasn't Terry."

At that moment Michael's mobile phone rang. "Hello Michael Fitzallen."

Out of earshot to Sandra the caller identified himself as

DCI Kim.

"How can I help you Sir?"

Kim requested details about who organised the installation of the new locks at the Sealand building.

"I thought that was all over Inspector."

Sandra realised immediately who Michael was talking to.

"Well Sir nothing is ever over if there are some loose ends to tie up."

"What on earth do you mean?"

"Specifically Mr Fitzallen I need to know how many sets of keys there were for the unit."

"I seem to recall telling you this before. There were two sets as we had an extra set cut. I had a set and Terry had a set. That's two sets, okay?"

"So you say you got a set cut?"

"Yes Terry did that."

"I don't suppose you know who did all this work on the locks?"

"I don't and I suppose the invoice would have been destroyed in the fire."

"Thank you Mr Fitzallen, I will make some further enquiries, I know how to contact you should I need more information."

"Thanks Inspector."

"Just to confirm you are certain an extra set was cut by someone."

"Yes, yes, look I am at lunch with a colleague, I can't help you any more."

"Oh you have helped me greatly, goodbye."

The two continued their lunch. Sandra said nothing about the phone call but realised the police were still trying to put some loose ends to bed, or at least DCI Kim was. She knew he was a good man. If he was not happy about any aspect of a case he would certainly rummage around until he had satisfaction. She wondered what had triggered some further thoughts in his mind.

"Sorry about that Sandra, the police never leave some things alone, yet if you have a burglary at home, it takes ages to get anything done."

"Yes I know, but they are obviously not satisfied with something."

Michael took a long slow drink of his glass of white wine, nearly draining the glass. Without any instruction within a minute of him finishing his wine, a waiter appeared at Michael's elbow to refill the glass.

"Thank you" said Michael, "would you like some more wine Sandra?"

"No, no thank you Michael I have to catch a train."

"So do I but I needed to relax, and with your company that is just how I now feel."

"Are you sure it isn't the wine and not me?" she enquired.

"I confess it is a bit of both, but it is great to see you again."

"Yes Michael, time flies, I find it hard to believe that it is nearly ten years since my father was murdered on New Year's Day 2000."

"Is it that long, I really can't believe where the time has gone?"

"Well when Dad's time was up it was an enormous shock to us all as you can imagine, followed reasonably shortly by the death and murder of his business partner

Roger Whiteside. He was pulled out of the River Dee at the side of the racecourse. I don't like to talk about this much in fact I don't think I have discussed those events since they happened. It's odd but I feel quite a sense of relief by talking to you now about what happened to our family."

"How did Whiteside die? I assume because of his death that is why you came to the rescue of the company with Sienna?"

"You are quite right."

"So how did Whiteside die?"

"That is very painful to me, but a dear friend and our GP was so angry that Whiteside had apparently killed Dad, that he took it upon himself to kill Whiteside rather than have the family dragged through the courts and for Whiteside with a clever lawyer to either escape justice or have a shorter sentence than he deserved. Uncle Frank took the view an 'eye for an eye' was the only way to find a just settlement."

A waiter cleared the empty plates. "Would you like a sweet?" addressing them both.

"Not for me thanks."

"Nor me," responded Michael after Sandra had declared no interest in a pud.

"Just a coffee please," said Michael.

"And herbal tea for me," Sandra joined in.

"So if it's not too painful Sandra do tell me how Whiteside met his fate?"

"No I don't mind telling you it was in all the papers. The sadness was that Uncle Frank was arrested eventually and found guilty. What we didn't know at the time was that as a GP he was aware he had cancer. He didn't have that much longer to live, his last act was to right a wrong."

"So how did he do that?"

"Essentially it's a long story, but one night he followed Whiteside as he was walking home. His route took him over the suspension bridge over the Dee to Handbridge to his flat. Frank hit him on the back of the head and threw him in the river. Unbeknown to Frank the river was flowing up stream due to the tidal effect. The tide was coming in and the body was swept upstream. Eventually shortly after high tide the body drifted downstream but it took a few days to end up where it was found by a dog walker."

"Good lord. I bet Frank had no idea that the tide would have an effect?"

"No I suppose not"

"So with both your father and Whiteside out of the way the opportunity for you to run Wall's with Sienna was immediately available to you?"

"Well no. There was an illegitimate son of Whiteside's, who turned up following an advertising campaign to find a next of kin. Our solicitor, of course you know him, John England, did the correct thing to try and find any relatives, hoping none would turn up so the coast would be clear."

"So this long lost son appeared, I bet you were not happy about that?"

"No, but in fact it all turned out all right as Rhys Williams, who was confirmed as the son after DNA analysis, was very helpful. All he really wanted was some money so he could go travelling."

"His lucky day then?"

"Yes he received just over a million pounds."

"Wow that was a pay day. So how did your mother end up owning the premises at Sealand?"

"She was a beneficiary in my father's will, and she

purchased the half share from Whiteside's estate, to the benefit of Rhys. The rent was significant from Wall's Holdings which set Mum up nicely."

"Oh I see and I understand why she would be upset at the loss of income."

"Exactly Michael. We seem to have come full circle. I don't want to discuss the fire anymore. In fact it is high time I went."

"Well that was a most interesting lunch I look forward to seeing you soon."

"Thanks for lunch Michael."

"Michael, like it or not we are in business together. You have an excellent income from the flats so don't let's fall out."

"I don't want to fall out – I've enjoyed doing business with you and I enjoyed our brief relationship. I'm sorry it seems as though we will not be able to pick up that thread of our friendship."

"Correct. What was your motive for lunch?"

"Motive? You sound like a policeman."

"Okay then, you indicated you wanted to talk business – what is it you have in mind?"

"Well I recall that you still own five flats in Chester – Squirrels Chase Development. Will you be prepared to sell them?"

"That is the long-term objective."

"Will you take a million for them now?"

"That's only £200,000 each, Michael, they're worth at least double that."

"Maybe, but not in the current market."

Sandra knew he was right. She, or rather Wall's Holdings, still owed the bank £350,000 on overdraft they were having to pay off which was significantly reducing the take from Manchester.

"How about buying three for a million?"

"Are they all let?" enquired Michael

"No. There are three at £550 a month. We have two vacant." Advised Sandra.

"That makes the five worth no more than about £700,000 and are you sure you don't want to accept my million? I want one to live in so vacant is fine by me."

"Michael, it's a very tempting offer – I need to consult with Sienna and my mum who are shareholders and if they will do the deal I will phone you."

"Fair enough – I have the money."

"No mortgage?" enquired Sandra.

"No, no mortgage, the money is in Santander bank you were with me when I was making the arrangements to set up the account."

"You mean I was asleep in your apartment when you went to make the arrangements."

"Okay – here's my current mobile number," and Michael handed her a card which looked as though he'd had printed by a machine at a motorway service station.

"I must go – I'm on the 3 o'clock back home. I'll ring you tomorrow." Sandra permitted a peck on the cheek and left Michael to finish his bottle of wine.

Sandra got up and left slightly annoyed that she had given away so much information to Michael. It was only history and it was quite a long time ago. "Get over it girl," she muttered to herself as she left the Grosvenor to find a taxi. I have possibly sold some flats though, which put a grin back on her face.

*

Damn, my coffee has gone cold. Kim muttered to himself. He drank it all despite the tepid nature of the liquid.

Tests had been carried out to see if fingerprints or a DNA match could be found on the Police DNA database. Nothing was found. It appears she was dead before facial mutilation took place.

"Why would anyone do that?" Kim asked himself.

"Tarrant can you spare a moment please?"

"Have you read the PM Report?"

"No Sir, what does it say?"

Kim explained the salient points. "Can you get the PR officer to issue a press statement please?"

Kim explained what he wanted. He wanted to find which M&S store the clothes had been bought from. He also needed to know who she is. Try and work into your press release that we need details of any female of between 23 and 28 who has gone missing in the last few days.

"It says she has been badly disfigured in the facial regions. I would prefer we don't mention this just now. What I would like to concentrate on are the clothes: there are pictures in the press release – a beige colour pair of M&S chinos waist 36, M&S boxer shorts, an M&S polo shirt in white, a blue 'V' neck sweater – she wore no shoes or socks," said Kim.

A press conference was arranged in the press briefing room at Police HQ. The press statement gave all the details Kim had requested should be in the statement. It went into some detail as to where the body was found and when, the garments she was wearing and her approximate age. The press and TV were assembled and Tarrant ran through the contents of the press release

"Are there any questions?" enquired Tarrant.

"Yes, Julian Friend, BBC North West Tonight. Why have you not released a picture of the girl, or even given her a name?"

"She has not yet been formally identified so until that occurs for the benefit of relatives we are not releasing that information at the moment. If there are no more questions, the press conference is over." Kim, Tarrant and the police PR Officer got up and left the room.

"I hope that brings some response, Sir."

"I agree, Tarrant – without a photo it's difficult to jog someone's memory the clothes are hardly unique."

"No, Sir, but you never know."

It was about an hour after the press conference when a member of M&S's PR department rang wanting to speak to the detective handling the case.

"Yes, Tarrant here. How can I help you?"

"Yes, Tarrant, I think it's the other way round. I am from M&S PR department. If you can read the barcode on the garments it should be possible to say which store sold them and maybe even which month, certainly which year. All our clothes carry some unique markings for stock control purposes. We thought this might help you."

"It would but how do you know about this?"

"Granada TV has phoned us with the questions and have given me your contact number."

Tarrant agreed to allow someone from M&S to identify the clothes. The clothes would need to be taken to the nearest M&S store in Warrington. A member of the police forensic team took the clothes and handled them with gloved hands and did not allow anyone else to touch them.

"Thanks, can you tell me when and where we might have some information?"

"Give me 10 minutes, Sir, and I'll tell you now."

CHAPTER 4

"Tarrant – how're you doing with the car that was discovered abandoned? Have SOCO turned up with anything yet? Apparently there was plenty to go at."

"Yes, Sir, we expect the report later today."

"What about the owner?"

"Warrington police have interviewed him. Mr Hussain – a small time butcher with a small shop in the suburbs of the town. He didn't report the car stolen as there is no insurance and thought he would be in trouble."

"Yes, he is right but in the current circumstances it seems rather heartless to pursue that charge."

"Yes, Sir."

"Why was it left in Chester, do you think? And why was the body dumped in the car park of The Swan? It seems that we have so many unconnected bits of this puzzle – we need to find the missing link."

"I agree, Sir. I'll check if we have any further reports on the phone line concerning a missing girl."

Jon spotted the note he had written to himself about the locks at the Sealand Building.

"Is that the fire investigation department? This is DCI

Kim of Cheshire CID."

"Yes Sir how can we help you?"

"Can I speak with someone who is familiar with the fire investigation at the Wall's building at Sealand in Chester?

"You are speaking to him, we don't have the luxury of receptionists Sir."

"Good, I need to know the name of the manufacturer of the locks on the main doors of the building."

"That's easy I recall them very specifically. They are ASSA locks."

"Oh, never heard of them, what, if anything, is special about them?"

"They are high security seven lever locks, and importantly the keys cannot be cut without the formal consent of the main key holder who would have a unique security card bearing a code for the locks."

"Well that is amazing, excellent news. I don't suppose you know who might have been the locksmith in Chester who dealt with these?"

"I don't know for sure, but there is a long-standing locksmith's with a shop in Baughton, Baughton Locksmiths, who I think hold the agency for these locks."

"Thank you very much, very helpful," Kim made a note of the details on his pad. "I must ring them when I have a moment."

*

At her apartment in Chester Sandra rang Sienna to see if she and John would be around later only to discover that both of them and James had gone to the hospital for a check-up for James. Dot, the England's daily help, was full of information as she had been a tower of strength during

James's abduction and now the new parents go together with James when he is out of the house.

"I'm sure that won't last, Miss Sandra," the faithful daily advised.

"Will they be back at lunchtime?"

"Yes, I should think so."

"Can you let them know I need to speak to them quite urgently and I will call round about two o'clock unless they ring me?"

"Very well – I will tell them."

Sandra set off to see her mother who she had established was at home in Church Cottage. She was always delighted to hear from her oldest daughter – a cup of coffee and a chat was just what Ann enjoyed. After the initial discussion between the two Sandra broached the subject of the financial position of Wall's Holdings and the still outstanding overdraft with the bank on Squirrels Chase. Ann saw the sense of selling, yes, the scheme had her vote.

"Oh I haven't mentioned it to anyone but I am a witness to a murder."

"Mum, you have kept that a scret. You just pop out with it like that. What is it all about?"

Ann spent the next half an hour explaining what she had found behind The Swan and what followed.

"Mum that's terrible, please keep me posted on how this develops. Promise?"

"Promise."

Ann waved goodbye with a smile which was saying to herself how lucky she was to have two caring and considerate daughters to look after her.

*

Just after two, the rattling of the cattle grid at Long Acre Farm Sandra jumped from her car, swept little James into her arms as he came unsteadily towards her with Sienna as the chaperone standing in the doorway. After being swept in Sandra's arms for a big cuddle and kiss Sandra presented him with a small plastic push-and-go car she'd acquired in London. Suddenly James lost interest in Sandra and the car was the centre of attention.

"My, how he's growing up! Hi Sis."

"Yes, every day now we see a change – it's amazing."

"Is he okay? I gather you had to go to the hospital with him."

"Oh yes – just a routine check."

"Sorry I'm late but I have been to see Mum and what a story she had to tell me. I will fill you in when we have sorted out Squirrels Chase."

It didn't take Sandra long to explain the potential sale of the five Squirrels Chase flats to Sienna and John. Whilst the price in theory was less than had hoped to make, the outstanding overdraft would be paid off and some capital would be released. The bank have no further interest in Wall's Holdings and debentures and personal bank guarantees would be cancelled – a benefit in itself, advised Sandra. She had total agreement to the plan within an hour.

"So what's been going on with Mum?" Sienna enquired.

"You won't believe it but she discovered a dead body at the back of The Swan walking home from the shops, apparently a murdered body."

"Oh my goodness, whatever next?"

Sandra went on to fill in the gaps in the story in so far as she knew it.

"Okay, we had better keep an eye on Mum."

"Yes I must go, things to do."

"Bye," said Sienna as Sandra got in her car, waved and drove off.

Sandra headed back to her apartment.

"Michael, it's Sandra."

"Any news?"

"Yes, reluctantly you can have all five apartments for one million."

"Okay that's a deal. Please ask John to do the paperwork. I will use Mersey Law again – I'll give them a ring now. I can complete as soon as you like."

"Okay Michael. Can you send £100,000 to John's firm as a 10% deposit?"

"Don't you trust me, Sandra?" She didn't answer that question.

"I'll get things underway, Michael. Bye." Sandra got set to create the details of the transaction and e-mail them to John at Bennetts and Mersey Law.

"Tony Munsford, please…Tony, it's Sandra Wall."

"Good to hear from you, Sandra. How can I help you today?" He was always the helpful bank manager but his wings had been severely clipped by Head Office's new regime to tighten up the control for the bank. They required all managers to report everything to Head Office for loans and overdrafts for detailed scrutiny by Head Office.

"Tony, this news should delight you. We have agreed to sell the five apartments at Squirrels Chase for a million with completion in a month."

"That's good – sounds a bit cheap to me."

"Yes, but a bird in the hand – it's a cash deal and will wipe out the remaining overdraft to allow the bank to release all the charges and personal guarantees. The account will be in credit so we will not need an overdraft."

"Oh, but what happens if you want to trade again?"

"I will try and find someone more amenable than the senior credit manager Mr Capstick. The bank can only apply that pressure on me once – it will never get a second chance."

"I understand, will you please write to me with the official request to release securities. I have to pass these up to Head Office but don't anticipate any issues here."

"Neither do I. Thanks, Tony."

*

The SOCO team member walked into Tarrant's office with a report in his hand and a grin on his face. "You look cheerful, David – what's made you like that?"

"Here's the report on Room 6, the car and clothes."

"That's great. In view of your cheerful disposition, clearly you have discovered something of significance."

"Why, yes. The back of the estate car was covered in remnants of blood."

"Yes, so I hear – presumably the victim's."

"No – cow and lamb."

"What!" exclaimed Tarrant.

"Yes, that's right. The blood is mainly cow and sheep with a bit of pig."

"By God! No sign of blood of the victim?"

"No, none at all." David went on.

"Well that puts a spanner in the works. We can't be sure that this car was in fact the car used to dump the body."

"No, sorry, we can't find a trace. Mr Hussain who owns

the uninsured car is a butcher, hence the blood!"

"Anything else?" enquires Tarrant.

"Yes. The clothes were bought during the last month at the M&S superstore in Warrington."

"Ah – by whom?"

"Well, we can't tell you that it's impossible to say."

"I thought so – only half a story!" quipped Tarrant

"Do you know how many people shop there each day?"

"I was only pulling your leg. Thanks anyway. Will you tell Mr Hussain he can collect his car once it's insured?"

"Yes, okay," confirmed David.

"And that is all they can tell us?" enquired Kim.

"Yes, that is all," advised Tarrant.

"Umm - I think we need a review. Any news from the missing person line?" went on Kim.

"They did have a number of calls: one about a young lady who had not turned up for work for more than a week but phoned back later in the day to say they had a text message with a faxed medical certificate to say she will be off a month."

"A month – that's an unusual certificate. What was the matter with her?" Kim enquired.

"Apparently, severe morning sickness. She had apparently gone home to her parents in Preston."

"When did we get this call?"

"Yesterday." Advised Tarrant.

"And the text message and medical certificate – when was that received?"

"Late Friday."

"Okay. That's not our girl – she was dead then. So she could not have done either of those things."

*

Mersey Law phoned Michael on the number Sandra had provided in her particulars of sale.

"Michael, I see you are buying again."

"Yes. Can you do this and I'll send you £100,000 deposit and in a couple of weeks the balance will follow."

"Okay, I'm not sure this will all happen in a month because the vendors want all the charges removing and so do I. Banks are not being as quick as they once were."

"Okay, no matter so long as we get the contract quite quickly before the vendors change their mind."

"Yes, I understand. It is a good price – you should do well with these."

Sandra e-mailed a letter of request for all securities to be released on sale. John England sent out the preliminary letters of confirmation with the bank's agreement so that completion could take place. £350,000 would be sent directly on completion. Sandra received e-mailed confirmation.

*

"Now Tarrant, so what have we?" The three of them reviewed all the threads of information they currently had. "This doesn't add up to a bag of beans, does it?"

"No, Sir. We need a break."

Jon's phone rang. "I'm in a meeting. Is it urgent?"

"Yes, I think so, Sir. It's the call centre – we have a call we think you should take."

"Hello, Jon Kim here."

"Hello, are you the detective looking for the identity of a dark haired girl?"

"Yes, how can I help you?"

"My name is Raquel, the manager of Allen's Lettings in Manchester."

"Yes?"

"Well we reported earlier in the week that a member of staff, Denise Ward, had not arrived for work for several days and then said she had received a text and faxed medical certificate telling us she was off for a month and visiting her parents in Preston?"

"Yes, I recall the report."

"Well, Sir, we've just had a phone call from her parents trying to contact Denise as they have tried her mobile for a few days now without success. They say she normally phones them daily."

"Can you get a copy of the text message and medical certificate? If so, can you please send them to us immediately along with her address and mobile phone number?"

"Yes, we can do that. Do you think she might be the person you're looking for?"

"Too early to say. Thank you for calling."

Jon relayed the information to his two detectives. As soon as we have her address, I want you to go there and see if she's in – better get a search warrant. The information came through inside ten minutes.

"She must be missed for them to act like this – I think they fear it could be her."

"What's hyperemesis gravidarum?"

"No idea, why?" responded Sullivan.

"It's what the girl is suffering from according to the

medical certificate. Google it."

"It's severe morning sickness what women get sometimes when they're pregnant. It can be fatal if not attended to according to Wikipedia. I hope she hasn't expired in her house. Should we contact the local bobby and see if they can get there before us?"

"Yes, good idea but ask them not to go tramping around all over the place if there's no one in."

It was nearly an hour later when DS Tarrant and DC Sullivan arrived at Denise's address in Warrington. The local PC was on site. The local cops had already gained access.

"Hi." The two detectives showed their warrant cards. "How did you get in?"

"We used a key."

"What key?"

"The one hidden under the plant pot."

"Will people never learn?"

"Apparently not, Sir. There is no one at home."

"Okay. We have a warrant to search the place."

Donning vinyl disposable blue gloves and over-shoes, the two set about going through the two bedroomed Victorian terraced house. "Clearly a female lives here," one said to the other, "all neat and tidy." The two spent an hour going through the place and found nothing of any significance except for an album of photographs some of whom were likely to be Denise. They bagged them and left a card and locked up leaving the key as before. They were just about to get into the car when a neighbour opened their front door to enquire who they were and what they were doing.

"We're the police," said Sullivan showing his warrant card.

"Can I help you?" said the neighbour.

"No, just keep an eye open for Denise. Have you seen her recently?"

"No I haven't seen her for more than a week."

"Do you see her often then?"

"Oh, yes. Daily normally."

"Will you have a look at this photo album, please? Don't touch it – I will turn the pages" his hands, re-gloved.

"That's Denise, her mum, dad and their dog."

"Thank you very much, that's very helpful."

"No harm has come to her, has it?" the enquiring neighbour questioned, anxious to know all the facts.

"We hope not. We're just making enquiries as to her whereabouts."

"I knew something would happen – I didn't like the look of him when I saw him."

"Who?"

"The young man she has been seeing for a few months now."

"Do you know who he is?"

"No, sorry, I don't. He goes snooping, you know," continued the neighbour.

"In what way?"

"Oh if he is passing he will call, collect the key, as you did from under the plant pot and wander around her house – snooping I call it."

"I see," said Tarrant, "did you confront him ever and

ask what he was doing?"

"Oh no. It's none of my business."

"When was the last time you saw him snooping?"

"He was around sometime over the weekend."

"Which day? Do you know his name?"

"No, no idea."

"What does he look like?"

"He's foreign."

"What do you mean by that?"

"Well his isn't white, you know he is foreign."

"Does that mean he is African or Asian looking?"

"Can't recall."

"Try; an African person would have dark skin and possibly curly hair and an Asian-looking person would be brown with straight hair."

"Asian then."

"Okay, thank you. Can I have your name, please?"

"Yes. Jennifer Cook, Mrs."

"Thank you." Noting this down in his notebook, Sullivan and his colleague returned to HQ in Winsford.

CHAPTER 5

Jon Kim was extremely interested in the findings of his two detectives.

"Get a copy of the picture of Denise circulate it, concentrate on local forces in Greater Manchester Police. Also send a copy to Dr Hughes, the pathologist."

The phone rang. "Jon, it's George Hughes."

"George, you must be telepathic – I was just talking about you."

"I hope it wasn't derogatory."

"No, not at all. I was just asking Tarrant to e-mail you a photograph of a young lady who may be the victim. Your thoughts would be appreciated."

"Okay, I will have a look at it. What I was phoning you about is that we have the DNA results back from the foetal blood."

"And?"

"Well, the parentage is mixed Anglo-Saxon and foreign."

"How do you mean 'foreign'?"

"Probably the Far East – India, Pakistan, Bangladesh. Any of the locations like Indonesia etc."

"Now that points it nicely."

"Is that a sarcastic response?"

"Well yes and no – it's more than we knew before. Thanks anyway."

"Sullivan, make sure you send a copy of the photograph to Manchester Letting Agents asking them to confirm the ID and get the address of the parents if the ID is positive. We will have to send a local officer to see them."

"Very well, Sir."

Jon considered all the new evidence which was a great deal more than they had yesterday. He felt there was more to find out from The Swan staff and the residents over the last month. It all appeared to check out. There didn't appear to be anyone who might fit the profile of the murderer but he was keeping an open mind. He decided to turn up at The Swan later to see who he could talk to and hopefully extract more information.

The employers of Denise, Allen's Lettings, quickly confirmed her identity. Jon left his two detectives to other duties and drove to Tarporley. It was just four in the afternoon on a Thursday when he drove into the car park at the rear.

"Can I speak to the manager, please?"

"Sorry, Sir, it's his day off."

"I'm DS, no I'm not, I'm Superintendent Kim the senior detective dealing with the murder of the young lady found in the car park two weeks ago."

"Yes, Sir, how can we help you?"

"I need to speak to whoever of the staff are available. I'm quite happy to wander around and be discreet."

"I'm sure that will be all right, Sir. Is there anything we

can get you?"

"No, not at the moment. I may need something later. It all depends on how long I will be staying."

"Please help yourself, Sir."

"Well, can I start with you? I can see you work behind the bar – is that the regular job for you?"

"Regular part-time, Sir. I only work on Thursdays, Fridays and Saturday and Sunday."

"Okay. Let me have your name and address." Roger gave his details. "Were you here when the body was found?"

"Yes, Sir. I had a lot of regulars complaining they couldn't get in the car park."

"When I was here two weeks ago the manager was here then so does his day off change?"

"It can. I don't recall why he was on duty on that Thursday. Maybe he had Wednesday off."

"Okay. It's not important. Do all the staff get on well together?"

"Oh yes, but we have different roles so we don't often meet."

"How do you mean?"

"Well, bar, restaurant and kitchen are effectively a unit and the hotel is a different unit."

"Okay, is there anyone in the hotel side now?"

"Oh, yes I can send for Bozena, the main chambermaid. She will still be here. She works very long hours and very hard. She is allowed to use a room late afternoons for a nap. She's Polish and I think she has no proper home to go to."

"By 'proper' you mean a flat or something?"

"Yes, I think she lives in a B&B near the village."

"Very helpful of you, thanks."

Kim wandered out into the hallway which was furnished with a small dark brown oak desk. Sitting on the desk was a blotter, a bell and numerous brochures – mostly about The Swan – in a leaflet stand. Either side of the desk was a large oak chair in the Jacobean style, probably Victorian, Kim mused. The stairs to the upper floors were encased in what he assumed was a fireproof screen. "An ugly but essential precaution," he muttered to himself. Under the stairs was a cupboard unlocked which housed the keys and secondary keys for each room. He noticed that all the main keys were present but the secondary keys for Rooms 6 and 10 were missing. He knew where key 6 was – who's got key 10?

Kim walked up the stairs to the first floor landing where the first six rooms of the hotel were situated. He knew what Room 6 was like so he explored a little further up the second set of stairs also enclosed in a fireproof screen up to the second floor. He realised that when the building in years gone by, the top floor was servant's quarters – only four doors were available to him.

The door to Room 10 seemed to be unlocked but only just. He pushed the door which screened him for a moment from the interior.

"Come in darling you are ..." The voice petered out as soon as the occupant saw Jon Kim standing there.

"I'm so sorry Miss, I did not realise this was the room you use for your siesta."

A woman with a thick Polish accent was only partially dressed in her pants but little else. Jon thought nothing of this as it was known that she had time in a room for rest. She was clearly about to climb under the duvet and have a sleep.

"It's okay, Sir," she responded in tremulous voice, Kim

hardly able to understand her in her Polish accent.

Kim introduced himself and he showed his warrant card.

"Can we have a talk?"

"Yes Sir."

"What is your name?"

"I am Bozena, sir."

"What is your full name?"

"Oh. Bozena Bania."

*

In the kitchen Ali Hussain arrived with the meat order for the weekend.

"I see you have a new car, Ali," observed the chef chatting to Ali as he packed the meat delivery into the large fridge.

"Yes, I had to get a new one, the last one was stolen."

"They must have been desperate for a car, Ali."

"It wasn't that bad!"

"We've got the police here again. Roger popped in a little while ago to say the top detective is prowling around."

"Oh, that's a nuisance."

"Yes, thought you should know. He went upstairs – he's probably talking to Bozena right now."

"Come on, Ali, you can't fool us. We all know that there is something going on between you and Bozena."

"What of it?"

"Nothing. Good luck to you both I say, but it might not be the most convenient time to pop upstairs."

"I had no idea you knew."

"Oh, yes. Nothing goes on around here that we don't get to hear about."

"I see – I won't be so discreet in future," said Ali.

"You do what you want to do, Ali. How much do we owe you?"

"£86.50 – that includes for four full fillets."

"Good boy. The boss left you £100 quid – make the bill out to £90 and we both do well.

You get a bit more and the boss can see I did a good deal - £10 under his expectations."

"Thanks, chef." Ali did as he was bidden and left.

*

"How long have you worked here, Bozena?"

"Two years, Sir."

"When do you start work?"

"Seven in the morning."

"And finish?"

"Oh well, it depends on how many guests we have and if I'm required to wait on in the restaurant. I very often have to do that at the weekends."

"You work weekends?"

"Yes, Saturday and Sunday."

"Do you get time off?"

"Yes, if I want."

"Do you want?"

"No, not often."

"Do you ever feel a little nervous, Bozena? It wasn't me

you were expecting was it?"

"No, Sir."

"Was it your boyfriend who was coming?"

"Eh, yes."

"Is he late now?"

"Yes."

"Who is your boyfriend?"

"I would rather not say. I will be sacked if the manager knew."

"Okay – do you have sex in the afternoon when the manager is off?" She turned bright red and nodded. "Do you ask for money?"

"No, but he gives me some anyway."

"So how much have you lost by my being here?"

"Fifty."

"£50? Do you provide that service for any of the guests?"

"Sometimes if they're nice."

"How much do they pay you?"

"Oh, more. It's more dangerous for me."

"£100, £200?"

"No, £100 maybe, a bit more – it depends on what they want." Bozena was getting quite brave and somewhat brazen with her responses now, thought Kim. "Do you want sex?"

"No I don't, thank you. I think it's best for you this conversation remains between us."

"Oh, are you going now?"

"Yes. Thank you for being so frank." Kim slowly wandered down the stairs. It was 5.30 already and preparation was at full tilt in the kitchen. The chef was in charge and he introduced Kim to the two helpers that came in for three hours per night to help with the preparation.

"Do you have any other part-time help?"

"Just a dishwasher person – they work from 9.00 to midnight. I finish at 10.30."

"What happens if a late arrival wants food?"

"There is always something in the fridge. Bozena or someone will rustle it up for them."

Kim asked the chef the unusual question he had asked Bozena about hours and days at work.

"Do you like working here, chef?"

"Yes, it's one big happy family. We all get on together."

"Oh, I would have thought bar, restaurant and kitchen would be one unit with the hotel side separate."

"No, who told you that?"

"No matter. Has anyone else been here whilst I was upstairs?"

"Like who?"

"Like anyone. Deliveries, staff you know the sort of people who would pop in and out?"

"Oh, I see. Well, the butcher came to deliver the weekend meat. Do you want to see it?"

"Yes, why not." The chef opened a large fridge door and brought out pre-butchered meat in plastic packs. "It's good – it all arrives ready to cook?" enquired Kim.

"Yes, Ali's good like that – always good meat and well-butchered."

"Do you know who is Bozena's boyfriend?"

"I think you should ask her that question."

"I'm asking you."

"Well who is to know? He may not be."

"Who?"

"I really shouldn't say. It's something the staff know but the manager doesn't – she's a very nice girl and I don't want to get her into trouble."

"Very well, we will find out. Sorry."

*

Back at the station Tarrant had returned. He had managed to obtain the confirmation that the photograph they had was Denise Ward.

"That's good news Tarrant. I have looked at the PM report and in particular the DNA report on the foetus, there are some interesting facts."

"Can I see the report Sir?"

"Yes Tarrant," Kim replied handing over the file.

Tarrant took the file away and read it at his desk.

'The DNA of the foetus points to the fact the father was of Asian origin.'

Mmm, Tarrant mused to himself. The neighbour of Denise said she had an Asian boyfriend. It is likely he is in fact the father.

CHAPTER 6

"Kim, it's George."

"Hello, do you have something for me?"

"I may have. I'm not prepared to put this in writing but I'm having second thoughts about the time of death about your girl from The Swan."

"Oh, in what way?"

"Well, there are various tissue changes which I put down to cold weather but thinking more about it, and I know it is a strange thing to suggest, but I have a hunch that she may have been in some sort of refrigerator for a while."

"You mean a deep freeze?"

"No, definitely not a deep freeze, that has very obvious traces. It's a tissue that was absent in this case."

"So what?"

"Restaurants, butchers and so on have what they refer to as a cold room. It's one down from a commercial refrigerator – it just maintains tissue in meat in a better stable condition, no freezing involved and no deterioration either."

"I see, so what would that put the time of death?"

"That's a good question because the chilling is so delicate and not obvious in the tissue. It could maintain the tissue in the same state for, say, a week."

"A week?"

"Yes, a week."

"That would make a considerable difference. Is that why there was hardly any blood at the scene?"

"Yes, I guess the vehicle that brought her to the car park would have little or no blood deposit at all. She may not have travelled too far and if there was no heater on the body would still be chilled. Lying in the car park for say an hour would start a very slow thaw."

"Thaw! It was cold that day."

"Yes but warmer than a cold room."

"So the bit of bodily function you had was as a result of a slight rising in temperature. So we found her say at 5 o'clock in the afternoon on Thursday, two weeks ago. Do you think she could have died a week earlier?"

"Yes, I would also speculate that she took the ecstasy tablet, Sky or Ees as they are called, with alcohol at a nightclub on Friday night. It's the usual place where these people get the drug."

"Interesting. After taking the drug and alcohol, how long before they die, if they are going to die, that is?"

"Usually 24 hours – it all depends on how much exercise they have after taking the drug."

"Dancing, you mean?"

"Yes and/or sex."

"You didn't mention in your report that she had recently had sex."

"No, impossible to tell after such a period of time."

"This has opened up a whole new line of enquiry."

"It's unofficial, Jon, as I am unable to scientifically quantify my thoughts."

"Yes, I see, George, but thanks anyway."

"Sullivan, Tarrant my office, please."

"I've some additional information on our girl." Jon explained what he'd heard. "Now I need Denise's photograph circulated in nightclubs tomorrow and Saturday night but I also need to see the CCTV from any club within 10 miles of Warrington for three weekends ago."

"There are not that many large clubs around. There is only one big one in Warrington and a couple of small ones. There are probably 10 maximum in your range excluding central Manchester."

"Okay, well let's get on with it. You two deal with the CCTV requesting information, uniform can do the photo ID asking punters and the nightclub staff ..."

"One more thing, Sir," Tarrant interrupted, "I have heard from Preston police. They have a firm ID from the parents who are now desperately upset in case some harm has befallen their daughter."

"Okay, we need to keep them informed. Somehow we need a positive ID. We can't ask them to identify the body. She may have some marks that can be used to identify her. There were none mentioned in the report."

"With a DNA test of parents they should match the daughter, Sir."

"Yes, Sullivan, there certainly would be a correlation. Will you ask the boffins to get on with the task?"

*

Sandra phoned Michael over in Spain to advise him his

solicitors had the contract but John England had not received the deposit.

"The deposit has been sent, Sandra. It's with Mersey Law."

"That wasn't the deal, Michael. John was to receive the deposit."

"Okay, I'll get them to send it to John."

"Thanks. Everything is moving well here so we should be able to complete in a month," crossing her fingers as she spoke as she expected the bank to be the main factor in any delay.

"I'll be over next week, Sandra, to sign the contract. Any chance that I can get into one of the empty flats? I have to see what I have to do to make one of them comfortable for me."

"Yes. Let me know when you want to go – I'll meet you there with the keys."

Michael considered asking for a bed for the night but decided against it in case it upset the deal.

*

Tarrant and Sullivan had each taken two nightclubs and went armed with an array of recording devices to enable them to download a copy of the CCTV they needed for their investigation. Some more modern units don't use tape but back-up their images to a computer hard drive so a USB data stick would do the trick as long as there was a port available on the computer for them to do that.

At the end of a long night for the two but well before closing time for these establishments, they had their copy data. Saturday had to be used to trawl through hour after hour – not always quality video. Both of them thought that had seen Denise. They looked at each other's images. After this they were down to two short bursts of video both from the same nightclub. The interesting thing is that she wasn't alone – she was in a group of four or five people usually more girls than boys. With the TV exposure and now the name available as well as a photograph, why had not these people come forward?

On Sunday morning Kim ran the tape. No one on the video meant anything to him – certainly on the first run through. He enlarged the image and lost a lot of the clarity but he could not identify beyond doubt two of the people in the group. He was pretty sure one was Denise and thought the other he could identify was Bozena – she looked so different. It was not easy to be sure. We have to wait for the technical experts to clean up the image if they could. Kim started to consider if it was the two girls, who were the common link? Would it be Bozena's boyfriend? If it could be – I need to know who he is. Is he in these pictures?

*

Michael arrived to collect his Range Rover from the storage facility near Manchester airport. He paid the bill and collected the parcel they had taken in for him from a parcel delivery company. He tipped the receptionist £20 for which she was very grateful. People rarely tipped in the car storage business. Having had enough of Travelodge accommodation, he booked himself into The Swan at Tarporley near enough to Chester but far enough away. It was a delightful pub/hotel, excellent cuisine and comfortable beds.

He arrived at The Swan just after six in the evening on Monday.

"How long will you be staying, Sir?" enquired the manager doubling as receptionist.

"I've booked in until Friday. If I wanted to stay any

longer, would that be possible?"

"At the moment yes, Sir but we often get booked up at weekends. If you want to stay over the weekend, I suggest you let us know by Wednesday at the latest."

Michael settled in and came down to the bar for a drink before a meal. He was conscious that two ladies in the lounge area had a small child - it was becoming a little fractious. He decided to remain in the bar. He could see the hallway from the bar stool but not the lounge itself. He was just taking another draught of his beer when Sienna and another lady and a child in a pushchair walked by. He almost blurted his beer all over the bar!

"Sienna."

"Michael," she said astounded, "what brings you here?"

"I'm buying the five apartments at Squirrels Chase."

"Sorry, how rude of me. This is my mother Ann and this is baby James who, as you can tell is keen to get home."

"Yes, sorry, I won't keep you. I'm meeting Sandra tomorrow."

"Good. I'll look forward to hearing the deal's gone through."

Ann just smiled then James screamed so the three of them went.

"Do you know Mrs Wall and Mrs England, Sir?"

"Yes I do – I've known them some time."

"They're regular clients. Mrs England has had a terrible time: her son was kidnapped."

"Yes, I heard – a terrible thing."

"Yes, and the old headquarters in Sealand burnt down I believe?"

"Yes, they've had a bad time."

Michael decided to sit somewhere other than the bar to avoid being dragged into a conversation he would rather not have. He decided to send a text from his iPhone.

I'm at The Swan. I'll be here Thursday. Bring your offering. I have the parcel. M.

In a moment the text reply came: *OK. A.*

The cryptic messages exchanged would pay for Michael's trip with at least some funds left to allow him to buy some bits and pieces for his new flat.

*

"Sandra, good of you to come in person. I can't wait to see the flats. Which one's vacant?"

She avoided the niceties of the meeting advising Michael that there was a 2-bed on the ground floor that was empty with the only penthouse in the development occupying the top floor which was also empty.

"Too expensive for most tenants, I assume."

"That's what you would like for yourself?"

"Sandra you had never told me there was a penthouse."

"Yes, it was a mistake. It has never been let although we had some offers to let it but at ridiculously low rents."

"Okay, let's see the standard lettable units." Sandra clicked the button on the key fob to open the security front door to the block. She then opened Flat 2. A riot of magnolia and beige carpets with little to enhance the box-like rooms: two double-ish bedrooms, two small bath or shower rooms, a small hall, lounge/dining area, and a bar/kitchen all part of the same room.

"Hmmm, not the most exciting flat I've seen."

"I'm sure you can make it more interesting, Michael."

"Yes. I think I could."

"Do you want the stairs or lift to the penthouse?"

"Oh, let's go in the lift."

"It was specifically for the penthouse. The door cannot be opened unless you hold the fob for the penthouse over the panel."

They went slowly to the second floor. The lift door opened into a lobby with one door which needed a key to open it. The penthouse, spanning an area roughly of four standard flats, immediately endeared itself to Michael. Three double bedrooms all en-suite, the master bedroom was enormous as was the lounge, the balcony with French doors allowed a certain amount of outdoor space with views much better than he expected with the buildings of the city of Chester to the right and the Welsh hills beyond and to the south.

"This is great – I'll enjoy this!"

"Good, all you need to do is sign the contract and do as you said with the deposit and send it to John."

"It will be done this very afternoon unless you delay me by allowing me to buy you lunch."

"Nice try, Michael but I must get back."

"Well, thank you Sandra this is an unexpected bonus. I'm really excited by the purchase now."

CHAPTER 7

Ali was at the meat market in Manchester as usual very early in the day. He'd recovered his old car from the police pound having insured it and thanked the police for finding it. He returned the hire car, the company charging him extra for cleaning the car.

"It smells like a butcher's shop."

"Probably because I am a butcher and used it for deliveries."

"If we had known that we would have suggested a van."

"Not ideal for taking a girl out, a van. Okay get on and clean it let me know what you hit my credit card with." Ali stormed out of the office back to his shop.

*

Kim had expected to obtain clearer CCTV images now, the tech boys said they had cleaned the image as best they can. Tarrant had been pressing the technocrats for pictures but nothing had turned up.

"Tarrant, have The Swan had their CCTV repaired?"

"I don't know, Sir. I'll ring the manager now."

"They're repairing it now, Mr Tarrant do you want a copy of any pictures before it went off?"

"Yes, that would be useful – say, for the month before it went off."

"Okay, I can e-mail the video to you."

"You can?"

"Yes, it's a digital system – it's useful in that way."

"Okay, let me have the video as soon as you can."

Tarrant now accompanied by Jon Kim looked at the video images they had been sent.

"Try looking at every Thursday."

"Why Thursday, Sir?"

"Well that's when Bozena's boyfriend visits for the most part. I would like to see who it is."

"By God, CCTV is boring hour after hour of nothing! Wait, what was that? Go back."

Tarrant stopped the fast-forward and returned to mid-afternoon two Thursdays before Denise's body was dumped in the car park.

"It's the butcher by the look of it."

"Yes, Sir – it's his car."

"Is that the same white car that was stolen and left at Chester station?"

"It might be – I need to check the index number."

Whilst Tarrant was away looking for the car's number, Kim continued watching. It was a gloomy rainy day and a person carrying bundles of something ran into the back door. It was impossible to get an identification of him or her.

"Yes, it's the same car, Sir – it's the butcher."

"Oh, that's what he is doing." Kim explained what he had seen. Fast-forwarding, they saw the white estate car leave.

"Tarrant, what time was that?"

"Not long, Sir, after it arrived."

"Check the timeline."

He went fast-forward. "About an hour, I think, Sir."

"An hour to deliver meat! Check the Thursday before and the one before that."

Sure enough there was the same person running in to deliver packets and leaving an hour or so later.

"The butcher was not just delivering meat – he was visiting Bozena Bania, the chambermaid."

"What if he was, Sir?"

"I don't know yet. I'm possibly just grabbing at straws. However, I would like to go and visit the butcher and see if he confirms that he is Bozena's boyfriend."

"Okay, Sir – anything else you would like to know?"

"Just what room numbers they had used on the last few occasions."

"At The Swan Hotel?"

"This is DI Kim, can I speak to Bozena Bania, please?"

"I'm sorry, Sir, she left early today. She will be in tomorrow." Advised the voice at the Swan.

"Do you have a mobile or phone number for her?"

"No, sorry, we don't."

So why has she left early this Thursday?

"Tarrant, when did The Swan say they were having the CCTV fixed?"

"This morning, Sir – why?"

"Give your man a ring and see if they can e-mail the images for today, please."

The manager of The Swan was as good as his word. The images were with Tarrant in 20 minutes.

"Let's have a look at these from say, 4.00pm onwards. Yes, there's our friend the butcher – the image is much clearer."

"Yes, Sir, we can see that he is Asian."

"Yes, Tarrant, and that he left today after only 10 minutes. We know Bozena is not in – so what do you make of that?"

"I don't know what to make of it, Sir, other than maybe they are meeting away from the hotel."

"Exactly, Tarrant. What time is it now?"

"Quarter to six, Sir."

"Damn, we've probably missed them. Anyway you go and see the butcher tomorrow – what's his name?"

"Mr Hussain, Sir."

"Okay, I suppose we should have known he was of Asian origin from the name."

*

Michael spent the morning with Mersey Law signing the contract and the conveyance documents ready for when it was needed.

"I'll forward the £950,000 when I get back. £50k is your fee including VAT?"

"There is the small matter of stamp duty, Michael."

"Yes, okay, how much is that?"

"I'll try and get approval for stamp duty on the penthouse only, the other four if we take £50,000 off the value of each will be below the stamp duty threshold. The penthouse will then attract duty at 2% being £400,000."

"When you say 'try' is it not then done that you can elect for duty on each unit? Not the sum as a whole?"

"No, I think we may in the end have to pay the higher rate."

"Well, I don't want to get carried away then I want to buy in separate transactions for apartments at £150,000 and then the penthouse at £400,000. Do I need to sign some more contracts?"

"Yes, you will, Michael and the conveyances will be wrong."

"Okay, copy five signature pages of each – I'll sign each one and you do the rest. You'd better phone John England and say that's how it's going to be. If they agree, send the £100k, if not say you have instructions only to do it that way and until agreement the deposit can't be released. I'll speak to Sandra, can you do that?"

"Yes, Michael, I have to warn you it might still backfire but we shall try."

"Damn right you will – it will save a fortune."

Driving his Range Rover back to Tarporley, Michael phoned Sandra, explained the stamp duty issue and how the sale would now be constructed.

"This is not what was agreed, Michael."

"No, but the stamp duty is a great deal of money for nothing. If you want the deal, that's the way it is."

"Very well, I'll notify John that he needs to create five transactions, not one."

"Correct. Thanks, Sandra."

He carried on to Tarporley, his next assignation in mind. It was just after three when he drove into the car park. He lifted the parcel from the boot and took it to his room with his briefcase. It was about 4.30 when the knock on his door came.

"Come in Ali, how're things?"

"Could be worse, Mr Michael."

"You're not in trouble, Ali, are you?"

"No, Mr Michael, I've just had my car stolen. That's all."

"Did you get it back?"

"Yes. It's amazing isn't it – I think the police are wonderful."

"Look, Ali, this is the parcel. One is 5,000 E's – they are the best. Retail at £5 each – you understand?"

"Yes, Mr Michael. How much do you want?"

"I want £2 each now and then a £1 each next time we meet. If this goes well, I'll bring some more of the same stuff."

"Are these different from the last lot I had?"

"Yes, they have a 'PMA' in them which makes them stronger. The last lot were a bit dodgy. They said they had 'PMA' but I'm not sure. I don't think they were all the same strength – a bit of a botch job. However, the punters seem to like them, don't they?"

"Ehm, yes. Dodgy ones cause trouble, you know. What is 'PMA'?" enquired Ali.

"It's a synthetic drug, some call it 'Dr Death'. Anyway here are 5,000. You owe me ten grand now. Next time we meet another five grand."

"Yes, Mr Michael."

"What's troubling you Ali? You seem a bit hesitant."

"Well, a girl I know died recently. She'd taken some E's from me."

"Oh, I'm sorry to hear that but it's a risk these kids take, you know. They mix them with alcohol and the rest is history."

"Yes, Mr Michael." Ali took several bundles of notes out of a plastic shopping bag and gave them to Michael who gave Ali the unopened parcel.

"Mind how you go, Ali, no speeding now."

"No, Mr Michael."

"Ali come back, I forgot something." Michael removed the parcel from Ali's bag and cut off the address label. "Can't have that there, can we?"

"Oh no, Mr Michael, I must go now." Ali virtually cantered down the stairs nearly knocking Roger over in the process.

"Hey! Steady on Ali – someone chasing you?"

"Sorry, Mr Roger – I'm a bit of a hurry." He sped out of the car park and at the end of the High Street stopped at the bus stop where a young lady got in.

CHAPTER 8

Parking his unmarked car a little down the street from Mr Hussain's butcher's shop, it was half past nine in the morning but the shop was not open. Strange, Tarrant thought to himself, these guys usually get up early. He rattled a door to see if he could raise anyone. Nothing. "Damn," he muttered to himself. He spotted a drive-thru McDonalds on the way and so decided to go back and have coffee and maybe a muffin and come back in an hour.

Sure enough at half ten the door was open and lights on. Not much to see in the window - a few cuts of meat and sausages and that was it.

"Hello, how can I help you today, Sir?"

Tarrant showed his warrant card and introduced himself.

"If it's about the car, I now have all the insurance. I have the papers if you would like to see them."

"No, no it's not about your car."

"Then what is it?"

"We are investigating a suspicious death and you supply meat to The Swan in Tarporley. Is that right?"

"Yes, but I'm not sure anyone has died from eating my meat."

"No, that's not the issue. Why do The Swan choose you to supply their meat?"

"Oh, I supply a number of pubs and restaurants. You see, when they built the new Morrisons down the road all my trade went. I nearly went bust. I had to find other customers. I had my credentials with the wholesalers in Manchester so to avoid the publicans having to get up early and going to the market, I do it – butcher and prepare the portions and deliver to them what they want."

"Is that why you were not open at half nine?"

"No, no, gracious me. I was not at the market on Friday. I go very early on Thursday and do the butchering in the morning and deliver in the afternoon. It's a very tiring day on the Thursdays. So I open late on Friday."

"All makes sense. Tiring, I suppose Mr Hussain because you have a friend to visit on Thursdays as well."

"How do you mean?"

"Does the name Bozena Bania mean anything to you?"

"Ah, have you been spying on me, Mr Tarrant?"

"It's not a secret Mr Hussain, it's well known in the hotel you visit when you deliver the meat."

"Oh dear! And I thought our friendship was a secret. People get the wrong idea, you know."

"When you meet with her at the hotel, do you use a room or do you go to her place?"

"Oh dear me, I do hope this is not going to get Bozena into trouble. She's a good hardworking girl. Yes, we use a room she has not prepared so it varies."

"I see. Did you see her about three weeks ago?"

"I may have done. I can't be sure. We don't meet every week, you know."

"Okay. What room were you in the last time you met?"

"Well, I'm not sure – they all look alike, possibly 10."

"Okay. Where do you live?"

"That's easy – I live, as they say, over the shop."

"You have a flat here?"

"Yes. It's not very big. Just one bedroom and a living room, kitchen and bathroom – big enough for me."

"And your car - where do you keep that?"

"It goes on the road round the side."

"Is that where it was when it was stolen?"

"Yes, I'm sure, yes."

"How did you do your rounds and get to the market if it was stolen, Mr Hussain?"

"I went in my car as usual – it wasn't stolen until later in the day, early evening."

"I see. You didn't think to report it?"

"No. You see, I didn't have insurance and it's not worth much so I decided to let it go."

"You have it back now."

"Oh yes – I was very pleased. I hired a car for a while - while your officers said they needed my car for tests – fingerprints, I suppose, to find the thief."

"Yes, yes, Mr Hussain. Can I have a look at your flat?"

"Well, it's a bit of a mess but I see no reason why not."

Tarrant went out of the shop to a side door which led to a flight of stairs up to the flat.

"That's handy having a separate entrance."

"Yes, when things were bad I thought of letting it and

then I got some contracts with pubs which ensured my business was saved."

"You're right, it is a mess. I see you like old cars."

"How do you know that?"

"Well, there's some classic car magazines under the TV," said Tarrant.

"Anyway, Mr Hussain thank you for talking to me. It has helped a lot."

"Has it? Yes, we now know that you are the boyfriend of Bozena. Thanks."

Tarrant sat in his car for a good 15 minutes or so and wrote a detailed account of his interview with Hussain. "Damn, I never asked for his Christian name – it will be on the DVLA website," he muttered to himself.

Ali was highly relieved when Tarrant was gone. He was astute to realise Tarrant had tried to make a connection between him and Denise without actually asking the question. He was glad he had cut the cable for the CCTV camera. No evidence of him being there the night he dumped Denise in the car park. Then it struck him, no one that is except for Bozena if she talked, would put him at the right place at the right time and they would start to put two and two together. Ali was concerned – he needed to make plans.

*

Michael had checked out of The Swan and was back at Manchester airport, his Range Rover placed back into the care of the storage company, his Easy Jet flight was on time and hand baggage made the whole experience much easier. Once back in Marbella he phoned Goose to arrange to meet him. It was fixed for the following morning. Goose was keen to know how the merchandise was going. He was a little concerned that a death had occurred and he put it down to alcohol and E's and probably too much of each.

"It's going well, Michael. Your sales seem to be finding the right markets. Did you get your apartments?" enquired Goose.

"Well, nearly – the legal work will take a little longer because to try and save on stamp duty I am buying five different units in five conveyances, each one as an individual purchase rather than all as one."

"Tax. You don't want to be paying tax, Michael." Advised Goose.

"It is unavoidable in the UK on property deals. The Revenue have the lawyers on their side."

"Typical," muttered Goose, "we can be doing with opening a second front. Do you think your contacts in England have another reliable distribution network in the Midlands? If that goes well, we can then try a London one."

"London would worry me, Goose, too many organised crime syndicates there. If we trod on the wrong toes we could be looking at funeral bills not £50 notes."

"Okay, let's concentrate on what we have and not be too greedy. Have you my money?"

Michael handed over £7,500 – that was the full amount of the last delivery. Michael was allowing Ali credit of £1,000 until the next time he saw him. Michael declined Goose's invitation to stay for lunch, he wanted to do some planning. His thoughts of spending some years with Sandra were now at an end. He needed to decide what he was going to do with his life. He had the insurance money from the villa, a steady income from Manchester and soon to be the Chester flats and the pills – they were good for spending money, cash. Should he build a new villa in Benahavis or should he simply sit on the cash or spend it on travel? He contemplated all these possibilities. He didn't need to make a decision now but he realised that if Ali got into trouble the domino effect might implicate him and Spain was not an ideal place to be in those circumstances. There would be extradition warrants available to authorities which now made Spain not such a safe haven. Maybe Goose has the right idea – a motor yacht, no fixed abode, not easy to spot where you are – maybe I should consider that. He went out to get a pizza and stopped at the newsagent in the port and purchased a couple of boating magazines. If nothing else, it would be something interesting to read over lunch.

*

"How did you get on, Tarrant?" Kim wanted to know the latest findings so he could run them through his personal database of a brain.

"Fine, Sir. No doubt Mr Hussain is the boyfriend of Bozena Bania. There is one other thing that has been bothering me, it hit me when I checked Mr Hussain's Christian name with the DVLA – it's Ali. Does that not ring a bell with you, Sir?"

"The only Ali I recall was the Ali that didn't exist in the arson attack on the Wall's premises in Sealand."

"Exactly! And when I found his name and put that together with a poster in his flat depicting an e-type Jaguar, and a couple of classic car magazines then I immediately put two and two together."

"Hope you didn't make four because the hypothetical connection is extremely remote even accepting, which the jury didn't agree that there was a Mr Ali involved. Anyway that Mr Ali, according to the fanciful tale from Terry Pritchard would have had to have known Michael Fitzallen and how would he know him? No, there can be no connection. Forget it. Let's find the person behind Denise West's murder. If not the murderer the person responsible for subsequent mutilation and disposal of Denise West's body if that is who she is."

"Very well, Sir – just a thought."

CHAPTER 9

Ali was back to his old routine. Instead of staying with Bozena the following Thursday, he arranged to take her out on the town.

"I'd love to do that. I don't have any clothes to wear."

"Don't worry about that. I'll take you to M&S in Warrington – they will be open until late. I'll treat you to some party clothes."

"Wow! Thanks, Ali."

Bozena was in her element at M&S at Warrington. She bought more than just party clothes but Ali didn't seem to mind. When he'd forked out the cash, the couple left and went to Ali's flat. Bozena gave Ali a striptease and fashion show with alternate garments. He loved every minute.

"Have a drink."

"I don't drink."

"Why not? You're a Pole – don't Poles drink vodka? Warrington is the home of British vodka, Vladivar."

"Okay, Ali, I'll have a vodka."

"It's really good with any of my special pick-you-up pills."

"What are the pills, Ali?"

"Speed, you know, they give you a high and me too – we'll have one each. Okay?"

"If you say so."

They took the pills and Bozena also drank several shots of vodka. Within half an hour they were having sex – sex like Ali had never had before!

"Stop, stop Ali – I'm blowing up, my skin is so too small for my body." She screamed a scream to curdle the blood, then she was still. No movement. Nothing. Ali put his hand on the side of her neck to try and find a pulse.

"My, God, she's gone!"

Ali checked her pulse again she was dead, very dead. He was sure it was the new E pills but he didn't have any strange feelings, maybe he was lucky. Once again Ali was faced with the disposal of a body. This was becoming a bit too routine. Upset, shocked and now very frightened he knew he needed to put her in the cold room naked as soon as he could. He knew the naked body would react better to the cold. It would keep it in good stable condition. She will be missed, he thought to himself, how to tell The Swan? Not easy thought – they must try and work it work it out but if they reported her missing to the police they will come round here now they know the connection. How to get rid of her? That was the issue. He thought the unthinkable but it was the perfect solution – it was just the clothes he would have to get rid of.

*

At The Swan Hotel the manager was frantically trying to locate Bozena – she had never missed coming to work. It was Friday and they were fully booked for the weekend.

"She may be in later," Chef merrily suggested knowing that she had gone home earlier than was her normal pattern but perfectly entitled to do so. He suspected with the recent revelations and police activity that she and Ali had gone out together. Eventually the manager contacted a stand-in chambermaid who filled in when they were exceptionally busy – she could come in at 10 o'clock as she had to get the children off to school but she had to go home at three. The manager knew it was just possible to get through servicing all the rooms by that time.

By noon no sign of Bozena, so the manager called in extra part-time waiting staff. The Swan was really busy and once he had enough staff to serve the guests his concerns for Bozena evaporated.

*

"DCI Kim the CC would like to have a word with you. Can you be free in half an hour?"

"Yes, I'll come up then."

"Kim, I've had a chat with the Chairman of the Police Committee. We both feel that we should like you to stay as the most senior able detective in the Force. The opportunity to save your costs in these times of belt-tightening have also to be considered."

"So what you are saying, Sir, is no I can't stay?"

"In a nutshell, yes."

"That is incredibly disappointing, Sir. I may decide to refer this to the Police Federation to see if they can negotiate a position for me."

"Well, if you feel that strongly you must do so if you think fit."

Back in his office, Kim was contemplating what his reaction should be to the CC's news or what alternative career he might pursue when he was disturbed by the phone.

"Yes?"

"Sir, it's Tarrant. I've had a call from uniform, there have been a number of incidents in the region recently with young people taking ecstasy tablets. The hospitals have reported that some of the symptoms are the same and the pills these youngsters have got hold are much stronger than they have seen before. I thought you should know."

"Yes. Any ideas as to the source of these tablets?"

"Not at the moment. The most likely are clubs and disco pubs."

"Have we arrested anyone with these new stronger tablets on them?"

"Don't know, sorry."

"Can you find out? If you can get me one or two samples, I'll see if we can get them analysed. It may be the same strain that was responsible for Denise Ward's death."

*

"Michael, its Ali."

"Why are you ringing me? I told you never to call me unless there was a real emergency."

"There has been another death associated with these new pills. They are very dangerous, Michael."

"It's how these kids use them, Ali, believe me. Too much alcohol, too many pills, that's it."

"Yes, I know, my girlfriend just died."

"Oh no, Ali, where?"

"In my flat."

"Bloody hell, Ali, you need to do something and quickly."

"Like what, Mr Michael?"

"Get rid of the pills – get rid of them as soon as you can preferably this weekend. Tell your people if they don't have the money they can take the pills and pay when they are sold."

"I see – why do that?"

"Well, if the police come calling, you don't want to be found in possession of any of the pills do you?"

"And the body?"

"That's for you decide but don't call me again. Just sort it, Ali."

Michael realised that if life in the UK gets a bit difficult, he should remain in Spain for a while and once the purchase of the Chester flat was completed, he might treat himself to an extended holiday. The thing was, should he take his Spanish Range Rover and drive or fly to a new location somewhere on the planet. He could always rent when he got to where he was going. At this point the destination was under review, although Ali's phone call made the decision on location more urgent. He paid the bill at The Swan and left losing the old phone down a grid in the road so it was out of action as Goose had suggested.

*

Goose, on the other hand, was always keen to keep a few jumps ahead of the authorities. He decided it was probably time to go. He wasn't keen to remain whilst there was a whiff of trouble – where to go was the issue? He liked the Mediterranean, a port out of reach of the European authorities might be best.

"Captain, I think in the next few days – say a week from today – we should set sail. Perhaps bunker in Gibraltar and then head for Tripoli in Libya."

"Is that wise, Sir, it's not noted for its welcome?"

"Ah yes, I'm sure Colonel Gadhafi will authorise our visit. I'll see if I can arrange it whilst you make your plans."

*

The Swan operated all weekend without Bozena. The part-timers and stand-ins were fine but somehow the speed of work did not match that of his Polish full-time girl. Monday morning and still no Bozena. The manager thought he should go and check her lodgings – the girl may be ill and need help.

"No, dear, I've not seen her since she left for work last Thursday. Is there a problem?"

"No, I hope not. I'm her employer, it's just unusual for someone not to communicate with their employer if they can't come to work."

"Yes, I know but she was foreign – she probably had a problem back in Poland and just left."

"Has she cleared her room?"

"I don't know, dear. It's not my place to see – she's paid the rent to the end of the month so I can't go snooping."

"Okay, yes, you may be right – she may be back any time."

The manager returned to The Swan and made arrangements for the next week with the prospect of help being required for the week after that. He explained that it was possible that she had to return to Poland in a hurry and without a mobile was not able to make contact.

*

"Mark Feathers, please. Mark, it's Jon Kim in Cheshire."

"Hello Joh, how can I help?"

"I am not sure if the Police Federation can help me much but I would like to see if you can."

"Can you let me have the details and I will let you know if we can help."

Jon laid out his predicament and the mandatory retirement next Christmas when he will be nearly 56. He explained that he was not interested in retiring and would like to carry on.

"Interesting question this! I can tell you the Government is about to extend the mandatory retirement age so the date you get your State pension in civy street is, as it were, will be 67 and as for our part in the Police, our position is to try and resist any extension of the years to be worked whereas your request is the direct opposite. Are you sure you don't want to retire – most of our members can't wait for their day?"

"No, I'm not married, no family, I enjoy my job, I have at least another ten years to give."

"Your request might not be easy to fulfil and may take some time. It could also mean a move to another division. If we have a situation where an officer wants to retire earlier than normal, I could suggest you are the ideal person to fill the gap but on a longer contract."

"That would be a solution, Mark. There is no immediate hurry – let me know how you get on."

CHAPTER 10

Nearly three weeks had gone by since Bozena Bania walked out of The Swan and had not returned – no message, nothing. The manager spoke to his solicitors to see if he could legitimately employ somebody else. They advised him he could but put them on, say, a three month contract to begin with and maybe if nothing is heard then take them on full time. As a consequence of the advice he had received the manager placed an advert in the Chester Chronicle, jobs available section, and hoped for a response.

To cover all bases the manager also placed an advert in the newsagent's window whilst asking his stand-in help if they would like to be considered for the full time position. He hoped ideally that Bozena would return but if not, he would have a solution. He couldn't continue with the temporary staff as good as they were.

Bozena's landlady not having heard from her and her rent now due decided she couldn't afford not to have rent so she packed Bozena's stuff into two black bin bags sealing them with tape and put them in the cellar. After cleaning the room she hung the little slip under the B&B sign advertising vacancies. She was cross Bozena had gone – she was a regular long term tenant and gave good income. One or two night people who pay more are okay but long term regulars she found were the best.

*

The e-mail to the Harbour Master in Tripoli was responded to in formal but firm language: *The Port is closed to unauthorised vessels.* How to get authorised was the issue. Perhaps if he went first to the neighbouring port of Tunis it would be best – he could perhaps get clearance when he was near there. In the end the e-mail was sent to the Harbour Master at Tunis.

The reply was instant and helpful: *We will be delighted to welcome you, please advise your expected time of arrival.*

"That's more like it," Goose said to his Captain, "let's get ready to sail."

*

Ali was pleased that he had heard nothing from the police. He assumed no one had reported Bozena missing so no connection had been made.

"The deliveries don't take so long now, Ali," remarked the chef at The Swan.

"No, I don't have time to dawdle."

"She isn't here, did you know she's gone – she just vanished one Thursday. You didn't take her with you, did you?"

"No, why ever would I do that?" said Ali in a rather uncomfortable way.

The chef thought Ali's response was less than truthful. He thought he had hit on exactly what had happened.

"I bet you have her locked up in your little nest in Warrington, Ali."

"No, no that's not right at all."

The chef now knew he was lying. Ali was so jumpy.

"I must go, chef. Got lots to do. See you next week."

When Ali had gone, the chef wondered what he should do. Ali seemed like a kind man. If he did have Bozena in Warrington, what of it! He thought no more about it. "Not my problem or business," he muttered to himself.

*

Michael, just to let you know we have completed the purchase in 5 units today, said the e-mail. *I've tried phoning you but your number is out of order.*

Michael e-mailed back to thank Mersey Law but not to provide his new number.

"Sandra, we've completed," said John England on the phone to his sister-in-law, "where do you want me to send the proceeds?"

"Well John I guess they should go to Wall's Holdings, I will sort out an appropriate distribution when the overdraft is cleared."

"Good as done, see you soon."

*

"Sandra, do you know I have completed the purchase?" Michael had phoned Sandra from Spain.

"Yes, Michael, I know, I tried to ring you but your phone doesn't work. Have you changed your number?"

"Yes, I had a problem with the old one."

"Okay, it happens. Are you coming over to England soon? I need to give you all the keys."

"Yes, I'll be over next week."

"That's good, let me know when you're here and we can meet up so I can buy you lunch."

"Ah, is the ice melting?"

"Possibly."

"That sounds favourable. I'll book in at The Swan, perhaps we can meet there. The food is excellent."

"Yes, okay. See you next week." Sandra had a slight tingle of excitement when she put the phone down. Maybe she had been too hard on Michael. She was looking forward to the meeting.

*

Jon Kim, meeting with DS Tarrant and DC Sullivan, reminded them both that little or no progress had been made on the Denise Ward case assuming that the PM and all the tests tell the right story.

"No, Sir," agreed Tarrant, "we've come to a halt after what looked like a promising start. The uniform branch has advised that there is an increase in deaths associated with Ecstasy. They think the strain is more potent than the previous pills they've confiscated."

"Did they give you some?"

"Yes. I sent them away for detailed analysis and they sent the report to the pathologist, George Hughes. He phoned earlier to say it was quite probable the Ecstasy digested by Denise is from the same batch. These had similar characteristics in the chemistry. He cautioned saying that some drugs can sometimes be altered from the original formulation by the enzymes of the person ingesting the drug."

"That seems to make sense, Sir, but it still means we are no nearer finding the source of the pills or, indeed who disfigured her body and dumped it in The Swan car park."

"Tarrant, maybe we have missed something at The Swan. I spoke with the housekeeper, the Polish girl, Bozena Bania. She is the only person to own up to doing something not strictly in accordance with her job. She, as you found out, is the girlfriend of Ali Hussain but we don't know if that takes us any further. Is there any possible connection between Denise Ward, a letting agent working in Warrington now working in Manchester, and Ali Hussain a butcher in Warrington? The town's a link but not really relevant and Bozena Bania, a Polish worker, and a pub hotel in Tarporley."

"My God! I'm stupid!"

"Only just realised that, Tarrant?"

Smirks broke out on the faces of the other two.

"No, you just mentioned Denise was a letting agent. Ali said he had thought of letting his flat when business was bad. Could it be that Denise went round and maybe became friends or possibly lovers? If so it would explain how Denise was pregnant. The foetal blood seemed to indicate a father who was of Eastern extraction."

"Good thinking. Don't go bounding in. You need to contact Denise's company. Was she ever employed at Warrington? If so, did she visit Hussain's flat? You do that Tarrant as it's your brainwave – let me know when you've got some answers."

"Okay boss."

"Sullivan any progress on the pubs and disco pubs which might be the source of the supply of the Ecstasy tablets?"

"No, Sir. It's no good going during the day – it's an undercover operation we need to mount. Unless we intercept a transaction and get offered some pills. Management of all these places say that drugs and amphetamines of any type are prohibited on their premises. They even have notices saying that anyone dealing or taking such things will be expelled."

"Yes, very moral I'm sure, but that's where the pills are. Maybe, if we don't make much progress in the next week we shall have to consider raids on some of these places. The problem with that is if we don't find anything we only drive the pushers underground and they will surface somewhere later which will not help our cause."

"Yes Sir," said Sullivan, but we should consider an undercover operation. A young female PC with some male back up would be the way to go."

"Very well Sullivan I will get authorisation for such an operation."

*

Back at The Swan, a rendezvous was in progress.

"Michael, how good to see you again." Sandra allowed a kiss this time. She was carrying a large envelope which he assumed contained all the keys.

"Have a drink."

"Oh, only a small white wine thank you Michael."

Michael ordered a small white wine and a pint of beer for himself from the bar. They found a window table which enabled them to have a little more space for Sandra to spread out the contents of the envelope.

"Cheers. Thank you." They smiled at one another.

"No problem. It's great to see you again especially so as you are not apparently cross with me anymore. I'm sorry about the Chester offices and the store. These things happen."

"I know. I don't hold you responsible Michael, but something unexplained went on. Maybe we shall never know so let's move on."

"Yes, good philosophy, Sandra. What have you got for me?"

She tipped the contents of a large padded envelope on

to the table and began to sort them into groups.

"Pay attention, Michael."

"Yes, Miss," he said with a grin and Sandra reciprocated.

"These seven keys, one for the front door of the block, each is a key and security fob."

"Seven. Why seven?"

"Five spares, three properties that are let. There's a key for each of them. Then two each for the flats that are not occupied. So when they are all occupied you will just have five spares. Get it?"

"Yes, I see. There are three sets of keys for each empty flat and a set each for the flats that are let. Very efficient!"

"Even more efficient, Michael, they are all labelled. Here's a copy letter for you which I would like you to sign to confirm I have given you all the keys today."

"Don't you trust me?"

"No, it's not that – it just completes the file."

"Okay." Michael signed his name on the bottom of the letter, scooped up all the keys into the envelope.

"Those are the only keys there are, Michael, so don't lose them."

"Would I do that?"

"Well, yes you may."

"Now, will you come with me tomorrow to help me choose furniture, carpets and curtains for the penthouse?"

"I will but why don't you use an interior designer? That way you'll get a really cohesive design – I'm not that sort of person."

"Anyone in mind?"

"Sienna used to use someone on show flats and houses

who seemed pretty good. Shall I ring Si and get the contact?"

"Yes, please, that would be great."

The call was made and then to the designer and arrangements were made to meet up at Squirrels Chase in the morning.

"That's great. How about lunch?"

"I can't stop for lunch, Michael. I must get back to Chester."

"Oh, you promised."

"I know but some things have to be done." In fact, she had an appointment with Tony Munsford for lunch and she was probably going to be late but she didn't want to miss it.

"Dinner tonight, then? I'll come to Chester – we'll go to The Grosvenor."

"That's great. What, 8 o'clock?"

"I'll be there and I'll book the table."

Michael and Sandra embraced and Sandra sped off to Chester.

"Tony, my apologies for being late. I hope you got my message."

"Yes, I did and it's fine. It's good to meet up under less stressful circumstances," said Tony.

"For you Sandra" he said handing over an envelope, "Yes, and before we go any further all the letters of satisfaction signed and stamped by the bank are in this envelope. You and Wall's Holdings have no more obligations to the bank and the bank no longer holds any charges, debentures or personal guarantees from you or any of the Wall shareholders."

"That is an event in itself, Tony I can tell you. We are a

fraction of what we once were but at least our heads are above water."

"Yes, I can't tell you how pleased I am."

"Thanks, Tony."

He handed Sandra a menu. "This one's on the bank."

She really felt like milking it but as she had a big dinner to look forward to she had some fish and salad and after that she returned to her flat, had a brief nap and a period of grooming for what could turn out to be a special night out.

CHAPTER 11

Tarrant called on the Warrington branch of Allens, the letting agents that Denise Ward had worked for. He enquired if she had ever worked at the Warrington branch. The manager, who seemed to be in a great hurry, confirmed that she had not – she had been a Manchester employee and if the police needed any more information, that's where they should go. The manager made his apologies but was late for an appointment and left. Tarrant stood in reception rather nonplussed at the attitude of the manager:

"Don't worry. He's always like that," said a young lady sitting behind one of a number of desks in the front office – she appeared the only employee left in the place.

"Oh, are you on your own now?"

"Only for a little while – one of the negs will be in soon."

"Negs?"

"Negotiators. Would you like a coffee?"

Tarrant accepted and sat on the opposite side of the desk whilst the coffee was produced.

"He's wrong, you know."

"Sorry, who's wrong?"

"The manager. Denise did work here for three weeks when Cheryl went on honeymoon."

"Cheryl?"

"Oh, she's a neg and got married last summer. As a rule there is only two weeks holiday at once but Cheryl was getting married in Barbados and wanted a week there before the wedding with a two week honeymoon afterwards. Would you like to see the photos? She looked gorgeous."

"No, no, no thanks – that won't be necessary. So how long ago about would it be that Denise was here?"

"Last June – no doubt about it."

"Okay, what did she do?"

"Oh, viewings and vals."

"Vals?"

"Valuations. She went to see a property and put a rent on it, hopefully to put it on the market to let."

"I see. Do you know if she went to see a flat over a butcher's owned by a Mr Hussain?"

"Hang on, have you the postcode?"

"Yes, I might have." Tarrant consulted his pocket book and gave the receptionist the code.

"Yes, Mr A Hussain, one bed, first floor flat over a shop, £400 a month but we never took it on. I expect another agent got it."

"Have you any details about the appointment – like, when it was, what time of day etc."

"Yes, it was at 5 o'clock on 6 June last year."

"That's excellent, thank you and the coffee was good too." Tarrant was pleased with himself as he had now proof that Ali Hussain had met Denise.

Back at Police HQ, Tarrant acquainted Jon Kim with the news.

"I think that you and I need to go and see Mr Ali Hussain."

"When are you free, Sir?"

"At 5 o'clock. It would be better to go when his shop is shut."

"Yes, Sir – fine by me."

*

A loud banging on the side door alerted Ali that someone was knocking and it sounded important.

"Mr Ali Hussain, my name is D C I Kim and this is DS Tarrant who you have met," Kim said, holding his warrant card.

"We need to have a word with you. May we come in?"

"It's not very convenient just now, can you …"

"No, Mr Hussain, this is important. May we come in?"

"Very well, so long as you don't take up too much time as it's Wednesday and I have to be up at three in the morning."

"It needn't take too long, Mr Hussain," Kim said as the pair followed Ali up to his flat.

"Sit down Mr Hussain." Kim found another chair but Tarrant remained standing.

"You have a nice little flat here. I understand you thought about letting it out last summer."

"Yes, that's right. It isn't against the law."

"No, no – I agree but tell me, Mr Hussain if you will, why were you thinking of letting it out and what did you do?"

"Oh, I asked a number of agents to come and look at the flat and tell me what the rent might be."

"Did you go to the firm of Allens?"

"Yes, I believe I did."

"Can you recall who came to do the valuation?"

"No, it was a young lady – they all were."

"Do you recall this particular young lady?"

"No, no - I don't."

"Are you sure, Mr Hussain?"

"Yes, I'm sure – I have no recollection of her name. I'm sorry."

"So if I told you it was Denise Ward, does that mean anything to you?"

"No, why should it?"

"Because I believe there have been programmes on the TV and in the local papers about her."

"I recall seeing something but I never made the connection."

"Why do you get up so early on Thursdays?"

"Oh, that's easy – I go to the meat market in Manchester and buy meat for my customers and deliver it to them on Thursday in the afternoon."

"And is The Swan Inn at Tarporley a customer?"

"Oh yes – a very good customer. I think I told that to that gentleman last time we met," Ali said pointing at Tarrant.

"So the fact that Denise Ward's body was found in the car park shortly after you left The Swan is a total coincidence?"

"Yes, yes it must be. As I say, I don't recall her at all."

"You are lying to me, Ali. We have CCTV from a number of clubs on Friday, seven weeks ago that show you and others in a group and in that group is Denise Ward."

"Inspector, I assure you I do not know her. Until you told me she was the person who came to tell me the rent on my flat I had no idea what her name is – you know these girls change their appearance when they go out."

"Okay, it may be circumstantial so that we can eliminate you from our enquiries regarding Denise Ward, we need you to give us a DNA sample?"

"Oh, I don't think I like needles!"

"It is not a needle, Mr Hussain. It's just a cotton swab on a long stick – it just takes a swab of saliva and goes into a sealed tube for analysis."

Tarrant took the sample and placed it in the tube. Kim and Tarrant bade Mr Hussain good evening and left.

"If the DNA sample matches the other elements of the foetal blood, he's our man – we need to get that tested as soon as possible."

Ali was extremely nervous now – he wasn't sure what he should do. He tried to phone Michael but his phone was out of order.

"Oh, bloody hell – what should I do?" he asked himself. He was up as usual at three in the morning. He had hardly slept. He could not see how they could link his DNA with Denise – he was sure they couldn't. "Don't panic – carry on," he said to himself - so he did.

*

It was just gone eight when Sandra walked into the Arkle Bar at The Grosvenor Hotel. Her escort for the evening was already there and partway down a flute of champagne.

"Sandra, you look fabulous!" She felt all the work in preparation had been worthwhile.

"Thank you, Michael. You don't look too bad yourself."

"Champagne?"

"Thank you."

Michael motioned to the bartender for another glass which Michael handed to Sandra. The bartender followed them to two leather armchairs and placed the champagne bucket and stand at the side of Michael's chair. Michael motioned with his hand that was enough – the bartender retired. The two made conversation over pre-dinner drinks, mainly about the interior designer who had been to the penthouse.

"Michael, what did she suggest?"

"She had some general ideas but said it would be Tuesday next week before she had a detailed design and prices."

"So are you staying then?"

"Yes, I thought I would. It seems the sensible thing to do. I can also speak with the agents about the letting and management of all the apartments at Squirrels Chase."

"Good – you'll be around for the weekend. Why don't I take you to see my stud and livery stables? We can go for a ride if you like."

"I don't know one end of a horse from another."

"That doesn't matter – they can find you a docile beast. All you need is some appropriate clothing."

"And where, pray, do I get that?"

"We can go shopping tomorrow – you can't have anything else to do."

"I do need to see the agents."

"Go there on Monday."

"Okay, let's do it – something I've never done before."

The two walked into the restaurant for dinner.

*

Ali was on his way home having finished his mammoth Thursday rounds. He couldn't be sure but when he was leaving The Swan late today at about 7 o'clock he thought he saw Michael: he was in a black Range Rover just driving out of The Swan car park as Ali was walking to his car. He thought about this for a while but put it down to hallucinations as he was extremely anxious to find Michael. What could or should he do to avoid being caught? The obvious thing to do was to leave – but leave for where? Whilst he was of Indian descent he was English: he had no connections, no family, nothing in India - it's a big country so he would be hard to find. The more that he considered this, it seemed like the most obvious thing to do. He knew people go on holiday to Goa so maybe it would be a good idea to go on a flight to Goa. Ali was not very technical so he stopped at a local Co-Op travel agent on the outskirts of Warrington. He advised the young lady behind the desk that his grandfather had just died in India and he wanted to go to the funeral in three days.

"We really only do packages but I'll see if there are any seats available on flights to India. Where and when do you want to go?"

"It's urgent. The funeral can't be delayed so I'm happy to drive to any airport. Are there any available flights tomorrow?"

The receptionist went to her screen. After a short while she advised Ali that there was a seat on the Thomson's flight to Goa on Sunday from Gatwick. "The flight takes off at 6 o'clock in the morning."

"How much is it?"

"For a return flight only it is £850."

"Okay, that sounds fine. I assume I'll be able to get transport when I get there," he said, lying through his teeth – he had no idea where he would want to go when he got there. "Okay, I'll go for that. I need to get cracking."

Ali paid for the flight by credit card – the most he had ever spent. He received a bundle of papers from the girl and was told to collect the tickets at the airport. Ali realised he needed to leave his flat by lunchtime Saturday at the latest. He could park his car at the airport. Back at his flat he started to gather things together and pack a case. He emptied the fridge – but what of the unsold meat and items in the cold room? How could he get rid of these? Maybe he just would leave everything in the cold room – it would stop anything going off.

*

It was late morning on Saturday when he loaded his luggage into his estate car and drove off towards London. On the way he stopped for something to eat at the motorway service centre: there was a police car at the entrance to the car park – he could feel the policeman's eyes burning into his back but nothing happened. Arriving at the M25, he'd never seen so much traffic but he pressed on and took the turning for Gatwick. He thought it would never arrive but it did. On the outskirts of Gatwick there were dozens of hotels. He spotted the Hilton Hotel and drove in.

"Have you a bed for the night? I haven't booked – it's all been a bit of a rush for me."

"Yes, Sir. Just one person?"

"Yes."

"Do you have a car?"

"Yes."

"Do you want to leave it here for the duration of your holiday?"

"It's not a holiday, my grandfather has just died – I'm going to his funeral."

"Oh, I'm sorry but would that help to leave your car with us?"

"How do I get to the airport? I need to be there at 4 o'clock in the morning tomorrow."

"We have a courtesy bus, Sir. I suggest you get the bus at 3.30."

"Oh, that's good."

"Here's the key card for your room. Take the luggage to your room and then park your car in the yellow car park. Here's a sticker for the windscreen."

Ali did as he was told and couldn't believe how easy all this was. He was beginning to feel quite cheerful at the prospect of going to India.

*

On Monday morning the details of the DNA test on Ali Hussain were back. There was an exact match to the foetal blood DNA.

"That's our man," said Kim. "Right let's get him. Tarrant, Sullivan get a warrant for a full search of the premises and organise SOCO also to get some uniform boys to be with you, possibly to gain access by force."

The team arrived at Ali's shop at 10 o'clock to find no one at home and the shop shut. Tarrant immediately phoned Kim to advise who in turn put out a 'wanted' message through the system to cover airports and ports including the Channel Tunnel. Tarrant and Sullivan had a good look round but it was a pretty ordinary flat with nothing of note. On the mantelpiece were some odds and ends and a small bowl containing a pair of dice, a whistle and some keys. Tarrant picked them out and wondered for a moment which locks they might fit. He then spotted the plastic label simply bearing the name 'Sealand'.

"I knew it, I knew it - Ali is Mr Ali!"

"What are you on about?" enquired Sullivan.

"Ali is Mr Ali – the guy Terry Pritchard had said removed all the cars from the depot at Sealand and, according to Terry, had set the place on fire."

"Seem to be getting a whole load of information from one bunch of keys."

"No, Sullivan, it all fits – I'm sure it does but let us get on with this job. We need to get back there is nothing here. An empty flat - an even emptier butchers shop. SOCO will do the technical bit. Let's go."

CHAPTER 12

"Mr Fitzallen?"

"Yes. Who's this?"

"It's Pam from Pam's Pads."

"Pam's Pads? Do I know you?"

"Yes, I'm the interior designer – we met last week."

"Oh, Pamela – I'm so sorry, I'd not fully taken in your name. How are you doing?"

"Well, I did promise to phone you today, Tuesday, so here I am."

"Have you a design and costings?"

"I have."

"Would you like to meet me at the Penthouse – I think it would be a lot easier to imagine the proposal inside the Penthouse."

"Okay, shall we say 2 o'clock?"

"Yes, that's great – see you."

What a woman! Who would have come up with a name like Pam's Pads? It sounds more like a pedicure for dogs, Michael mused to himself.

*

Kim was getting very frustrated. They had their man and now he had slipped the net.

"Tarrant, stop messing about with Ali's possible conviction with a case that's dead – let's get on with this case."

"Okay, Sir but we have no leads at all."

"It's combined brain power that's needed. He is a single English guy of Indian extraction; he knows he is in trouble so where would he go?"

"Well, Sir, he's taken most of his clothes."

"What's left?"

"What do you mean, Sir?"

"So what clothes did he leave behind?"

"Overcoats, anoraks, sweaters – that type of thing."

"What does that tell us?"

"Going somewhere hot?"

"Yes, of course. Well, as it's winter it would be reasonably far away and as he's Indian extraction – why not India? You two, get hold of all airlines that fly to India and see if Mr Ali Hussain was a late booker and has flown out of the UK since Thursday. I'm certain he will have done his deliveries on Thursday – it's money in his pocket."

"Blimey, Tarrant, there's dozens of airlines flying to India."

"Which bit of India might help?"

"I agree and to find a Hussain in India is like finding a Jones in Wales."

*

Michael met Pamela at the Penthouse as agreed. She turned

up looking decidedly sexy in blouse and tight-fitting jeans. Her hair was brushed back with specs balanced in her hair.

"Michael. Good to see you again. I have the most fabulous design for your new bachelor pad."

"Good, let's go and look at it." Michael was nearly overcome by Pamela's perfume in the lift.

"Now, Michael," she said as she produced her portfolio of designs, fabric swatches, material and furniture design. She explained what colours went where, what furniture and in the bedroom she said it was necessary to have a cool sophisticated space that was sexy too – so she had a massive female nude proposed for the wall behind the king-size bed which she had finished with grey sheets and crimson throw and cushions.

"What do you think?"

"It's a bit over the top."

"Oh, Michael, if you have a girlfriend and then bring her back here this will be a perfect ice-breaker."

"What makes you think I do that sort of thing?"

"You're the only handsome eligible bachelor I've met who wouldn't. Oh my god, you're not gay are you?"

"No, no I'm not. I'm amused by the total scheme but how much including your fee?"

"£25,000." They shook hands and smiled. Pamela was hoping for a kiss – in fact, Pamela was hoping for a roll in the bed once installed!

*

"Got it!" exclaimed Sullivan, "Sunday from Gatwick; Thomson holiday flight to Goa; Mr Ali Hussain; booking agent Co-Op Travel, Warrington. The boss has certainly go the knack of picking the right ideas."

"He's no fool our boss."

"Whose 'no fool'," enquired Kim as he came into the detectives' office.

"We have – or rather Sullivan has found that Ali flew out by Thomson's on a flight from Gatwick on Sunday to Goa."

"Well done. Alert the Indian police. There may be a lot of Hussains in India but not that many staying on UK passports in Goa."

The SOCO report hit Kim's desk as he arrived back in his office at about 3pm on Thursday.

"Sullivan, Tarrant, my office now," was the phone message delivered to Tarrant and Sullivan. The two men raced up to Kim's office aware his tone was angry so best not to keep him waiting.

"What the hell were you doing when you went to Ali's place?"

"What do you mean, boss – what were we doing?"

"It's a simple question, Tarrant. What did you do at Ali's?"

Tarrant explained that they had looked around, found the Sealand bunch of keys and looked into the shop which was completely empty.

"Did you look everywhere in the shop?"

"Yes, Sir – I think so, Sir."

"How about the cold room?"

"No we didn't go there – that's where the butcher keeps his meat."

"And the corpse of someone he may have murdered."

"What?"

"SOCO report that the partially dismembered body of a young lady was found wrapped in plastic in a bundle at the back of the cold room."

"How disgusting! Who is it?"

"I don't know. You are the detectives who missed the obvious."

"Sorry, Sir but …"

"No 'buts' Tarrant. If you want to stay on my team thoroughness at all times is what I expect."

"Very well, Sir. Who's the girl?"

"How the hell do I know? The body will be with George in the morning so perhaps he can help."

*

"Sandra, it's Michael."

"Hi, how are things?"

"I must tell you about the meeting with the interior designer."

"Okay, press on."

"No, I mean we should meet. We should go to a bistro, you know where we went before – it seemed like a cave, I can't recall the name?"

"Yes, sure – when, tonight? I can't recall the name either but I know exactly where you mean."

"Why not. The procedure on the sale of the flats is now complete – I'm a footloose man about town."

"That's great."

"You haven't told me how you felt following the horse riding."

"I felt, shall we say, sore or stiff – all in the wrong places on Monday. I'm okay now."

"Good, let's meet. Say, at eight at the bistro?"

*

The two met as arranged and Michael explained the basic proposals for the decoration of the penthouse. Sandra laughed at the bedroom proposals and Pamela's sudden thought that he was gay.

"I've heard some funny things – but, you gay! Never."

"Me neither."

"Well, you say that but I have to tell you in all confidence," said Sandra, "that I once did have a lesbian relationship with a PR girl in Chester."

"Oh, and did you enjoy it?"

"At the time I did – it was uncomplicated and very satisfying."

"I see – so why did it end?"

"I don't fully recall but she was a bit of a mixed up girl and I think I didn't need that sort of thing. It wasn't long after my father had been murdered so I guess I was looking for some solace. Anyway business took off and I was fully occupied with running the firm."

"Hmm, that's strange – we all have a secret side. I must say, I hadn't got you down as being a lesbian even for a short spell of time," replied Michael, "it's the second time you have mentioned your father was murdered, what happened?"

"It was a very gruesome event. I am sure you don't want to hear it Michael."

"Yes get it out, tell me about it."

"Well it was New Year's day, about eight o'clock in the morning. Dad had a habit of driving Jumbo, that was our old Land Rover with no roof, up the long meadow to the

118

oak tree at the top, usually with Purdy, our dog, as a passenger."

"I get the picture."

"Well as it turned out later Purdy had been drugged, certainly Dad did that before fireworks were let off. Despite being a gun dog, Purdy was very upset by fireworks. It seems however that someone else had added to the dose, so Purdy was not with Dad on this his last trip up the hill."

"Ah, I see, go on."

"Well, it seems that the murderer who we now know to be Roger Whiteside, Dad's business partner, had hidden himself in the back of Jumbo, the Land Rover, and hitting Dad over the back of the head as soon as Dad got in. Whiteside then drove to the tree at the top of the hill. Using the wire from the winch at the front of Jumbo made one end fast to the tree and put a noose made from the wire rope around Dad's neck."

"No, I don't believe it?" interjected Michael.

"Well that is what happened. Whiteside set Jumbo off down the hill, it kept in the ruts it had made over the years as if they were tram lines, at the fateful moment halfway down the hill the noose tightened and Dad was decapitated. Jumbo came to rest at the stone gatepost at the bottom of the field."

"Good lord how frightful."

"Yes it was a terrible day, I recall it as if it were yesterday. The way he had been killed made it look just like suicide. The coroner was about to give suicide as his verdict until John and Sienna told the police it could have been Whiteside. They discovered a flight to Manchester from Zurich and back, would have allowed Whiteside to commit the crime and return to Zurich in time to finish his holiday. I am certain he was convinced he had the perfect alibi."

"Well that was very clever of John and Sienna."

"Yes their suspicions were raised when the hostess at the hotel in Zurich which was the same one Whiteside had stayed in, told them that Whiteside had unexpectedly missed the New Year's Eve party."

"I see, so there is no such thing as the perfect crime?"

"No and I really don't want to be reminded of it, so it's your turn, what's your secret side, Michael?"

"What makes you think I have one Sandra?"

"I've been around long enough to know everyone has a secret that could involve shattering a relationship or a friendship – a thing you have done that maybe only you or the person you shared it with knows. It's part of their secret side."

"Well, Sandra, if I have a secret side and I tell you what it is it will no longer be a secret."

"That's a cop out if ever I heard one. I know you hide a secret, Michael – I just can't figure out what it is. It would do you good to share it. You know, in fact, regarding the lesbian relationship I'd never told anyone about it, but telling you now seems to have lifted a weight I didn't realise was holding me down. So, Michael, come on - it's your turn."

"There are some secrets that I just can't tell."

"Why is that Michael?"

"Well they will be self-incriminating. I would put the listener in an invidious position. They would be in possession of knowledge they knew was wrong but out of loyalty to their friend they wouldn't say anything to anyone. That would make them a liar in certain circumstances."

"Blimey, Michael, that's all a bit deep. Do you mean you've committed a crime and no one has discovered what it is, so is that you're secret?"

"In a way but I really can't tell you."

"Have you nothing which is a secret which is not incriminating but you've just kept quiet about Michael?"

"I suppose I could say that the whole Inside Property Investment Company was set up to exploit the market and make as much money as we could in the shortest possible time."

"Hmm, not really a secret that, Michael. Have you had sex with anyone who blew your mind so much that you have hidden it in the secret side of your memory?"

"Oh, yes there was a time at Dunmore Hall with Sarah Polaki, she was Niall Phelan's assistant – he financed us to start IPI, when we had sex when everyone else was out. She only marked me 5 out of 10."

Sandra laughed and laughed. "You're a real card, Michael. No, this is not what I call your secret side. You know very well what I mean. I know you have secrets – anyway I will leave it there on one condition."

"And what's that?"

"You come to my bed tonight."

"Is that our secret?"

"If you like but it is not something I will be broadcasting but I know I'll enjoy every minute. I can score you much higher than Sarah whatever her name was."

"It's a deal and it's our secret."

*

"Sir, the photograph of the corpse from the coroner has come through, may I bring it …"

"Yes, yes. Good Lord! That's Bozena Bania."

"How do you know that?"

"Because, Tarrant, I went to some trouble to talk to a few members of staff at The Swan. She was having a fling with Ali every Thursday afternoon."

"It looks like he's murdered her just as he murdered Denise Ward," said Tarrant.

"Hang on, I'm not saying Ali murdered Denise, he may have mutilated her body post-death."

"Oh, yes. George said she had taken a drug-Ecstasy pill or something like it."

"Correct, and how do we know that that isn't the case here?"

"We don't, Sir but I guess the PM may take some time with the body being so well disfigured."

"Disfigured? You mean dismembered, Tarrant. She was in the process of being cut up – no other way of putting it."

"Yes, Sir."

"Keep up the pressure on the Indian police, Tarrant. We need this man back here as soon as possible. I'm off to The Swan to speak with the manager."

"I gather Bozena may not have been at work recently?" Kim enquired of the manager.

"How do you know that?"

"Because she's dead."

The manager suddenly went pale. "My God, how awful! Here's me calling the poor girl for not appearing at work. When she was here she was as good as two and I've been chastising her for weeks. I just don't know what to say."

"Firstly, you can give me the address of her lodgings."

"Oh, yes, Sir – I can do that." The manager opened a

drawer of his filing cabinet and took out a buff file from near the front of the cabinet – 'B' for Bozena. "Here we are." He wrote the address on a compliment slip.

"Thank you. Have you any idea why she left and didn't return?"

"Well, no but everyone knew her secret."

"Her secret? You think she had a secret?"

"Doesn't everyone, Inspector, have a secret that they are unwilling to reveal?"

"But you know Bozena's secret!"

"Yes, everyone did."

"Not much of a secret then!"

"Well it was, in a way, because no one would let her know that we knew."

"Okay, what was it?"

"She had what you might call an assignation with Ali Hussain, our butcher, every Thursday."

"Do you mean that they met for sex?"

"Yes, that's about it."

"I see. I will come back, or one of my officers will, to obtain formal statements from all the staff, but for the moment, if you don't mind keeping this information confidential."

"Certainly, Superintendent, our secret," the manager said with a wry smile on his face, despite being shaken by the news.

Jon Kim found his way to the bed and breakfast establishment. The landlady opened part of the door and he introduced himself. Once inside, he explained why he was there.

"Oh, my goodness. How awful and her so young as well!"

"Yes. I wondered whether I could see the room she occupied."

"Well, that's a bit difficult – I have re-let it."

"Oh, without knowing what had happened to her?"

"Well I needed the rent. I had to clear all her stuff out of her room. There was quite a bit of trouble and I had no rent for two weeks until I re-let it."

"What did you do with her belongings?"

"I still have those. I have two bin bags in the cellar."

"May I see?" Kim took one look and told the landlady he would be keeping them. He placed the bags in the boot of his car.

He entered the police station in Winsford and handed the bags in and asked them to inspect and bag them in the Bozena Bania's case, they could be evidence.

*

Sandra and Michael were breakfasting late after a wonderful night. Sandra was glowing with delight. Then there was a ring on her doorbell. "That's very unusual. I hardly get callers."

"The only way of knowing who it is, is by answering it," grinned Michael.

Sandra went over to the phone which serves as a video and answerphone; she could see a middle-aged man in a less than smart suit. "Hello, can I help you?"

Tarrant held his warrant card to the camera and announced his name and rank.

"Come in, Sergeant." Sandra pressed the button to let him in.

"Who the hell is it?" demanded Michael.

"It's the police, Michael. I have no more idea of what they want than you. I'm just going to put some jeans and sweater on. Let him in when he arrives."

The doorbell rang and Michael answered the door.

"Oh, I think I may be at the wrong door."

"No, Sandra Wall is just changing. She will be here in a minute."

"I'm DS Tarrant, Cheshire Police. Who are you please, Sir?"

"I'm Michael Fitzallen, a business associate of Miss Wall's."

"Oh, I see."

Sandra reappeared looking a more soberly dressed than when the bell rang.

"Mr Tarrant, we met a number of years ago."

"Yes, Miss – I'm very sorry to bother you but I need some information."

"Okay, ask away."

"Is it in order to discuss a confidential matter or …," Tarrant enquired looking towards Michael.

"Oh, yes. We were only saying last night how we may have our secret side but, in fact, we probably don't have many secrets from one another."

"Well, that's alright then. What I wondered was – well it's an odd request, but do you by any chance have any keys for the building that burned down at Sealand?"

"I don't think I do but you must have some, Michael."

"Well, why would you have some, Sir?"

"My company was the tenant but, in fact, I gave all my

keys to Terry Pritchard. He's in prison now for arson, you know."

"Oh, I know – I helped put him there."

"Very good. It cost me quite a lot of money that fire." Sandra shifted uneasily as Michael said this as she recalled in a flash the car journey in Spain from the town of Rhonda and Michael's concern at the time about something she thought he knew – the building was being set on fire.

"Oh, I'm sorry to trouble you. Do you know how many sets of keys there were?"

"Why?"

"I can't answer that at the moment, it is just to assist us with our enquiries Sir."

"Try to recall Michael," implored Sandra.

"There were definitely only two sets. They were special security locks, the keys could only be copied by the manufacturers, and subject to my signature."

"Is there any possibility that a third set had been cut, Sir?"

"No, not without my consent and signature."

"So, as far as you know there were only ever two sets."

"Yes, correct." Michael smiled and looked at Sandra as if to say, I've nailed that one.

"If that is correct, Sir, the set Terry Pritchard said was recovered from his house along with other items before he was charged was one set."

"Okay, yes that would make sense," said Michael.

"So, who had the second set?"

"I had them most of the time but think I must have lent them to Terry at some point."

"Why, Sir, would he need two sets of keys?"

"You know, I just can't remember."

"Would you recognise the set of keys if you saw them again?"

"Oh yes, definitely."

"Did you put tabs on them to identify them?"

"Yes, I had the orange set and Terry had the blue."

"What was written on the tabs – can you recall?"

"Yes, that's easy – not terribly secure but as they were the only two sets it wouldn't be an issue: the word "Sealand" was all that was written. It seemed appropriate that anyone who stole them would simply not know which building in the Sealand Estate they fitted but were easily identifiable by Terry and me."

"I'm grateful, Sir. Thank you. Terry suggested before and again at his trial that a Mr Ali was the man you had told him was going to have access to the Sealand site whilst Terry was on holiday. I recall you were at the trial, Sir, and gave evidence. Do you recall?"

"Yes, I do and I said no such thing and I stick to that."

"You're quite sure, Sir, that at no time you told Terry Pritchard that a Mr Ali would have access to the premises whilst he is away?"

"That's correct. I gave evidence under oath, you know."

Sandra was listening intently. She felt very uneasy as Michael was reiterating everything that had been said previously, and that Terry had vehemently denied but his testimony was not as strong as Michael's and the rest was history.

"Michael Fitzallen, I'm charging you with perjury and contempt of court and anything you may say will be taken down and may be used in evidence against you."

"What the hell are you talking about, man? This matter is settled: it went before a jury - Terry was guilty of arson."

"And you denied you had met or even knew someone called 'Ali'."

"Correct. So withdraw the charge."

Tarrant pulled a bunch of keys from his pocket and dangled them in front of Michael. "Mr Fitzallen, these keys have been recovered from a flat in Warrington belonging to a Mr Ali Hussain. They have been forensically checked and are an identical match to the keys recovered from Terry Pritchard's house."

Michael lunged at Tarrant and pulled the keys from his hand and rushed to the open patio window balcony and threw them into the undergrowth.

"Now prove it Mr Policeman!"

"Do you expect that I would have brought the originals with me? They were a copy made up by our Forensic Department. Anyway your perjury has been witnessed by Miss Wall, a solicitor." Tarrant radioed for assistance and within ten minutes three uniformed officers arrived and arrested Michael and took him to the Police HQ in Winsford.

Sandra was left dazed. She could not believe what had happened. She felt uneasy about the fact she had unwittingly been a witness to the lie Michael had told the police officer leading to a perjury charge.

"John, is that you?"

"Yes Sandra good to hear from you, how can I help you today?"

"No actually I need your help once again."

"Why whatever has happened?" enquired John as he detected sobbing at the other end of the phone.

Sandra explained the circumstances of the past hour and how now she was sure Michael had ordered the arson of the Sealand building, whilst she and Michael were in Spain.

"Good heavens, the police will charge him and put him before the magistrates. I suspect he will be given bail, but possibly have to surrender his passport."

"Could I be in any danger John?"

"Well I don't think Michael is the violent type, fraud deception white collar crime would be his speciality, no I don't see that you are in danger." John spent a few minutes chatting to Sandra and then passed the phone to Sienna who had the whole story repeated.

"Come round this afternoon and have supper, you don't want to be on your own tonight."

"Thanks Sis, will four o'clock be okay?"

"Yes that's just fine, you can bath James, wear something you don't mind being splashed, he makes quite a splash now!"

"Great thanks, I will see you then."

CHAPTER 13

Rhys Williams arrived back at Manchester Airport at midday. He was amazed at how the airport had changed since he had been away for nearly ten years. Ten years since he sold all the inherited shares in Wall's Holdings to the Wall family, banking well over a million pounds.

Not bad in your early twenties, he reminisced to himself. He didn't have too much luggage; mainly a big rucksack and a smallish wheelie suitcase. He managed to understand the new geography of the place and realised there was a railway station now as part of the airport complex.

"Can I get a train to Chester from here?" he enquired at the ticket office.

"No Sir not a direct train, but I can sell you a through ticket. Change at Manchester Victoria for the Crewe to Chester train which stops on the hour at Victoria."

Thanking the ticket clerk and parting with eighteen pounds Rhys went down to the only platform for trains from the Airport train station to Manchester Victoria.

"I must remember to get off at Victoria," he mumbled to himself. There was a train in the station, and he considered if he should get on this train.

"Scuse me, is this train going to Manchester Victoria?"

"Yes," said a uniformed official with 'Virgin' written on his breast pocket.

Rhys took the advice and boarded the train, thinking to himself that some of the places he had visited in the world, no one would be seen dead wearing a jacket with 'Virgin' written on the breast pocket.

As the train moved off the guard announced the stops and final destination of the train. Warning passengers to have tickets available for inspection or they would have to pay the full price on the train if they didn't have a ticket. Rhys's ticket passed muster. He got off as instructed at Victoria, walked across the platform and joined train which left the station only minutes after he boarded the Chester train.

"Looks like someone has this train link sorted out," he muttered to himself in an incredulous way.

On the journey Rhys had time to reminisce on how it was he had ended up travelling the world, with a million pounds safely tucked away in a savings account. He remembered as if it were yesterday that when his father, who was not married to his mother thereby making him illegitimate, had been killed by the local doctor for the murder of Peter Wall. A crime of passion, one man's love of another and the respect in which the doctor had held Peter Wall.

Working in the forensic lab at Chester Police headquarters, as his first job from leaving university, which at the time was in Chester, he had helped deal with analysis of the samples in the death of Peter Wall and Roger Whiteside. He was amazed to learn that he was the only heir, despite being illegitimate, to Whiteside. That caused a bit of concern in the Police as the DNA evidence was the confirmation the lawyers to Whiteside's estate needed to make Rhys the legitimate legatee. There was an extremely complex legal arrangement as to the split of shares between Peter Wall and Roger Whiteside in the event of the death of one of them. The situation was that they were both dead. Rhys could have taken shares in Wall's the family firm but decided to take the money and leave the family to sort out the running of the business.

He felt he was coming home, the area in which his life was changed, changed for the better. He determined to go and pay his respects to his mother and his grandparents all of whom were dead, by placing flowers on their graves. In fact his mother died in giving birth to Rhys and was brought up by his grandparents for whom he had great affection.

Leaving the main station building in Chester and joining the throng of people mostly heading back up to the station, he found his way down on to the station approach past a line of taxis. Damn it, I am not lugging this lot half way across Chester, he thought to himself. So Rhys jumped in the first available taxi.

"Where to young man?" came a jovial request.

"The Blossoms Hotel please."

"You been away a while? It's the New Blossoms now very smart. It will be six pounds."

Waiting for confirmation that the fare was accepted, which Rhys agreed, the taxi moved off.

A young porter type person in uniform met Rhys at the door of the taxi and took his bags as he settled with the driver, who seemed a bit sniffy at only getting a pound tip.

At reception Rhys indicated he did not have a reservation, but wanted to stay for several nights. A room was found, credit card duly swiped and the livered young man escorted Rhys to a fourth floor room with a double bed and en-suite bathroom with a shower. Another pound disappeared in the direction of the porter.

Rhys was delighted to be back home so to speak. He had things to do, including meeting his bank manager to discover how much money he had left.

Rhys unpacked some of his clothes and put others in the laundry bag for room service to launder for him.

"I need to get myself some decent clothes if I am to make an impression at the interview, which I must arrange," he said out loud to himself.

Turning to the carefully folded copy of *Horse and Hound*, he found the Chester number he wanted.

"Hello, you had an advert in *Horse and Hound* for a manager for your stud and livery stables."

"Uh, oh yes, yes I did. Sorry I am in a bit of a fluster, it's been an unusual day."

"Would you rather I phoned back?"

"No, no," came the female voice, "can you come to the farm and stud at Tarporley this Saturday say ten o'clock?"

"Yes, yes I can. I will see you there then."

The phone went dead at the other end, but he was firmly of the view he had established the fact he had an interview. Feeling suitably buoyed up by the call, he decided to shower and shave prior to a wander around the city centre. The weather was quite pleasant so he couldn't think of anything better to do.

It was four o'clock on Tuesday, too late to fix appointments with the bank and his accountant, but time enough to do some clothes shopping. He had never treated himself to good quality clothes. Rhys wandered into the Grosvenor Shopping centre and found Gieves and Hawkes, gentleman's outfitters. They looked like the sort of shop that he was looking for.

As he walked in he suddenly felt scruffy in jeans, t-shirt

and sweater. The reception he received from an elderly man in a black three piece suit was not exactly welcoming.

"Can we help you Sir, we don't sell many casual clothes."

"I have just returned to Chester from an around the world trip, so my wardrobe was designed to fit that activity. I am now about to go on an important interview and need to be dressed accordingly." Stick that in your snobby pipe, Rhys thought to himself.

"Oh I see, how exciting. Please come with me upstairs. We can fit you up perfectly."

"I don't want a pinstripe suite, its more sports jacket etc that I am after, as the job is in agriculture."

After about two hours as the shop was about to shut Rhys emerged several hundreds of pounds lighter, clutching four carrier bags full of his new clothes. He was excited, and couldn't wait to try them on. Straight back to The New Blossoms for a private showing.

"Hi hun, how are you today?"

"Rhys, how wonderful to hear you it's been two days."

"Sorry my love I have had a great deal of travelling, shopping and appointments to fix up."

"Have you managed to get an interview?"

"Yes my love on Saturday."

"That's great." The two chatted on as lovers do about nothing in particular.

"I must go, this call is costing a fortune Francesca with you being in Mallorca. I will ring you on Saturday afternoon when I have been for the interview. Bye."

CHAPTER 14

Sandra didn't need to knock on the door of the farmhouse, she was expected.

"Hi Sis, long time no see, you will stay for supper won't you?"

"Oh yes please."

"That'll be lovely."

*

Despite it being Saturday, Tarrant and Jon Kim were in work. They were about to interview Michael Fitzallen. He tried to obtain his own solicitor but Mersey Law don't do criminal work and John England thought it professionally wrong to represent Michael as there could be a conflict of interest. He eventually obtained the services of a solicitor from the Panel. The nominated solicitor was less than pleased to be in Winsford on a Saturday morning sitting with a new client whilst the police drew out the information they hoped for. The whole of Tarrant's discussions with Michael the previous day were rehearsed again and recorded on tape.

"This looks like a possible perjury case which, whilst serious is not criminal in the sense of a crime against a person, Inspector."

"I don't think a judge will be quite as charitable as you!" retorted Jon Kim.

"The point I'm making is that the allegations made against my client still need to be proven. The burden of proof lies with you, Inspector," said Michael's solicitor.

"We can prove our case. Don't worry about us."

"My point is really that there is no need for my client to be locked up. He should be granted bail immediately. If you cannot agree to that I'll go to judge in chambers and get an order for bail," the solicitor persisted.

Jon knew a good solicitor would achieve bail via a judge. He of course, was correct, Jon mused. We still had to make the case. For that we needed Ali and preferably the lorry drivers and crane drivers who did the job, the shipping manifests for the containers – all this would take time. Bearing in mind Michael was a resident in Spain, Jon Kim was concerned he would skip bail.

"Very well, we won't oppose bail and will even go as far as to allow police bail in this case as long as Mr Fitzallen's passport is surrendered for the period of bail. We can wait for Magistrates' directions and any other terms next week."

"May I have a word with my client?" Michael and his solicitor were left alone for a short while when the interview resumed. They accepted Jon Kim's offer. The practical point was that Michael's passport was at The Swan in Tarporley and his Range Rover was at Sandra's – both items he needed.

"Very well," agreed Kim, "please give us the keys for the Range Rover and I'll arrange for an officer to collect it and your passport and bring them both here. When they arrive the formalities can take place: you surrender your passport and agree to attend the Magistrates' Court in Chester on Monday."

"You have all the cards, Inspector. Here are the Range Rover keys."

"Where is it exactly?"

"In a visitor's bay in the basement of the flats Sandra Wall occupies where we unexpectedly met yesterday, Mr Tarrant."

"Have you Miss Wall's number? I need to ring her and let her know we're coming."

Michael took his mobile from his pocket and started to flip through his contacts.

"I would like to see that phone," demanded Kim.

"I'm not sure you're allowed to look at my phone."

"You are charged with a serious offence – we are entitled to search you and look at your phone's contents."

Michael looked for support from his solicitor but none was forthcoming – the phone was handed over. Tarrant flipped through the contacts and as 'Wall' was at the end it took a few moments to get her. He noted the number – he kept on searching. The second name on the list was 'Ali'.

"You've someone called Ali on this phone, Mr Fitzallen. We'll keep this and pass it to our forensic team."

"You can't do that!"

"We just have. This interview is at an end."

Tarrant and Kim left the interview room. The PC who stood quietly in the corner opened the door for the solicitor to leave and then escorted Michael to the Charge Room where the formal charge was read to him. Kim had already notified the Duty Sergeant of the bail conditions.

Until Fitzallen appeared before Magistrates on Monday a member of the SOCO team was taken to Sandra's flat. She was waiting for them to collect Michael's Range Rover and then Tarrant drove the Range Rover to The Swan at Tarporley. Tarrant, on presentation of his warrant card, found Michael's passport where he indicated and had a good look round as he had been instructed to do. On returning to Winsford, the Range Rover was placed in the police garage and SOCO had a good look round. In the void for the spare wheel covered with a towel was a parcel from Spain addressed to Michael and an address in Manchester which, from the title, was the car storage company.

"Sir, it's SOCO here. We have found a parcel from Spain concealed in the Range Rover spare wheel cavity. What do you want me to do?"

"Can you X-ray it and let me know what's in it?"

Half an hour later SOCO rang Jon at home. "It's a parcel of loose pills."

"My God, I bet they're Ecstasy. I don't suppose you can somehow get the pills out and replace them with paracetamol or something without damaging the packaging?"

"I think we can. How long have we got?"

"A couple of hours."

"Yes, we can do that – I think we should put a micro-tracker in the parcel as well if you like."

"Okay, but don't keep it any longer than is necessary. When you get the pills out, can you count them and send some away for analysis. Take lots of photos as well."

"Very well, Sir. I will let you know on Monday what sort of pills they are."

Kim was grateful to this SOCO officer. It will be interesting to see exactly what these are.

*

"Sorry I'm late, I had to wait for someone," Sandra explained.

"You look a bit flustered. Come in."

"Hello John – ahh James." Sandra picked him up and gave him a big cuddle and a kiss then kissed John and Si.

"Drink?"

"Oh, yes please John. Have you a white wine?"

"I have, Sandra." All three had a glass poured. "Hope you don't mind but we fed James so I will put him in his cot and we can then have supper and a chat."

After supper Sandra explained the last 36 hours beginning with the meal at The Grosvenor and her belief that perhaps Michael was not involved after all in the fire at Sealand including the disappearance of the classic cars.

"The day ended with us being together in my flat," she explained with a slightly broken smile on her lips, it would have been a 'Cheshire Cat' smile but for subsequent events, and the arrival of DS Tarrant.

"He called to see me to see if I had any keys for Sealand. The last person he had expected to find was Michael." She explained the conversation that took place between the two men and how Tarrant had eventually extracted the information from Michael as to who had the keys to the workshop.

"Then Tarrant showed Michael the keys he had brought with him. Michael flipped, snatched the keys from Tarrant and threw them into the land at the back of the flats from my balcony."

"My God, so there is a Mr Ali and Michael is involved."

"Yes and Terry was telling the truth all the time."

"Where's Michael now?"

"He's with the police."

"He spent last night in Police HQ presumably in the cells."

"Yes, that would be normal. I popped into the office as I had a call that I was trying to be contacted by Michael. Apparently he wanted us to act for him but I told my staff to refuse due to potential conflicts of interest."

"I'm sure you did the right thing, John. But what a mess! Will he be given bail?"

"Almost certainly. It's not the sort of crime that demands custody during the pre-trial period."

"Oh, Sis, what a rollercoaster of a day, whatever next!" consoled Sienna.

"I really don't know other than the fact that my suspicions have been confirmed. I'm not interested in Michael Fitzallen anymore. All I'm interested in is getting Terry out of jail as there has been a miscarriage of justice here."

*

"Sir, its SOCO. All those pills have been extracted and replaced by a placebo pill we have in stock."

"In stock! You sound like a shop."

"You'd be surprised what we have for eventualities like this! The parcel's back in the Range Rover."

"Did you put a tracker in it then?"

"Yes, Sir. I will let you know where it moves to."

*

Michael was released from Winsford Police HQ and bailed to appear before Chester Magistrates on Monday. He drove back to Tarporley his mind in a total spin. He checked back into The Swan but was at a total loss without his mobile phone. Fortunately, he had Pamela's phone number so used the hotel phone.

"Pamela, its Michael. I need to get into my apartment

very quickly. Can you have it finished by this time next week?"

"You don't want much! I can but at £25,000, Michael, maybe some of the finishing touches will have to be left until later. I'll see if I can get the decorators in on Monday and carpets Thursday furniture Friday. I'll pick up pots and pans, crockery and bed linen etc. as I go. The curtains may be the problem. Shall I put up blinds as a temporary fix?"

"Yes, just do what you can."

"You sound a bit down."

"Yes, I am a bit but I will survive."

CHAPTER 15

"Thank you, thank, you – yes we will, yes thank you."

"Who on earth are you talking to, Sullivan?" enquired Tarrant.

"The Indian police in Goa have found Ali. I'm not sure what they have said to him or done for that matter but he has agreed to be allowed to fly home," advised Sullivan.

"Now that's a turn up – it could have been a year or more before extradition proceedings. When's he coming back?" enquired Tarrant, "Ali has probably experienced an Indian jail for twenty four hours. I suspect that would have persuaded him to return to the UK as soon as possible."

"They put him on the 3 o'clock flight Indian time today."

"So when does that come in and where?" enquired Tarrant.

"Tell me more. Are you volunteering, Sullivan, to go and get him?"

"One o'clock in the morning tomorrow at Gatwick," Sullivan replied.

"Oh blooming hell – can't we get the airport police to hold him until some sensible hour?"

"Good thinking. I'll fix that. I will go and get him in the morning," volunteered Sullivan.

"Sir, it's Tarrant."

"Okay, what news?" enquired Kim.

"Ali is on a plane back to Gatwick. Sullivan will collect him with a uniformed officer in a marked car in the morning to bring him here."

"I won't ask how the Indians did that but it will save us a great deal of trouble."

"I agree, Sir. I will arrange for the airport police at Gatwick to meet him off the plane and hold him until Sullivan collects him."

*

Michael was wondering what to do. It was Sunday – should he stay on at The Swan or move? He had no idea what would happen in court at 10 o'clock on Monday. He hoped to be allowed the bail to continue. If he could negotiate a cash bail he could have his passport back. Maybe he could hitch a ride with Goose somewhere.

"Oh shit," he said out loud, "there is the parcel in the boot. I bet the police have got that now but if they didn't find it or even look for it I could get rid of it and avoid any connection with E drugs."

After an excellent breakfast, he decided to check the boot. The parcel was still there just as he'd left it.

The goons, he thought to himself, they didn't even find it. He decided there and then to take it to Ali's when he removed his address from the outside of the package. Ali wasn't at home, he was gone. Blast! He scrabbled around in the centre arm well locker of the Range Rover. A single Yale key. He was about to turn the lock when the door opened. He jumped backwards in fright but no one was there – the lock had been broken.

He's been burgled – where is he? Michael decided to stop worrying about Ali and just put the parcel on the table in the living room – he would know how it got there. At this moment payment was not the issue. He tried to shut the door as best he could and make it look locked from the outside. He drove away immediately. He suddenly felt alone - but now where to go? He had all the rest of Sunday. He couldn't call anyone or go and see anyone. Back to The Swan – I can watch some sport on Sky – there must be a match on. He collected the key from Reception.

"There's a message for you, Sir. Can you ring this number?"

Intrigued, he took the message to his room and before doing anything else he phoned the number. "Hello, this is Michael who is this?"

"It's Pamela, Michael. I was wondering whether you were at a loose end today or if you would like to come over. It will be a late lunch but you must have left early. I got no response from your mobile."

"Oh, sorry, yes I lost my mobile. I had an errand to run. A late lunch sounds fine. I'll come right away if that's all right."

Michael set off to the easterly outskirts of Chester to a modern estate not far from the Countess of Chester hospital. One of those estates where there are small roads off the estate road without pavements and cars are left all over the place. Pamela's place seen from the outside was at least a 3-storey townhouse. Inside, after an extremely warm welcome from Pamela, the living room was a 2-storey height room which made what was actually a small room seem extremely large.

"This is a fantastic house, Pamela."

"Thank you. I hope you like it. The design of the interior, of course, is mine."

"A glass of wine, Michael?"

He was not generally a wine drinker but on this occasion, why not!

"Red, please."

There was to be no match on Sky for Michael this afternoon. A brunch type lunch of bacon, eggs and other trimmings was soon demolished by the pair. The first bottle of red wine was entirely empty.

"Let's finish this bottle and sit in the lounge – it's far more comfortable." The sitting arrangement was an L-shaped settee which left little choice for Michael other than to sit with Pamela! He knew exactly where all this was leading – all that was missing was a 'Take Me to Bed' sign on her forehead. Halfway down the second bottle the invitation came that he had been expecting.

"Oooh, I've not shown you the rest of the house. Come and have a look." Pamela led up the stairs and, on purpose, Michael thought. He had a perfect view of her G-string because her very short skirt and tight t-shirt left very little to the imagination. She had a nice figure, on the plump side Michael mused to himself, but some rumpy-pumpy for the afternoon would certainly take his mind off what was to come tomorrow.

*

At 10 o'clock on Monday morning the Cheshire Police were involved with two men who were linked to a crime of arson and maybe the deaths of two girls but that was a guess as far as Kim was concerned. The first was the Magistrates' hearing when Tarrant gave evidence for the police; the second was Sullivan's date at Gatwick where he and uniform traffic officers collected Ali from the airport police.

Both tasks were executed satisfactorily. Michael was bailed in terms sought by the police to appear at the Crown Court for committal proceedings in one month.

Ali got a free ride back to Chester but he faced a significant amount of interviewing before the day was out. When he arrived, he was nearly asleep complaining of jet lag. It was decided to book him in and commence the interviews tomorrow.

"Sir, I've just had a report from SOCO."

"Yes, Tarrant."

"The parcel of pills have turned up at the location believed to be Ali's flat. That means Michael has been supplying pills to Ali."

"Hey, Tarrant, that's a neat trick: Ali supplied meat to pubs and clubs as well as Ecstasy. Of course, that would make sense."

"Shall I re-arrest Michael Fitzallen, Sir?"

"No, not yet – we need to get Ali to confirm being the distributor and from whom he gets the pills. We should have that confirmation from Ali tomorrow, assuming he sings like a canary once we have that and then we can go after Michael. It looks like an early night. Be ready for a very long day tomorrow."

*

Michael returned to The Swan still without his mobile phone. He was very frustrated: he couldn't phone Goose or anyone. He could always phone Pamela – no, he thought better of that. If he wasn't careful she would move into the penthouse. Roger was working on reception at The Swan.

"Am I all right staying for the rest of the week? My apartment is still not quite ready to move into yet."

"Certainly, Sir. Can you please renew your booking with a card payment?" Roger tapped in the amount for a stay including Sunday and to include Saturday night.

"Can you put your PIN in, please?"

Michael did as he was asked – then to his amazement the payment was declined!

"Ah, you must have a dirty strip on the card. This happens sometimes." He tried again. "No, sorry Sir, it isn't working. Do you have another card?"

"No, what do I do now?"

"Can you pay cash?"

"Well for tonight, certainly. I need to go to my bank in the morning and find out what is happening."

Monday was going to be a busy day.

*

Kim requested that Ali be brought to the interview room at 9.30. He was to be offered a solicitor. They needed to be there at that time as well. Kim and Tarrant made their way to the interview room only to be advised by the Duty Sergeant that Ali was not well and they'd called for a doctor.

"Damn, that's going to make life difficult," said Kim. "Very well, let me know just as soon as you know something, I need to interview this man as soon as possible." The police doctor examined Ali and discovered by questioning that he had taken two Ecstasy tablets whilst on the journey from Gatwick. There could be another 24 hours before he came back to being cogent. Kim was less than pleased.

"Didn't the Indian authorities think to search him, and why didn't our lot do the same? My God what has happened to standards!"

*

Michael presented himself at the Chester branch of the Santander bank: he gave them his credit card and demanded to know why it was no longer working.

"Wait a moment, please Sir, I will make enquiries." Michael was left standing at the cashier's window for what seemed like ages. Just as he was about to start asking what on earth was going on, a smartly dressed young man with red tie and dark suit appeared at the front of the counter.

"Mr Fitzallen, I'm the Assistant Manager, would you like to follow me and we shall see if we can sort this matter out." Michael's blood pressure rising but desperately trying to maintain his cool, followed the young man to a small cubicle entitled 'Interview Room'.

"Please have a seat, Sir."

"What is the issue with my card?"

"Well, Sir, I'm afraid you've exceeded your limit."

"That's absolute rubbish – I've done no such thing. I have a significant balance in your Marbella branch. If what you say is correct, ask them to wire some money over."

"That will be possible, Sir. Have you any ID – passport, for example?"

Michael could feel the colour drain from his cheeks.

"That will be impossible to produce." Thinking on his feet, so to speak, he responded:

"No, I don't have my passport on me but I do have some letters, maybe even a bank statement."

"No, Sir. It has to be a photo ID. Do you have a photo driving licence?"

"No, I don't. I don't drive in the UK much so I've never applied for one."

"I'm sorry, Sir, there's nothing I can do. When you get your passport, please return and we can sort this out." Sheepishly, Michael left the bank. He had £25 in his wallet and a useless credit card. He was nearly out of diesel, he needed to pay for his hotel and there was no prospect of getting any petty cash – what a bloody mess!

∗

"Inspector, I'm afraid Mr Hussain is deteriorating – I'm sending him to hospital as an emergency. An ambulance has been called," advised the Police Doctor.

"How long do you think he will be out of action?"

"I'm afraid I can't say."

"Can't I have a brief word with him before he goes?"

"Very well, just a minute."

"Tarrant bring a hand-held recorder."

Ali looked terrible. Kim told him who he was. Tarrant switched on the recorder.

"Ali, I won't keep you long – you are going to hospital to get you better. If you will, can you answer these questions? If you don't feel like speaking, just nod or shake your head to indicate yes or no." Ali nodded.

"Were you employed by Michael Fitzallen to move all the classic cars from Sealand and then set fire to the building?" Ali nodded and in a quiet voice said "Yes."

"Did you give Ecstasy pills to Denise Ward and Bozena Bania?" He nodded again and Kim indicated his nodding for the recorder.

"Did you disfigure Denise and dump her body at The Swan?" Ali nodded again.

"Did Bozena die in your flat after taking a pill?" Ali nodded.

"Are the pills you gave the girls the same ones you have taken?" He uttered a "Yes".

"Did Michael Fitzallen give you the pills?" Ali's eyes rolled like he had stopped breathing. "Tarrant get the doctor quickly."

The doctor rushed in and tried to revive Ali with CPR but no luck. He turned to Kim and said, "he's dead, Superintendent."

"A customer for George Hughes the forensic pathologist. Thanks for your help, doctor."

Kim and Tarrant returned to Kim's office, delighted that they had settled three crimes in one short session.

"The question we didn't get an answer to, the question I would like to have got was the one that implicated Michael Fitzallen."

"We can still get Fitzallen, Sir. He doesn't know we have Ali and he's dead. We also know that Fitzallen left a package of pills at Ali's flat."

"True, but as the door was broken down and not re-secured it could be argued that anyone could have put the pills there."

"We have the details of the tracker as evidence Sir."

"Not sure how the DPP would handle the issue of covert surveillance in this case. I can see a defence barrister having a field day with this."

"We need a conference with the DPP and their barrister before we make any further moves. We must get our story straight before we make the next move," advised Kim.

"Very well Sir, shall I make an appointment with the DPP Sir?"

"Yes Tarrant."

*

It was ten thirty exactly when Rhys drove into the stable yard at the livery stables and stud in Tarporley on Saturday morning for his interview.

He was smartly dressed wearing his new purchases. A harries tweed sports jacket with double vent at the rear, cavalry twill trousers, tattersall check shirt, and suede desert boots in brown. Quite the man about the country.

The groom was busy preparing horses for owners and casual riders to take them out this fine Saturday morning.

"Hello have you come for a ride?" she enquired of Rhys.

"No, no I have come to meet Sandra Wall, we have an appointment."

"I am afraid she is not here at the moment. She usually appears on a Saturday morning. She has probably got held up. Feel free to have a wonder around, oh my name is Daisy, I normally work during the week, I'm just helping out this weekend."

"Rhys, Rhys Williams," he replied rather taken in by Daisy's good looks and trim figure in her jodhpurs and riding boots and polo top.

"Thanks I will. Don't worry about me it looks as though you have lots to do."

"Yes, busy day Saturday. It starts a bit later on Sundays." Daisy carried on wheeling the barrow full of horse muck to the tip.

Rhys did as he was invited and had a look around. It was quite a set up, and it looks as if Sandra has the builders in. There were piles of sand and limestone and empty paper bags which had contained cement. There was also a pile of white polypropylene bags which held a ton of building material of some sort.

The four square farmhouse was on the right hand side of the yard. He knew from a previous life these buildings dated from the latter part of the eighteenth century. A room on each corner is was what 'four square' eluded to.

There was a small flower garden to the front of the house surrounded by a picket fence. The gap between the house and the brick outbuilding was gated by a large tubular metal five barred gate. Rhys had a squint over the gate and it was obvious this was one of the access ways to the fields that were part of the establishment.

The brick outbuilding was a substantial two storey building which had probably been a machinery shed with loose boxes and stalls at the far end. There was a large opening in the side with wooden full height double doors. The first floor had a staircase up from a personnel door at the front next to the gate. Rhys tried the door but it was locked. Looking at what was going on it seemed as if the first floor of the building was being converted to a flat.

At the opposite end of the building was a lean to shed of a building a bit like a garage but access was denied as straw bales were stacked up outside the doors. The two long rows of timber loose boxes, one set with their back to the road, the other row of the same length constructed opposite. The yard between was rough concrete to provide grip for the horses. Each end of the yard was gated in case animals escaped whilst their box was being cleaned.

Rhys counted ten loose boxes per row, so the capacity was for twenty horses.

"Potentially a good steady income for livery," he muttered to himself. He carried on wandering and the manure heap and a midden were situated behind the inner row of loose boxes. He could see a ménage in the field adjacent.

"Quite a setup, what a good place to be, and surely a chance to grow the business," Rhys muttered to himself.

"No sign of Sandra yet Rhys?"

"No Daisy, it's half eleven now. I have tried her on her mobile but there is no response."

"Oh dear," sighed Daisy, "look come into the tack room office and write down your number on the diary and when I see her I will say you called. I am so sorry there must have been a very good reason not to come and meet you Rhys," said Daisy with a grin.

"That's very kind of you."

Rhys left feeling rather dejected and unfulfilled but his appetite to work and be part of the business was very tempting.

*

Sandra had stayed the night at Long Acre Farm, as they talked long into the night. She was so tired that she overslept and didn't wake until nine fortyfive. Then a shower and breakfast. A good farmhouse breakfast with all the trimmings. She and John and Sienna were still sitting at the kitchen table at eleven fortyfive when Sandra suddenly jumped up.

"Oh my god," she suddenly exclaimed," I agreed to meet a guy who had answered the advert in *Horse and Hound* for someone to work in partnership running the stud and livery, I totally forgot."

"Don't worry," said Sienna, "you have had a lot on. Have you his number?"

"No I was distracted when he rang."

"Perhaps Daisy will have the number if he called."

"Good idea Sis." Sandra rang the stables and Daisy gave Sandra Rhys's mobile number.

"Hello, my name is Sandra Wall, I gather you are Rhys

according to Daisy at the stables?"

"Yes I turned up this morning, but I guess you had an emergency."

"You're so right, I am dreadfully sorry. Can we try and meet again?"

"Yes of course I am free, I have been abroad and just returned to the UK this week."

"Well I am free this afternoon if it's not too much to ask for you to come back to the stables?"

"Yes I can do that. Shall we exchange details in case something else goes wrong?" suggested Rhys.

"Good idea," said Sandra and they started to exchange information.

"Good lord, you aren't 'the' Rhys Williams are you?"

"Well I am not sure about that description but if you mean was I once a shareholder of Wall's and you purchased my shares then the answer is yes."

"Good lord, Rhys how fantastic that you are back in touch. Look I am at Long Acre Farm in Tarporley at the moment, which is where my sister Sienna, John England, her husband, and James their son live now. Why don't you come here first and meet the family again and then we can go to the stables."

"Well if that is alright, yes let's do that. I will get my car and be with you in about half to three quarters of an hour."

"Great, see you then Rhys, bye."

"Who was that on the phone? I must say you seem very cheery now."

"You will never guess?"

"No I can't who was it?"

"Rhys, Rhys Williams, you know the guy who inherited Roger Whiteside's shares when he was murdered. We bought his shares and he has been travelling and saw the advert and is interested in a partnership in the stables."

"Good heavens that is amazing, I would love to see him again."

"That's good as I have just invited him round he will be here in half an hour."

"Oh Sandra I have nothing for lunch, the place is a mess, what were you thinking of?"

"Hey slow down Sis, everything is just fine. It will be you, John and James he will want to meet not your hoover!"

They both laughed. It seemed like no time at all when the cattle grid rang out its welcome. Rhys drove his second hand dark green Land Rover Freelander into the yard.

The two sisters stood at the kitchen window watching this young Adonis with a bronzed face get out and walk towards the house. They almost fell over one another in their struggle to be first to greet Rhys.

CHAPTER 16

Once the sisters had overcome their excitement like young school girls welcoming a pop star, they resumed their decorum and invited Rhys into the farmhouse. John England had been doing a bit of work in the office over the barn, and heard the arrival of a car and a certain amount of commotion in the yard. He couldn't concentrate without knowing what was going on. He switched off his computer turned off the desk light, raced downstairs to see what was going on.

He could see his wife and sister-in-law shaking the hand and giving a most fulsome welcome to a young man who was obviously the driver of the Land Rover Freelander. Who is it, was the question that flashed through his mind.

"Oh John, you will never guess who has just arrived," exclaimed Sienna in high excitement.

"Correct, I can't guess." At that moment Rhys turned to greet John.

"Blow me down with a feather, it's Rhys isn't it?"

"It most certainly is John," said Rhys holding out a strong and bronzed hand to shake John's outstretched hand. Firm handshakes were exchanged and much patting on the back.

"To what do we owe this honour? It must be nearly ten years when you made your fortune and left to explore the world."

"Yes John, nine actually, but it seems just like yesterday."

"Come in all of you the kettle will be on or there is something stronger if you prefer."

Once inside the farmhouse they repaired to the lounge; teas and coffees were served by Sienna and Sandra, the boys declining a drink of beer due to Rhys's requirement to drive back to Chester.

"Rhys what can I say about this morning? I am so sorry. It's a very long story and of no consequence to you, but I was really held up."

"Please don't concern yourself, it's all over and I am here now."

Sandra explained to the others. "I had an appointment to meet with someone, I now know to be Rhys this morning to look around the house, stables and livery business. Rhys was responding, by coincidence, to an advert in *Horse and Hound* for a partner for the business."

"Oh I see," interjected John, "did you get a look at the place Rhys?"

"Yes I did John and what a great place it looks. It seems as all the loose boxes have occupants making weekly payments which must be a great start to the business, allowing other activities to be addressed to make more money."

"You seem to have got the picture of the place very well Rhys."

"Well Sandra, Daisy was more than helpful, but as she was very busy I didn't take up too much of her time, just obtained some basic facts."

"Having done that Rhys is it the sort of business you would like to get involved with?"

"Yes it certainly is. You see I have been travelling for seven and a half years. The last eighteen months I have been in Mallorca helping to run a very similar establishment."

"Oh I see, bit warmer there?" commented Sienna.

"Yes but I have been all over the place, and horses seem to have been the common denominator."

"Oh, tell us more Rhys I am fascinated to hear what you have been up to," said Sienna.

"Well maybe another time but suffice to say I worked on a racing stud in Kentucky, a polo ranch in Argentina, a sheep station in New Zealand which was all horseback stuff, then to a racing stables in Melbourne, Australia where we had some beautiful horses. We had a winner the year I was there in the Melbourne Cup."

"That's all very exciting Rhys, with Chester racetrack so close and enough land at the stables with a gallop already established, your experience would be invaluable, and perhaps we could find a winner of the Chester Gold Cup?"

"Well it's possible, who knows? It's really a case of building a reputation. The basics are in place so yes, I am extremely interested."

"Would you be on your own Rhys or do you have a partner?"

"I have a long term girlfriend who I think would love to come and join me here. Will the flat be available?"

"Yes it certainly would be, I have the key if you have time we could go and have a look at it, and I can show you around the house."

"Is it appropriate now to ask what you plans are for a

partner, the cost etc?"

"Quite appropriate Rhys. John would be acting for me, and you know he has had your interests at heart as well, right from the beginning."

"Yes I know I will be eternally grateful to you John for getting me off a hook not of my making."

"I had in mind a payment for half of the business of sixty thousand pounds."

"What about the property and what security would I have for my investment?"

"You have learnt a lot on your travels Rhys, good question. I had in mind living in the house, but the flat and outbuildings can be an asset of the business and a share of the value can be added to the price so you would in fact own half the premises except the house."

"That all sounds extremely interesting. Have you any accounts for this year and previous years Sandra?"

"Yes I do they are in the office over the yard here. I can get a copy for you before we move off to have a look round. This is a good time as all the horses will be back in and Daisy will have gone so we will not be disturbed."

"Well, much as I would love to stay and tell you about all my travels, I am excited to see around the stables again, can we go?"

"Of course Rhys, let's hope all this works out. Where are you staying now Rhys?" enquired Sienna.

"I am at the New Blossoms Hotel."

"Are you planning to stay in the area for a while?"

"Well yes, what I want is to find a business for the future so I don't want to move."

"Well," said Sienna, "whilst Sandra is copying the

accounts let me show you the flat we have over the barn here. It could be yours on a short term lease to suit you. The rent for a month would equal the cost of staying in a hotel for a week. Would that be of interest?"

Rhys accepted the invitation to use the apartment at Long Acre farm. He then joined Sandra in convoy to the stables.

Eventually Rhys returned to the New Blossoms Hotel in Chester. He advised the reception clerk that he would be leaving tomorrow, Monday, so could they make up his bill to then and he will pay on his way out.

"Francesca, is it you darling?"

"Si si, yes Rhys it is. What news?"

Rhys spent an expensive half hour on his mobile phone to Mallorca explain everything that had happened during the day. He was so excited Francesca could hear it in his voice.

"I am moving into the flat at the farm tomorrow, the farm owned by John and Sienna England. You must come over I can't wait to show you."

"I will, I will, just not sure how soon I can get time off. I will phone tomorrow."

The young couple spent several minutes just saying goodbye, neither wanting to be the first to end the call.

CHAPTER 17

It was mid-afternoon before Michael managed to find a phone, then rang Sandra.

"You've a bloody nerve! Why are you ringing me?"

"I need some money, to put it simply."

"Oh, spent all your share then?"

"No but my credit card is up to its limit and I don't have my passport to prove my ID so I am skint and have no way of getting any money. Can you let me have £10,000 and deduct it from my share of the rent?"

"Why should I?"

"For old times' sake. I've made some silly mistakes but we were friends."

"Okay, Michael – it will be tomorrow I've a lot on today. Let me have your number. As soon as I have the cash I will call again."

"It's Tuesday tomorrow, can you get all the money then?"

"Probably I can let you have a couple of hundred if you want I am in Tarporley I can call at The Swan soon."

"Okay, that will help. I will stay here until you arrive,"

he muttered to himself as he put the phone down. Michael went down to the bar to find Roger to say that he was expecting a call and could he take a message.

Michael spent most of Sunday night in his room. The following day he decided that some human company might be preferable to morning TV. Michael was at the foot of the stairs near the bar, which fortunately was nearly empty when a voice assailed his ears that he knew only too well.

"So I have come to you as promised," said Sandra in an extremely cross voice. She was livid and started to shout at Michael, "go on, cough it up. What the fuck have you been doing?"

Michael, quite involuntarily, started to cry and fell to his knees.

"Get up you big sissy. I think you owe me an explanation."

"Have you got a drink? Gin, whisky, anything?"

"Bloody hell, Michael you do push things to the utmost limit don't you?"

"Sandra, sorry I need to explain everything."

"Here's a G&T, more G than T."

"Thanks."

She let him steady himself – he'd stopped crying and after the second slug of his drink he set about telling Sandra the awful truth of what he'd been doing.

"You mean not only did you set up this thing with Goose, whoever he really is, but you meant all along to defraud the owners of the cars."

"No one was defrauded – all the owners got their insurance money."

"Your perjury in court has led to an innocent man going to jail."

"Okay. That's right."

"But why are you apparently on the run now?"

"I'm not on the run I have bail an orderly trial will begin later. I have a defence. You see Ali, the butcher, supplied pubs and clubs with meat. Goose and I thought it was the ideal distributor for the pills."

"So not only do you perjure yourself in court, you are now a drug dealer and how many lives have been lost as a result of your activities?"

"Oh don't pin that on me. It's up to the kids – they buy the stuff and they use them."

"Umm, a moot point Michael – that will not wash with the police. Anyway why did you fall on your knees crying?"

"I need cash I have no money. I owe the hotel, the Range Rover needs fuel."

"Why do you need so much cash are you going to abscond?"

"I have a plan, it will be best if I am not around."

"What the hell does that mean, who else are you drawing into your web of criminality and deceit?"

"Just give me what money you have now and I will come to your flat tomorrow for the rest is that alright?"

"I guess so Michael."

Sandra went to the bar and spoke to Roger to say that Mr Fitzallen would be leaving in the morning, and as his business partner she would like to settle his account now, if that be possible. Sandra did just this and told Michael the hotel was all paid for until after breakfast tomorrow.

"Look Michael, here is £200, I will get an extra eight thousand from the bank in the morning. Come round when you have finished with the court, police whatever."

"Only eight thousand I had hoped for ten?"

"Don't look a gift horse in the mouth Michael, it's the best I can do right now."

*

Later in the day Sandra phoned Tony Munsford at the bank, and explained she needed eight thousand pounds in cash. She arranged to collect the cash at eleven o'clock. Tony being Tony arranged for a junior member of staff to accompany Sandra back to her car so he could be satisfied that she had arrived safely. Once back to her flat she put the money in a plastic bag and placed it in the sideboard cupboard.

Sandra being a solicitor knew she could be culpable if she just handed over the cash to Michael so allowing him to break his bail conditions and disappear. She decided to call DCI Kim a friend of John England's and explain the situation.

"Sorry mam, all the officers on that case are out, shall I ask one of them to contact you on their return?"

"No, no it's alright. If I need any help I will call again."

Her solicitor training made her write down what she was expecting what she anticipated Michael was about to do, and the fact she had tried to report her feelings to the police.

Michael arrived early afternoon as arranged to collect his money.

"What will you use this money for Michael?"

"None of your business."

"It is my business, I assume because you are here you have been allowed to continue your bail pending a full trial in a few months' time - right?"

"Yes."

"But I know, or rather I think I know you are not planning to be around when the trial is due to start. Is that correct?"

"Might be, but who knows."

Sandra picked up the phone and dialled 999, Police, was her response to the question. She was just about to say that she had Michael Fitzallen in her flat when he wrenched the phone away from her and hit her across the face.

"Michael don't you dare you bloody fool!"

Michael pushed her down on to settee and pulled his tie off and bound her legs tightly together. Sandra beat him about the head making little or no impact on the man.

"Stop hitting me you bitch! Now where's the cash?"

"Haven't been to the bank yet."

"Liar! You were there yesterday. Where is it?"

Sandra didn't answer so he hit her really hard. She started to cry and realised in his heightened state he could do anything.

"It's in the sideboard – it's the small plastic bag."

Michael looked wild. He rushed to the sideboard, grabbed the bag and checked quickly the contents.

"Where's your car key?"

"On the table in the hall."

"Is it still the red Audi TT?"

"Find it yourself," she said in a very angry voice.

He picked up the keys and then with the money raced to the exit and the lift to the underground car park. He wasn't exactly sure – there were two red cars. He was wild. He pressed the open button on the key fob. Sandra's car kindly acknowledged him with a flash of its headlights. Once in the car he drove as quickly as he could to the barrier and pressing the key fob for the barrier kept on a small ledge by the gear lever. The barrier went up. He got into gear and gunned it just as a police patrol car drove in impaling the Audi right on to the driver's door making it impossible for Michael to move as the airbag had deployed momentarily pinning him to his seat. Another police car arrived in minutes from the opposite direction. All four officers leapt at the Audi and dragged Michael out through the passenger door. They read him his rights as he was handcuffed.

One of the officers went to Sandra's flat. The front door was open. As he entered he could see Sandra struggling to undo Michael's tight knot. Within a few minutes or so it seemed to Sandra a plain clothes officer arrived and then a WPC. The detective took a detailed statement of what had happened whilst the WPC intervened with suggestions of cups of tea and a trip to hospital to get checked out. Eventually Sandra managed to persuade her that she was fine but did agree a phone call to her brother-in-law to take her to his house might be appropriate.

John England arrived in about three quarters of an hour after the incident. As soon as Sandra saw him she hugged him and started to sob uncontrollably. He had only the slightest indication of what had happened from the police officer at the door.

"Come on now, I'll take you to Long Acre and we can relax and sort everything out there."

She was so grateful for this kind and generous man to take control for her. John explained to the officer where they were going proffering the address and phone number.

"Don't worry, Sir, the lady's car will have to go to the Police Station. We can sort out what happened later."

"Michael's Range Rover is in the visitor's slot. It would be useful if that could be moved."

"Don't worry. We'll sort it all out."

Sandra left the key and garage fob for the officer at the door then left with John.

Sienna couldn't believe her ears when she heard what had happened.

"I'll get some arnica because you are going to have a corker of a black eye – the bastard!"

James toddled over to Auntie Sandra. She picked him up and cuddled him tightly. Sandra stayed the night and in the morning true to Sienna's predictions, she did have a corker.

*

Tarrant and Sullivan were in the conference room with Jon Kim and Julian Radley of the CPS

"What a shopping list you have for Fitzallen! I'm not sure where to start."

"So Julian. The first step is put right the miscarriage of justice and get Terry Pritchard out of jail."

"Agreed, but that is really a matter for the DPP – they will have to go to the High Court for a hearing to get the judgment set aside. I doubt they will seek a retrial involving Terry but a trial there will be with Fitzallen in the dock for perjury."

"We had an opportunity to interview Ali Hussain minutes before his death. Tarrant was with me and we have a recording of his answers and my description of his responses."

"That's very helpful but a dead man can't give evidence. Neither can he stand trial for the crimes he has committed."

"Understood, but surely we can get Fitzallen on a drugs charge."

"Not on the evidence of two police officers interviewing

a dying man. A man who was suffering from a drug overdose of narcotics. He could have been hallucinating and it wouldn't take very long for an average barrister to knock that one on the head. No, you need an acceptance on tape preferably in front of his solicitor that he was delivering drugs to Ali to distribute. What would get the pulse racing is if you get this Goose man to the dock. How you do that, I don't know, but ideally that's what you want."

Kim spoke to a counterpart in the Guardia Seville in Marbella to see what they could do in assisting Kim and his men arresting Goose. They needed more information than Kim had to date but if they had a witness who could identify Goose and confirm that he and Michael were associates there would be a chance that a European extradition warrant could be obtained.

"My God," Kim muttered to himself with a spark of inspiration.

"Sergeant, can you tell me where Sandra Wall went after the incident at her apartment yesterday?"

"I don't know, Sir but I will find out."

Not long afterwards Kim had what he needed. He phoned to make sure Sandra was still at Long Acre farm. He knew that Sandra would be his star witness.

"DI Kim, just to let you know I am back in Chester now in my flat, tidying up after the events of the other afternoon. Do you mind coming here?"

"Miss Wall, thank you for agreeing to see me. I can see you came off rather badly in the exchange with Fitzallen."

"Yes. It's a mess and it hurts."

"I'm sure you will be willing to give me some background on Michael Fitzallen. In particular, his relationship with a man called Goose."

"Certainly, Superintendent. I hope you have a large notebook."

"Even better, I have a digital recorder. Do you mind if I record our conversation?"

"No not at all. Where to begin is the thing."

"You start where it suits you."

"Well D I Kim…"

"Oh please call me Jon it is far less of a mouthful, and I think we know one another by now."

"Very well Jon. After my father Peter Wall was murdered, my sister and I took over control of the Wall's contracting business. As a commercial solicitor it was decided I should run the overall company, whilst my sister, a Chartered Surveyor, was ideally suited to run the property development division. I converted Wall's into a holding company with two major subsidiaries, contracting and development. Sienna was Managing Director of Development.

Once we got underway the property market started to expand, and frankly we just couldn't build houses and flats fast enough."

"I guess that was a very profitable time."

"Yes it was," confirmed Sandra, "so much so we were able to sell property 'off plan'. That meant we had contracts for the sale of flats and houses before we had even started building. The furious rate of activity of course attracted entrepreneurs into the market. One of these was Inside Property Investment. A new company founded by Michael Fitzallen and Wayne Lamb. They were two estate agents who wanted to get into development. Michael had a contact in Ireland, who introduced him to Niall Phelan a wealthy business man, racehorse owner and fierce advocate of the abolition of drugs. He had started a drug supply business

169

which he said was selling a placebo and helping youngsters kick the habit. Subsequently we now know that was all a lie. He himself was a drug dealer, sourcing his supplies from Spain."

"Yes I was aware of him, however he was killed in an explosion at his magnificent Dunmore Hall, as I recall," interjected Jon.

"The funds for the new property investment company set up by Michael and Wayne was Niall Phelan. It transpired that all their profits were sent to Spain. The idea was that Inside Property Investment would teach prospective landlords how to invest, raise the capital to buy investment property, so helping the expansion of buy-to-let properties. Wall's became a main supplier of properties to IPI who signed option agreements at a price we were very happy with. IPI then packaged the flats as individual investment opportunities, by having the apartments furnished and offering a guaranteed rent for two years. This enabled the client to obtain a substantial mortgage, because of the guaranteed income. Frankly we couldn't build the properties fast enough at one point."

"That sounds like a wonderful business for you and Wall's Sandra. What went wrong?"

"Well for reasons not clear to me, the boys split up geographically. Michael remained in the UK with an apartment in the converted warehouses at the Albert Dock in Liverpool. Wayne lived near Marbella in Spain, where the boys had built a villa. Apparently one evening returning to the villa with a girlfriend Wayne was in a fatal car crash. His passenger Sarah was very seriously injured and rushed to hospital. Michael had to go to Spain to identify the body and at the same visit went to see Sarah, who was seriously poorly. Michael was required by the Spanish police, to attend an urgent meeting. He was informed that the car crash had been caused by the brakes on Wayne's Ferrari being tampered with. The police were now dealing with a murder enquiry."

"That must have been a huge shock for Michael?"

"Yes it must have been. Michael decided to stop trading and wound up IPI. There were significant funds as I understand it in Spain."

"I see, there seem to have been a number of fatalities in this story Sandra?"

"Yes Jon, in fact Sarah died, and was apparently killed, possibly by Niall Phelan or an associate. However before he could be questioned on the matter Phelan was killed in an explosion at Dunmore hall. The Irish Police were convinced that the IRA were to blame. They assumed Phelan was causing problems to the drugs business which the IRA believed to be their business and no one else's."

"So Sandra what happened to bring you back together with Michael?"

"Well, as was chronicled in the press the banking crisis caused builders and developers serious problems. Wall's were not immune to the problems. We had a large block of flats in Manchester built but undergoing finishings, and a small block at Squirrels Chase in Chester. All but three of the apartments in Chester were contracted to be sold. John England, Wall's solicitor who you know," Jon nodded in agreement, "managed to get completions on all the contracted flats in Chester in time for the year end in 2009. The Bank were pressing hard for all borrowings to be paid off by the end of January 2010. The opportunity to sell the flats in the Manchester building was very hard. In fact investors were failing to complete and giving up their deposits. We were down to two contracted flats so we sent their deposits back and cancelled the sales, apparently much to the delight of the investors. I did this to allow us to deal with the whole building. In the mean time I had made all except one employee of Wall's redundant. You will recall the kidnapper of young James Wall from Sienna, which in the end the reason was the kidnapper was trying to punish IPI and Wall's for the lost money on the investment on six flats in Manchester. The bank were really pressing for repayment of a great deal of money, about three million."

"I hadn't appreciated that both sisters were under terrible strain at the time of the kidnap?"

"Well we were Jon, I was not much help to Sienna."

"I think you were if I recall you were the one who spotted the error on the police photograph that led us to the kidnappers and the return of James."

"Yes the return of James was indeed a bright point in the gloom."

"So how did you pay the bank back?"

"I was pretty desperate, so I resorted to putting adverts in various papers and the Estates gazette offering a fifty percent stake in the building for three million with significant income from rents as soon as the flats were let. Well I had only one response and that was from Michael. Cutting a long story short he purchased half the block just before the end of January and I was able to repay the bank."

"That must have been a huge relief Sandra. Where did Fitzallen get three million from?"

"I am not clear on that other than it was probably the proceeds that had accumulated in Spain from the activities of IPI."

"So there will be a record in the Spanish bank of the transaction?"

"I doubt it, the money came from banks in various tax havens, to John England's client account."

"Did that seem strange to you?"

"A little but knowing Michael I wasn't exactly surprised. I discovered later that Goose, the man whose name I have never known managed to put the money on one side for Michael when it was recovered from Niall Phelan. I'm sure there is a great deal more to Michael's background that he will admit. His secret side, you know Superintendent."

"I see, I assume he must have some cash in Spain to live off."

"Yes as far as I know there was about half a million over from the money that came from the various off shore banks, and John England was required to send it to Spain in Marbella. I am sure John can give you the details."

"Have you ever met Goose Sandra?"

"Yes, I have. I had dinner, in fact, on his yacht in Puerto Banus."

"Oh, and who was there?"

"Just Michael and me and, of course, Goose."

"Do you recall what his boat was called?"

"Yes. It was called The Flying Swan."

"I see. It seems appropriate somehow!"

"Have you any idea of Goose's real name?"

"No I've no idea."

"Do you recall discussions over dinner?"

"I do and with hindsight all the strange talk of cars and merchandise distribution, insurance claims, Middle East markets makes sense. At the time I rather switched off because unless you knew what they were talking about it made no sense at all but it does now."

"What we want to do is to try and incriminate Michael

and Goose from their own mouths so that we can bring them both to trial and end this awful business and get these pills we are certain they have been selling, off the streets."

"How do you intend to do that Jon?" enquired Sandra.

"Well we need an intermediary who could meet with Goose, we think we have enough already on Fitzallen. As far as Goose is concerned we need to get him to say he was involved with the drugs, money laundering the arson of the Sealand premises and sale of cars to the Middle East. What we need is a recording of Goose confessing to everything he was doing with Fitzallen."

"Have you anyone in mind for this role Chief Inspector?" said Sandra with a glimmer of a smile on her lips.

"Well Ms Wall, would you be prepared to do this for us? This is a big ask for a girl to undertake Sandra, it could be extremely dangerous."

"I know that but if it will help close these people down then I will do it," said Sandra.

"Thank you dear lady. We need to work up a plan, a reason for you going to see Goose and of course we will need the help of the Spanish authorities. It will take a few days to fix up, so it may be the end of next week, hopefully Goose will still be in port."

"Are you satisfied that after your meeting with Goose you will be able to give evidence in court that will persuade a jury that the classic car business was a scam at the outset? That in addition Goose was aware or more likely that someone else was the source of the Ecstasy tablets that Goose distributed through Michael Fitzallen?" requested Jon Kim.

"I believe I could, yes and I would. People like this need removing from society – they poison the lives of young people which can lead to occasional tragic deaths," said Sandra.

"Good. We may need you to meet with the barrister of the CPS to help in the formation of the European extradition warrant. Will you do that?"

"Certainly. I'm sorry Superintendent would you like a drink?"

"No, no dear lady. You are too kind. I must go now."

CHAPTER 18

Michael Fitzallen had little hope of returning to The Swan any time soon. He had been taken before the Magistrates on a charge of actual bodily harm and stealing a motor vehicle. He was remanded in custody for seven days pending further enquiries.

Sandra realised that if she was to be involved in the entrapment of Goose and get him and Michael convicted, it would involve quite a bit of time and a trip to Spain. She had better get the stables deal settled as soon as possible if Rhys wants to go ahead.

"Rhys, it's Sandra. Hi, look I am not trying to put you under any undue pressure but I have to be involved with a complex arrangement to help the police. It will involve me going to Spain for a while. It is a potentially dangerous task I am being asked to perform, so I want to be sure you have the deal on the stables before I go, if that is what you would like to do?"

"Oh, well yes, yes I do want to do the deal. It's a matter of price and the property, also I want Francesca to see it before I sign."

"When can she come over?"

"I don't know but any day now."

"Okay Rhys, let's get together I will draft a partnership agreement, and I can put you in touch with a firm of solicitors if you wish to be represented?"

"I am prepared to trust you and John absolutely. I assume the agreement will be in plain English so as soon as you have it let me see it and we can move on."

"When are you moving to the flat?"

"Today, actually. I am due to leave the hotel any time now."

"That is excellent as I use the other flat as my office. We can meet quite regularly and go through the document over the next few days. Would that meet with your approval?"

"Yes I will phone Francesca tonight and see if she can get an early flight to Manchester."

"Very well Rhys, I may see you later."

*

"John, are you free at some point today for about half an hour?" enquired Sandra.

"Yes sure give me twenty minutes or so, then pop in."

"I will be there within the hour as I am still in Chester."

"Okay, that's fine."

"John, I want to chat about the partnership arrangement with Rhys, and the property side of things. Can I set out my thoughts and then you can pick away at it?"

"Yes. Fire away."

"Well I have drafted some heads of terms, your views would be appreciated."

Sandra handed John a sheet of paper containing the bare bones of a partnership arrangement with Rhys Williams.

Proposed partnership between Sandra Wall and Rhys Williams.

The partnership will be a 50/50 arrangement between the parties.

The business has a value of £60,000.

The premises excluding the house but including all land save for one acre to remain with the house have a value of £200,000.

Banking and cash at bank will be an asset of the partnership and will not be denuded before completion.

The assets of the business will remain and the value is included in the price.

Animals consisting of four riding horses, and five ponies, will be included in the sale.

Other clauses to be considered: insolvency dissolution and disposal of partnership share on death or incapacity to work in the business.

"In a nutshell that would seem to put the bare bones of the deal in order. What about the house? I know you are going to live in the house, but you are a fair bit older than Rhys, who I assume would ideally like to acquire the house eventually."

"Yes that's a good thought John. I guess an option for Rhys to exercise in the event I didn't want the house for whatever reason."

"Yes that's a way of doing it. The value should ideally be the average full market value of three independent valuers."

"I would need to make reference to this arrangement in my will, wouldn't I?" enquired Sandra.

"Yes, and you will also need in the agreement a way of settling disputes between you. Also it would be a good idea to have cross insurance on eachother's lives to cover the cost at least of acquiring the other half of the business either way."

"That's a great help John, I will add the appropriate bits to the list and give it to Rhys, and if he is in agreement I will draft the full document. I guess I should tell you, not sure you will want to pass this onto Sienna I will leave it to you, I have spent a few hours with Jon Kim today. The end result he has asked me, and I have agreed, to go to Spain and arrange an interview with Goose. The idea being that a secret microphone, a wire microphone, will pick up the conversation with an aim to entrap Goose leading to his conviction."

"My god Sandra that could be extremely dangerous. People like Goose don't like being trapped."

"Oh I will be alright. It will be a success if I can get Goose to spill the beans on his operation."

"I will not tell Sienna until you have gone, but for god's sake be careful."

*

Rhys arrived towards the end of the afternoon, and John took him to his new home, showed him where everything was. John took a meter reading.

"Do you want a deposit and a signed agreement John?"

"No not in this case Rhys, I am more than happy to do this informally. You will have to pay for the electricity and the rent, four hundred a month, and if you put a TV in you will have to pay the licence fee."

"All very straight forward John, will a cheque do for the rent?"

"Yes that's fine. Can you make it payable to Sienna England? Technically she is your landlord."

Rhys did as requested, and unpacked his meagre belongings as soon as John had gone. He checked the fridge was plugged in only to find some basic provisions eggs, bacon, tomatoes and some bread. Also two bottles of wine.

"What are these people like?" Rhys muttered to himself, "they are generous to a fault."

*

"Rhys it's me! I have a flight to Manchester arriving at three thirty tomorrow afternoon, can you meet me?" said Francesca.

"You bet, which airline?"

"Jet 2, Terminal One."

"That's brilliant there is so much to talk about and see I am so excited, can't wait to see you. Bye."

As Rhys had put the phone down there was a quiet tap on the living room door.

"Hello."

"Hello Rhys it's me the front door was open - hope you didn't mind me coming up?" said Sandra.

"No, not at all."

"Good I won't keep you a moment but I have drafted what are essentially the documents to put the deal in place. If they are acceptable or you need to discuss changes then please let me know. I may have to be away on Wednesday and I hope to get this agreed and signed before I go. So I have printed off two copies of everything so you can study a copy."

"That's quite quick, are you sure you need to do this quickly?"

"Well I know what I am being asked to do, I will tell you one day but should it all go wrong and I don't return I want you to be able to carry on and not lose out because of my activities."

"Gosh it sounds pretty dangerous whatever you are up to."

"It could be, look here are the heads of terms have a look through this evening, and give me a ring if you need to discuss anything. I will be back in my flat tonight in Chester, so if you are not clear on anything give me a ring."

"Sandra this is a dream, I can't thank you enough."

*

A conference had been arranged for the CPS, Julian Radley, a barrister, Jon Kim and Sandra Wall. The whole scenario that Sandra had outlined to Jon Kim had been put in a document prepared by Jon Kim to all participants before the conference.

"Is this an accurate statement, Miss Wall?"

"Yes it is. Perhaps it would help if I tell you that I'm a solicitor although I stopped practising in commercial law when I took over the running of my father's business some ten years ago."

"Yes, that's helpful – I will choose my words more carefully. I didn't want to imply the statement wasn't true."

"That's fine – I hope you didn't."

"Can we get back to the case instead of dealing with legal niceties?" interrupted Kim.

"What I need is some hard evidence that this Goose character is involved in the drug trafficking and the classic car scam." Insisted the barrister.

"Why don't I go and see him and tell him more or less what has happened to Michael? Perhaps I could wear one of those discreet recording devices. That might get you what you want."

"What is your professional view of this, Kim?"

"I'm not happy about that, Sir. It could be an extremely risky, not to say a dangerous episode. I don't think we should let Miss Wall walk into this."

"Why ever not? Please let me go – I'm sure I can get what you want."

"No. It will have to be an exceptional warrant from the Spanish police to enable you to do this. I would want to be there as well. In addition, any recording equipment mustn't be on Sandra's person. A microphone and transmitter so the conversation could be recorded nearby."

"Can this be done?" enquired the barrister enthusiastically, "if so then we would have a real chance of nailing Goose – indeed, cooking his Goose!" They all groaned and the meeting broke up.

*

The DPP applied to the High Court for an annulment to the charge against Terry Pritchard and a complete discharge with no stain on his character. They persuaded the court that it was urgent and a gross miscarriage of justice that had occurred. Terry Pritchard was brought to the court in Manchester to be party to the proceedings. Michael Fitzallen was not in the dock but was referred to regularly through the proceedings. The Judge was satisfied with the overwhelming weight of evidence and Terry Pritchard was a free man again. Dot, the England's daily help with her daughter were at the court to hear the result. Tears and laughter all round. Terry just couldn't believe what had happened. It was all so sudden and he still wasn't sure what had happened. When he got into the car to go home, he met with Nicola and their son James – a family complete.

*

Rhys had made sure he was at Manchester Airport in plenty of time to meet Francesca off the Jet 2 flight from Mallorca. He settled down in a coffee shop adjacent to the arrivals gate. The indicator board showed that the flight had landed at three twenty. From experience Rhys knew only too well it could take another hour before she would clear passport control and baggage claim before people would start arriving through the gate.

Rhys was more than surprised when at ten minutes past four Francesca appeared. He left his coffee and they embraced completely oblivious to hordes of people trying to manoeuvre their way past them. When they came up for air Rhys took her luggage in one hand and her hand in his other the two made their way to the lifts and the short stay car park.

The two of them looked like they had won the jackpot, smiling from ear to ear like two Cheshire cats.

On the way back to Tarporley starting off down the M56 They couldn't stop talking. So much so Rhys made a wrong turn and had to double back. Not concentrating! As is always the case the cattle grid rattled as they drove into the yard.

"This isn't it is it?" enquired a wide eyed Francesca.

"No, this is the flat I am living in for a while, it is owned by the sister of the lady who owns the stables. They aren't far away, I will show you later."

No sooner had Rhys shown Francesca the flat and there was the sound of feet on the stairs.

"Hello Rhys, it's Sienna and my James."

"Sienna how great to see you, this is my girlfriend Francesca."

"Hello and this is James."

Francesca was immediately attracted to James. "Can I pick him up?"

"Yes of course."

"He's beautiful," and James chuckled.

"Sorry but I can't let you have a drink I am not that organised yet."

"Not necessary, just popped in to say hello, don't hesitate to call at the farmhouse if there is anything you need."

"Thank you Sienna, bye James."

"What a lovely lady and little boy," remarked Francesca.

"Yes they are a wonderful family. Look I have the keys for the stables and the house in fact. There will be no one there. When we have been to see that we can pop into the general store in Tarporley for supplies and then have some supper at The Swan. I think that will probably do for the day."

"Yes darling that is just wonderful. Let me go to the bathroom, and I will be right with you.

*

Francesca was really excited at the prospect of helping run the stables with Rhys. She loved every aspect of the place and the opportunity to live in their own flat in the country - what could be nicer?

"Shall I ring Sandra and confirm we want to go ahead?"

"Oh yes please darling. Not sure what mum and dad will say, but it's my life."

"Sandra it's Rhys."

"Hi, have you taken Francesca to the stables?"

"Yes we are here now, and yes we would love to go ahead."

"That's great Rhys, fantastic. I will let you have the draft partnership agreement probably by Tuesday. Is that okay?"

"Yes that's fine, but please don't bust a gut on our behalf. I am not going cool on the deal but I do want some time to take advice before I spend a considerable sum of money. So when you get back from whatever it is you are going to be doing, I hope we can then progress. I will have some points to discuss, possibly. So you do what you are going to do and we will do what we have to do, is that a deal?"

"Yes that's fine by me. I will ring you on Tuesday so we can meet and I can hand over the document. Have a great weekend you two."

"Thanks Sandra we will."

*

On Sunday as arranged Sandra met with Rhys and Francesca for a run through the documents of the proposed partnership agreement, a contract for the sale of half the business, and a draft option agreement giving Rhys the right to purchase the farmhouse subject to certain conditions.

"Wow, this is a lot of paper, have you drafted all this in a few days?"

"Oh yes, don't forget Rhys it was my job as a commercial lawyer this was meat and drink to me. In fact it is a small document compared to some I have drafted in the past."

"Well that's great I am glad we have a bit more time as we will need it to take all this in."

"Take all the time you want I need to feel you are happy with the deal."

Sandra returned to her apartment, expecting to hear from Jon Kim about some training on the recording equipment. As she was thinking about the potentially dangerous excursion she was about to embark on, the phone rang. She answered it in the full expectation it was Jon Kim.

"Sandra Wall."

"Ah you are still on the same number that's good."

"Who is this?"

"Jo Stafford."

"Good lord Jo, are you out of jail already?"

"Yes there is something called parole you know," Jo said sarcastically.

"I do know Jo, what can I do for you?" Sandra responded in a formal voice.

"I want my money."

"What money do you mean?"

"The money you paid for the stables when you robbed me whilst I was in prison."

"What on earth are you talking about?"

"Well you took advantage of me when there was nothing I could do about it so I need my money, and I need it now."

"Look Jo, let me remind you that you had been arrested on drug smuggling and disposing of a body. You rang me from prison asking for my help. Your firm instruction to me was to sell the stables. You were in no position to do anything having witnessed the explosion that killed Niall Phelan and two of his employees."

"I know but I didn't expect you to nick the place from under my nose when I couldn't do anything about it."

"You are quite wrong. The whole place was a mess, the house was uninhabitable and the business was going downhill, especially after you were arrested, lots of customers withdrew their horses. What I did, Jo, was to get in three estate agents to give me valuations on the place. I took the average of the three valuations and added twenty five thousand to indicate that I was not 'ripping you off' as you contend. I sent a contract for you to sign and you did. It was witnessed by the Governor of the prison. I completed the purchase, and paid off the mortgage with the Chester Building Society. With arrears I seem to recall you owed them about one hundred and twenty thousand pounds. I then asked Bennett's solicitor who handled the transaction to place the balance of funds in a savings account pending your release from prison. Did the prison return your passport?

"No."

"Where did you keep it?"

"I kept it in the cab of the horse box as I was always going back and forwards to Ireland."

"Yes, ostensibly to transport horses, but in fact you were transporting drugs for Phelan."

"Okay, okay, that's enough, I have done my time. What do I need my passport for anyway?"

"So you can prove who you are to the bank where your money is, and Bennett's can take you there and transfer the account to you."

"You people are all the same, all tied up with red tape, you bitch, I want my money and I need it now."

"Don't you talk to me like that Jo, I have done more than you asked for. I had to sell the horse box as it was a wreck. I got eight grand for it and put that money into your account. I am about to go away any day. Give me your phone number and I will ask John England of Bennett's to arrange for you to go to the bank. But you will need your passport, I suggest you speak to the police. If they can't help ask John England if he can get it for you from the police."

"Thank you for fucking nothing." The phone went dead.

Sandra was a bit shaken by the call. She rang John England and recounted what had happened. She explained Bennett's may get a call.

"He was extremely angry, I was a bit upset, and I really don't want to meet him as he thinks I have done the dirty on him, and of course he now needs money urgently."

"Leave it with me, I will sort it out."

"Thanks John that is a relief."

CHAPTER 19

Sandra was taken to Police HQ at Winsford and given a crash course on what she was about to do; how to handle the equipment and where it would be secreted. Her handbag was the chosen location for the microphone with the battery pack built into the base of the bag and an aerial was slipped into the handle.

"Don't you think it's a bit obvious? I am not normally a handbag person."

"Well," said Tarrant, "you will have to carry the returned packet of pills in something."

"Yes I suppose so but I am not a natural handbag carrier. Can't we put the electronics somewhere else?"

"Yes we can but where do you suggest?"

"Well why not my bra?"

"How do you see that working?"

"Well I thought you could put the microphone in the cleavage and the transmitter and batteries in the strap."

"Yes alright but that is going to delay issues, you will have to let us have the bra you plan on wearing."

"You mean like this one?" Sandra produced a bra from her handbag, the bag she normally doesn't carry.

The technicians, experienced in this mini microphone, expressed surprise and delight that they could start on the mechanics immediately.

"Is the microphone directional?" enquired Sandra.

"Are you sure you haven't done this before? You seem to have thought this through quite a bit."

Sandra just grinned.

"No it isn't directional – it will pick up sound wherever the subjects were. It is susceptible to wind but we may be able to filter that out."

The recording would be taken by a static receiver possibly in a van on the quay. Ideally a marine services van. It had to be a firm known to the harbour authorities as it was important no one knew what was happening, or become suspicious of the van.

On the flight to Marbella, Sandra had a frisson of excitement. She tingled at the thought of what she was about to do. On the same flight were the policemen, Jon Kim, DS Tarrant, and the sound technician: he had a suitcase with equipment to install in a van when he got to the destination. Unbeknown to Sandra, he had a bag which also contained a tracker so they could keep a track of her. She had to be natural, not give any hint of what she was really up to.

Sandra had with her Michael's mobile phone and his keys to his apartment. Jon Kim had the money, which also had a tracker in the small bag that contained the notes. The Spanish authorities had been alerted to what was happening and their customs officials were not to intercept the team and possibly disclose their cargo.

On arrival in Marbella, Sandra rented a car for herself. Jon Kim and team collected a minibus. Sandra drove straight to Puerto Banus whilst the police went to Police

Headquarters so they could work out their strategy and back-up. Kim and his team needed a day or two of preparation before the visit to Goose was to be made. The marine services van had already been acquired by the Spanish authorities. Kim's technology expert got to work on installing his listening device and to make sure it was all working as expected.

Sandra opened the door to Michael's flat with apprehension. She wasn't sure what she would find. Despite her concern she was pleased to find the place in reasonable order for a man! There was still some crockery on the draining board that he hadn't dried but was dry now fortunately, and nothing in the sink requiring attention. She threw the shutters and window open to the balcony and the afternoon sun flooded in.

Now is the moment to make the call, she thought to herself.

Pressing the number for Goose in the contacts list on Michael's phone, it rang out loudly.

"Michael! Where the hell have you been? I've been trying to contact you."

"It's not Michael, Goose. It's Sandra."

"Sandra! Blow me down! Where are you and why have you got Michael's phone?"

"It's a long story Goose but I'm in Michael's flat. I have something for you but I can't discuss it now."

"No, no dear girl – you must come for dinner."

"That's very kind of you but not tonight. I've a few things to do but I would love to see you tomorrow."

"It's a date. Say 7.30 – come for a drink and then we shall eat on board," demanded Goose.

The die was cast. She tingled when the call ended.

Suddenly the implications of what she was about to do hit home.

Kim rang later to check Sandra was established and also to discover that she had been invited to dinner the following day. "You know the drill, Sandra."

"Yes."

"We will park near the flat tomorrow afternoon and check the transmission from your transmitter to the van. We'll ring you when we're ready."

Sandra decided to go for a walk then have a pizza in the Italian on the dock followed by an early night. She tossed and turned. Her mind was turning over and over with everything that was about to happen tomorrow.

*

Michael had been put before the Magistrates again – this time for assault. His bail was revoked and he was sent to Risley Remand Centre to cool his heels until the committal proceedings. There remained the small matter of importation of drugs. Did he collude with others to bring drugs into the UK illegally and organise their distribution and sale? That interview would have to wait until Kim and Tarrant returned from Spain.

*

At Long Acre Farm John and Sienna were extremely concerned for Sandra's safety. They had taken the decision not to tell Ann Wall as it would only distress her. Sandra rang them and mentioned she had returned to Michael's flat just to reassure them that she was okay.

*

In the morning Sandra, having slept fitfully in a bed she had occupied before, woke to another stunning morning. The sea beyond the harbour shimmered in the morning sun with wavelets refracting the morning sunshine. The harbour itself was mirror flat, the yachts and super yachts at their moorings. Not many people were about this early, she noticed, as it was not in season the crews enjoyed an easier life than when the owners and guests were not aboard. The Flying Swan was moored nearly opposite the Port Office as were the two super yachts on either side, one even longer than The Flying Swan, her teak and bright stainless steel fittings glinting in the morning sunshine. Despite it being January there was a delightful warmth in the air.

Toast with a poached egg, orange juice and a black coffee were prepared and taken on the terrace in full sun. No concern now about needing Factor 30 sun cream! Whilst warm, the power of the sun was diminished by the angle the earth presented itself to the sun. She knew that the southern hemisphere received the full force of the rays at this time of the year. Maybe a trip to Australia might be a good idea after all this is over. Perhaps a cruise far more leisurely and who knows she may meet someone.

At about ten o'clock, as arranged, the marine services van appeared on the private road by the port outside Michael's flat. The ring on her mobile phone gave the signal. Kim instructed Sandra to switch the microphone on in her bra, which she was not wearing. When she had done that she had to read a few sentences from whatever she had to hand.

"Perfect," the technician declared, "that is just what we need." Kim advised Sandra that they would be in position from 7.00pm that evening and the Guardia would have their troops in place by the same time.

Sandra had made an appointment to have her hair done. So after a light lunch she settled into the stylist's chair to have a makeover.

"How would you like your style to be?" enquired the

young man dressed all in black.

"I want my hair to be long and sexy. I want to impress the man that I'm meeting later."

"Oh, that sounds exciting. What are you going to wear?"

"Well, dinner is on one of the super yachts in the port. I'm torn between a completely vampish backless dress with a plunging neckline with silver glitter and matching shoes or something far more nautical - tight trousers and see through blouse and blazer. I thought deck shoes would be best here."

"Oh, darling, the latter has to be the one. These boat owners are fanatical about their decks. You can't go trotting around in Jimmy Choo's high-heels on those decks can you?"

"I'm sure you're right but what about my hair? It never seems to have significant volume to look good when it's long."

"Oh, darling, you leave that all to me. Enjoy your coffee and then we shall get started."

Three hours later and a few hundred euros lighter Sandra made her escape from the scissors, dryer and the rest of the paraphernalia but she had to agree he had transformed her and she did look like a sexy vamp.

The tight white trousers and see through blouse with the minimal bra left nothing to the imagination so the royal blue little blazer with brass buttons covered most of her modesty but only when she stood up straight. She really was looking forward to seeing Goose's eyes pop out when she arrived. The £10,000 she brought with her in a small leather bag was to pay Goose for the latest and last consignment Michael had received.

Sandra decided on the trousers, blazer and see through blouse giving a tantalising glimpse of breast would certainly keep Goose's attention. Seven thirty arrived so she left

Michael's flat and walked slowly but purposely down to the port and along the main quay. Parked cars caused some obstruction. The projecting gangplanks of the super yachts had to be manoeuvred along the walkway. It was a cool evening but clear the night stars shining bright in the clear sky. Some of the boats, The Flying Swan in particular, had been lit up and looked wonderful with their illuminated shapes reflecting in the mirror flat harbour.

The handbag over her shoulder was quite a burden with £10,000 in £50 notes being the payment she was to make to Goose on behalf of Michael. Passing the marine maintenance van, she hoped against hope that the van could pick up the signal. It was reassuring to see it there knowing that Kim and the Spanish police were all stationed and ready to pounce when the time was right. The gang plank (passerelle) was lowered so access was easy. The blonde crew member, body builder type, stood at the head of the passerelle and welcomed Sandra aboard.

"Good evening, Madam. May I take your bag?"

"Oh no thank you, I will keep it with me, thank you."

"Please take a seat in the saloon," he indicated the way to go.

Sandra decided against a seat on one of the three large settees but opted for a single leather armchair. She felt more secure without the opportunity for Goose to cuddle up if that is what he decided to do. Sandra placed her bag beside her. She wasn't sure what to expect and nothing much happened for some time until she noticed the super yacht next to The Flying Swan move. She was intrigued so went to the window to see it go. Amazed and then concerned when she realised that it was The Flying Swan that was moving.

"God," she muttered to herself "why didn't we think of this? Where the hell are we going?"

She moved her position to look aft to the large patio windows over the quarterdeck. The quay was receding quickly. As the boat turned, the other boats in the port came into view. She could see the marine services van disappear as they slipped through the harbour entrance into the black Mediterranean night.

"Sandra!" boomed a voice from the little man, "how good of you to come."

CHAPTER 20

"Goose," she said, "I see we're off to sea. Where are we going?" there was tension in her voice.

"Don't worry, Sandra. I thought this would be a treat for you."

"A treat?"

"Yes, ladies usually like treats."

"Oh err, yes," she responded clearly concerned. Sandra tried her best not to allow the new situation give Goose any clue as to her real motive for being on board.

"We're going for a moonlit dinner and a mini cruise. Don't be concerned we will return." Goose's manner was now firm and authoritative.

"That's good because all I have is what I'm standing up in."

Goose laughed. "You girls, you always worry about what you wear. No, you'll be back in time for bed."

Sandra's mind was racing. The carefully rehearsed presentation of the money and the conversation, where she hoped she was going to get an acknowledgement from Goose that he was in fact the Mr Big of the drugs cartel that Michael was involved with. Would all this be for nothing? Had Goose rumbled the plan to record what was said? She didn't know. What was she to do now for best?

"Sandra, we'll be steaming for about an hour so let's sit down and have a drink and a chat so we can have dinner whilst we're stopped. I've asked my captain to moor off Gibraltar in a quiet anchorage so that we sit on the quarterdeck and admire the stars – the moon will be up soon. If you've never seen the sky whilst at sea you really don't know what you've missed."

The two returned to the seating area in the saloon. Goose pushed a button at the back of the settee – a steward appeared almost at once.

"What will you have to drink, Sandra?"

"A gin & tonic will be just the thing." She didn't explain why but she felt it would settle her nerves and she would relax. Nothing for it now but to sit back and enjoy the experience. The police could do what they wanted but Goose had once again avoided their gaze. Once the drinks were delivered (Goose drinking only Coca Cola) Sandra took a long drink of the cold G and T.

"Tell me what has happened to Michael," enquired Goose.

"Oh where to start! He's currently in custody with the police."

"Tell me all about it Sandra." And for the next hour Sandra explained all she knew and what had happened to her premises in Sealand. "The arrest of Ali Hussain was a breakthrough for the police because it enabled them to nail Michael. He was released on bail but got himself in trouble for assaulting me so his bail was cancelled."

"He assaulted you?"

"Yes and it hurt. He was not rational."

"I would say not. Are you okay now?"

"Oh yes. Pride I guess was hurt more than my black eye would indicate."

"Did Michael give you anything for me before you eh... fell out?"

"Yes, don't worry Goose, I have it here."

"What do you have?"

"I believe it to be £10,000."

"I think that will do – I think he owes me a great deal more but it sounds as though he will be out of action for a while."

"Yes he will. Did you put Michael up to the classic car scam, Goose?"

"Scam! My dear Sandra, it was a perfectly executed business arrangement. There were no losers - no one got hurt."

"Oh." Sandra stopped herself from mentioning Terry Pritchard as that in Goose's eye would simply be a minnow in the plan and dispensable. "How do you mean "no one got hurt?""

"My dear lady, insurance companies are set up to compensate people for loss. In every case in this arrangement all those who suffered loss will have been compensated."

"Really?"

"Yes. You will or have been paid out for the premises. The cars would all be insured and the owners paid out."

"So where did the cars go, Goose?"

"Dubai. I'm not sure of the final destination."

"How did it come about that you decided to send five classic cars to Dubai?"

"Oh it's a long story but we were in port in Dubai for a month or so a few years ago I was approached by a dealer who had a market for classic cars. It's too complicated to try and buy them and sell them – there is insufficient profit in it anyway."

"So you sold them?"

"No Michael did that. He paid me a commission on the sale."

"So you received 100% of the cars' value."

"Yes. Simple wasn't it?"

"When you put it like that, yes."

"Good - Sandra we're coming in to anchor now. Let's get ready for dinner. I'll freshen up. If you want the rest room, it's just there."

*

Jon Kim and the Guardia immediately sprang into action the moment The Flying Swan started to cast off. The marine services van shot to the opposite end of the port and the Guardia commandeered a small fishing boat. The owner was about to set out to commence a nights fishing, but not now! The listening devices were hurriedly transferred to the fishing boat complete with operator. A police officer also boarded the fishing boat which putted its way out of the harbour and in minutes they were following quite some way behind The Flying Swan. The absence of buildings and vehicles to obstruct the signal ensured that a perfect reception was obtained despite the distance from the super yacht. It was agreed that radio silence would be maintained until they had recorded everything they needed. The conversation about the classic car scam was indeed useful but not as toxic for Goose as an admission of supplying drugs – maybe that would come.

"Everything all right Captain?" enquired Goose before

he returned to the saloon.

"Yes, Sir. Nothing around just the odd fishing boat but they're always about."

"Okay. If you get any other type of activity, let me know immediately."

Back in the saloon Goose joined Sandra and sat in state on the quarterdeck. Sandra was concerned it would be cold but as the ship sat at anchor head to wind the quarterdeck was protected. The partial glass screens either side of the deck ensured not even the slightest draught crept around the corner. The Flying Swan had overhead heaters to ensure a warm area. The dining table was set for al fresco dining.

"This is marvellous, Goose. I had no idea the sky could be so amazing. There are millions of stars."

"Yes. We all think we have seen the sky at night but until you have seen it at sea you have only seen a fraction of the night sky. Blame electric light pollution! Look back at Puerto Banus in Marbella if you want confirmation of that."

Sandra did as he suggested and the orange glow of the town was obvious.

"Dinner is served, Sir."

"Thank you, Carl. Let's sit and look aft, Sandra. It will also be warmer and out of the draught."

The two of them sat on the forward side of the large red teak table on the quarterdeck looking aft. As was normal when the sun was down and it had been a hot day the onshore breeze reversed in the evening to be an offshore breeze. The view therefore was seaward towards North Africa. The odd light flickered on the horizon. A few ships passed by lit up looking like massive wedding cakes.

"Lobster tails to start – is that alright?"

"Goose, you certainly know how to flatter a girl." A cold

Chablis was poured as well as an iced glass of water in a crystal goblet. There was little conversation during the starter.

"That was gorgeous, Goose. Thank you."

"No problem. It's good to have a companion for dinner."

"How did you first meet Michael?"

"Oh it goes back a long way. We were introduced by an intermediary in Spain who initially introduced me to Sarah Perlaki who had a problem with a guy in Ireland. She was going out with Wayne. I wasn't aware of the relationship at first, then I discovered much later Wayne's partner, Michael. Wayne was killed in a car crash and Sarah badly injured. She subsequently died. The police decided it was murder because the car had been tampered with."

"I see, but how did you help Michael?"

"Phelan needed a large consignment, so I supplied him, but not exactly what he was expecting."

"Niall Phelan?" enquired Sandra.

"Yes. Do you know him?"

"Oh yes he financed Michael and Wayne in their business of Inside Property Investments. At Wall's holdings or rather the development company we sold a large number of apartments to IPI and their clients. It was a very profitable time."

"Well he was introduced to me as you do in business. He needed to recover a significant sum of money from Niall Phelan. I agreed to help him do that in return for a commission."

"So how exactly did you do that?"

"This is strictly between you and me Sandra. I have a facility to supply certain products that Phelan needed, he used to buy from me quite regularly."

"So how did you get Michael's money back?"

"Pudding?"

"Well after the lobster and the steak which were simply delicious I don't think I can eat another thing. May I have a black coffee?"

"Of course my dear."

As soon as the coffee had been served and the staff withdrawn Sandra returned to the main topic of conversation.

"Go on it doesn't matter anymore Niall Phelan is gone and Michael will be in jail for some time I think, tell me what you did?" she demanded.

"Well it's complicated but I fixed up a shipment of product to Niall in exchange for a sum slightly more than Michael was owed. One of the packets of the product was laced with explosive and a pressure switch. As soon as the parcel was opened 'bang' and that was that." Goose laughed and laughed.

"Goose, I have to give you the ten thousand pounds Michael asked me to give to you, also a packet of pills that were never distributed as Ali has died."

"Well ten grand is too little but I guess you have to be thankful for small mercies. Sorry to hear about Ali. Are both items in your carrier bag?"

"Yes Goose."

"Can I just take them to my office? I won't be long."

As Goose was leaving his office having carefully secured his cash and ecstasy pills or so he thought, the steward intercepted him.

"Pardon me Sir but the captain requests your attendance

on the bridge."

Within minutes of the steward and Goose disappearing from the saloon, three armed men all dressed in black arrived on the quarterdeck, having disembarked from a RIB via the swimming platform.

They hustled Sandra down to the water's edge and literally threw her into a black rigid inflatable boat which sped off in the direction of Puerto Banus but slowed and stopped so that Sandra could watch the next instalment of the operation from a safe distance.

Sandra could hardly believe what was happening, being lifted off the back of The Flying Swan was so effortless with these large men lifting her as though she was no weight at all. When she regained her equilibrium, she looked around from the comparative safety of the inflatable boat bobbing up and down in a slight swell on a calm Mediterranean night. There were at least three other of these RIBs at the back of The Flying Swan. Once her eyes became accustomed to the dark she made out two larger boats – speedboats really.

"Here Miss put this life jacket on please." She was surprised to hear an English voice. She did as instructed. Suddenly the whole of The Flying Swan was lit by floodlights from the two speedboats and also from a larger vessel further out to sea that Sandra had not seen.

"Wow, this is quite an operation. What will happen next?"

"We are just securing the vessel and arresting everybody on board. They will be taken to one of the other RIBs."

"I see. It's a shame The Flying Swan left harbour as you will not have been able to record any of the conversation I had with Goose."

"Oh we did! It caused us a bit of a panic but we

managed to get the listening kit transferred to a fishing boat. It's over there."

"So what will happen about Goose?"

"The Spanish police and the Guardia are on board and will arrest everyone. They will bring them off in a minute. We want to wait until they are off as we want to go back on board to conduct a search. We will do that in the morning."

"Are you going to take the boat back into port?"

"Yes, possibly. We need an experienced skipper for that. Look here – they've got Goose and the crew."

As the officer spoke Goose and the blonde crew member and a girl who Sandra had never seen (she assumed she had been a stewardess) and the captain clearly evidenced by his uniform. The four of them were handcuffed and unceremoniously loaded into two RIBs. The big coastguard cutter still had The Flying Swan totally floodlit.

"It's quite a sight floodlit! Will they standby all night?"

"Yes, I imagine so."

Goose and the rest of the crew in the other two RIBs, the fishing boat with the listening equipment and Sandra's RIB with the police officers started to return to port. They all moved off together at a steady pace but not rushing along as these boats will do. Sandra looked back on The Flying Swan as she was receding into the distance. Just as they were entering the harbour, there were two enormous explosions from out at sea.

"What was that?" exclaimed Sandra.

"I don't know. It came from The Flying Swan," responded the English policeman.

All the RIBs and the fishing boats stopped. The occupants stared at The Flying Swan. There were trails of smoke from the bow and stern of the boat. Slowly, almost imperceptibly she started to lean to port. Little by little the angle increased. Then a high lurch and the ship was nearly capsized. They all looked transfixed at what they were witnessing – lit up for all to see by the searchlights from the coastguard cutter.

Everyone except Goose, who started to laugh a loud hollow laugh, were transfixed and to some extent sad to see this beautiful ship sink. Such a loud mocking laugh that the gaze of everyone was momentarily diverted from the ship to Goose.

"The bastard!" uttered the English policeman. As they were all looking The Flying Swan slowly sink beneath the calm black Mediterranean Sea and all that was left was a collection of flotsam and smoke floating around the sea. Nothing left, just the cackle of the mocking laughter floating over the waves.

*

In Chester despite the hour, they were monitoring the events in the Costa del Sol. The last communication they had received confirmed they had Goose and Sandra was safe and a good voice recording was achieved – that was good enough. The duty sergeant was about to text John England to report that Sandra was safe as had been agreed. On arriving in port Jon Kim turned on his phone to discover he had received and e-mail from the Chief Constable:

Dear Jon,

Following on from our earlier conversations on your retirement, I have a proposition for you. Please make an arrangement to come and see me.

Jim.

Jon was somewhat taken aback: he'd never had a Chief

Constable call him by his Christian name and never had he signed off using his Christian name. Was this a softening up process for what was come or did he have some good news for Jon? He would have to wait.

*

"Good morning." Kim was phoning Winsford Police HQ. "Jon Kim here could I make an appointment to meet with the Chief Constable?"

"Yes, certainly Sir, he is expecting to see you. Would next Monday be convenient for you?"

"Eh, yes I think so. What time?"

"Oh, two in the afternoon." The arrangement was made – no hint of what was to come.

"Stop worrying about it," he said to himself, "just get on with the job."

As he was running the possibilities of the CC's offer through his brain, the phone interrupted him. He jumped slightly as the bell interrupted his thought process "Hello. Jon Kim."

"Morning, Sir, I just wanted to inform you of what happened in Spain."

"Oh, Sullivan. It's you."

"Well the most important issue is that The Flying Swan has sunk," Sullivan advised Kim.

"Sullivan, I am here in a RIB, watching the thing sink. Are you off your rocker?"

"Sorry Sir, I had pressed the wrong button I wanted to report to HQ!"

"Okay. What about Goose is he with you?"

"Yes, I am with him at the Guardia Office. The good news is he has agreed to return to England. He signed a statement to the effect that we do not need to wait for his extradition."

"Good. When are you returning?"

"Hopefully some time tomorrow. We'll bring Goose to Chester HQ and he can be held until Monday. I guess we will have to charge him and put him before the Magistrates' Court."

"Yes, okay. Will you accompanying Sandra Wall back to the UK tomorrow as well?"

"I have yet to discuss that with her. I have to be back in the UK on Monday I have an appointment with the CC in the afternoon."

As the various crews disembarked from their boats back in Puerto Banus Kim went along to see how Sandra was.

"I am fine thanks Jon, nothing a stiff drink won't cure. It all became frenetic at the end. A situation I had not expected. I assumed for some reason you would arrest Goose when we came back into harbour."

"Well," said Kim, "it's just as well we didn't as he would have blown up half the boats in the harbour."

They both laughed, a nervous laugh, a laughter of relief.

"Come on there is an all-night bar on the corner of the port, let me buy you that drink."

Sandra didn't refuse.

"When will you want to return to the UK Sandra?"

"Well I need to catch up on some sleep, and then I need to have a rummage around Michael's flat and get it ready for returning it to the landlord."

"Will you be happy to come back on your own, as I have to get back and I will be flying tomorrow?"

"No I will be fine. It may well be the middle of the week

when I get back."

"Well Sandra I cannot thank you enough, your testament will be most useful and hopefully put these guys away. You will I am sure have to testify it was you and all that those who were on The Flying Swan but there is plenty of time to sort that out."

"No problem Jon. I have time on my hands once I have cleared up all the loose ends."

Jon Kim's phone rang "Sir it's Sullivan. Will Miss Wall need a seat on the plane back to the UK?"

"No Sullivan she is travelling back mid week."

"See you on Monday morning."

"Yes okay, she wants to go to Michael's apartment to see if there any papers of documents she needs. Something about a loan Michael made to Wall's."

Sullivan set about arranging transport and the statement for Goose to sign.

Sandra went off to Michael's apartment. She slept like the proverbial log, not wakening until nine thirty. When she did awake with a start she didn't know for a moment where she was.

It was as she knew it a two bedroom apartment with a wonderful balcony. She flung open the windows and shutters and the Mediterranean sun flooded in. She showered, and washed the previous night and salt water out of her hair. Then an omelette breakfast and coffee on the terrace.

She knew she had to end the tenancy on this flat as for sure Michael would not be coming back. She also wanted to find Michael's copy of the loan agreement on the Manchester block if she could.

Sandra methodically went through the apartment room by room, cupboard by cupboard, drawer by drawer. She emptied everything putting all the clothes in suitcases – the papers she inspected and tried to find the agreement for the apartment with no luck. She felt she should terminate the lease as the landlord wouldn't get any more money from Michael. No luck! What was she to do? The main line phone rang.

"Hello, is Michael there?"

"No, I'm afraid not. Who's this calling?"

"I'm Manolo, his landlord. It's just that he hasn't paid the rent."

"Are you nearby Manolo? I'm a friend of Michael's and I need to have a chat with you."

"Okay, Senorita, I will be there in an hour."

Sandra abandoned her search for the agreement – a discussion with Manolo would be ideal. She continued the search emptying all Michael's effects and placing them either in suitcases or bin bags. Just as she was finishing the doorbell rang.

"Hello, are you Manolo?"

"Yes, and you are?"

"Oh, yes, I'm Sandra. I was Michael's girlfriend at one time but we have split up."

"Oh, so why are you in his apartment?"

"It's my good deed. He's in prison in England for drug smuggling. He was involved with a man called Goose."

"You mean the man with the super yacht that sank last evening?"

"Yes, that's right."

"Well goodness me, so what is going to happen?"

"Well, Manolo, there is no prospect of Michael

returning for a number of years so I thought the best thing to do was for me to clear the flat and give the keys back to you so that you can re-let it."

"That's very good of you. I have a deposit but I think I will keep that to pay for the unpaid rent."

"Good idea. I will have all this lot out of the way by tomorrow. Do you know of a lockup or storage place I could use?"

After a long chat Manolo gave the information to Sandra that she needed. He also told her what to do with the key and he also gave her his mobile number. Manolo smiled and was glad to have the uncertainties sorted out and for him to get his flat back.

"Adios, Senorita Sandra."

"Adios,Manolo."

That agreement suited Sandra perfectly and she wanted to spend the rest of the day looking through Michael's papers. She found a good number that could be very useful in the future but there was an even bigger pile that was of no use at all: utility bills, credit card statements and the like were all committed to trash. Michael's bank statement was interesting – there was nearly €200,000 in it but who or when that would next be touched was anyone's guess. The next decision was should she hire a car or get a taxi to the storage unit. On balance, after checking there was not much in the price, she opted for a taxi. The driver was really helpful and assisted Sandra with the suitcases and bags into the unit. Sandra signed the papers and gave her credit card for payment for a year. She told them they could extend the period by charging her card. At the back of her mind she knew this was a winning move despite the fact that it would cost her a few hundred euros each year.

After a good night's sleep, Sandra departed for the

airport to catch the plane home to Manchester. Goose had flown back to England on Monday morning with the other three crew members from The Flying Swan.

After detailed interviews with the crew of The Flying Swan, they were not charged with anything and were allowed to go: they had little money and nowhere go but at least they were free.

Goose was remanded in custody and charged with money laundering, drug smuggling and causing death by proxy of Niall Phelan. He was remanded in custody pending a trial at Chester Crown Court.

*

"John, its Rhys Williams."

"Hi Rhys, what can I do for you?"

"Well you have done more than anyone for me, but I wondered if I could ask you one more favour?"

"Yes of course, what do you want me to do?"

"It is probably very improper, but I trust you. Would you be good enough to go through the documents Sandra has drafted before I sign?"

"Well Rhys I will do this as a friend, if there are areas that could be difficult for us both then I will have to advise you to go and seek independent professional advice."

"No I fully understand."

"When do you want to meet?"

"Just as soon as you have a moment, I would like to bring Francesca along as well, would that be alright?"

"Yes fine why not come to the farm at say four o'clock today. I will be home early and we can spend an hour going over the documents."

"We will be there, thank you so much."

As arranged Rhys and Francesca arrived on the dot of four o'clock at Long Acre farm. John came out of the farmhouse to meet them and suggested they went to the office, being the other flat over the barn, now converted to an office jointly used by Sandra and John.

Rhys and Francesca followed John up to the office and all three sat around a circular meeting table. Rhys laid the documents Sandra had produced on the table. John picked them up and had a swift glance at the documents.

"Right you two, we have here a full set of documents for you to buy half the business of the stables, a partnership agreement, this document," John waved it slowly in the air, "the last document, is an option to purchase the farmhouse under certain circumstances."

"I understand," said Rhys. Francesca sat and listened.

"So," continued John, "let's look at the contract for sale. It is a straightforward document which says you Rhys, or both of you as you decide, will buy half the business from Sandra Wall. The price to be sixty thousand pounds payable on completion. The price includes half of all the assets equipment and animals belonging to Sandra, as well as the cash at bank."

"I see," said Rhys, "so really the value of the whole thing is one hundred and twenty pounds?"

"Yes that's correct Rhys."

"What happens if either Sandra or I want to sell our share?"

"Good question, the document does not mention anything about that, because this is the sale now of half. The answer to your question is covered in the next document which is the partnership agreement. The partnership agreement deals with each parties conduct after the sale of half the business has been completed. In essence it allows the profits to be split fifty fifty, it deals with what happens if the business runs out of money, what happens if one or the other partners are ill for a long time, or become mentally incapacitated or god forbid either one of you dies. In those cases there is a formula for dealing with the share of the person who can no longer be involved in the business. There is a timescale for the other partner to bid for the remaining half and the representatives of the other party have got to agree that offer, if not they have to buy the remaining persons share at the price you have offered for Sandra's share if that is what happened."

"I see could insurance be taken out by the company to cover the cost of buying the other out?"

"Yes absolutely, good question."

"So all the running of the stables will apparently be down to me and Francesca, and we can live in the apartment over the barn. Will that be rent free?"

"Yes absolutely that if you like is part of the extra compensation for you in the deal. If you don't mind me saying so to get a deal like this which will possibly see you earning at the moment forty or fifty thousand pounds for an outlay of sixty is really good."

"Yes I agree. Can you explain the last document?"

"Yes, that is an option for you to be able to buy the house, should Sandra decide she doesn't want to live there anymore."

"I see," said Rhys, "how will that work?"

"Very much like the partnership agreement Sandra or her representatives invite you to make an offer for the house. They then get three independent valuations and take the average and will sell to you at the average. You will have to decide if you will pay more or possibly less to get the house."

"I see, so the house cannot be sold without me

knowing?"

"Correct. You seem to have got a grasp of the whole thing quite well Rhys. How much cash have you still got left? If I recall you ended up after inheritance tax with a million pounds."

"Yes that's right. I put half of it in a five year investment bond with a fixed two percent interest rate. The rest I gave to an investment company to invest for me for income, which had to be paid to my bank account. In total with the fixed interest bond there is five hundred and fifty thousand there, and despite me getting about three thousand a month, there is still four hundred and eighty thousand with the wealth management company. So in total I have just over a million, one million and thirty thousand pounds to be exact."

"Well you have done spectacularly well, considering the way the financial markets have behaved."

"Well John without your help and advice and interest you took in me at a very difficult time, I wouldn't be in this position now, so we really do want to proceed."

"When you say 'we' do you mean just you or both of you?"

"No both of us."

"Am I right in thinking you are not married?"

"Correct." Francesca was quite flushed at the thought.

"Well forgive me but if you take my advice you have an agreement between you as to how the transaction will be handled, you need to think about what might happen if you fall out and Francesca wants part of the value of the business she has helped create. How would that leave things, unless you have agreed now how it should be sorted in such circumstances?"

"Good advice John," said Rhys, "I have a solution for that however it is not for now."

"Are you two going out now or will you be staying in the flat her at Long Acre farm?"

The two looked at one another and grinned. "We will be staying in the flat now," advised Rhys.

"Well in that case you must come over to the farm and have a drink. Say half an hour?"

Rhys and Francesca returned to freshen up at the flat.

"Rhys, what did you think about Daisy at the stables?"

"She seemed fine to me, she could be a real help going forward."

"Mm, well she told me that she was very cross with Sandra because she had kept the stables running in Sandra's absence and had hoped she would be offered the flat and a manager's job. She was quite off hand with me as if it was our fault she was being pushed out. She was clearly very angry towards Sandra."

"Well people do get funny ideas, it's Sandra's property she can do what she wants with it. All we have done is to answer an advert. Don't worry about it she will get over it."

"Okay Rhys, just thought you ought to know."

"Yes, but don't mention it to anyone. It will all sort out eventually."

"It's just that she had expected to have the flat, and now we are stopping that happen."

"Well that can't be helped, we are not moving into the house, that's where Sandra will live. Don't worry about it darling, it's time we were back to the farmhouse."

CHAPTER 21

Monday morning as usual was a hive of activity at Police HQ to parade the arrested individuals over the weekend at a preliminary hearing before Magistrates. Jon Kim was not involved in this mayhem – he was interested in only two things today: Goose, or whatever his name is, and his appointment with the Chief Constable to see what he has managed to work out to permit him to stay in work.

Two o'clock arrived before Jon realised it. He presented himself at the CC's office ready to hear his fate.

*

On arriving at Manchester, Sandra picked up a taxi at the entrance of the airport requiring her to be taken to the city centre. She booked into The Midland hotel where she indulged herself with a top of the range meal in the French restaurant. A Jacuzzi in her room after dinner - a deep comfortable bed with a feather pillow saw her to sleep in no time. The following morning she took a taxi to her apartment building surprising the commissionaire who was pleased to see her.

"Joshua, would you mind putting my bags into your office for a few hours. I need to go and do some business and I don't want to be walking around with this lot."

"Certainly, Ms Wall."

Sandra walked to the agent's office on Deansgate to meet Denise, the property manager who was in charge of letting the block. The office explained that she was no longer working at the office and had left but they didn't explain why. A young lady called Raquel was taking over the management of the block for the time being.

"Why don't we offer a discount on rent for a longer let?" suggested Sandra.

"Yes, we can do that – in fact, up to three years. Your bank might not be happy as there is usually a clause in the mortgage that prevents lets of more than a year at a time."

"Don't worry, there are no borrowings on this building with any bank."

"Oh, that's excellent. We often get asked for longer lets."

It was agreed Sandra looked at the schedule of lets and could see opportunities to get one hundred percent occupancy.

"That should please Michael," she muttered to herself - although why she was worrying about him she wasn't quite sure.

*

The Chief Constable was pleased to meet with Jon again welcoming him to his office with a handshake and an offer of a cup of coffee which was accepted.

"Now, Jon I've discussed your retirement with the Police Committee and they, like me, will be sad to see you go but we are constrained by the rules laid down by the Home Office."

"I thought the answer would be no, Sir. I was prepared for that."

"Yes, Jon it's a terrible waste. That is why I discussed your case with the Chief Constable of Greater Manchester."

"Oh!"

"He, likewise, is constrained by rules so when you retire you will have to draw your pension like all other police retirees."

"Oh, I see, Sir."

"Jon, in your case, however, the Chief Constable of Manchester and I have come up with a scheme which may be unique but the rules do permit the police authorities to appoint on a temporary contract individuals who are over 55 years of age. The rules are intended for backroom staff but there appears to be no restriction on employing detectives. Should I say the regulation is silent on the matter?"

"I see, Sir, so what exactly do you have in mind?"

"Well, Jon, Manchester and Cheshire will jointly appoint you as a part-time detective on an as-and-when required basis."

"Really! That would be interesting but how would I integrate with full-time detectives, who would run the investigation and what powers would I possess?"

"I knew you would have these questions. The joint CCs will appoint you as a Detective Chief Superintendent whilst working for either Manchester or Cheshire. You'll have full police powers and your rank will denote that you are in charge of any investigation. You will be paid a retainer of £40,000 a year and depending on which force you are working for on a case they will be paying you £10,000 per case. We don't expect that there will be more than six cases in a year if that were the case your total remuneration could be £100,000, over and above your pension."

"I see, Sir, that all sounds very interesting. What if I'm not required to deal with a case?"

"Well, Jon, you will be at liberty to take private detective work or any other interest you may have subject to the overriding obligation to be available for the police when you are required."

"Can I think this very interesting prospect over, Sir? I am extremely interested."

Jon left the CC's office to his surprise with a grin on his face and a spring in his step – he was really delighted at this unique offer made to him, because of the financial constraints of the police budgets. He was flattered to be considered for the post, they must think I am worth it, he mused to himself. He couldn't get it out of his mind. He then thought he didn't ask about how long the arrangement might last and if he would get expenses.

Back in the office he quickly realised he had unfinished business with Mr Goose or whatever his real name was - he didn't even have a passport to indicate nationality and indeed without his real name it was not really possible to establish much about him.

*

Sandra returned to her apartment in Chester with a plan maturing in her mind. She was furious with Michael Fitzallen for allowing Terry to be sent to prison for arson and she planned to get Michael prosecuted and sent to jail which would also be beneficial for her and the Wall family. The call to Police HQ met with a degree of resistance in that she was unable to speak to Jon Kim, the man she felt sure would want the information she had. At Police HQ Jon Kim had commenced interviewing Goose to try and move the investigation forward. The Spanish police had carried out investigations in Puerto Banus to ascertain if any materials were loaded onto The Flying Swan when she visited. The Spanish authorities were arranging for the wreck of The Flying Swan to be investigated by divers.

They were keen to find documents, cash and any other objects that might incriminate Mr Goose.

"So, Mr Goose, this interview is being taped. You and your solicitor, should you employ one, will get a copy of the tape, the second tape is retained by us." Goose nodded in acceptance. "Please tell me your full and proper name, date and place of birth." Nothing – no response at all. "Did you hear the question?" Goose did not respond. "This is going to be a long day, Goose. We can keep this up much longer than you. What I will tell you is that you will be taken to court tomorrow to face charges. Later today we will charge you with a number of offences so I suggest you consider co-operating. The courts take a dim view of the silent approach. We are going to process you now."

Jon asked the duty sergeant to process Goose which involved a set of photographs, fingerprints, a DNA sample. That done, Goose was returned to his cell.

Checking the national database, with the benefit of police photographs and DNA to compare against the passport office records they managed to discover who Goose really was. A copy of his passport application papers were retrieved. A further check on him revealed his past under various names.

*

"John England, please," requested Sandra on ringing Bennett's solicitors.

"Sandra, good morning, welcome back home. What can I do for you today?"

"John it's a strange request but I need to speak directly with Jon Kim. He has Goose in custody and I have some further information that could be extremely useful to him. Could you please use your contacts to see if you can get him to ring me?"

"Sure. Are you in the apartment?"

"Yes, I will be here all morning."

"I will ring him straight away. I must tell you that I had a meeting last evening with Rhys and Francesca. I was not giving them legal advice but they asked if I could explain the various documents to them. I hope you don't mind?"

"No not at all in fact I am sure it will be most helpful to all concerned, thanks John. Oh did you hear from Jo Stafford about the money for the stables?"

"Yes, what an objectionable man. He certainly doesn't like you much. I spoke with Jon Kim and he authorised the release of his passport to him. Clearly the police had recovered it during the search of the stables and the horse box a few years back. They have sent it to the Chester police station. I gather he has it now as I think he spoke with one of our clerks to make arrangements to go to NatWest and change the name on the account to his, so he could get his money and spend it as he wishes."

"More thanks again John, look forward to hearing from Jon Kim."

*

It must have been gone 11 o'clock when Jon Kim phoned Sandra. She explained what additional information she had on Goose and on Michael Fitzallen, not just to do with drugs either. They agreed to meet later in the day at Sandra's apartment when Jon Kim had finished his work at Winsford Police HQ.

"Ms Wall, it's Jon Kim," he announced to the door intercom system.

"Come in."

"Ms Wall, please call me Jon."

"Sandra, likewise."

"What can I do for you?"

"Well, Jon, it's a long story but I have information you will find useful not only in the prosecution of Goose. You will have the recordings taken on the boat but in addition I know a few things - also I need to add a name in the frame, Michael Fitzallen."

Sandra explained the relationship and all she knew about the relationship between Michael and Goose. She also gave details to Jon of the whereabouts of a suitcase in a lock-up in Puerto Banus full of papers belong to Michael. She explained he was in England currently and where he was staying.

Jon Kim was aware that once again Fitzallen had been allowed out on bail but he had to report to the police every week.

"That's useful. I will need to act on this. I will arrange for Mr Fitzallen to join us in Winsford. You realise that you'll certainly be called as a prosecution witness at any trial."

"Yes, I'm aware of that. It may be difficult but if I have corrected a miscarriage of justice that is my reward."

"Apparently the recordings obtained of you talking to Goose, need to be corroborated by you in court, otherwise, it may not be admissible."

*

Back at HQ the following day, Jon arranged to see the CC.

"Sir, I've decided to accept the kind offer. Could you please confirm the expenses issue and how long the contract will be?"

"The contract will be as long as you like. Let's try it for a year and see how we go. Of course, all expenses will be paid."

"Very good, Sir. Let's begin."

"Well, I would like you to complete the case you have on at the moment with the man called Goose."

"That's fine, Sir. I have, as a matter of fact, additional information that may involve a third party and re-opening the arson case of Wall's premises at Sealand. It seems, if my information is correct, there is a third party involved in the theft of the classic cars, the mastermind if you like. I am delighted the original suspect Terry Pritchard has been pardoned by the courts. I suppose it is possible there might be a claim for compensation from him, as it transpired he was totally innocent."

"Looks like you have a lot on. I will arrange some documentation for you and will let you have it shortly."

Jon returned to his office instructing Tarrant to contact the Spanish police to recover the suitcase of papers Sandra had left in Spain. Jon was anxious to read the contents.

"Now Mr Goose, shall we try again? I know who you are."

"In that case there is no more for me to say."

"So you do have a tongue!"

"Oh yes. Who am I?"

"Julian Archibald Lenwell. With a name like that, I'm not surprised you've changed your mind on what you want to be called."

"Cheek! I like my name."

"So why 'Goose'?"

"Well, it's easier."

"Easier for what?"

"Well, people remember me better."

"What sort of people?"

"People."

"Goose, let's stop kidding one another. We have a recording of a conversation with you and Sandra Wall on The Flying Swan. There's no doubt that you were involved with supplying drugs to Niall Phelan. The last large order you double-crossed Phelan on behalf of a new client, Michael Fitzallen who was owed about three and a half million euros by Phelan. You organised a drop of the drugs, except they were packets of cement. The exchange took place off Southern Ireland. One of the packets contained explosives which were triggered by a pressure switch when opened it would explode. The resultant explosion killed Niall Phelan and two of his staff."

"That's quite story, Inspector, but you can't prove any of it."

"Oh, I wouldn't be too sure of that Goose. We have substantial evidence."

"Well, if you have you'd better get on and charge me. Let's see if your charges stick. I have a very good lawyer who will rip your case to shreds."

Jon was not prepared to be intimidated.

"Are you saying you didn't act for Michael Fitzallen in the recovery of his cash?"

"Yes."

"Well can you please explain how it is that Fitzallen paid into his bank in Spain the sum of half a million euros the week after Phelan was blown to pieces?"

"I don't know. You'd better ask Fitzallen."

"Oh, we will. In fact, he's in the cells right now."

Goose didn't reply.

*

"Michael Fitzallen, you are charged with assault, stealing a car, damaging a police vehicle and most importantly, distributing a banned substance namely Ecstasy tablets. How do you plead?"

"Your Honour, I plead guilty to the provoked assault and taking my girlfriend's car but the police cars ran into me not the other way round. I plead not guilty to distributing Ecstasy."

"I see, why have you pleaded guilty to the lesser charges?"

"Sir, I am guilty of these. I was drunk, flew into a temper when my girlfriend wouldn't give me the £8,000 she had taken out of our business account for me. I was furious. I accept I hit her for which I apologise and yes I took her car but in fact it was owned, as is mine, by our joint company so it was hardly stealing something owned by a company of which I am a shareholder."

"Good point, Mr Fitzallen. What have the prosecution to say to this?"

There was a hurried conference between the solicitor and the barrister for the CPS the result being that they agreed to withdraw the lesser charges. The Judge in the Crown Court was less than amused.

"Why can't you people check your facts before wasting the court's time?"

The barrister apologised profusely to the Judge.

"Now, on the more substantive case you plead not guilty, Mr Fitzallen. Is that correct?"

"It is, my Lord."

"Very well, this will have to go to a trial and I hope the CPS will have a case this time. Now, Mr Fitzallen, I gather you have been held on remand."

"Yes, Sir."

"Well, in view of your earlier statement and you have not been in trouble before I propose to set bail at £10,000. Are you able to obtain such a sum?"

"I am, my Lord, but only if the police return my passport as I need photo ID for my bank who have a branch in Chester – my money and account is in Spain."

"Very well, I order that you shall be freed on bail, that your passport be returned to you but only if you are accompanied by a bail officer of this court when the money is paid and your passport no longer required you are to surrender your passport to the court. Understand?"

"I do, your Honour, sir. Thank you."

The CPS and police were furious. "We'll have to make damned sure we have a watertight case when he is tried," said Kim as he left the court.

CHAPTER 22

Sandra spent the next weekend at Long Acre farm with John, Sienna and James. She had been somewhat nervous about spending time on her own since she had been attacked by Michael. She was even more nervous when she discovered thanks to a tip off from Jon Kim Michael had been allowed out on bail after he admitted hitting her. Ann came for Sunday lunch and the Wall family were gathered again at the location where all their troubles began.

"You've all had a terrible time recently. It's hard to believe rational people can get involved with a kidnapper, arson, theft, drug smuggling and murder. The good thing, that is young Terry Pritchard has been freed and pardoned," said Ann.

"Yes, Mum," pondered Sienna, "but I think we want to put all this behind us."

"I wish I could," said Sandra, "until Michael Fitzallen is behind bars I'll not sleep soundly. I am also very concerned about Jo Stafford who is now out of jail, when he rang me he was very threatening."

"Yes, dear, I do understand," said Ann.

"Mum, you are a rock. Thank goodness that we can all see that there is an end in sight."

"Yes, just Michael's trial. I want to tell you I hope you don't mind, John, but I want to put the apartment in Chester on the market." Said Sandra as she changed the subject.

"Well, that's a surprise. Where will you live?" enquired John.

"Well, at the livery stables eventually. Currently they are being run by part-time staff, that can't go on forever. Hopefully Rhys and Francesca will take over very soon. I want to be involved and live in the house. At the moment it is my view uninhabitable, but it shouldn't take the builders too long to fix it up."

"That sounds a great idea!" They all spoke at once.

"Good, I'll get the apartment on the market tomorrow. If it sells before I get everything sorted at the stables can I rent my old flat back?"

"Yes that's always a possibility, but don't forget your new business partner Rhys and his lovely girlfriend Francesca, they are living there currently."

"Oh? What's all this about?" enquired Ann.

"Mum I am so sorry, events have overtaken me. Yes, out of the blue Rhys appeared."

"Rhys? I seem to think I know that name."

"You do, he was the young man who turned out to be the son of Roger Whiteside, and he managed to walk off, all by agreement of course, with about a million pounds. You may recall as he was the only living blood relative of Roger Whiteside he inherited forty percent of Wall's shares. He could have demanded a seat on the board. Well luckily for us he didn't want that, just the money so we paid him a million for his share of the business. He was delighted and we got away very cheaply. It appears he has been on an extended world tour, his interest has been mainly horses.

He saw my advert for a partner in *Horse and Hound*. The rest simply is that he wants to buy part of the business and run it with his girlfriend who I suspect may well be his wife before long."

"Oh, do you think so Sandy? That would be great, another wedding in the village."

"I wouldn't get your hopes up, she is Spanish and may want to get married in her own country," advised Sandra.

"They are a lovely couple, I spent some time with them both simply helping them to understand the documents Sandy had prepared. They are clearly very much in love, and really looking forward to moving in," advised John.

At that moment there was a knock on the back door. As Purdey had come to the farm with Ann she barked, but that was it.

"Purdey, you silly dog you are too old to be chasing after people."

Knowing exactly what Ann had said the old dog looked knowingly at Ann and sat down again with a few wags of the tail. John opened the door and there were Rhys and Francesca.

"Hello you two, please do come in."

Reluctantly they both moved into the kitchen.

"Is it Sandra you need to see?"

"Yes if it's not too inconvenient."

"I am sure it isn't, in fact we have all just finished lunch, come in to the dining room, I will find you a couple of wine glasses and you can join the merry band."

"Look everyone, just as we were discussing them, look who has appeared."

Rhys and Francesca, moved quietly and timidly into a

room mostly of strangers who were all very happy having full stomachs and their fill of wine. There was a veritable cacophony of sound as everyone started to speak at once.

"Hang on folks they have really come to see Sandra."

"Do you want to go into another room if you want to discuss business?" enquired Sandra.

"No, oh no, please don't upset the party on our behalf," replied Rhys.

"It's just that Francesca and I have decided we definitely want to do the deal with you Sandra. There is just one question?"

"And what is that Rhys?"

"Will you be responsible to the refurbishment costs of the flat at the stables?"

"Oh yes certainly. In fact I am hoping that the alterations will be complete in a week or two."

"Oh that's great," responded Rhys. "Can we sign up as soon as possible as we have other plans to arrange to fit in with everything?"

"Yes we can sign up on Monday if you like. Do tell what other plans you have?"

"That's a bit cheeky Sis," Sienna butted in.

"No, it isn't, because what I want to tell you will involve you all anyway," said Rhys.

"Really you have us very curious now Rhys."

"Well the seed was sown by John who was talking about a contract between me and Francesca as we are going to live and work together. So I decided the best contract was a wedding contract, so I asked Francesca and she agreed. She has agreed to be my wife."

Well the whole room erupted with joyful woops of

delight. Francesca turned bright red in embarrassment, and Rhys had a smile as wide as the Cheshire Cat's. He planted a great big kiss on Francesca's lips, and they both laughed and smiled.

"Luckily I have a bottle of Champagne in the fridge. Darling can you get some more glasses out I will get the champers."

"Oh John I had not expected this you are all so good to me, and now Francesca."

"Do tell me," said Sandra, "when and where will you get married?"

The happy couple looked at one another with a sheepish grin.

"Well," said Francesca, "I have always dreamed of a country wedding. My mother and father are not very well off," continued Francesca in her endearing Spanish accent, "so Rhys has kindly agreed to pay for the whole thing. My family and friends can come over, there won't be too many of them, so we wondered if you would allow us to put a small marquee in the long meadow and have the reception here?"

"Where would you get married?" enquired Ann.

"Well," continued Francesca, "we would love to get married in Tarporley church, but we don't know how to go about that."

"Can I ask dear, are you a Roman Catholic?"

"No Mrs Wall, although I was christened in that faith I have never been a practising Catholic, so I would love to become a member of the Church of England."

"Well you have certainly thought this out, now there will be lots to do and sort out, I have good connections with the Church in the village and I would deem it an honour if you would look on me as a surrogate granny, and let me do some of the organising for you, I would love it."

"Oh Mum," said Sandra and Sienna in unison, "what are you like?"

"Mrs Wall I would very much like that and would be extremely grateful for your help," said Francesca coming to Ann's rescue.

John was busy pouring the champagne and passing the glasses around.

"A toast, to Francesca and Rhys for all the luck in the world, and happiness on their wedding day and reception in our field."

They all cheered raised their glasses and drank to the happy couple's health.

"Have you any plans as to when the wedding might be, either of you?"

"Well we have decided we would like to get married before we start work full-time at the stables, so as soon as it is possible to get everything organised, but so as not to interfere with your arrangements for holidays and so on John."

"Hee hee, that's great, a new outfit new hat how wonderful," chirped in Sienna.

Chairs were pulled up for Francesca and Rhys whilst their new companions at the table were subjected to a barrage of questions. The excitement of the afternoon faded into the evening whereupon Rhys and Francesca were invited to have supper with everyone. James was woken at the appropriate time and showed off his tentative walking skills to a very happy audience.

Before the day broke up diaries were produced and a number of appointments pencilled in and mobile phone numbers swapped. Ann confirmed that her primary duty was to organise a meeting with the vicar for the happy couple and then organise a date. Once that was set, everything else would fall into place.

*

The weeks passed and there seemed little progress in the case against Michael Fitzallen. Sandra had heard nothing but as she was now preoccupied with her new project, the completion of the alterations on the flat over the barn, and then the refurbishment of the farmhouse. She had little time to consider Michael's trial.

She arranged with Si and John to come and live back at the flat as soon as the flat over the barn was ready, and when it was Francesca and Rhys could then move in. It was more convenient for Sandra to oversee the development of the farmhouse living at Long Acre Farm. She had contemplated moving first into the apartment over the barn at the stables, but in view of the forthcoming wedding she thought it best to allow the newlyweds to move in and be the first occupiers. It was better to have the Chester apartment furnished and empty so she didn't have to keep tidying it up all the time. Agents could have a key and accompany viewers as and when they liked.

*

The papers Sandra had placed in storage in Spain had arrived. Tarrant had been delegated to sort through them and schedule them and file them for easy reference. Any specifically interesting papers should immediately be brought to the attention of Jon Kim.

Jon Kim for his part listened, and listened again to the tapes recorded by Sandra on The Flying Swan. The evidence was reasonably conclusive although Goose never actually agreed that he was transporting drugs to Niall Phelan– this might be an issue for the CPS. There was an interesting credit of half a million euros to Fitzallen's account which would coincide with a payment from Goose, but it wasn't from Goose, but Bennett's Solicitors, there was no indication as to where Bennett's received the money from. A question for John England.

"Tarrant, I've had a listen to this section of the recording. Is this confirmation of Goose loading a package with explosives?"

After a couple of re-runs of the recording, Tarrant agreed it was prima facie evidence of the context of the conversation. Later in the day after consultations with the CPS and the Irish Police, Jon Kim charged Goose in his real name with drug trafficking and the murder of Niall Phelan and his two colleagues. Goose was furious but knowing what he did know he could have been charged with many more offences. Fortunately, due to his foresight, the evidence was locked in a safe inside The Flying Swan at the bottom of the Mediterranean.

Jon Kim had been requested to attend at the Chief Constables office that afternoon. Once he had charged Goose he was free to go to the CC.

"Good work, Kim," said the CC.

"Here are the papers creating your new position. When you've had a read through let me know if there is anything you are not sure of and we can discuss it."

Jon Kim thanked the CC and knew there was a mountain of work to prepare for the two trials of Michael Fitzallen and Goose.

"It may be a while before I am able to come back to you Sir. There are two large trials to prepare for."

"I understand, there is no hurry."

*

"John, its Jon Kim."

"Jon, good to hear from you, what can I do for you?"

"Well it's a personal and yet a police matter. I could use some advice on a new position in the Police Force I have been offered."

"Happy to help when do you want to come?"

"Can I come back to you on that because we have a mountain of work with two big trials coming up fairly soon. I also have a question for you John, about monies your firm transferred to Michael Fitzallen's account in Spain. Half a million euros. What was that for and where did the money come from John?"

"No worries, you just let me know when you want to meet. As to the other matter regarding Michael Fitzallen, it was money received legitimately from foreign banks for Fitzallen's purchase of half of an apartment block which Wall's owned in Manchester."

"I see. I will need a formal statement from you John and copies of the amounts and where they were from, can you arrange that for me please?"

"Yes no problem I will let you have the information in a day or two Jon."

CHAPTER 23

Sandra, Rhys and Francesca found a convenient day for them all to sit around a table and thrash out the final points of the partnership agreement, the contract to buy half the business and the option to buy the farmhouse. Rhys was not sure on the farmhouse arrangement.

"How long will we have to make up our minds to put an offer in for the house Sandra?"

"I think I have drafted an initial two months, but if you would rather have three, then that wouldn't be a problem."

"Okay, can you please just talk us through the process?"

"Yes certainly Rhys. What happens is that if one of the trigger events occur which is that I die, or I am incapable of looking after myself at home, or I just decide to move away for whatever reason, then either I or my representatives serve a notice on you – it's just a letter – confirming that the house will be put on the market for sale unless you decide to trigger your option to buy within the three month period starting with the day of the notice."

"I see," said Rhys. "Do you understand darling?" he turned to Francesca.

"Well yes, but what price will the house be?" she asked.

"Ah," replied Sandra," we cannot know that now it may be many years in the future so there is a provision for either side to get a valuation with a third valuation from an agreed impartial firm so there would be three values. The price of the house will be the average of the three. Once the price is established, and that has to be done within a month of the 'counter notice' from you to say you want to buy it. Once the value is established you agree the price suggested or not. If you don't agree within fourteen days of the price being established than the property can be put on the open market, and your special position has gone. There is nothing to prevent you making an offer for the house when it is on the open market, it's up to you to gauge the position."

"I see, it's quite complicated?"

"No not really, what it does do is to give you an opportunity to buy the house, and it also gives you time to fix up a mortgage and so on as you wish."

"Sandra it may be that the house comes on the market because you are moving away. What happens with your half of the business then?"

"Well Rhys if you look at the draft partnership agreement there is a provision for the other partner to acquire the share from either the deceased partner's estate or the gone away partner. Bear in mind Rhys it could be you who want to move away, so I would be in the same position as you would be if I moved away. There is a formula to arrive at a price. That formula takes the last three years profits and finds the average profit over those three years then a multiple of one point five is applied, to arrive at a price to include the goodwill and all assets of the business."

"I understand, but what happens if this scenario occurs before three years accounts are available?"

"Then Rhys the part of the partnership acquiring the

other half will pay one year's profit based on the average profits since the partnership started up to three years when the other calculation will kick in."

"I've got it, are you happy with all that darling?"

"I am, but you understand it better than me but it all seems very fair."

"Thanks Francesca I want it to be fair."

"Can you please arrange to complete the documents so we can sign them? Francesca and I we are going to Mallorca next week to meet with Francesca's parents and her sister to talk weddings and so on. Can we sign up before we go?"

"That might be a bit difficult. I will see what I can do, if I can't arrange the formal signing I will drop you a letter today and confirm the deal as drawn up is agreed. Would you both like to sign the front of these drafts to confirm your agreement so that we have a basis should the unthinkable happen?"

"Yes of course. That is excellent as it gives us and you time," advised Rhys.

"I need to create a new will, I may suggest you two do the same, so there is no problem should the worst happen."

"Good idea Sandra. We must go we have to meet Ann and then the vicar."

"How exciting hope all goes well."

*

Rhys and Francesca arrived at Ann's cottage on the dot of five as agreed. Ann was overjoyed to see them, their wedding had certainly given Ann a project. What she needed was a date then she could get quotations for all the various elements required for a wedding.

"Hello you two," Ann said planting a granny kiss on

each of their cheeks.

"The vicar I am sure is waiting for you I will show you where he is, and when you have finished you must come and see my cottage, agreed?"

"Yes," they said in unison.

As expected the vicar's wife answered the door and ushered the happy couple into the vicar's study. Rhys was not to know, but this was the same performance that Sienna and John had been through, if they had been able to ask them, they would discover the vicar's study was just as untidy now as it were then. The cat had since died, so chairs were piled high with books, rather than one being occupied by a cat.

"What a lovely room," remarked Francesca, "every wall covered in bookcases except for the bay window wall." It had a lovely window seat with a fitted brown velvet cushion now showing its age. The two of them decided to perch on the window seat due to the absence of a clear chair.

Five minutes later the vicar burst into the room apologising profusely for not being on time.

"Has anyone offered you a cup of tea?"

"Err, no but really we don't need one thank you Vicar," responded Rhys.

"Now I love weddings and Ann Wall has told me the fascinating story of how you managed to inherit a share of Wall's Holdings. What a story, Francesca isn't it? When did you two meet?"

Francesca decided this was her moment to join in the proceedings. She told the vicar how they met in Mallorca where Francesca was working for the summer having finished university. She loved horse riding as did Rhys. They both went to the same stables at the weekend to ride. As they say the rest is history.

"Wonderful. Now Francesca I gather you were brought up a Catholic is that right?"

"Yes, my word Mrs Wall has briefed you well."

"Yes she is very reliable. Well I am pleased to say that causes me no problem at all. Have you discussed this with your parents?" enquired the vicar.

"No we are seeing them next week," advised Rhys, "do you think this might cause a problem?"

"Well it all depends on the attitude Francesca's parents have on this matter. Something you need to sort out as amicably as you can. You don't want to start off in married life with a rift in the family. Now when had you in mind to get married?"

"Well we thought," they both started to talk excitedly at once, "next June if possible."

"Oh what a wonderful month for a wedding, the weather and the flowers are, or should be at their best. Now let me see. Would the twelfth of June twenty ten be acceptable? Furthermore there is a full moon that night so you and your guests will be able to dance under the stars."

"That sounds wonderful Sir, can we book that please?"

"Yes my dear boy. What time do you think, say two o'clock which means we may get the service going by two thirty, brides are always late! Please let me know how your visit to Francesca's parents goes, then I will arrange for the bands to be read."

"What is that please?" enquired Francesca.

"It is a formality in the Church of England giving the whole area, well those that come to church at least notice of the intended wedding. You will come to church won't you, you will hear them read?"

On their way out walking towards Church Cottage they

were in heaven, grinning from ear to ear, having fixed the day for their wedding.

As arranged they knocked on Ann's front door which was opened without any hesitation.

"Come in, come in tell me all about it. I have some tea and scones ready for you."

*

Jon Kim arrived at John England's office around eleven o'clock. They met in the ground floor boardroom. Three of the walls were covered with bookshelves, holding copies of law reports from the year dot.

"An impressive set of books John!"

"Yes, but quite useless. I can find what I need on the internet quicker than it would take me to walk downstairs."

"Amazing, but I assume every reported case in the English courts is recorded in these books year on year."

"You have it Jon, it shows how busy we lawyers are."

"Well John I guess we should look at my little job."

"Very well Jon, I believe you have been offered a pretty unique deal?"

"Yes, should I spell out the deal as I understand it, then perhaps I could leave the documents with you to see if they reflect what I understand? It would also be useful if you could spot any issues that I hadn't thought about, also if you could consider what clauses should be added that aren't there."

Jon Kim started to explain why and how this special arrangement had come about. The force didn't want to lose him, and he didn't want to go, but police rules required him to retire at fifty five, albeit he would be nearly fifty six by the time he had to leave.

"You see John, the police budgets are under extreme pressure and are being cut all the time. This arrangement would allow me to work as a part-time detective either for Cheshire CID or Greater Manchester. That way the two forces can share the cost. Strangely back room part time staff are allowed under the rules, but the rules are silent when it comes to employing police officers on the same terms, so in the absence of anything to the contrary the police authorities think they can get away with this."

"Very creative thinking Jon, I will have a careful look at the papers. I will come back to you when I have done that. It might be best if we meet again."

"Well John thank you for the document and attachments on the Fitzallen money. Were you in a position to do a money laundering check?"

"Thought you might ask that," said Jon. "In the end I took the view that the half a million euros which went via me to Fitzallen, a known director of our biggest client Wall's, was nothing more than a normal transaction the like of which had taken place many times over the years."

"And the three million John?"

"Three payments into our client account each one from a legitimate bank, for the purchase of half a share of a property seemed to me not to need further investigation."

"Even if the money was the proceeds of crime?"

"Well had I asked that question I guess the answer from respectable banks would have been a denial. The money was required very quickly to avoid the property in Manchester being seized by the bank, which would have been a crime."

"Well John I will not raise the matter with the authorities, I guess the penalties about to be handed down to Fitzallen and Goose will be retribution enough."

"That's good of you Jon, I will let you have my thoughts on your matter as soon as I can."

The pair agreed, and Jon Kim left to return to the grind of putting the cases together against Goose and Michael Fitzallen.

*

A month passed. Sandra was pleased with the progress the builders had made converting the farmhouse into a home for her. It would be a beautiful home when the builders had finished with it. The good news was the stables were full and they had a waiting list for space. Rhys and Francesca will be delighted when they get back from Mallorca she said to herself. Daisy and the others were working hard to keep the place going.

Sandra, wanting to ensure the builders completed the farmhouse in accordance with her wishes, spent many an afternoon at the farmhouse. She knew in her mind how it was to look once completed, it was just a matter of transmitting her ideas to the builders. She would make sketch drawings in the evening and when at the farmhouse she tried to impart her ideas to the builder's foreman. He seemed to always have reasons, of a technical nature, that made her ideas less practical. "This is not easy," she muttered to herself.

Having had an extensive discussion with the foreman on the details for the master bedroom and en-suite bathroom, Sandra was left to consider the practical points the foreman had raised. As it was gone four thirty all the builders' workmen left site for the day, leaving Sandra to ponder.

"Hello, are you in?" came a call from below.

"Yes I'm upstairs," she called back, assuming it was either a builder or possibly Rhys. To her amazement around the door came Jo Stafford wielding a large length of wood.

"Got you, you thieving bitch. You will regret you ever bought this place as a 'steal' when I have finished with you."

"Jo Stafford if you assault me you will be returned to jail immediately, and they will throw away the key."

Stafford lunged at Sandra with the stick, as he did so she jumped to one side. They were jumping around like a couple of foil fighters in a competition. Sandra's disadvantage was that she did not have a 'foil'. Only Stafford did with his wooden weapon.

Sandra was continually shouting at him to stop and put his weapon down. Whilst she had his attention she managed to manoeuvre herself into the landing. He kept trying to hit her making as he missed large holes in the fresh plaster on the walls. Then he hit her, hard on the right arm, blood streamed out. This put more energy into Sandra's defence. He lunged again and the stick passed under her right arm. She held on. As they were now joined by this wooden 'link' she managed to arrange herself in such a way that Stafford was now at the top of the stairs. With an almighty push Sandra managed to make Stafford lose his balance and he hurtled head first backwards down the stairs. Watching him go, in what seemed like slow motion, she hoped against hope he wouldn't get up. She began to shake violently and cry.

Stafford lay motionless for what seemed like ages, but Sandra was not happy about following him down in case he was bluffing. She shut the bedroom door, and then went into the bathroom, which had been fitted with a lock. She locked herself in and collapsed onto the WC.

"John, its Sandra," she said sobbing into her phone.

"Sandra whatever is the matter?"

Sandra explained briefly what had happened.

"Stay right where you are I am on my way."

"Sienna, can you phone the police? Sandra has been attacked by Stafford at the farmhouse. Can you get an ambulance and the police as soon as possible?"

"My god John, whatever next?"

"Yes I know I am going there now."

"Be careful darling."

"I will," he called back as he raced across the yard to his Range Rover.

John England arrived at the stables before an ambulance or the police. A quick assessment of Jo Stafford at the foot of the stairs ensured that there was no life present in the corpse. A long piece of timber laid nearby covered in blood at one end. Climbing the stairs and reaching the master bedroom, John could hear the continual sobbing of Sandra.

"Where are you, it's John?" he called out.

"I'm here," a weak voice emanated from the bathroom. The door was shut and locked. When Sandra was sure it was John she unlocked it. She rushed out at John and flung her arms around his neck sobbing her heart out.

"Hello, it's the police."

"Up here in the bedroom, mind the body at the foot of the stairs."

One police officer leapt over Stafford, up the stairs to the bedroom.

"So what's gone on?"

John explained who he was and that he had just arrived to find his sister-in-law in this state.

The police officer tried to get an explanation from Sandra but she was clearly in shock, and was not able to communicate in any lucid way.

The paramedics, arrived one stopped to check the condition of Stafford and was able to confirm he was dead. The two paramedics then came together in the bedroom, again realising that Sandra was in severe shock, they thought some gas and air might help. They put a blanket on the floor allowing Sandra to lie down. They dressed the wound on her arm and suggested they took her to hospital for observation overnight.

"No, no I don't want to go to hospital, I will be alright soon, and it has been a terrible shock."

Realising the patient was making more sense the police officer asked what had happened. John England gave their names and addresses, Sandra briefly explained what had happened.

"Why did he do this?" enquired the officer.

"I don't know. I need some rest. Can I tell you in the morning?"

"Yes, yes, but it really is best for you to come with us in the ambulance. Your family can come and see you in the morning."

Sandra had no fight left, she allowed the ambulance crew to carry her downstairs to the waiting ambulance. The two Police officers advised John that they would have to come to the site, possibly with a pathologist.

"Very well, I can wait until it's all over." Which he did, locking the house up as he went. He phoned Sienna several times to acquaint her of the events of the night.

*

The following morning Sienna, John and baby James, arrived at the Countess of Chester hospital to see how Sandra was. To their surprise she was sitting up in bed having a breakfast and managing to eat with her newly bandaged arm.

"Wow Sis, I didn't expect to see you so chirpy this morning?"

"They gave me a tetanus injection, and a sleeping pill. They re-bandaged my arm this morning. I have a massive bruise, but they say they x-rayed it last night and it's not broken, so that's a relief."

"Oh, good. What a night."

"Yes one I would like to forget. In fact they need the bed so I can come home, can I cadge a lift?"

"Don't be daft of course we shall take you home."

John went to see the ward sister who confirmed that Sandra could be discharged. She was taken back to Long Acre farm, and propped up on pillows in the lounge with a fire burning. The room was warm and comfortable.

*

Later in the day D S Tarrant arrived to take a statement from Sandra, about the attack Stafford had mounted on her the previous night. Sandra explained how she became to own the stables and house. How she was meticulous at buying the property at a fair price, how the money was put on one side for Stafford, which the firm of Bennett's had now arranged access to the account.

"I think as soon as he had the money, always thinking he would have a great deal more than he thought, despite the fact he signed the legal documents with the price on, in the Governor's office in prison. I suppose he thought he could threaten me and get some more money."

"It's lucky he fell down the stairs. If he had connected with your head with that lump of wood you would be in the morgue and not him."

Sandra decided to leave it at that, not mentioning the fact that she had manoeuvred Stafford to the stairs and gave him a shove to send him on his way. She had never meant to kill him though.

*

The coroner gave an accidental death verdict having heard the police evidence. No further action was ever contemplated against Sandra.

It must have been a month before Sandra felt like getting into the swing of things again. She did however pop up to the house to see progress.

From time to time Sandra kept in touch with Michael really to discuss their joint business. The apartments in Manchester were now all let thanks to Sandra the suggestion of offering longer lets at a discounted rent, had worked.

"Can I come and to see you and what you have been doing at the stables and house?"

Sandra was in two minds about meeting with Michael. She relented – what could he do that would put her in harm's way? She had already had a dose of Stafford. Michael couldn't pose anything like the threat.

"Yes Michael – come over on Friday I'll show you around."

"Sandra, can you arrange to get some money out of the bank so I can collect it from you when we meet?"

"What's the matter with your bank Michael?"

"They are not keen to provide me with cash above a couple of hundred pounds."

"Well that's what happens when you are a naughty boy. Yes I will get some cash for you. How much do you want?"

"Ten thousand will see me right."

"That's quite a lot Michael. What's it all for?"

"The final sorting out of the penthouse."

"Okay let's say about three thirty at the stables?"

"Suits me, see you on Friday."

CHAPTER 24

The trial against Michael Fitzallen was scheduled to take place a month before the trial of Goose. Michael was due in court in two weeks. The charges were drug trafficking, arson, theft of classic cars and money laundering. Some of these charges had been added following the police's forensic sector having gone through all the papers Sandra had kept from Michael's flat in Spain. His solicitors had been advised and requested details of the case, they also requested a delay to the start of the two weeks set down for the trial because of this late addition to the charge sheet.

"Michael, we need to speak," advised his solicitor.

"Why what has happened?"

His solicitor went through the basis of the additional charge, and how they have come to light, when Sandra went to sort out his flat.

"What! The bitch. Why has she been rummaging through my papers?"

"Apparently she had to clear the flat in Puerto Banus as the rent had not been paid, and the landlord wanted possession of the flat so he could re-let it. I think she thought she was doing you a favour."

"Bah! She wouldn't know the meaning of the word. She

was grubbing around to make life more difficult for me. Also did you know I lent her, well Wall's Holdings, about three million pounds to get the bank off their back? They are paying me back, but there is a get out clause that if I am convicted of a crime the loan agreement ceases and no repayments of capital and interest ever need to be paid again."

"Why did you sign that Michael?"

"I wouldn't had I thought all this stuff would come out. I did say at the time I was not happy about the clause, and the response was "you are not going to break the law are you Michael?" which is a hard one to argue against."

"I get your point but it's a good point to bring up at trial as it could be argued that Sandra was deliberately trying to get you convicted. In fact she seems to be involved in your case and Goose's case. Tricky customer, Sandra."

"You got it," confirmed Michael.

Michael parked his Range Rover (now released back to him by the police) in the farmyard almost amongst the builders' equipment, piles of sand and stone. Sandra's question only moments after she said hello as Michael got out of the car, was: "How are you feeling about the trial, Michael?"

"You don't let anyone settle for long do you Sandra? It's good to see you." He offered a hand which was not accepted.

"You're a cool one today, Sandra."

"I've nothing but contempt for you Michael."

"Short memory. How about the millions I lent you to get you out of a fix?"

"I accept that you did that Michael, however your actions in leasing my premises, burning them down and trying to blame Terry were despicable. In addition you have been dealing in drugs that kill people. Have you no morals, Michael?"

"I had hoped we might get over our little difficulties, Sandra, but clearly you are determined to make my life difficult."

"It is only what you deserve. It is all of your own making."

Michael didn't reply but allowed Sandra to take him on a conducted tour of the building works. The builders were not at work today because one of them was getting married on Saturday and the boss of the firm had given them the day off.

"Did you bring some money, Sandra?" Michael asked.

"Yes, Michael, I did. No point in giving you a cheque so I drew it out in cash, £10,000. What on earth will you spend it on when you've got every prospect of going to jail in a few weeks, I don't know."

"That, Sandra, is for me to know. It's a secret. I have a secret side, you know and no one knows about it."

"I see – that's all very intriguing."

"I think most people have deep secrets that only they know," said Michael.

"If you say so, Michael."

"What's that over there?"

"It's a midden. It was there after the former owner left the place. They had pigs and this tank holds the waste."

"It's very smelly. Are you getting rid of it?"

"Yes, we shall."

"Umm – quite a job to get rid of that tankful."

"Yes, thank goodness someone else will be doing that." The two walked back to the yard in silence.

"What do you think?"

"It's very good, Sandra. You will enjoy living here. I hope you will think of me when I'm not here."

"You mean in jail?"

"Maybe."

"This money – you're not going to skip bail, Michael, are you?"

"What if I did? It's really nothing to do with you."

"Don't forget I'm a solicitor. I can't stand by and watch someone break the law."

"You wouldn't stop me would you?"

"I will be forced to advise the authorities …"

"Well you can relax – I've no such intention." She's a bitch, Michael thought to himself. She will make sure I am locked up.

"Good."

Sandra bent down to her car to open the door to hand Michael the bag containing the money when she felt a massive blow on the back of her neck. Michael had hit her with a brick on the back of the head as she bent down to collect the money. She collapsed immediately a small trickle of blood fell down her face from the laceration to her skull. Surprised at his ability to do what he had just done, he then started to think quickly. What the hell to do with the body?

He looked around and there was a pile of empty one ton bags which bulk building materials were delivered in. He picked one up which had a few small holes where stones had poked out. He picked up Sandra, who was no weight at all. He thought she was still breathing but she was out cold.

He wasn't going to hit her again. That would be messy.

"The bitch," he said out loud, "she was going to shop me for certain. My plans are too advanced to allow her to throw the proverbial spanner in the works." As his solicitor had told him Sandra was involved in rather too many aspects of the case against him, and Goose.

Michael placed a number of bricks and brick ends in the bag, before he placed Sandra in the bag. He rolled the whole lot together. He found a length of builders twine so strong he couldn't break it so he used all there was to tie up the parcel. The shape of a body was obvious but he hoped it would remain submerged for a very long time.

It may have been adrenalin or the realisation of what he had done, but he needed to hide the evidence. Michael picked up this large 'person parcel' weighted with bricks and slid the whole package into the midden. The tank was about five feet tall and nearly full of pig slurry up to the brim.

"Oh my god," he said to himself, "it's floating." The air trapped inside the bag held the body and the bricks afloat. Then bubbles started to appear. Slowly, very slowly the whole package started to sink below the surface. Then all of a sudden the body stood vertically and then totally submerged. The weight of the bricks was keeping the body down.

Michael was shaking. This was a girl he had made love to on more than one occasion. How could he have done this? "The bitch," he said out loud. She would have seen me put away for years, and stolen all my money by a clever legal document. No thank you.

Christ what about her car? Michael recalled on the conducted tour that the wooden lean to garage at the end of the barn was apparently empty. The doors were obstructed by four large bails of straw. Again his adrenalin kicked in.

He moved the bails. He drove the Audi TT into the wooden garage, covering it with an old brown tarpaulin, probably used for covering haystacks in the fields. He shut the door and replaced the bails.

Standing back surveying the scene, everything looked very much as it had done before he arrived.

"Hello," a girl's voice called out.

"Oh, hello," replied Michael possibly visually shaken, "who are you?"

"I am Daisy, I work here. I forgot to take my coat and I have come back for it."

"Oh, I see. Have you found it?"

"Yes, yes where is Sandra?"

"Oh, she had to pop back to Long Acre Farm she had forgotten some papers we needed for our chat."

"I didn't see her car down the road."

"She must have missed you she has been gone some time."

"Oh, well then I had better be going. Are you okay here on your own?"

"Yes Sandra will be back soon."

"Okay, I will push off."

Christ they are a nosey lot round here, thought Michael.

Jumping into his Range Rover, Michael realised that his mobile phone was still with him, and potentially a trace on his movements. He switched off the phone and removed the battery. Getting out of the car he threw the two items into the midden to join Sandra. He realised also by habit he still had the keys of the Audi TT, so they went into the midden as well. Was there anything else, he asked himself?

Michael had the money in a Tesco bag, but there were so many of those around it was hardly a clue for anyone. He removed some of the money from the bag, putting the majority of it still in the Tesco bag into the boot under the boot floor.

Michael had about a million or so euros in the bank in Spain. He had emailed them to send the money to a bank where he had an account in Bolivia or so he hoped. He understood that the money had been sent.

Michael needed to disappear. It would be a short while but for sure the Walls would start a hunt for Sandra and eventually she would be found. He needed to get away pretty quickly. The problem he had was that he had no passport having had to surrender it back to the authorities so they could be sure he would not be able to abscond. "What they didn't know," Michael muttered to himself, was that he had Wayne's passport, and as is the case with most passport photographs it doesn't take much imagination to accept the person in front of you is the person shown in the passport photograph.

Wayne Lamb (Michael Fitzallen) drove his Range Rover to his penthouse in Squirrels Chase, packed a suitcase of clothes and toiletries, and collected Wayne's passport before driving to Holyhead. He purchased a car and passenger ticket in the name of Wayne Lamb to Dun Laoghaire. The ferry port for Dublin, southern Ireland.

Michael arrived late on Friday night. He checked into the Imperial Hotel near the port. Mr Wayne Lamb was shown to a double en-suite room on the fourth floor. Michal/Wayne ordered a snack from the room service menu. He was very tired and went fast asleep. At about three in the morning he awoke having had a terrible dream that he was pushed into a pit and he was drowning. Would this dream ever leave him?

Wayne drove south on Saturday morning having devoured a very hearty Irish breakfast. That would keep him going all day, he mused to himself.

In Wicklow he purchased a completely new set of clothes, a soft bag with wheels was purchased from a charity shop – it had that 'used' look about it and a new mobile phone with a year's contract pre-paid from Irish Telecom.

At the travel agents in Wicklow he purchased a Ryan Air flight to Paris the following day Sunday. Wayne Lamb boarded the flight to Paris from Cork Airport at 07.00 in the morning. He left his Range Rover in the long stay car park having paid for its stay for a month at the service desk in the airport. He looked like a tourist with casual trousers, a shirt with a waistcoat type garment festooned with pockets. He had a fabric bag slung over his shoulder whilst his baggage was in the hold. He had purchased a savings card in euros from the Allied Irish Bank and paid in sterling – this effectively operated like a credit card but the money was already on the card. The balance of his funds were variously secreted in his jacket and in his holdall. The flight left nearly on time and took only an hour and a half to land in Paris Beauvais Airport - an airport Michael (he should now think of himself as Wayne) had never heard of.

It transpired it was 60 kilometres from Paris. No matter - deep into France, a stay there would not be a problem. He knew from previous enquiries Air France only flew to Bolivia once a week on a Friday. He'd missed this week's flight and as it was Monday it would give him time to purchase flight tickets for Friday. He found a small pension in town and became a tourist.

CHAPTER 25

On Friday evening John arrived home early to spend the weekend with Sienna and James. He was welcomed home like a long lost relative. Sienna and James were thrilled Daddy was home. The weather was fine and quite warm for May.

"Let's go for a walk up Long Meadow, bring Cadbury as well."

Cadbury was the dog Sienna had longed for when her mother moved out to Church Cottage. Cadbury was a year old now but still a puppy. The family walked and skipped up to the old oak tree. Cadbury had developed some of the habits of Purdy running into the copse and picking up rabbits which she played with and let go.

"Have you seen the improvements to the stables Sandra is doing up?" John enquired.

"No, darling. I've been too busy with one thing and another. When Sandra comes home we must ask if we can go and have a look."

"Good idea. It will be interesting to see what she's doing."

"She said to me that she had a plan when Michael was convicted. Do you know what that might be?"

"No, sorry. She said nothing to me. If it was legal she would be more likely to speak to you, John."

The couple wandered down Long Meadow back to their farmhouse for tea and a bath for James. A well-earned glass of wine for John and Sienna. The air had turned cold so they were glad to be inside. There was nothing much on the TV so they retired to bed after the 10 o'clock news.

On Saturday morning Sienna let Cadbury out for a run only to see that Sandra's car was not in the yard.

"John, Sandra's car isn't back."

"Well, she probably decided to stay in Chester – she still owns the apartment."

"Yes. You're probably right – you usually are."

The weekend slipped by with shopping trips to the big Sainsbury's outside Chester, a visit to Tarporley and their favourite butcher and a visit to Granny for James and some tea.

*

Jon Kim on Monday morning had a conference with the CPS where they discussed the upcoming trial for Michael Fitzallen and Goose. The barrister for the CPS was present who started to pick holes in the evidence, that was his job. Kim knew that but it was incredibly frustrating.

"This Goose character is suspected of all the crimes you've listed but I'm not happy with the quality of the evidence." The CPS solicitor looked at Kim requesting a response but without uttering word.

"Sir, the Spanish Police have produced affidavits from the crew of The Flying Swan regarding the loading of the materials including the explosives that killed Niall Phelan. The recorded conversation with Sandra Wall surely will be the evidence you require, Sir."

"No, there isn't a killer blow. What we need is Michael Fitzallen to give evidence against Goose which I'm certain he could do. In return we could negotiate a lighter sentence for him."

"Very well, Sir. Would you like to us to re-interview him and put it to him that he could get a much lighter sentence for co-operating in the trial of Goose? He needs to give evidence to the fact that Goose was instrumental in the murder of Niall Phelan and was the Mr Big behind the drug dealing enterprise."

On Tuesday, late morning, Sienna received a phone call from Tarrant at Cheshire Police enquiring if she knew where her sister was. He thanked Sienna but he was not concerned saying that he felt sure she would turn up. Tarrant phoned Michael Fitzallen's mobile phone but there was no answer. "I'll try again later," he muttered to himself. He returned to his other duties.

*

Wayne Lamb found the pace of life in the small French town very enjoyable. It was big enough for all the services to be available but small enough so that he could visit all parts of town in an afternoon.

French Telecom had an office in the main square where he purchased the pay-as-you-go phone (his, Wayne's, passport was sufficient for this purpose). Being a smartphone he was able to view the Internet as well and set up an e-mail account but he couldn't see why he would need one so he decided not to bother. He wandered around and visited the Saint Pierre cathedral to pass the time.

*

"Yes Mr Tarrant can I help you?" John England had answered the phone at home as he was spending the day considering Jon Kim's new contract.

"Yes, I hope so. We would like to speak with your sister-in-law Sandra Wall. She is a witness in two cases shortly coming up to court and she is a key witness. The barrister for the CPS would like to speak to her."

"Well, Mr Tarrant, I wish we could help you but we haven't seen Sandra for three days now and we are getting a little anxious because she is not answering her phone."

"Please don't be anxious. I'm sure there is a totally reasonable explanation. If we find her we will ask her to contact you and likewise if you find her ask her to contact us please."

"Sienna, I'm worried about Sandra. She seems to have disappeared. The police want to talk to her about the upcoming trials. What do you think we should do?"

"Let's go to the apartment, I still have a key, and check she isn't there. You've checked the stables so if we get no clue we'll have to assume a missing person and notify the authorities."

The two of them, accompanied by baby James went to Chester, John having eaten his evening meal in a hurry. James was put out; bath and bed were the normal activities at this time of the day. There was no sign that Sandra had been anywhere near the apartment. The three of them returned to Long Acre farm with James falling asleep in the car seat.

"Shall I phone the police when we get home, John?"

"No, let's give it one more night and I shall speak to Jon Kim in the morning."

James was quickly bathed and put to bed – he fell asleep almost immediately. It was around half-past nine when the phone rang. Both John and Sienna jumped – it was very unusual to get a call at this time.

"Is John England there, please?"

"Yes. It's Sienna speaking. Who shall I say is calling?"

"Jon Kim."

"Okay, sorry – I didn't recognise your voice."

"John, I'm phoning to let you know we are putting out an all persons search in the UK and Interpol for Sandra and Michael Fitzallen."

"Good Lord! Do you think they're together?"

"Frankly, John, we don't know. What we do know is that they are both missing. Can I come over in the morning and speak to you and Sienna regarding the last known movements of Sandra?"

"Yes, of course."

"Nine o'clock okay?"

"Yes."

True to his word, Jon Kim arrived at Long Acre Farm to interview John and Sienna.

"When was the last time you saw Sandra? Do you know where she went after you saw her? What has she been doing recently?" These questions set the conversation off. They talked for an hour, Sienna explaining where Sandra lived at the moment, the apartment over the yard, the other flat was now an office. The flat at the stables was being occupied by Rhys and Francesca, but they were currently in Spain visiting her parents. Kim then wanted to inspect both apartments whilst he was here.

"What about the stables, John?"

"Oh, they are just the other side of Tarporley. I can take you there after you are done here."

"Thanks, John. What else do you know about her relationship with Michael Fitzallen?"

"She didn't have a relationship with him," interjected

Sienna. "She did go and live with him in his apartment in Spain for a very short while."

"Yes, I know as she thoughtfully put all Michael's papers in a suitcase and put them in store. We have them all. Interestingly there is correspondence about the transfer of a large sum of money to a bank in Bolivia. Does that mean anything to you? advised Jon Kim."

"No, nothing at all – never heard of it being mentioned."

"Okay, we'll keep an open mind on Bolivia then."

Jon Kim and the Englands looked around Sandra's apartment at Long Acre farm and found nothing of interest except there was washing up in the sink, her bed was unmade (obviously in a hurry) and papers on the table all about the lettings of the apartments in Manchester. Jon Kim had a good look at the papers and discovered a Mortgage Deed for three million pounds loaned by Michael Fitzallen.

"Do you mind if I borrow this?"

"Well without Sandra here it is difficult. I have photocopier at the farmhouse, can I make you a copy?"

"Yes that will do fine, Sienna."

With the copy document in hand Jon Kim followed John England to the stables leaving Sienna behind to look after James. The builders were hard at work in the yard. It was full of workers' vans, piles of sand and stone so the two men had to park in the road.

"Can I help you?" enquired a worker.

"Yes, I'm Jon Kim and this is John England, Sandra Wall's brother-in-law. I'm a police officer," he said proffering his warrant card.

"Oh, can I help you? I'm the site manager."

"When did you last see Sandra Wall?"

"Last week. She comes here every day."

"Oh, so why didn't you say yesterday?"

"We haven't seen her since last week."

"What day?"

"Thursday. We didn't work on Friday."

"So it's nearly a week since you've seen her?"

"Yes, that's right."

"Could she have come on Friday when you weren't here?"

"Possibly. The stable girl might have seen her."

Jon Kim and John went in search of the stable girl who was working on one of the empty stables. On enquiry about Sandra, the stable girl Daisy admitted seeing her last Friday just after lunch with a man she'd never met before.

"Oh, and what happened then?"

"I was on my way home when they arrived in separate cars so I just said hello and explained to Sandra that I was finished and was going home. Saturdays and Sundays are our busiest days so I can take half days off from time-to-time to compensate."

"Okay, thanks. What sort of cars were they?"

"Sandra in her red Audi TT and the man had a black Range Rover."

"Did you see where they went?"

"Yes. They walked all around the stables, and the house which is being converted for Sandra. I assume they went into the house but I'd gone by then."

"That's helpful, thank you. Did you go straight home?"

"Yes but I came back after about an hour and a half as I had left my coat here."

"Oh, were both cars still here, did you see Sandra?"

"There was only one car here, the Range Rover. I didn't ask the man but he volunteered that Sandra had gone to Long Acre Farm for some papers. Strange though, I didn't see Sandra as I was cycling back here."

"That's very observant of you, but of course she may have left for the farm soon after you left in the first place?"

"Possibly, it's just I didn't see her car on the road at all."

"Thanks Daisy if I need to speak to you again can I call you here?"

"Yes anytime Sir."

"Let's have a walk around, John, do you know the layout?" enquired Kim.

"Yes, follow me."

The two men walked unknowingly retracing the steps taken by Sandra and Michael a few days earlier.

"What on earth is that?" enquired Jon Kim.

"That's a midden, Jon. The farm used to have pigs before horses and all that slurry from the pigs was put in here. They used to pump it out and spread it on the land."

"Does that still happen?"

"No, Sandra was going to have it pumped out and the tank taken away."

"Good idea – it stinks!"

"Yes, strange I've never seen the liquid surface before – it normally has the crust on the top. The builders must have put some rubbish in it."

Having gleaned nothing from their visit, the two men

exchanged pleasantries and went their separate ways.

*

At the small travel agents in the French village Michael made a discovery. The receptionist confirmed she would be able to check out flights from Paris to all destinations. So she checked on her system.

"I'm afraid, Sir the Air France flight to Bolivia was suspended some months ago. It's only Iberia who fly to Bolivia."

Wayne was a bit taken aback by this information. He decided to move to Paris. He checked into a small boutique hotel on the West Bank for three nights which could be an ideal location: there were wine bars, cafés, restaurants as well as ladies of the night – what else could he want! He would make enquiries about the flight tomorrow.

CHAPTER 26

Rhys and Francesca were exploring Francesca's village where her mother and father lived. It was a small hamlet not far from Binisalem a well know wine producing region of the island. The whole area was steeped in history. The Jacques, family house or rather smallholding was a long two storey building with walls limewashed an off white colour. The roof was pan tiled. Around the house to front and back was an area of land used by the family for growing vegetables and fruit. Chickens pecked around the front of the house and a pretty informal flower garden set off the front in a haphazard sort of way.

"This is just beautiful Francesca," commented Rhys.

"Yes Mum and Dad are really very fond of the place. My dad was born here."

The couple walked hand in hand down the rough drive way to the front door, carrying their rucksacks as they were used to this sort of travelling.

"Mamma?" called out Francesca, speaking in Spanish.

"Ah mama mia, Francesca, you look beautiful." (All spoken in Spanish)

"Is this your young man?"

"Yes mother, he is a little older than a young man."

"Yes you are right but most attractive."

Francesca's mother held Rhys's hand and gave him a kiss on each cheek.

"You are Rhys," she said in perfect English as she continued to hold his hand.

"Yes I am and I am delighted to meet you."

"What's all the commotion out here?" said Francesca's father as he came out of the house.

"This is her young man father."

Her father grabbed Rhys by the hand and gave him a very hearty handshake.

"Welcome Rhys, and of course Francesca also."

"Thank you, thank you so much," said Rhys, "it really is wonderful to meet you."

"Do you like rugby Rhys?"

"Well yes I do, my name is Welsh and we have been known to play rugby!"

Francesca's father burst into laughter.

"Sit down, sit down," he pointed to the long table and chairs which clearly spent a goodly part of each year outside.

Whilst the guests were being seated, a bottle of red wine without any label was placed on the table and small utilitarian glasses spread around. Snr Jacques filled up everyone's glass as full as they would go, and said: "A toast, to Francesca and Rhys. Enjoy the wine, I made it."

They all drank and laughed. The wine was excellent. The bottle was soon empty, Mrs Jacques ushered the two upstairs to their bedroom. Dinner would be in an hour.

Rhys and Francesca took their rucksacks to a first floor bedroom.

"This used to be my bedroom," she announced with glee.

"And what a lovely room it is. I love your mum and dad, they are lovely."

Francesca bounced on the bed inviting Rhys to do the same.

"No we can't, not here someone is bound to walk in on us. It doesn't seem right," advised Rhys.

"You old fuddy duddy, ok come here and give me a kiss."

Well before dinner was due to be served the two love birds were downstairs dispelling any notion, or so Rhys thought, that they had been up to no good.

"Let's walk around the garden," suggested Francesca.

"What do you think your parents will make of us getting married in England?"

"Oh they will be fine, not sure what Grandpa will think but we will cross that bridge. I think he will be here tonight."

"Does he speak English?"

"No not a word."

"Ah, that will be a bit difficult, stay by me," implored Rhys.

"That's the whole idea of getting married staying by one another."

"Correct, come rain or shine. Sounds like it might be a bit showery tonight."

Rhys and Francesca ventured into the kitchen asking if there was anything they could do?

"Yes, that's wonderful, can you please take out three bottles of wine, two red and a white and seven glasses. Francesca can you please lay the table." The couple did as requested.

Within half an hour Francesca's Granny and Grandpa came down the path.

Francesca ran towards them and gave them a big cuddle guiding them back towards the table and Rhys.

"This is my fiancé Rhys, he is a wonderful man, I hope you will love him just as much as I do."

"Hello young man and welcome," said the grandfather.

"Help me, what now?"

"He said he is fine and hope you and your wife are too." Francesca laughed, Grandpa had it all wrong. They all smiled at one another, Grandpa headed straight for the wine on the table and poured himself a glass of red and a white for his wife.

"What have I been saying?"

"Oh just that Granny and Grandpa are alright too."

"We are going to get on famously tonight I just know it Grandpa."

"That's good, otherwise it will be a boring evening."

"Oh don't say that," said Granny, *"you are an old bore yourself."*

Francesca and Granny laughed, Rhys joined in but had no idea what the joke was about.

Mrs Jacques came out of the house to join in the revelry.

Olives were passed around, Mr Jacques arrived and so did Francesca's younger sister Suzanne. Mrs Jacques had roasted half a lamb or so it seemed. There were potatoes roasted and green beans. Father Jacques carved and great portions were handed around. Not much conversation was passing between everyone whilst they were gorging on the beautifully sweet lamb. As the plates were being taken away by Francesca and Suzanne, Grandpa asked where they were going to get married. Rhys realised it was a question about

271

the wedding but as Francesca was elsewhere it was up to Mrs Jacques to give a reply.

"They are going to get married in a lovely English village church. We shall all be able to stay at the local hotel and restaurant that Rhys has organised for us."

"What is the matter with Mallorca?"

Francesca returned just in time to parry this one. *"Well Grandpa, Rhys and I have bought a house stud and livery and we shall be working together in England. My home will become England. So I think it is appropriate to start off married life in the place where we shall make our home."*

"Where has all the money come from?" Grandpa was clearly keen to dig into the details of Rhys.

"Well, he inherited a lot of money about nine years ago, and has been travelling, that is how we met in Mallorca where I was working. He invested the money well and only spent the interest."

"How much did he inherit?" Grandpa pursued the questioning.

"That's not a very polite question Grandpa," said Mrs Jacques.

"Maybe it is but it's relevant we don't want our Francesca working for a pittance her with a degree and everything."

Francesca repeated the question to Rhys. "What do you want to say?"

"Ah a wise question, and one I am delighted to answer. It is important that we all understand where we stand. I inherited a million pounds."

Francesca translated for the grandparents. Mother and father had not been aware of this figure either and were suddenly very impressed at their future son-in-law.

"That's a great deal of money, you look after it young man," Grandpa responded.

Mrs Jacque wanted to know if they had fixed up a date for the wedding.

"Yes," responded Francesca as excited as anyone could recall. *"It's the twelfth of June next year."*

"Wow," said Suzanne, who was fluent in English despite never having been there. "Who are your bridesmaids going to be?"

"Well if that isn't a fishing question I don't know what is. You will be my main bridesmaid if you will agree?"

"Oh yes, yes how exciting, I have never been a bridesmaid before."

Mother and father Jacques were sipping their wine and beaming at the joy their two daughters were currently displaying.

"Are you a Catholic Rhys?" enquired Grandpa.

"No he isn't" responded Francesca on Rhys's behalf.

Rhys was ignorant of the bombshell Grandpa had just launched into the proceedings.

"You know that you should not marry a man who is not a Catholic Francesca. He should convert to the faith."

"Grandpa, I need to tell Rhys what you have said."

Francesca relayed the essence of Grandpa's interjection. Was Rhys going to convert to a Catholic as Francesca was a Catholic?

"I am not sure how to say this gently and with respect to your grandfather but the short answer is no. We have discussed this and we had decided this was not a problem. Our vicar at home is perfectly happy to conduct a mixed ceremony."

Francesca gave Grandpa a potted version of what Rhys had said, in the hope he would not pursue it.

"Well as you are both here I think it is essential you go and see Father Peter at the church, probably after the service tomorrow, and explain what you propose to do."

"Yes Grandpa we will," responded Francesca.

Francesca explained to Rhys what she on their behalf had agreed to do. All it will take is a phone call to arrange the appointment. The meeting was set for noon, presumably after the morning service which Francesca said it would be a good idea to attend.

"I am a bit nervous of all this, we are going to do what we are going to do, aren't we darling?"

"Of course, we are just satisfying grandparents and possibly my parents although they have never mentioned anything."

"Okay I will go along with it. Don't forget I was brought up by my grandparents, and I went to a Welsh Methodist chapel. We used to go every Sunday morning. I was sent up to the age of fourteen to the Sunday school. Not the best way to spend Sunday I can tell you, in fact the whole thing put me off religion."

"I know," Francesca responded, "I was required to attend church every Sunday, and then a Sunday school in the afternoon. It would have been so much better if I had been able to make up my own mind, but I was forced to go."

"Seems like we have had a similar beginning to our religious upbringing."

"It will be difficult to go to church on Sundays Rhys once we are running the stables, Sunday is a busy day."

*

Now Wayne was in Paris, the first thing was to book a ticket to La Paz. The Iberia office was just off the Champs Èlysèes so with cash card available he requested his ticket.

"Very sorry, Sir, we only fly to Bolivia once a fortnight."

"What? Are you sure?"

"Yes, very sure, Sir." The smartly dressed Iberia representative spoke in perfect English with a French accent. Very sexy, thought Wayne.

"So when is the next flight?"

"A week on Monday Sir."

"Very well I will buy a ticket for that."

"The flight leaves from Madrid sir, so you will need a connecting flight to Madrid as well?"

"What is the nature of your visit, Sir?"

"Oh, I'm a tourist. Why do you ask?"

"You only need a tourist visa."

"Oh, I hadn't thought of that."

"Wait a moment, Sir - I'll see what we can offer you."

The visit to Iberia took over two hours. Whilst all sorts of permutations were discussed and information gleaned. Michael thought that staying in Paris for so long would be a gift to the authorities. He decided to make his own way to Madrid by train staying in small hotels as he went. In the end he was booked on the flight to Lima in just over a week on the following Monday. He would arrive in Lima at 18:00 hours local time and the flight to La Paz would be on Friday at 10:00 hours and Wayne was booked into a hotel in Lima. Once he'd paid €2,360 with his card he was handed an Iberia folder with all the necessary documentation enclosed.

"Just one last thing, Sir."

"Yes, what's that?"

"Can you please look up now? Thank you."

"What was that all about?"

"Oh, we always photograph our passengers who come direct for security purposes. The information will be kept confidential, Sir."

Not sure if he should kick up a fuss or simply accept what had happened. He chose the latter course and left somewhat uneasy – he had now left a trail of where he was. This vindicated his decision to get to Madrid by train. He couldn't change his appearance as that would raise suspicion. He consoled himself by the fact he had changed his name and hoped it would be sufficient and put people off the scent. Wayne told his hotel his plans had changed and he would check out the following day.

*

The Jacques family including Rhys all walked to the centre of their little village to the Catholic Church for the Sunday Mass at ten thirty. Despite having been indoctrinated into the faith Francesca was a little uncertain about the service and what she should do, and when. Some came back to her, as for the most part she tried to follow her parents lead. Rhys was stumped; firstly the service was in Spanish and secondly even if he had understood the language he was certain he didn't understand the religious rites and practices. Rhys didn't like the smell of incense which is a feature of Catholic services, it made him sneeze. Francesca was very amused by this but couldn't laugh so she held his hand and squeezed it tight. They smiled at one another which said it all.

After the service it was ten to twelve and they were exiting the church and shaking hands along with all the other parishioners; Granny and Grandpa were just ahead of Rhys and Francesca.

"Just pop back inside in a minute and we can have a chat," indicated Father Peter.

Francesca told Rhys what they had to do, but Rhys wanted to smell fresh air for a moment or two. Once Rhys was clear of the incense he was fine and then returned to the church to meet with Father Peter.

"This will of course be all in Spanish darling, but I promise I will translate it all for you."

They grinned at one another.

Shaking Father Peter's hand, they both felt a genuine warmth and a welcome.

"Now Francesca this is your man?"

"Yes Father, his name is Rhys, Rhys Williams. He is Welsh."

"Excellent, now I gather Rhys is a Welsh Methodist, is that correct?"

Rhys understood all that as there clearly is not a Spanish translation for Welsh Methodist.

"Now you are to be married, in England I gather. So it will be a marriage of a Catholic and a Methodist?"

"Yes father."

"The church you are to marry in, is that a Catholic church?"

"No Father it is a Church of England country church. We have met the vicar and he is happy to conduct the service."

Francesca explained what had been said to Rhys.

"Yes Father, there is absolutely no problem."

"Well Francesca, the Catholic church wishes all its members to marry other Catholics and procreate children, bringing them up in the Catholic faith. Will Rhys become a Catholic?"

"No Father he won't," Francesca said firmly.

Again Francesca reiterated what had been said in English for Rhys's benefit.

"You are quite right darling, I am not converting to

Catholicism."

"Will this cause a problem in the family?"

"No Father everyone is delighted. It was only Grandpa who suggested we came to speak to you Father."

"So what are we to do Francesca?"

"Oh Father we would love your blessing, but we are a couple, we shall have a lovely new home in Cheshire. We are going to be running a livery stables so as many of the customers want to go riding on a Sunday, it will always be difficult to go to Church on a Sunday. We are both Christians, we love one another and we do indeed expect to start a family."

"Now Francesca, I know many people think I am an old stuffed shirt, but I am quite up to date with the laws and teachings of the church and the Holy Father's teachings."

"I am sure you are Father."

"Well my darling Francesca," Father Peter said holding her hand and Rhys's hand, *"I will be the last person to stand in your way. Of course you will have my blessing. Furthermore if you can arrange transport and somewhere for me to stay I would love to give an address at your wedding. I won't interfere with the marriage ceremony, but I will want to give you my blessing and support on this your most important day."*

A tear trickled down Francesca's face, so much so that Rhys was concerned that something wrong had occurred. Francesca immediately put him at ease and explained what Father Peter had said.

"That is wonderful, of course we shall provide the transport and the accommodation for Father Peter. In your honour darling I would like to make a generous donation of one thousand pounds to this church. Would that be acceptable?"

When Father Peter heard this news from Francesca he

was overjoyed. He hugged and kissed the two of them.

"We are going back to my house Father, you are most welcome to come for some lunch if you like?"

"Oh yes please, and I will explain my decision to your parents and grandparents."

"Thank you Father that would be wonderful."

Father Peter closed the church doors and walked hand in hand with Francesca with Rhys holding her other hand. He acknowledged many people on the short walk to Francesca's house. There was a small gathering outside the house, sampling Monsieur Jacques's best wine.

Francesca explained everything to Rhys on the way. The sight of Father Peter hand in hand with Francesca and Rhys was a signal for all those gathered that the blessing of the church was to be bestowed on the young couple.

CHAPTER 27

John and Sienna felt they should tell Ann about their concerns for Sandra – it all seemed very strange and totally out of character.

"I agree darling," said John, "but I don't think it is something that should be said over the phone. I will drive over and see her, if appropriate I will bring her back here."

"Good idea John, I will expand lunch as I am sure she will not want to be on her own."

Ann was very, very upset.

"Look Ann, why don't you put some things in a small case so you can stay at Long Acre Farm for a while until the situation becomes clear?"

Ann did as suggested, Purdey jumped into the back of the Range Rover. She was hugged and kissed by Sienna and James when they arrived at the Long Acre Farm.

*

Jon Kim notified the CPS and the Chief Constable that he had two missing persons; one a bail absconder and the other the key witness to both trials.

"Kim, this is the CPS. I've spoken our barrister and without Sandra Wall he doesn't think we have a case."

"A case against whom?"

"Well Goose and Michael Fitzallen. They tie together."

"No, you must have – the recording and everything," said Kim.

"They're fine in themselves but without Sandra Wall to fill in the gaps, the body language, the knowledge she has of Fitzallen and so on, the evidence so far will not withstand any form of cross-examination as there is no one to examine."

"What do you advise?"

"Find them both, and quick."

Jon Kim was mortified: how to find two people apparently just disappeared would be an uphill task. He restudied the documents Sandra had taken from Fitzallen's apartment.

"Tarrant, can you look at the possibility of Fitzallen being on his way to Bolivia. See what you can find out as quickly as you can."

Jon Kim also made arrangements with Interpol and The European Security Force to issue arrest warrants for Sandra Wall, a missing person, and Michael Fitzallen, a felon who has jumped bail. The international warrants were despatched as soon as the various organisations had all the information they needed.

Tarrant was aware Interpol had a missing person's request, that someone wanting to travel to Bolivia surely would not be too hard to find. He searched the Internet with the help of Google to discover that the only airline to go to Bolivia from Europe was Iberia. He could find a flight from London so that surely was how Fitzallen would go.

"Sorry, Sir. It will be tomorrow before we can search the passenger list for the last seven days," was the response from Iberia.

Jon Kim was not impressed. At least the route out to the probable destination had been established. Would he get a flight without his passport? Jon enquired of the court office to check that they still had his passport.

"Sorry, Sir. That department is shut for the day. Can you ring tomorrow?"

"Bloody hell! Doesn't anyone work long hours anymore?"

*

Michael started his train journey from Paris, through to Bordeaux. The very heart of French wine. A day or two here would not go amiss. He checked into a small hotel and enjoyed the fruits of the city and the region for two days. Then back on the train.

He saw the irony of travelling to Bilbao, a place he had never been to but had subsequently discovered it was a destination of much of the money that IPI had made. It was syphoned off by Niall Phelan for his drugs company. The drugs from North Africa came ashore in southern Spain and were transported to Bilbao for a fishing trawler to take them to Dunmore East to eventually to be collected by Phelan. All this and the circumstances that had led him being in the fix he was now in, passed through his mind as the modern French train transported him from Bordeaux to the northwest Spanish fishing town now famous for its Guggenheim Museum. What to do and where to go when he got to Bilbao were questions that filled his mind for the rest of the journey.

A small hotel on the outskirts of the town of Bilbao was ideal. He caught a bus to the town centre. Meandering around, he found himself in the fishing port. The trawlers were enormous, so more than capable of navigating the Bay of Biscay, and he now understood why this was an obvious route for the drugs. Bilbao is a major train hub, so he was able to purchase a ticket to Madrid for two days hence, so he could arrive in the capital a day before his flight to Bolivia.

Wayne arrived in Madrid on Friday evening and booked into the Intercontinental Hotel. He had a day to cool his heels in Madrid. He thought it would be a worthwhile visit and his immediate issue was to acquire another cash card. This time denominated in US dollars being the official currency of Bolivia. Something for tomorrow – first a shower and a meal.

*

"Is that the department that handles bail applications?"

"Yes, Sir."

Kim introduced himself and enquired if they had the passport of Michael Fitzallen. After a few minutes wait the answer was ' Yes sir we have it.'

"Why has it taken so long to tell me?" Kim was irritated.

Kim slammed the phone down.

"Tarrant, Fitzallen doesn't have his passport it is still with the court."

"I suppose, Sir that could be helpful."

"Yes we need to check the ports and airports to see if they have a record of him going abroad."

Tarrant contacted the ports using the Ports notification procedure with the full details of Michael Fitzallen including copies of the photographs the police had taken when he was charged.

"Send it to all airlines as well, Tarrant. I guess we might get some reaction from them," instructed Kim.

The communication systems worked and within the hour copies of the wanted person's notice were arriving at port offices and airline offices throughout the UK.

"We'd better alert the duty staff that we are waiting for a sighting and to call us both at the moment something is reported," instructed Kim.

The weekend passed without any sighting of Fitzallen – the pressure was really on to find him. Kim was certain he had skipped the country.

"I would bet money on it he's in Spain. That's where his happy hunting ground is and he had an apartment there. Let's get the Guardia to do a search of his place in Puerto Banus – I bet he's gone there."

"Very well, Sir, but didn't the tenancy on the flat and when Sandra emptied the flat? Why would he go to the obvious place? His money is apparently in Bolivia. They speak Spanish there and the only intercontinental schedule flights are by Iberia but if he went to Spain to fly to Bolivia he would have to be in Madrid."

"Good thinking, Tarrant. Let's see if he has checked into a hotel there."

Two calls were made to the Spanish police.

The following day (Tuesday) there had been no reaction from Spain to their request. A further check produced nothing.

"Blast! The old method of police looking at passports of travellers would have flushed something out, I'm sure." Kim berated Tarrant.

"Shall I try all the European countries' airline offices as we think he is in Spain, Sir? We can't be sure. He may be sitting it out until Friday and then join the flight from anywhere."

"Friday?"

"Yes, Sir. There is a flight to Lima from Madrid on

Friday."

"Good man. Have you checked the passenger list?"

"Yes, Sir. I've spoken to Iberia bookings but he isn't listed."

"Do you have a copy of the list?"

"Yes, Sir." Tarrant handed it over.

"Whilst I have a look at this, get a notice to all European airline offices to see if they recognise Fitzallen." Tarrant did as he was bidden.

Kim read carefully through the airline booking list. There were five single men on the flight. In accordance with international regulations, everyone had to give their passport number when booking. He decided to get the authorities in the various countries to verify their passports.

Over Monday afternoon the various responses came in. Two men on the passenger list remained to be confirmed as genuine. Kim turned his attention to Sandra Wall as the cogs in the bureaucratic wheel ground slowly. He decided to get SOCO team to look at her flat at Long Acre Farm and to do a general sweep of the stables. There are so many people involved with this case he felt a full investigation by SOCO would turn up some information.

"John England, this is Jon Kim."

"Hello, Jon. How are your enquiries going?"

"Not very well, I'm afraid. That's why I've order a full search of the apartment at Long Acre Farm and general search of the stables. The SOCO teams will be at the farm shortly."

"Okay. If you think that will help, I will advise Sienna of this."

"Thanks, John."

The SOCO team arrived at 3 o'clock in the afternoon at Sandra's flat and went through it with a fine toothcomb. They couldn't find anything of particular interest. Fingerprints were taken from recently used unwashed glasses but on examination there was nothing which raised alarm.

On Tuesday, the SOCO team turned up at the stables for what was described as a general search rather than a forensic examination. The place was too large, too busy, too well-used by a multitude of people to warrant such a search. At the stables the SOCO team worked methodically from building to building.

"Any news yet, Tarrant, on our fugitive?"

"No, Sir. Nothing."

The phone rang.

"Jon Kim, please."

"Yes?"

"I'm from the SOCO team from the stables in Tarporley."

"Yes – have you found something?"

"We may have, Sir."

"Go on then tell me what you have found."

"A red Audi TT locked in the garage covered with a rough tarpaulin. Is that of interest?"

"I am sure it could well be."

"The DVLA confirmed its registered owner is Sandra Wall, Sir."

"Okay, but it's her place. She may well have left the car there. I think you should bring it back for a forensic examination," ordered Kim.

After a great deal of difficulty, the fact the car was

locked meant they needed the assistance of an Audi dealer to unlock and start the car. It took the garage all morning to come out and do this. The SOCO team removed the car from the garage and had it loaded onto transport for its delivery to Police HQ.

"Tarrant, SOCO have found Sandra's car. It's on its way back here. Any news on your side?"

"Possibly, Sir. There are two men on the Bolivia flight – amazingly both have passports that appear to be fake."

"That's extremely interesting. What are their names?"

"Daniel Evans – English and a Wayne Lamb, also English."

"Why didn't I spot that, it's Wayne Lamb. The cheeky bugger he is using his dead partner's passport."

"Shall I see if we can apprehend him off the plane?"

"Yes Tarrant, as soon as you can," instructed Kim.

SOCO took no time in identifying the fingerprints of Michael Fitzallen whose prints were clearly on the steering wheel and gear lever as the last driver of the Audi. There was also a small drop of blood on the driver's seat. So far SOCO had not been able to identify whose blood it was.

"Look at the DNA results for Sandra Wall, I am sure we took DNA samples from all members of the Wall family when we were looking for baby James."

Kim was delighted - some hard evidence at last but why did Fitzallen drive the Audi TT there, where was his Range Rover and where was Sandra?

*

Wayne was taking his time in visiting the sites of Madrid. He took the opportunity to purchase more clothes – smart casual as well as a business suit. A new suitcase to accompany his soft bag would be quite appropriate. He kept a low profile not attending any agencies like travel offices, flight offices etc. He was certainly pleased not to have been requested to hand over his passport. When you have nothing to do except wait time goes really slowly. He had time to contemplate the past as well as his future. Sandra Wall would make sure that he would be in prison for a long time – a prospect that did not appeal to Michael one bit. He had all but put aside the row with Sandra at the stables – it was now committed to the secret side of his mind, hopefully never to be retrieved.

As to the future, well he understood that Bolivia was on the up; he had money, a brain and surely he could put the two to work to make money. He knew property and development, he'd made a success of the business in the UK without any cash to start with, he was certain he could do it again now he had money – equally he was determined to be very careful who he did business with. He didn't want to meet another Niall Phelan or Goose for that matter.

Wayne was at the airport in good time on the Monday, and was ushered with others to the aircraft. The plane was large so it could make it all the way to South America. There was only about half a plane full of passengers.

They were up to an hour in flight when a message came through to the flight deck that there was an international arrest warrant out for Mr Wayne Lamb. The Bolivian authorities had been notified and requested to arrest him on landing.

The captain called the senior member of the cabin staff into the cockpit to give her the news.

"Please treat him in just the same way as any other passenger. There may well be police or security personnel coming onto the plane to arrest him once we arrive in Lima."

*

"Sir, Sir! I have an ID."

"What? Who of?"

"Michael Fitzallen, Sir."

"Tell me all."

"An Iberian booking office in Paris who booked a flight from Madrid to Lima then Lima - La Paz, Bolivia in the name of Wayne Lamb on Friday this week."

"How do we know it's Michael Fitzallen?"

"There is a security system in their office which photographs every customer. I have the photo here," Tarrant said, passing the print of the digital photograph to Kim.

"That's him. No doubt. We need him arrested."

"Well, Sir, he was in Madrid, the plane he booked on is now about an hour out of Madrid. I have requested that the authorities in Lima refuse him entry and return him to Spain on the return flight."

"Well done Tarrant, we need the Spanish police to put him on a plane back here. I think you and a uniformed officer should accompany him back to England from Spain."

Tarrant was excited at the prospect and looking forward to his trip to Madrid next Monday morning. The same plane that took Wayne out to Lima on its return leg, he assumed. The Police Inspector at Madrid made it plain that so long as a European arrest warrant was in place and brought to Madrid by Tarrant they would supply support and facilities to hold Fitzallen following his arrest.

*

In Paris the receptionist at the Iberian office was delighted to hear that her evidence was a help to arrest a felon. She couldn't help herself letting her journalist boyfriend know as soon as she knew. Journalists being journalists cannot help themselves when they get a story: by Wednesday morning the story had broken in Cheshire and on Granada TV. It was soon picked up by Sky News: "*A fugitive from justice, Michael Fitzallen, has been identified as currently flying to Bolivia under an assumed name of Wayne Lamb.*" The newscaster read and showed a photograph of him on the screen.

Wayne/Michael Fitzallen was oblivious to all this activity, as he sat back and snoozed his way over the Atlantic to Bolivia.

"Tarrant, how the hell have Granada TV got hold of this story?" demanded Jon Kim.

"I am not sure Sir unless it is something to do with the Spanish end had leaked the story to the press and it has been picked up."

"Yes you are possibly correct, no point in phoning Granada, they are no different to journalists the world over, they will not divulge their sources. Any further news on the disappearance of Sandra Wall?"

"No Sir, nothing."

"Well whilst we are waiting for Fitzallen to return see what you can find out about Sandra and any recent dealings she may have had other than the deal with Fitzallen."

"Anyone in particular we should interview Sir?"

"Well try Daisy at the stables she may know more than she has told us. Whilst you are at it go and see John England, he may know some of Sandra's recent activities."

Tarrant made his way to the stables. It being a Monday there were no owners of horses at the stables, just Daisy working hard clearing up after the weekend.

"Daisy?" called out Tarrant.

"Yes," she said as she popped her head out of a loose

box halfway down the row, "yes who is it?"

"I am DC Tarrant, Cheshire police, I need a word please?"

"Oh whatever has happened now?"

"Oh just a chat as it seems you were one of the last people to see Sandra Wall."

"I didn't know that."

"How do you get on with Sandra?" enquired Tarrant.

"I used to get on fine with Sandra."

"Used to, what changed?"

"Well, I had every expectation of occupying the new flat that has been converted over the barn, but she has let it to two people I don't know, who apparently have purchased half the business."

"Has that upset you?"

"I wasn't even consulted. When she told me I wouldn't be getting the flat I could have killed her."

"I see, did you?"

"No of course not."

"Could you have bought half of the stables?"

"I don't know because I have no idea what she wanted for it, I was never even asked."

"So you are cross, very cross about it," repeated Tarrant.

"Yes I am I feel totally duped, I work hard to keep the stables running, and just as the future was looking bright I got pushed to one side. I was furious."

"After you saw Sandra as you were leaving where did you go next?"

"I cycled home."

"Where is home?"

"I live with my parents, they live on the far side of Tarporley." Tarrant noted the address.

"How long does it take you to get home on your bike?"

"About twenty minutes or so why?"

"The black Range Rover you saw, what do you think that was doing at the stables?"

"I have no idea. Sandra doesn't discuss anything with me anymore, so I don't interfere, but I am very angry with her."

"Well if you don't like her anymore why do you stay here?"

"I love the job and there are no other stables around that I could get to easily."

"Did you return to the stables last Friday, after you had left?"

"No I didn't."

"So you went straight home?"

"No I stopped in Tarporley to do a bit of shopping."

"Are you quite sure you didn't return?"

"Yes, I am," she said crossly.

"Okay, we will check your story, I may need to speak to you again, unless you have something else to tell me?"

"Well you have reminded me that I did return to pick up a coat I had forgotten, but that was all. I then went straight home."

"About what time was that?"

"Oh, I don't know, I just do what I have to do, I don't bother about the time."

"When you came back it must have been an hour after you had originally left the stables, allowing for twenty minutes shopping and a ride home and then back to the stables. Was there anyone here when you came back?"

"No, no one here. I thought the new owners of half the stables were supposed to keep an eye on the place but they were not here either. Some owners they are turning out to be."

"Alright, I will be back to question you further, are you sure you didn't have an argument with Sandra when you came back?"

"No, as I say there was no one here." Daisy was angry now.

"Okay, I will be back shortly." Tarrant left the yard.

*

"Mr England please?" enquired Tarrant of the receptionist at Bennett's solicitors.

"Sorry Sir he is out this afternoon."

"Okay I will try again tomorrow."

It struck Tarrant that John England might be in the office at Long Acre Farm and as he was about to drive past the lane to the farm he thought he would call in on the off chance England was there. Tarrant's car made the cattle grid rattle. As he was parking his car outside the barns John England appeared at the door to the office.

"Hello, what can I do for the police this afternoon?"

"Ah, Mr England. My hunch was correct, I tried phoning you at your office, so as I was at the stables I thought I would pop in here on the off chance that you were here."

"Good thinking Tarrant. Is it a quick meeting or do we

need to sit down?"

"Well Sir I do have a number of questions you might be able to assist me with."

Sitting at the round meeting table, having both men supplied with a coffee by John England he asked the question, "What is this all about?"

"Well Sir I am making general enquiries as the disappearance of Sandra Wall, and I was hoping you could help me with a few issues."

"Fire away, I will do what I can."

"Well Sir it seems Daisy at the stables has had her nose put out of joint by the sale of half the stables to a stranger, when she felt she should at the very least been given the opportunity to buy half."

"I can see her point of view, in isolation, but I suspect she doesn't have the money."

"Well she was not happy about not being considered at all."

John went on to explain why Rhys and Francesca had bought the half share, not only were the two of them experienced horse people but Rhys Williams had the money.

"Rhys, is that by any chance the Rhys Williams who was found to be the heir of Roger Whiteside, the business partner and murderer of Peter Wall and Fred Appleyard?"

"My you have a good memory Tarrant."

"It's a case you just can't forget Sir."

"Well Tarrant you are absolutely correct, so you will see there is a long-standing connection with Rhys."

"I see. So when did Rhys buy the half share?"

"Only a matter of weeks ago, he bought it with his fiancé Francesca. In fact they are to be married in Tarporley next year."

"If something happened to Ms Sandra Wall, who I assume owns the other half of the stables, what would happen to her half?"

"You are thinking like a lawyer now Tarrant. I didn't create the documents, Sandra did, but I did have a meeting with Rhys and Francesca to explain the content of the various documents. I was not giving advice. I told them that they should seek independent legal advice, but they seemed very content, and excited at the prospect of owning half the stables. To answer your question in a simplistic way, Rhys and Francesca had an option to buy the other half of the stables and the farmhouse, on either Sandra's death or her decision to move elsewhere."

"So, there is an advantage to Rhys if Sandra is dead."

"That is a very simplistic statement Tarrant. They haven't even started working in the stables, far too early for them even consider such a thing. They need Sandra to help run the place."

"I see, but there is a benefit for them should Sandra not be around?"

"The answer has to be yes, but you are barking up the wrong tree."

"Very well Sir, thank you for your help."

Back at the police HQ Tarrant went immediately to see Kim. He explained the conversations he had had with Daisy and then John England relating to Sandra's relationship with each of the parties.

"Looks like there is a potential for either party or even both to seek the death or disappearance of Sandra, be it financial or jealousy."

"I agree Sir, but there are extenuating circumstances. I

don't think Daisy is capable of killing anything, she is a very caring person. As for Rhys and Francesca they are away in Spain so that really excludes them."

"Well they are suspects to be kept in mind Tarrant, I just need to interview Fitzallen first before extending the enquiry."

CHAPTER 28

In Tarporley Saturday was always a busy in the village and at the stables. The majority of horses were on livery so their owners would come at the weekends to ride them. One of the part time stable girls, Camilla, also gave lessons. They had four ponies for children to ride usually in the ménage to practise trotting and cantering as well and taking a few small jumps. The young girls (as they were mainly girls) who came enjoyed their time at the stables – they often fell in love with their favourite ponies. Camilla smiled to herself when parents came to collect their charges and were met with entreaties to buy a pony. She could recall doing the same when she was eleven. Most of the children were collected by car but one child rode to the stables on her bike – she only lived in Tarporley. She became an unpaid assistant at the weekends virtually living at the place nearly every weekend. Her parents berated her for not doing anything at home or her homework, but she was in love with the ponies and horses.

"You live at those stables, Jenny. You must do your homework," was apparently the regular demand from Jenny's mother.

It fell on deaf ears mostly as first thing on a Saturday morning she was off on her bike dressed in her joddies, boots and polo shirt and a Barbour jacket with her hard hat on which doubled as a safety helmet on her bike as well as a crash hat when riding. As she was an enormous help to Camilla, Jenny was allowed to have free rides whenever there was a gap in the bookings. Jenny was in heaven. The first job on Saturday morning was to muck out the four ponies who were used for children to ride. The larger horses on livery were mucked out and fed during the week by Daisy, these horses were taken over by their owners at the weekend. However, it was Jenny and Camilla who were the first into the yard to get ready for the first lesson at 9.30.

Jenny wheeled a full wheelbarrow of muck round to the end of the rows of the loose boxes to the giant manure heap next to midden. She added her load to the heap which would be collected in a week or two by a local flower nursery, they said it made the perfect fertilizer. Jenny's eye caught a glimpse of something. Someone must have thrown something into the midden. Her curiosity got the better of her and she took a closer look. She screamed a scream that would have sent shivers down the spine of anyone in earshot. Jenny ran away from the midden as fast as she could back to the stables into the arms of a now very curious Camilla.

"Whatever's the matter, Jenny?"

"It's in the midden – it's a body," she blurted out with tears streaming down her face.

"Whatever do you mean?"

"There is a strange object in the midden."

"No – can't be. You must be mistaken."

"It is a body. It's true, I swear." More tears and sobbing returned.

Camilla convinced that Jenny was not making this up

ran to the midden. When she got there she could only see the outline of a white object just under the surface. She was scared. It was very spooky. She ran as fast as she could to the office where she had left Jenny to recover.

"I must phone the police. Jenny can you close the yard gate this place will be swarming with police any moment and we don't want anyone coming in. I'll phone the children who are booked for lessons and cancel their lessons for today."

"Yes, we will have to look after the livery horses ourselves today."

"How do you know that a lot of police will come?"

"I was here when the previous owner was arrested. It became a real circus. I've never seen so many police vehicles in one place."

*

"Sir I am sorry to disturb you on a Saturday, but it is possible that a body has been found at the stables in Tarporley," said Tarrant.

"My God, no - that family! How on earth do you break the news to them if it turns out to be Sandra Wall?" exclaimed Jon Kim.

Within a quarter of an hour of the call to the police, two police officers and a squad car arrived and parked across the gate to the yard preventing entry to the yard by anyone. Within the hour a SOCO team had arrived, Jon Kim, Tarrant was following, the Home Office pathologist had also been called out and was expected soon. Kim realised as soon as he saw the task of recovering the body the fire brigade would be required – they would be able to do two things: recover the body and hose it down as it was going to be covered in pig slurry. Kim didn't need to wait for the full recovery of the body – he knew in his heart it was Sandra

Wall. He was about to do something he would not wish on his worst enemy – notify the family in person that Sandra was dead.

Jon waited for the Pathologist to undo the 'parcel' after the fire brigade had hosed down the 'package'. There was no doubt, it was Sandra's face rather disfigured and bloated by the slurry, but it was Sandra alright. Jon Kim left the stables leaving the enquiry in the hands of specialist teams, pathologists, SOCO and the fire brigade. Tarrant was on his way – Kim phoned him to tell him where he was going and gave him instructions as to what he was to do. Camilla and Jenny were stunned - they couldn't believe what was happening.

"Jenny," exclaimed Camilla, "we haven't attended to the livery horses. They'll be hungry and thirsty. Miss Sandra would expect us to look after them and Major, her horse, in particular."

"Yes. Let's go and do that." The two set off purposely to collect a sack of feed and to run the hosepipe along the stable runway.

"Hey! What are you two doing?" demanded a police officer.

Camilla explained the importance of what they were doing and carried on walking with the barrow.

"Oi! Stop! You can't do anything. This is a crime scene."

"It certainly will be if we don't feed and water these horses." She just carried on and the police constable ran off to seek a senior officer who immediately gave his consent for the girls to attend to the horses.

There were a lot of horses very pleased to see the two girls. There were a lot of frustrated and angry owners at the gate unable to get in.

Kim was not expected at Long Acre Farm. He thought it

best to simply arrived. He just hoped John and Sienna would be there. He'd not expected to see Mrs Ann Wall but she was there also. John England opened the door to Jon Kim and just by the look on his face John knew something bad had happened. All the family assembled in the kitchen where Ann, Sienna and James were finishing a late breakfast. Jon was invited to sit down but he preferred to stand.

"I have to inform you that we have found a body of a female this morning who seems to fit the description of Sandra. I'm very sorry."

"You mean she's dead!" cried Sienna trying to assimilate the policeman's words.

"Yes. I'm afraid so. I'm pretty sure it is Sandra but it does require a formal identification."

"I'll do that," said Ann in a steady voice.

"Are you sure, Ann? It's something I can easily do," responded John.

"No, John. She's my daughter from my body. It's my job to see her for the last time."

Both John and Sienna had tears running down their cheeks but Ann retained amazing dignity and showed no emotion.

"Are you all right, Mum?" enquired Sienna.

"Yes, darling, I am. Nothing can hurt me anymore."

Jon Kim was so impressed at the calmness displayed by Ann. He said he would arrange the identification as soon as possible and send a car for her.

"Will you be here, Mrs Wall?"

"No. I'm returning to Church Cottage this afternoon. I'll be there."

"Very well, Ma'am, I'll phone you and let you know

when a car will call."

"Thank you," she said in a most dignified way. "I think I shall go to my room now."

"Jon, a car will not be necessary, please advise me where and when the identification will take place and I will bring Ann."

When Jon Kim had disappeared, John and Sandra hugged one another until they could hardly breathe.

"Whatever next, John? Why us? What has this family ever done to deserve all this?"

"Darling, I really don't know. I am at a loss for words. What I do know is that your Mum is a very tough lady."

*

Back at the stables the day progressed slowly. Camilla and Jenny had managed to feed and water all the horses but none had been taken out for exercise.

"Would it be possible, Mr Tarrant, for the owners to take their horses out for exercise tomorrow? It's very important for these animals."

"I couldn't say at the moment. When I've spoken to my boss, I'll let you know."

Tarrant was able to confirm the owners could come in on Sunday. He would need a list of names, addresses and phone numbers of everyone who had a horse here. Camilla rang all the owners and notified them that they could come up for a ride on Sunday.

*

On Saturday afternoon John drove Ann Wall back to Church cottage. He was amazed at her stoicism. She never shed a tear. What a strong woman, he thought to himself.

"Now Ann when the police contact you to go and identify Sandra you must let me know. I insist on driving you, and accompanying you to the morgue."

"That's extremely kind of you John. You are our rock. This family would have collapsed without your strong and steadfast support."

John didn't reply. He let Ann out of the car carrying for her the small overnight case.

"Is there anything I can get for you?"

"No my dear boy, Purdy is here to keep me company. Everything is fine, you get off back to your family."

John left Ann at Church Cottage, wondering all the way home if he should have left her. She was not at all in shock or showing signs of grief. How odd, he thought to himself.

*

A few days later John was back at Church Cottage, to collect Ann to go to the mortuary to identify her eldest daughter's remains. She was still very brave and hardly shed a tear when the sheet was pulled back to reveal Sandra's face which had been cleaned and made to look as best a dead person could look. Ann did cry a little when leaving the mortuary and was grateful for the support John gave her. They drove back in silence to Long Acre Farm.

"I think I'll go back to the cottage this afternoon, John, now everything is over." John nodded. He thought her choice of words odd. "Over" – what did she mean?

"Will you be all right on your own, Ann?"

"Yes, John. It's been nearly ten years and it will be at the end of this year that Peter died and the whole sequence of tragedies that have beset the Wall family. I'm the only Wall left – I just want to live out my days in peace."

"Yes, of course."

They were nearing Tarporley village when Ann spoke again – only for the second time since leaving the Countess of Chester mortuary.

"If I tell you something, John, can I have your strict assurance that you will never mention this to Sienna?"

"Ann, keeping confidences is part of my job – you have my absolute assurance."

"Do you believe in astrology?"

"No, I don't think I do. I may look at my horoscope from time to time. Why?"

"Well, a week after Sienna was born I met a lady in Chester. We lived there then. She was an astrologist. She said she thought the little girl in the pram was beautiful, Sienna. Sandra was walking besides the pram holding onto the handle. She said "you", meaning me her mother, will endure terrible sadness when the two girls grow older; you will lose their father and the oldest daughter. She gave me her card. I thought it was a load of old rubbish. When I moved to Church Cottage cleaning out one of my drawers I found her card. I rang her and explained what had happened to Peter. She recalled our earlier meeting when the children were small. She told me that my eldest daughter would be the next to go. I dismissed it as rubbish but now I think I do believe in astrology."

"Good Lord, Ann – what a story! I am sure there may be something in astrology but, of course, there are rational reasons for what has happened."

"I know, John, but this is my secret. In a way I knew Sandra was dead – that was my secret and now shared only with you. The prediction is now cleared up. You won't tell a soul, will you?"

"No, you have my word – it's our secret. It's your secret. The secret side of you that will never be repeated." John now knew why the word 'over' had been used by Ann.

*

Kim received the pathologist's report on Sandra Wall. It seemed she received a sharp blow to the back of the head by a heavy sharp object then drowned in the midden. What a horrible death, Kim thought to himself.

"Sir, I have just had an email from the police in Lima saying they have arrested Wayne Lamb and have him in custody. They want to know what we wish to do with him?"

"Well that's a great relief. You had better get onto the CPS and give them all the information, advising them we need him back here as soon as possible."

Tarrant did as he was told, and awaited developments.

*

Wayne, or Michael as he will soon be called, being his real name, was not at all happy at having been arrested and put into a small jail near the airport. The local police had no instructions other than to keep him in custody. The jail was part of a police station. It stank of stale urine. There was little air in the place and no windows, for his cell anyway. The other two inhabitants of the same cell were clearly local villains, and judging by their bedraggled dress and beards had been here for some time. Michael tried talking to them but they didn't speak English, and he didn't speak Portuguese or Spanish. The two of them kept snarling at Michael like some caged wild animal. It was a very uncomfortable experience.

The following day a truck, that looked for all the world like an Army truck, arrived. Michael was handcuffed and put in leg irons. He shuffled out of his cell, and was ordered to get onto the truck. There was no way he could get into the truck so two soldiers picked him up and literally threw him in. He was covered in dust and dirt. His head had been

305

cut by hitting a metal bracket in the truck. The tail gate was shut and the vehicle shot off at what seemed like a great speed. Michael was shaken nearly to destruction by the time they arrived at their destination.

"Get out," was the order barked by someone out of his sight.

"I can't move."

"Get out," came the order again.

When nothing happened two soldiers were ordered into the truck to get him out. The reverse process was adopted. Michael was thrown out of the truck landing on his back on the ground.

"Get up," shouted the sergeant standing over him. "Get up," he shouted again.

Michael was unable to move, so he thought, he ached everywhere. A sharp kick in Michael's stomach was supposed to assist Michael in following orders. It did the reverse. He slumped and nearly passed out. The two soldiers were ordered to pick him up and pull or drag him to the jail house. It transpired he had been moved to this army camp as the civilian prisons were full. As he was a foreigner it didn't seem to matter to the authorities where he went. He was just a nuisance.

The CPS confirmed to Tarrant that the official extradition papers were lodged but the CPS had indicated it could take up to six months for the process to complete.

"Has Fitzallen been visited by anyone from the UK consulate in Lima?"

"I am sorry Sir I don't know."

"Well can you get the CPS to request a consular visit, so we know we have the right man, how he is and importantly would he like to voluntarily return to the UK?"

"Do you think that is likely Sir?"

"Well you never know. It's worth asking the question."

*

Francesca and Rhys said their farewells, Rhys having made his donation to Father Peter and the church. They all waved kissed and explained they were looking forward to the wedding.

"Oh, one last thing Rhys," said Monsieur Jacques.

"Yes Papa, what is it?"

"Well I have spoken to my employer to make sure I could get the time off. No problem there. However they have offered me as much Champagne as I want at cost, so Rhys that will be our present to you both on your wedding day."

"Monsieur Jacques, that is a wonderful gesture thank you so much. There will be quite a lot of bottles required knowing our friends."

Laughter all around.

The two love birds drove off to the airport in their hire car ready to get back to the UK and start running their business.

*

Rhys and Francesca having collected Rhys's Land Rover Freelander car at the airport, they were still on a high and couldn't stop talking all the way back to Long Acre Farm. The cattle grid announced their arrival. They both jumped out of the car, grins all over their faces, Francesca carrying a large bunch of flowers for Sienna and Rhys some bottles of wine for John. They knocked on the back door, and John came to welcome them home.

"Now you two, thank you so much for your gifts, but I

have some terrible news to tell you."

"Why what has happened?" They both realised by the look on John's face a terrible tragedy had befallen the family.

"What is it John?" enquired Rhys, both he and Francesca now in sombre mood.

"Sandra is dead."

The words were heard by the two but made no sense the statement John had just made was rattling around the room like some enormous echo.

"What?" Rhys asked.

"Yes I am sorry Rhys, Sandra is dead."

"Oh no." Francesca burst into tears the enormity of what she had just heard. Rhys had tears running down his cheeks.

"Come in both of you, Sienna and I are sitting in the lounge, let's sit down and have a cup of tea or coffee."

"Sienna, Sienna," Francesca rushed over to Sienna and hugged her like she was a sister.

"How awful, I can't believe what we are hearing."

"It's true Francesca, I am so sorry."

"This is tragic, how did this happen?" enquired Rhys, ever the practical one.

"We think she was murdered."

"My god who would ever want to do such a thing?"

"Exactly Rhys why, and what sort of person are they?" responded John.

"Would you like me to put the kettle on John?" enquired Francesca.

"Oh you would be an angel, yes please," said Sienna.

"There are so many questions and concerns but that isn't for now I am sure."

"If you are concerned about taking over the stables and the house, please don't be concerned. There is no doubt they are yours. What the final arrangements will be will have to wait until the dust settles, but Sienna and I want to reassure you both that your plans for the future are intact. Your future is secure."

Francesca heard most of the conversation including the important last bit as she was coming into the room with a tray of drinks.

"Francesca," said Sienna, "you are going to have to be my sister from now on."

"Oh Sienna, you are so kind, we love you both dearly. You have been our saviour on more than one occasion, Rhys has told me all about it."

There was silence in the room whilst hot drinks were handed round and enjoyed. A cry from upstairs broke the spell. Sienna went to collect James.

"Can I come with you?" enquired Francesca.

"Of course, yes please."

Francesca held James after Mum had changed him and organised him to be respectable to come downstairs. Walking into the lounge holding James, Francesca looked every inch a mother. Rhys knew that she felt like a mother. They wanted children more than anything.

"Just getting in some practice Rhys."

Everyone laughed. The sombre tone lifted. James did the trick. Rhys and Francesca stayed for another hour, the atmosphere was more relaxed. The burning question for Rhys was the stables, but it was just not appropriate to ask the question now.

"What will happen now Rhys?" enquired Francesca as the two drove to the Stables and their new flat.

"I don't know darling. I am sure the Wall family and John are honourable people and will wish to continue with the deal. However, you never know what may happen. I suppose the good news is that someone has to run the stables, without that the business will fade away."

The two had a light supper and an early night, although not much sleeping was done. They were both worrying about the stables.

"I know," said Francesca at some early hour of the morning. "Let us just go and run it whilst the family grieve and sort out matters. That way we can meet customers, and legitimately say we are taking over as was agreed with Sandra, before she died."

"Good idea, go to sleep brainbox."

CHAPTER 29

In the army barracks detention centre the benefit
Wayne/Michael now had, was that the cell was clean and
had a reasonably comfortable bed. The downside was he
was in effect in solitary confinement. The only people he
saw were the orderly with a meal tray. Within a few days he
was getting very disturbed about being on his own. Michael
was not used to isolation in quite this way. As his mind was
considering what he might do about the situation two
guards arrived with the keys. They unlocked the cell,
handcuffed Michael, and gestured for him to come with
them. After a walk down numerous corridors they stopped
outside a door. They opened it and pushed Michael in, and
locked the door from the outside. Michael, somewhat
surprised picked himself up and looked around, only to see
a smartly dressed man sitting behind a desk.

"You must be Michael Fitzallen masquerading as Wayne
Lamb?"

"Yes sir, yes that's me," said Michael suddenly realising
that this man spoke perfect English and Michael was for the
first time in a long time talking to someone else who could
understand him.

"My name is Andrew Masters. I am a member of the
British consular staff here in Lima."

"Oh so you have come to get me out."

"No Michael, my job is to arrange a lawyer for you as the authorities have been requested by the British government to extradite you back to the UK."

"Oh I see, may I call you Andrew?"

"Yes by all means."

"Well I have been in some pretty horrible places since I was arrested here. It was not my plan to be found but now I have been and there seems little prospect of escape I might as well go back to the UK, at least I can talk to people."

"Oh I see," said Andrew, "you don't mind going back to the UK?"

"No I don't want to stay here a moment longer than necessary."

"Well that could simplify matters a great deal. An extradition process could take six months or more. From what you say a stay here for six months is not a prospect that appeals to you?"

"You have a wonderful way of putting it Andrew, but please help to get me back to the UK as soon as you can."

"There will be paperwork Michael, but I should be able to get you on the next plane back to Spain. Leave it with me."

Andrew pressed a button on the table and the two guards came and collected Michael, returning him to his cell. Andrew returned to the consulate.

*

"Sir." Said Tarrant.

"What is it Tarrant?" enquired Kim.

"I have just received a fax from the UK consulate in Lima which says that Michael Fitzallen is a willing to be repatriated immediately."

"Ha, ha, I suspect he had not factored into his scheme a stay in the jails in Lima or anywhere else in that area."

"Shall I make arrangements to have him met in Madrid, as that is where his flight will come to, or will we take over in Manchester?"

"It all depends on how helpful the Spanish authorities will be. Get in touch and make some arrangements Tarrant, I will contact the CPS."

Jon did as he had promised and the CPS were very pleased Fitzallen was on his way back to the UK.

"The issue is Jon will he give evidence against Goose? Without that we have nothing on Goose and will have to abandon the case."

"That will be a sad loss, but we shall see what Fitzallen has to say."

*

The funeral for Sandra was currently being planned by Mr Cartwright the undertaker. The same man who had buried Peter Wall nearly ten years ago.

"Mrs Wall," said Cartwright in his undertaker's sycophantic manner. He stooped when talking, trying to show remorse for the bereaved. "I am so sorry to learn of the death of your eldest daughter. How tragic, how awful. I can assure you I will look after all your concerns."

"Thank you Mr Cartwright, most kind."

"Shall we arrange to collect the body and bring her to our Chapel of Rest?"

"Yes please but that will not be possible straight away as the police have insisted on further forensic tests before the body is released. They have assured me it will only be a day or two."

"Very well Mrs Wall. We can however make arrangements in anticipation of the release. Do you know if this is to be a burial or cremation?"

"No I don't, my son-in-law is looking for her will. If there are instructions in there, then we must follow the instructions. However if the will is silent, then I think a cremation will be appropriate. I would like her ashes to be buried in the church yard with a commemorative headstone."

"Yes of course. I assume the service will be at St Helens?"

"Yes you are correct and I would like the wake at The Swan."

"Of course. Do you have any proposal as to time? I suppose much will depend on the burial arrangements and the availability if appropriate at the crematorium."

"Yes, ideally I would like a lunchtime gathering so a morning funeral if it can be arranged?"

"Have you seen the vicar?"

"No Mr Cartwright, but I am expecting him shortly."

"Ah, dear lady, if you can possibly consider hymns and songs you would like to incorporate in the service, and any readings by family or friends then, when you hear from the police please let me know then I can start to put things in place."

"Thank you Mr Cartwright," said Ann as she received his business card. "I will be in touch."

Bowing low Cartwright made his exit.

If ever there was a man in the right job it is him, thought Ann. She had a little chuckle at the thought. Just as Ann was about to make herself a cup of coffee there was a knock at the door. Purdey just wagged his tail, rather indifferent to what was going on.

"Hello Vicar, do come in."

"Mrs Wall, or may I call you Ann?"

"No Ann please, I am just about to have a cup of coffee, would you like one?"

"Yes please just black if I may."

"Same as me and my son-in-law. I will use this coffee machine which my son-in-law gave me for Christmas. I think there was a hidden meaning there. I don't think he liked my coffee very much."

They laughed as the machine gobbled up a cassette of coffee followed by another.

"Clever aren't they, the machine shuts off just as the cup is full."

The two sat around the kitchen table, the atmosphere having been broken, the vicar sensed that Ann was not grieving in the way he had anticipated.

"How are you coping Ann?"

"I'm fine. I have attended more funerals and court cases for the murder of family or friends than I care to recall. I am hardened to the event."

"I am not sure that is totally wise, you need to grieve and have a cry to let your emotions out."

"There is nothing left, I have done all my crying."

"Sandra was your eldest daughter I think," enquired the vicar.

"Yes that's correct and a very clever girl. She qualified as a solicitor, and was lined up for a partnership at Spencer's when Perter died, and Sandra took the reins of the family firm Wall's, and had made a tremendous success of it."

"You obviously thought a lot of her?"

"Yes I did, but she never found a man that she could live with so she never married."

"In a way, grandchildren are very special. My youngest daughter who you married, Sienna, has a little boy James, he is a treasure."

"Yes I am sure. Have you instructed an undertaker yet?"

"Yes as a matter of fact he left moments before you arrived Mr Cartwright, I am sure you know him?"

"Yes of course, excellent firm."

"We are held up at the moment in making arrangements for the funeral as the police have not yet released the body. They say it will be in a day or two."

"Oh well I am sure Cartwright will contact me when he is ready to fix a date. I have brought a little pamphlet which might help you when it comes to considering hymns, prayers etc. There are several suggestions and a draft order of service. I hope you find it of help."

"Thank you vicar that will be most helpful."

"Do you want to say a prayer Ann?"

"Yes thank you that would be kind."

Once the prayer was over the vicar left. Ann finished her coffee, then rang John.

"Sorry to bother you but I wondered if you had managed to locate a will for Sandra?"

"Yes I have and it's no more than three weeks old. Sandra instructed my probate department to draft a will which we did and she signed it three weeks ago."

"That is very strange, do you think she knew something?"

"No it was all to do with the stables and making it clear that Rhys and Francesca were to take it over."

"Well, she was just a bit organised I think."

"Yes it's quite a long document and I haven't read it yet, but perhaps we should have a formal reading. When would it suit you Ann? If we did it at the farm you could stay for supper?"

"Yes, good idea. I am free tomorrow," said Ann.

"Fine I will get back to you and confirm it, bye."

*

Michael Fitzallen eventually returned to Manchester Airport and was met by a police van which transported him to the Cheshire Police HQ at Winsford. He had had a great deal of time to consider what he should do, own up and plead guilty or not guilty and face a trial and potentially a longer sentence. He realised that if he co-operated with the police and agreed to give evidence for the prosecution in the Goose trial, he could get a much shorter sentence. However Goose would not be thrilled, and could ensure through his criminal connections would give Michael had a hard time in jail.

The duty sergeant booked Michael into a cell, to await instructions from detectives about any charges. Jon Kim decided to let Fitzallen cool his heels in a British jail for a bit. They would interview him tomorrow. In the meantime Tarrant was tasked to enquire if Fitzallen wanted a lawyer, if so which one. If he did not have a lawyer to act for him, the police would call a duty solicitor to attend.

"No I don't have a solicitor," advised Fitzallen.

"Do you want us to request that the duty solicitor attends?"

"Okay, I may as well as it isn't costing me anything."

Tarrant made arrangements for the duty solicitor to

attend at four o'clock.

Jon Kim received the second forensic report on Sandra Wall. His suspicions were not supported by the findings. He had thought that Fitzallen might have given her one of his toxic tablets, in which case she might have been dead before entering the midden. There would however been little point in bashing her over the head with a brick if she was already dead. His mind was still working on this scenario when his phone rang.

"Kim?"

"Jon it's John England. I was wondering if you were in a position yet to release the body of Sandra Wall."

"Timely call John. Yes I can arrange that. I have just received the final forensic report on my desk. We have no need to hold onto the body any longer."

"Thanks Jon that is good news I will advise the undertaker."

John England phoned Cartwright and advised him the body is available for release. Details of the location would have to be obtained from the police. Having organised for the reading of the will at Long Acre Farm, Sienna had arranged a hotpot supper afterwards.

At five o'clock Ann arrived, followed almost at once by Rhys and Francesca. John had requested the partner of his solicitors practice to come and read the will. They all assembled in the dining room, all sat around the dining table. John England opened proceedings.

"Thank you all for coming. I have asked Andrew Clifford of my firm who is head of the probate department as his department drafted and secured Sandra's signature for her last will and testament. I have not seen the document and I have no idea what will be in it. Please can you wait until the end for questions. Andrew, over to you."

"Thank you John. As John has indicated as a partner of Bennett's solicitors I acted for Sandra in the creation of her new will, only three or four weeks ago. I will now read the salient parts of the will. I will miss out the legal jargon which is required, and very uninteresting. The document says:

My life has become rather complex in the recent past, so I felt it was necessary to renew my will. It takes into account all the changes that have occurred recently, and the change that will occur when Michael Fitzallen is convicted of money laundering and drug dealing. The relevance of this will become obvious shortly.

My assets are, an apartment in Chester overlooking the Roodee, a forty percent shareholding in Wall's Holdings Limited, the ownership of the freehold of the stables and stud, in Tarporley, and an insurance claim on the buildings at Sealand.

In the event this will is being read by someone who has no knowledge of the Wall's Holdings business and its residual asset which is a large block of apartments in Manchester, I will explain. There are no commercial borrowings on the building, but there is a private loan from Michael Fitzallen, in the sum of three million pounds. At the time of the loan the block had a market value of about seven million pounds. The loan is recorded as a registered loan agreement with the land registry, the original is in my safe in the office at Long Acre Farm.

The agreement allows for the loan to become null and void and no repayment to Fitzallen be made at all even in the future, should he be convicted during the term of the loan of a criminal act. As I am writing this will he has been charged with money laundering and drug trafficking. I am certain he will be convicted, and in that event there will be no charge on the block in Manchester. So, as there are no charges on any of the other properties my assets are totally free of loans and mortgages.

I now wish to bequest the following in this way:

The insurance claim money on the building at Sealand in total to go to Ann Wall, my mother. This is expected to be four hundred thousand pounds. In addition the land itself is for sale. The land is in the ownership of Ann Wall so the proceeds of that in future will go to her. Strictly this is not an asset of mine, these are mainly instructions for my executors, as I was handling the claim on behalf of my mother.

The forty percent shares in Wall's Holdings which are in my name to be split as to twenty percent to go to my beautiful nephew James, probably to be held in trust until he is older, but the share of the income from the apartments to be applied to this holding and held in a safe investment fund for James when he is older.

The other twenty percent to be split in half so that ten percent will go to my sister Sienna, and the remaining ten percent to John England, our rock who has held the family together in the last ten years.

The apartment in Chester or the proceeds from sale to go to the Chester Racecourse in exchange for a life time's membership of the course for all race days for John, Sienna, Rhys and Francesca.

Finally the stables, and stud. There are documents in place, but as I am writing this will, they are yet to be signed. My executors are therefore instructed in the event the documents remain unsigned, that they complete the transaction with Rhys and Francesca. However there is an option for Rhys and Francesca to purchase the house. If this will is being read then the trigger for the option is established and the purchase arrangements may proceed on the basis of the currently unsigned documents.

The purchase of the stables assumes under the unsigned agreements that fifty percent of the stables will be owned by Rhys and Francesca. By this will I hereby amend the arrangement in that Rhys and Francesca paying the agreed price for fifty percent will in fact receive one hundred percent of the stables business.

The money paid will go to two things. A payment of five thousand pounds each to all the grooms who have kept the business running in my absence. The balance to be invested into a pension fund for the grooms and staff of the stables.

Assuming Rhys and Francesca purchase the house then the proceeds of sale are to be split equally between Ann Wall, Sienna and John England.

"Thank you Andrew, I rather think a drink is called for after all that. Whilst I arrange a bottle or two feel free to ask Andrew any questions."

"Andrew, thank you for reading this rather unusual document, it is as if she almost anticipated her demise," said Ann.

"I agree Mrs Wall."

"Oh call me Ann please."

"Very well Ann. Yes, it is a very unusual document as it had anticipated future events, as did the loan agreement from Fitzallen. As I understand it Fitzallen is to be charged with Sandra's murder. There can be no doubt about refunding his money if that proves to be the case and he is found guilty of murder."

Ann smiled, the realisation that another member of the family had been murdered.

"Mr Clifford, may I ask a question?"

"Oh Andrew please, Rhys."

"Well, I don't want to appear pushy, but there are animals involved at the stables and the sooner we get involved the better, as there is an urgent need to buy more food for the horses, and so on. The staff also need certainty and paying, what can we do in the meantime?"

"Fully understood Rhys, there cannot be any actual transactions until probate has been awarded, that may take a little while as the value of this estate is quite considerable and whilst there are a number of cash bequests, the amount of inheritance tax to pay will be considerable. The good thing is that the biggest asset the building in Manchester is held in a closed company and the transfer between family members is an inheritance tax free event.

So really to answer your question Rhys, and subject to the executors' agreement, both of whom are here, you could take charge straight away and wait to complete everything, once probate has been obtained."

"Probate Andrew, what is that?"

"Oh its jargon Francesca, it is agreeing the tax on death and how much has to be paid. Once it is agreed then the wishes and bequests can take effect."

"There is a time limit on the option for the house, if getting probate takes longer than three months we may be out of the running on the house. What can we do to ensure we are able to buy it?"

"Well Rhys, Sandra had anticipated this problem and says in this will that the option agreement has been triggered. We cannot get at a price until we have an agreed valuation with the revenue. I suggest that no further work takes place on the house, so as to keep the value down. It will be up to the executors to say if they will sell to you at the revenue valuation."

"I don't see why we would sell to you at that price. We will obviously be fighting for the lowest valuation, so that will help you. It also helps us as the tax will be lower."

"Wow," said Rhys and Francesca was smiling all over her face. "It is wrong to be excited and joyful under such circumstances, but Sandra, bless her, has certainly helped us. Thank you Sandra."

"There is nothing wrong at all in that Rhys, I am delighted your mind is now at ease."

"Don't forget you two, I am more than willing to organise your wedding, we need to have a meeting, perhaps after the funeral okay?"

"Oh Ann you are wonderful. Thank you."

"Well I am hungry, and we all need that drink John promised. Francesca do you mind helping me plate up the hotpot and transporting it to the dining room?"

Francesca eagerly helped Sienna, as if she were a new sister.

CHAPTER 30

Fitzallen had spent a more comfortable night in the cell at Winsford Cheshire Police HQ. Jon Kim asked for Fitzallen to be brought handcuffed to an interview room, so that the cross examination might begin.

"Where are you taking me now?" demanded Michael.

"You will see it's only a short walk."

He was ushered into interview room one. The significance of this being that it had a viewing gallery of one way glass so police officers could watch the interview but not be seen. This room also had static video cameras so the whole room could be recorded in pictures and sound. Tarrant came into the room. Fitzallen sat quietly on a chair, still in handcuffs. There was a PC standing in the corner. He would be there for the duration of the interviews, with one exception. That being he would have to withdraw when Fitzallen's solicitor arrived, for an initial briefing.

"Your solicitor should be here soon, until you have briefed him, we cannot start."

Michael said nothing.

At twenty five to ten a solicitor introduced himself at the front desk as, "Paul March, Solicitor, I am here for a conference."

"Who is your client Sir?" enquired the duty officer.

"Michael Fitzallen."

"Do you have any identity Sir?"

March produced his photo driving licence and a business card.

"Very well Sir please take a seat. I will advise CID that you are here."

Twenty minutes passed. March was just about to get up and enquire why he couldn't see his client, when the side door opened.

"Mr March?"

"Yes," he responded in quite an aggressive tone.

"Follow me please Sir."

The PC took March on a walk behind the scenes of this large modern police station to interview room one. Opening the door the PC introduced March to Michael Fitzallen.

"Excuse me officer can you please remove the cuffs off my client. They will not be necessary."

The PC did as he was requested.

"This officer." He pointed to the young PC standing in the corner, "will leave now Sir, the door will be locked. If you need assistance or simply want to indicate the interview is over, just press the button under the light switch."

The two police officers left and the door was locked behind them.

Paul March introduced himself.

"Are you able to get me off?"

"Highly unlikely, the evidence I have seen would certainly put you in jail for life."

"My god, so what's the point?"

"What do you mean Michael?"

"I mean why don't I just plead guilty and get on with it."

"Well that would certainly save court time, but there is no way back from a guilty plea. At least with a trial there is always a chance we can at best reduce your sentence."

"So I am going down whatever, is that your view Paul?"

"Yes I am afraid so. I cannot see, unless you can give me some more information that can get you out of any of the charges."

"Well Paul, is it worth my while letting you have my take on things, and then for you to advise me what to do?"

"Yes Michael, by all means. I guess this will take some time, would you like a drink?"

Paul March ordered two coffees before they started to unpick the charges against Michael.

*

A conference was called by the CPS to discuss the charges against Goose.

"Now Kim," said the DPP, "have you any further evidence about Goose, as what we have at the moment, frankly doesn't add up to a row of beans."

"No Sir, we have tried to get Michael Fitzallen to give evidence for the prosecution with a deal on sentencing, but he wasn't for playing."

"Well if that is the last word on Goose, I think you had best let him go. We cannot prosecute him with no credible witness. Sandra was the ideal candidate for this, but she is no longer with us, so Goose gets off."

"That Sir is a great disappointment. He has been wanted for years but no one has been able to pin anything directly on to him. Let him go we will."

"Oh Sir, we now have Fitzallen back, his solicitor is spending most of today with him, so we hope to be able to interview him tomorrow."

"Very well Kim, at least we do have a strong case here."

*

Mr Cartwright had worked hard and arranged Sandra's funeral in a week. A Monday, not ideal for many people, but it is not easy to just choose your preferred time. As there were no instructions, it will be a cremation after the service.

A press announcement in the Chester Chronicle and the Daily Telegraph were made. The Telegraph picked up on the announcement and wanted one of their specialist reporters who wrote obituaries in the paper, to come and meet with the family. A young and not unattractive young lady arrived at Long Acre Farm where Ann, Sienna and John were assembled, to assist with the interview and the subsequent obituary that presumably will be published in the paper.

"This could be a very long story," said Ann, "do you want all the details of Sandra's life, including the death of her father which was the catalyst which started the Wall's Holdings rise to fame?"

"Yes please I would like everything. If I may I will record the conversation and I will where appropriate ask a question or two, is that acceptable?"

A unanimous 'Yes' was recorded, as the reporter placed the small recording machine in the centre of the dining room table. Everyone was sat around so hopefully the machine would catch everyone's input. After two hours the story was just about told, and the reporter was about to stop the machine.

"Isn't it important for you to know that Sandra was murdered by Michael Fitzallen?" enquired Sienna.

"Well yes it is, but as he has not been tried yet, we cannot say that. We will have a reporter covering the trial, so a small article will appear which will clear up the loose ends," she said with a weak smile on her face.

"Well, that was very interesting, we shall see what transpires," said John.

"I am not at all hopeful there will be anything printed. Having said that I guess it all depends on who else has died and if they have space for Sandra?" advised Ann.

"Do you want to stay for a bite of lunch Mum?"

"That's kind dear, but I have Cartwright coming at two fifteen to Church Cottage, I had better be there."

*

"Mr Cartwright, do come in," asked Ann.

"Mrs Wall, how are you keeping?"

"I am as well as can be expected, possibly better."

"Good, are you up to discussing the funeral arrangements for Sandra?"

"Yes Mr Cartwright I am. Do you have a date?"

"Yes Mam, I do. It is next Monday."

"That is quick, it is Tuesday today, not much time."

"All will be well I assure you."

"Yes, yes I am sure, now what do we have to do?" Ann responded in a rather irritated manner.

"Well choose some hymns, and if anyone is going to make an address it is always nice to have that reproduced in the order of service sheet. I would also like some colour photographs of Sandra, it just gives that very personal touch," advised Cartwright.

"Well, let me have a list of suggested hymns and the format of the service and I will consider them. I will also see what photos we have. Sienna, her sister, said she wanted to say something, but I am not sure she will have it fully written yet. I will ask and the photos and hymns will be decided upon by noon tomorrow."

"Oh, that is excellent madam. Can you please advise if there is to be an address so we can incorporate it either as a statement there is to be an address or a copy of it? Excellent.

Now what sort of coffin would you prefer?"

"A light oak I think, the usual brass handles. She was a solicitor you know so it would be good to have something to make that connection. Perhaps a wreath of flowers in the shape of the Law Society Coat of Arms for the coffin along with white lilies from me and Sienna, John and James."

"How many cars will be required Mam?"

"Just the hearse and one car to take the family to the crematorium, and then back to The Swan".

"Yes Mam, I can arrange all that. I will see you tomorrow."

Thank goodness that sycophantic man has gone. I have had far too many dealings with him for my liking. I guess he will see me off, but at least then I will not have to deal with him. Ann was just about to pick up the phone when it rang. She had quite a start.

"Ann Wall."

"Ann it's Margaret."

"Margaret?"

"Yes Margaret Stringer."

"Good heavens Margaret, how lovely to hear from you,

my mind was elsewhere."

"Don't worry Ann, you must be worn out I am so sorry to hear about Sandra."

"Oh my darling it's as if nothing else can hurt me now. It is a matter of whatever next?"

"Yes I know, life is a bitch sometimes."

"Margaret, why don't you come to stay for a few days. Come on Saturday, the funeral is on Monday. Would you do that for me?"

"Of course I will, we can catch up then. See you on Saturday, I will give you a ring when I am nearby."

"That's great see you then."

Ann was delighted to have an old friend by her side. Excellent, no one she would prefer more than to have Margaret with her. She knew what the pain is like. Now she said to herself with the phone still in her hand what was I going to do? Ann hung up the phone and walked back to the kitchen when the pieces in her mind joined up; phone Sienna.

"Sienna darling, sorry to bother you but I have a few questions for you, have you a minute?"

The two chatted for nearly an hour going over Cartwright's requests. "Oh, one last thing, Auntie Margaret is coming to stay for a few days on Saturday, isn't that great?"

Sienna could hear the joy in her mother's voice. "Yes that's wonderful. Mum I must go, I will bring the stuff you need mid-morning tomorrow."

"Alright darling, bye."

*

At Police HQ in Winsford a case conference was underway between Jon Kim and Tarrent and the solicitor and barrister for the CPS. The trial of Michael Fitzallen had been postponed because he had been at large. In view of the fact he was unlikely to be a credible witness now the murder (for that is what it was) of Sandra Wall had meant as a witness she was now out of the picture. The CPS were very concerned that without the two of these people the case against Goose was very thin. The chances of a successful prosecution were less than half. After much discussion it was agreed that the prosecution would not present any evidence. An application to abandon the trial would be made and Goose released from remand. Goose, of course, was delighted to be a free man but his connections in the UK were, to say the least, minimal and his money was far away. His cash at the bottom of the Med. What to do was the issue – who could he turn to?

Kim was in conference with the Chief Constable who was less than pleased to learn that Mr Big of drugs trafficking had again escaped justice. Equally, he was delighted that Fitzallen who had apparently escaped from the UK was now back in the cells, thanks in part to the good work of the consulate staff in Lima.

Goose tried some numbers in his mobile but found they didn't work. He tried Wall's but that was discontinued. Where to get money from was his biggest concern – without cash he was stuck. The police had not recovered anything from The Flying Swan so he had no passport, or credit cards – he was totally stuck. He knew there was someone who could help him somewhere but who? Michael was not answering his phone and Wall's were not available. Racking his brain for the name of the guy who ran the classic cars scam with Michael, Goose thought he might help. Eventually the penny dropped. Terry Pritchard, there can't be too many people with that name. With the hundred pounds in cash he had been given on release, everything he had in the world at that time, he used it to look for Terry on the internet, at an internet café. Fortunately he managed to track him down, and his phone number.

"Is that Terry?"

"No, I'm his mother-in-law. Who is this?"

"Goose."

"Goose? I've never heard of you."

"I was the man behind the classic cars scheme that Michael Fitzallen so foolishly wrecked and he got Terry put in jail. I was so angry about that."

"Quite right! He is out of work thanks to you and Michael."

"Is Terry there? I might be able to help him."

There was a long pause, and eventually Terry came onto the phone.

"Hello?"

"Terry, we have never met but we should, today if possible. I can help you get into business if that would be of interest?"

"It might, but I have been in jail you know."

"Yes, I know but you were not guilty, a miscarriage of justice. I might be able to help you get compensation. I assure you, Terry, the fire was nothing to do with me."

"Okay, so what do you want?"

"I want your help and I will give you one hundred thousand pounds if you help me."

"How much? Say that again."

"Yes, you heard right Terry – one hundred thousand pounds."

"No, no - there's a catch. No one phones me out of the blue with an offer like that."

"Look, Terry, I'm very genuine about this. Can we meet – today, if possible? I'm in Chester now. Can I come to your house?"

"Okay, I suppose so, there is nothing lost in that." Terry gave Goose his address and hung up. He told his wife, Nicky, and she didn't believe him.

"Stop playing tricks on me, Terry."

"It's true and he will be here in an hour."

"Oh, goodness I'd better tidy up."

*

"Terry, I'm Goose."

"Hello," said Terry rather diffidently not sure how to address someone with a name like Goose.

Once the preliminaries were over, which didn't take long as Terry didn't want Goose in the house any longer than necessary, Goose started his story. He had been wrongly arrested and brought to Chester from Marbella. His yacht had been sunk by saboteurs; his passport containing all his papers had gone down with the ship; he hadn't even a bank account in the UK to which he could retrieve some money sent from the Cayman Islands where he had some deposits.

"I don't even have a mobile phone and for someone who had the best of everything I now have nothing. It is hard, very hard indeed."

"Tell me about it, Goose, I know. I haven't been able to get a job since I was wrongly imprisoned. Everyone thinks I am a fire raiser – in fact, I'm a good car mechanic and I need a break."

"If you help me, Terry, you will get your break. Do you have a bank account?"

"Yes, I do."

333

"Will you be prepared to allow me to ask my bank in the Cayman Islands to send to your bank account £600,000 and when it is there you give me £500,000 keeping the £100,000 for yourself?"

"Is that it?"

"Yes, it's as simple as that."

"Yes, of course, but what do I do?"

Goose explained the process and what he needed to tell his bank. At the end of what had now become a very long conversation, Terry said "where do I contact you?"

"That, too, is a problem Terry as I've nowhere to stay."

"Well stay with us why not? It'll be okay with Nicola, won't it?"

"Oh, yes of course. I'll have to make up a bed in the spare room."

"Don't go to any trouble on my account, please."

"Oh, it's okay. We were going to have a takeaway pizza for supper. Will that be okay?"

Goose couldn't recall how long ago it was when he last had a pizza but he agreed. The next few days at Terry's house were hectic. Terry had a daunting task of speaking to his bank. He felt sure everything would be alright, the proof would be if the money came.

CHAPTER 31

Jon Kim at Cheshire Police HQ was licking his wounds at not being able to bring one of his fugitives to trial and having another murder upon his plate which he believed he had solved. He was nearing the time when he was to retire from the Force but he would not want to leave with an incomplete investigation especially as it was a murder and one of the Wall family who had suffered so much in the last ten years. Kim had placed a tail on Goose when he left prison and amazingly he seemed to have sought refuge in the house of Terry Pritchard who was wrongly convicted of arson. Kim pondered on the potential relationship of these two totally different characters – could it be that Goose without any assets or contacts and little money has bribed young Terry to do something to help him? He didn't have enough information to allow him to follow Terry. Goose was under surveillance twenty four hours a day. Jon Kim applied to a judge for an order to tap Terry's phone. Over the last few days, Kim had learned some interesting things.

First, Terry was expecting a large sum of money into his bank account. He had advised his bank that it was a bequest from a long lost relative who had recently died and the money, when it arrived, would mainly be shared amongst other family members but Terry would retain £100,000 in his account. The bank went along with this. Kim was keen to know if the bank had notified the serious organised crime agency SOCA. The reporting process should be carried out by a nominated officer of the bank. If the manager is suspicious he should advise the nominated officer of the bank. It seems that the manager didn't think that over half a million pounds being paid into an unemployed person's bank account was enough reason to report it.

Strange, thought Kim to himself. He let the transaction run. Terry was going to be £100,000 richer. Goose was to be in possession of half a million pounds by way of five bank drafts and £100,000 each in cash. Goose seems to have taken a shine to Terry and Terry to Goose as Goose remained living in Terry's house for some time.

Kim had placed a 'need to know' notice if an application for a passport from Goose in his full name was made and sure enough one came through. The passport office discussed the application with Kim but said there were insufficient grounds to refuse the grant of a passport. They said it would infringe his human rights if one was not provided. Kim was not very amused at this but it seems as if one half of the Home Office which dealt with passports and immigration has a totally different set of rules from the police who come under a separate section of the same ministry. "Very confusing," he muttered to himself in his Chinese dialect.

*

Sienna, John, Ann and baby James all attended Sandra's funeral at St Helen's church in Tarporley. Even the undertakers were amazed at the number of people who turned up – there was standing room only in the church. Every car parking space in Tarporley had been occupied. The thought provoking but moving service of thanks for a young lady struck down in her prime brought a tear to even the most hardened of mourners. The Swan next to the church provided a light buffet lunch. Roughly half the congregation attended. Mr Spencer, the senior partner at Spencer's was there, he sought out Ann Wall to heap praise on her eldest daughter. Ann thanked him but she felt that Sandra's death had an inevitability about it – she'd been so successful. Some people were jealous of others wealth in these difficult financial times. It had not surprised Ann that Sandra had become a victim. This sentiment stunned Spencer but at the same time was struck by the stoicism of Ann. As funerals do, there are always a few hardcore people who find it difficult to get the message that the wake is over. However, eventually everyone except Ann, Margaret John and Sienna, Rhys and Francesca had left. James had been taken home and looked after for the afternoon.

"I'm off to Church Cottage as this chapter in my life is over. I'm broken but not totally without hope for the future," said Ann who said her farewells to John and Sienna. The two went home to Long Acre Farm. Rhys and Francesca left for the flat at the stables, Margaret stayed one more night at Church Cottage with Ann.

"It looks as though I have a lot of work to do now."

"What do you mean, John?"

"The estate of Sandra's is quite considerable. The details will take some time to sort out. It is lucky she made a recent and up to date will."

"I see. There are, of course, the apartments in Manchester and Chester to deal with. The ones in Manchester are an asset of Wall's Holdings but the Chester apartments were bought by Michael Fitzallen."

"Yes, you are right, I need to look out the shareholder agreement and see what the provisions are and the situation with regard to the death of a shareholder."

"Will we end up with more, John?"

"That's a bit premature. Let's see what the documents say."

*

Goose meanwhile was going through the motions of getting hold of some of his money with the help of Terry. When the two of them turned up at Terry's bank to withdraw the bank drafts and £10,000 in cash that Goose required, they were ushered into a small side office where they met with the manager and were quickly joined by two officers from SOCA. After much discussion and some raised voices the officers accepted Goose's story that due to the unforeseen circumstances, the sinking of his boat with everything on board he needed some funds to enable him to live again. Not having a bank account in England required some lateral thinking. His friend, Terry, was happy to oblige hence the withdrawal today. The two SOCA officers had no reason to intervene when a private individual transferring his own money to someone else's account. The manager got a telling off for not reporting the transaction. The bank was reported and ultimately fined for not reporting it earlier.

Goose and Terry parted company after they had been to the bank. Goose wished Terry well and hoped he would be able to start his own garage with the money.

Goose for his part went on a shopping spree – his first purchase was a new Range Rover. The bank draft was very convenient and he was able to persuade the garage to provide cash for the change.

Some clothes, a suitcase, toilet bag and contents completed his initial purchases; a travel agent arranged a ferry crossing for him from Portsmouth to Santander. So within a week of collecting his money from Terry's bank he was at sea again, although not his boat, travelling towards Spain where he will be able to renew friendships, open a bank account and start to live again.

*

In Chester, Michael Fitzallen was questioned for two days by the police. Jon Kim, and Tarrant taking it in turns with Kim. Following extensive examination Kim and Tarrant were convinced Fitzallen was guilty, although there was no admission on his part to any of the charges against him. Following the cross examination Jon discussed the interviews at length with the Crown Prosecution Service. The decision was on the evidence the police had was to proceed with the prosecutions.

As is normal there was first, the day after the interviews Fitzallen was brought before magistrates, an initial hearing. He was remanded in custody for fourteen days when the CPS would seek a trial, having prepared an outline of the case. Fitzallen was not at all happy with all this, except he had to confess the jail was far better than anything he had endured in Lima.

The case was set down for the trial in the crown Court at Chester being the 14th of January 2010. Michael will have been on remand and in custody for nearly six months by then. It gave him plenty of time to discuss the upcoming case with his solicitor. The solicitor Mason, had the opportunity to put issues to Fitzallen that were part of the prosecution case. Fitzallen denied all the assertions regarding money laundering, drug smuggling and distribution, and finally murder. He gave his solicitor enough information for a defence to be created in answer to the prosecution case.

*

It was ten o'clock on the 14th of January 2010. The crown court in Chester was packed. The jury had been sworn in and were in their place. The press were present and in their seats, solicitors and barristers had taken their places as had the clerk of the court.

The public gallery was packed. John and Sienna, and Ann Wall, were all present. Rhys and Francesca asked to be excused as they needed to get on with everything at the stables.

"All rise," announced the clerk of the court.

The judge arrived in resplendent red robes and a long wig. He sat on his large chair on a high dais.

The clerk announced that the court was in session and the case was Regina v Fitzallen.

The prosecution barrister opened proceedings. "Ladies and gentlemen of the Jury, you will hear during the course of this trial, how the accused managed to avoid the tax authorities by moving considerable sums of money, on a regular basis, to Spain. In addition you will hear how the accused made money from importing ecstasy pills in large quantities to the UK and arranged distribution throughout the north of England. These pills were of such a strength that in given circumstances people died from taking them. The accused was supplied by a 'Mr Big' type character who will not be standing trial as the evidence against him has been withheld by the accused, and the murder of Sandra Wall by the accused has prevented recorded evidence from 'Mr Big' of his involvement in the trafficking of drugs."

"You will also hear how, desperate for cash, the accused met with Ms Sandra Wall, a business associate, who had obtained ten thousand pounds in cash on behalf of the accused, whilst he was on remand and his passport was in the custody of the court. Evidence will be brought forward to show how on a day in September last year the accused bludgeoned Ms Wall to death, leaving her body in a tank of pig slurry where she died. Her car was secreted on the farm. There are many witnesses and a substantial amount of forensic evidence which will show beyond doubt the accused is guilty on all counts on the charge sheet."

The defence barrister stood up to address the jury and the court.

"Ladies and gentlemen of the jury, my honourable friend has set out a set of circumstances which clearly occurred, but not at the hand of my client.

He is not a money launderer, neither is he a drug dealer, and neither is he a murderer. The prosecution have as they are required to do pre-trial, served details of their evidence on me so we can see the details of the prosecution case. It is a tissue of lies and inaccuracies relying wholly on police evidence. On none of the counts do they have a 'killer blow' to make their case watertight. It will be for you to weigh the evidence before you, to decide on what you hear in this court and nowhere else, that my client the defendant is not guilty."

The court adjourned for lunch whilst the participants took a break, solicitors and barristers in huddles discussing what they had heard and anticipating what was to come. They were all instructed to return for two o'clock.

*

John England's firm Bennett's had the job of sorting out Sandra's estate. In fact it was one of John's partners Andrew Clifford head of the probate department who did the main work on the estate. John England was a beneficiary so it was thought improper for him to be involved. The will Sandra had made was indeed very useful. As she had no children to leave anything to she left the majority of her estate to James England who had suddenly become a very rich boy.

The shareholder agreement with Michael Fitzallen was in fact a partnership agreement and had a very unusual clause which John suspected could have been the root of any argument the two had. The clause he had discovered was that if Michael was convicted of any criminal offence then he would forfeit the three million pounds he had put into the Manchester apartments and no further interest payments or share of rents will be paid. This meant that the whole of the estate in Manchester was available to Sandra and her estate.

Some of the bequests were straight forward so the payments to staff at the stables could be made from the cash in Sandra's bank account. Valuations of all the property Sandra owned, the flat in Chester, the stables and the house, all had to be valued. The land at Sealand was in the ownership of Ann Wall so the reference to this in Sandra's will was an error, but as she was dealing with the insurance claim for the fire, and the sale of the land under an agreement with her mother, she had clearly forgotten that the property was not hers.

Probate was granted in November 2009 which was quite quick for The Revenue, but it enabled the assets to be disposed of and the inheritance tax paid. The asset value as agreed by the district valuer for the Inland Revenue was £450,000 for the flat in Chester, and the stables were valued at £400,000 as the house was unfit for occupation and the stables were a business which had a poor profit record. The refurbished flat over the barn had pushed the value up, the total taxable amount was then £850,000. The shares in Wall's Holdings were exempt from tax as they were able to be passed to family members without a charge to tax.

The tax system allowed for the first £325,000 to be at a nil tax rate, the balance was charged at forty percent. This meant that there was a tax bill of £210,000.

"My god," exclaimed John England as he opened the post one morning at Long Acre Farm.

"Whatever is the matter John?" enquired Sienna.

"The tax on Sandra's estate is £210,000."

"Good lord. It's fortunate that Rhys and Francesca have paid cash for the stables and the house, so there will be money to pay the tax."

"Yes you are right of course darling, it's a great deal of money though."

"I agree, let us hope Fitzallen is guilty and the other half of the ownership of the apartment building in Manchester will come our way."

"Yes I agree, but what this all means is that we should take some tax advice on how we hold the bequests from Sandra. We don't want to burden James eventually with a massive tax bill."

"Not just James," retorted Sienna.

"Yes of course there is your Mum's estate to consider as well."

"I wasn't thinking of that." Said Sienna,

"Oh well what had you in mind?"

"I was thinking of any other little 'Enland's' that might come along"

"My god, you have kept that quiet, how wonderful darling, this requires some more champagne."

CHAPTER 32

At the trial of Michael Fitzallen the court had re-convened to hear the evidence for and against the accused.

The prosecution started the proceedings with their chief witness DS Tarrant. He took the witness stand, and took the oath to tell the truth, the whole truth. After the preliminary questions which the barrister asked to establish Tarrant's credentials and involvement with the case, the barrister started his examination in chief. Tarrant was on the witness stand all day, and half of the following day. To the amazement of the prosecution there was no attempt to cross examine Tarrant by the defence.

The next witness was the forensic pathologist who confirmed that the bloodstain in the Audi car was the blood of Sandra. He was also able to confirm that a hair discovered in the driver's seat matched that of the accused, as well as the fingerprints. There was no challenge to this evidence by the defence barrister.

"Can you please explain how the blood stain became to be in the car and where exactly it was found?" enquired the prosecution barrister.

"Yes Sir, the stain was discovered by the use of a 'Luminol' spray which highlights blood stains. The stain was on the front seat fob of the driver's seat."

"Why did you need to find it with a spray?"

"Well Sir when blood dries and soaks into fabric it changes colour to grey. It was a stain that was not obvious to the eye."

"What tests did you expose the blood sample to determine ownership?"

"Well Sir, we think the sample was between a week and two weeks old. Checking the blood as if it were a recent sample would not work, so we subjected the sample to DNA testing which confirmed that this sample belonged to the deceased."

"What do you suppose was the cause of this drop of blood?"

"Well Sir, we found a brick, with the same blood sample and the deceased had suffered a severe blow to the head, so the assumption which to us seemed perfectly reasonable that it had come from the head wound of the deceased."

"Could the blood stain have come from another source?"

"Well yes, if she had a cut or bled at some time prior to her death then the sample could have appeared that way. However I would have expected an older blood sample to be a different colour than the sample we obtained."

"How old can a blood sample be to carry out the DNA test?"

"There have been tests done on animals that are one hundred thousand years old, and the system still worked."

"Thank you doctor, I have no further questions."

The defence barrister sat in his seat not wishing to cross examine the witness.

"This is all going rather too well," the prosecution barrister whispered to the CPS solicitor sitting behind him.

"Let's see what happens with our next witness."

Called to the stand was John England. He explained his relationship to Sandra, his role in the affairs of Wall's Holdings and the advice he had given Sandra.

"Before we get into your evidence on the legal documents can you please tell the court how often you met with the deceased, and if you were aware if she had suffered any cut or damage before her death?"

"I met with Sandra almost every day, and no I don't recall any cut that she had sustained. She didn't mention it if that was the case."

"Thank you Mr England, now in the matter of the loan by the accused to Wall's Holdings in exchange for a half share in the block of apartments in Manchester, can you please explain to the jury firstly the need for the loan and how the loan was secured from the accused."

John explained the urgent need for the loan, to prevent the banks from foreclosing and taking all the assets of the company. Wall's were in debt to the bank at this point to the tune of about three million pounds. Michael Fitzallen, who Wall's had done a considerable amount of business within the heady days when house prices were rocketing up, was known to us and to Sandra. The benefit this deal was that Fitzallen had the cash, he knew the property and was comfortable in making the investment. He was to receive fifty percent of the net rent after costs. He was getting a considerable income.

"Was there a loan agreement and were you familiar with it?"

"Yes Sir there was. The idea Sandra had, bear in mind she was a qualified solicitor, was to create a company in which the apartment block would be the only asset and then the shares in the company would be owned fifty-fifty with the accused."

"Is that what happened?"

"No in fact the transfer of the apartment block into a company outside Wall's Holdings would have given rise to a very substantial stamp duty charge payable on the transfer of property from Walls to the new company. What happened in the end was a rather unusual arrangement where a partnership with the accused was set up with Wall's as the other party. There seemed no reason in law why a limited company couldn't form a partnership with a private individual, which is what happened."

"As with partnerships in general, Mr England, was there a partnership agreement?"

"Yes Sir there was."

"Were there any unusual clauses to give effect to the arrangement?"

"Well yes it was a rather bespoke document, a copy has been provided. It gave the accused the same benefit as if he had been a shareholder of a company, but only in relation to the block in Manchester. The partnership agreement also had, as most partnership agreements do, arrangements in the event of death, incapacity or falling foul of the law of the individual, and it set out the arrangements that would happen in each of these situations. This protected the Wall's shareholders from the accused should any of the events occur."

"I believe your firm acted for Sandra Wall in the creation of her will. Is that so?"

"Yes Sir."

"Were you or anyone else aware of the most recent will and its contents?"

"No Sir I had no idea that she had made a new will only

three weeks before she died."

"So it is unlikely if you didn't know, a partner of the firm drafted the document, no one else could be aware of it," asked the barrister.

"I cannot see how anyone else could have known. Yes Sir that is correct."

"Part of the bequests in the will relate to the stables in Tarporley. Is that correct? If so can you please explain the relationship to the beneficiary?"

"Yes Sir. The beneficiary in respect of the stables was Rhys Williams. A young man who had answered an advert for a manager of the stables. When he arrived everyone was amazed to find that Rhys Williams was in fact the man who had inherited his father's estate including a forty percent share of Wall's Holdings in 2001. There was a great deal of discussion at the time and it was finally resolved that Rhys didn't want to be part of running a business so he sold his shares to the company. He became very wealthy overnight. As far as I am aware he has been travelling the world since. He returned to the Chester area late last year with a view to finding a business which suited him. He had acquired a keen interest in horses and the job in Tarporley was ideal. In fact as he was known to the family, Sandra offered to sell him half the stables with options to buy the other half and the farmhouse in the event of Sandra moving away or her incapacity or death."

"Is that normal in such arrangements?"

"It is Sir, as I have explained earlier the partnership with the accused had similar clauses."

"Thank you Mr England I have no more questions."

The barrister for the defence rose to his feet and addressed the judge.

"Your Honour, there is clearly a need for me to have the

opportunity to cross examine Mr Rhys Williams. Can you please instruct the prosecution to call him as a witness?"

The prosecution barrister was on his feet before the judge opened his mouth.

"Yes?" enquired the judge.

"I cannot see, your Honour what possible use to either side Mr Rhys Williams can be?"

"In that case if there is nothing to concern you about him giving evidence I shall order that he be called as a witness in this case."

"Mr England," the defence barrister was now addressing John England.

"Can you please tell the jury who drafted the documents relating to the stables?"

"Yes Sir, it was Sandra Wall, as I have already said a qualified solicitor."

"I see, you are aware she no longer has a licence to practice."

"Yes Sir I was aware of that but there is nothing in the Law Society rules preventing her from drafting documents for her own affairs. Clearly she could not do that for third parties."

"Thank you Mr England, as Mr Rhys Williams will be a witness I will save my questions for him, but if I may your Honour," switching his attention now to the judge, "may this witness not be released as I may wish to re-examine him depending on the result of cross examination with Rhys Williams."

"Granted," said the judge who now adjourned the court for lunch.

Rhys Williams was contacted and he raced to Chester to

be ready to appear as a witness.

After reading the oath the barrister for the prosecution spoke to Rhys.

"Can you please give your full name and address and occupation?"

Rhys did as instructed.

"Now Mr Williams, can you please tell the court where you have been for the last two weeks?"

"Yes Sir, my girlfriend Francesca, now my fiancé, and I have been to Mallorca to meet with her family and to obtain the blessing of her parents, and of course the church for our wedding."

"When was the last time you saw Sandra Wall?"

"About two or three days before we left, it was a Wednesday. She was anxious that we should sign all the documents for the stables, and the option to buy the house before we went."

"What did you make of that?"

"Well I thought it was a very generous thing for her to do and typical of her consideration for others, that she wanted us to be secure in our future before meeting with Francesca's parents."

"I see. When did you return?"

"I am afraid I don't recall the exact date, but Sandra had already died and the stables were crawling with police. They also examined our flat over the barn."

"I see. Did you have any idea what the contents of Sandra's will were?"

"No Sir, absolutely not. Francesca and I were totally amazed at her generosity when we discovered the wills' contents when they were read out by the solicitor."

"Thank you Mr Williams, I have no further questions."

Council for the defence who had requested that Rhys attended and gave evidence, having heard what Rhys had to say simply said, "I have no questions for this witness."

"Mr McLeod, are you deliberately wasting this court's time?" the Judge demanded.

"No Sir, I am not."

"What then was the purpose of requesting Mr Williams to race here from Tarporley, no doubt in the midst of looking after the horses, to give evidence at your request and you don't even have one question for him?"

"I beg the courts indulgence your Honour, but in view of the fact there was an option agreement in the documents for the sale of part of the stables to Mr Williams and his now fiancé the benefit of the death of Sandra Wall would have in part been his, as he could have triggered the option agreement. No doubt he has. I had no idea and it was not in any of the disclosures that he was abroad in Spain. I apologise my Lord."

"Seems to me Mr McLeod that you are scratching around for a defence. Have the prosecution finished with their case?"

"Yes my Lord."

"Well then Mr McLeod it is for you to open your case."

McLeod, barrister for the defence called only one witness, the accused, Michael Fitzallen.

Fitzallen was escorted from the dock to the witness stand, where he took the oath. The formalities over McLeod started his cross examination.

"In the matter of the money laundering, were you deliberately laundering money to support the drug business of Niall Phelan?"

"No Sir. The business of Inside Property Investment was a legitimate company engaged in the buy-to-let business. We helped many hundreds of investors buy their investments properties."

"Despite the fact some have become bankrupt because of the investments they made?"

"I understand that is the case Sir, but that is a result of market forces not the scheme IPI had running."

"I see, so why was it necessary to send all the company's cash to Spain on a weekly basis?"

"Sir, my now dead partner Wayne Lamb and I were over a barrel. We started IPI with no money and we couldn't progress without capital. We had no assets on which we could borrow money, so were stuck with Mr Phelan and we had to do as he requested. He was only taking his share from the account in Spain. We suspected there was something irregular about his actions, but you must understand we were at his beck and call. We had no choice. The company's money, our share, remained in Spain."

"Were you surprised when after Wayne's death the balance of the monies in Spain were transferred in total to Ireland?"

"Surprised is not the word Sir, I was horrified and dismayed. I really had no idea what to do. You see I was never a signatory to the Spanish bank account. That was Wayne's end of the operation."

"So what did you do to recover the money that was rightly yours?"

"I was introduced to a man called 'Goose'. It was a nickname after his super yacht called *Wild Goose*. He said for a fee he could recover the money for me."

"Why didn't you go to Phelan and demand the money back?"

"I was nervous of travelling to Ireland. The IRA were still a force. I was not sure if Phelan was part of their organisation. I was a person on my own, there was every prospect I might have been killed."

"So Mr Fitzallen, you did receive your money back via your agent Mr Goose?"

"Yes Sir."

"Mr Phelan was blown up very shortly afterwards, do you know anything about that?"

"No Sir, I assumed it was an action of the IRA and I believe the Irish Police had a similar view according to TV reports."

"Very well, so now to the second charge of drug trafficking."

"Yes Sir, I accept that I was sent a package every month and I sold it to an established dealer Ali Hussain. I had no idea what was in the packages."

"Who sent you the packages?"

"Goose."

"So you say you had no idea what was in the package. Surely you were suspicious in view of the sums of money involved."

"Yes Sir I was, but I was acting as a courier. I guess they could have used DHL or some other company to make the deliveries."

"Do you admit to your part in the deliveries?"

"Yes I do Sir, I cannot deny it, but as I was ignorant of the content. I am not a drug dealer."

"Very well Mr Fitzallen, let us move to the substantive charge of the murder of Sandra Wall. Please tell the court why you were at the stables on that Friday afternoon?"

"Yes Sir, I was there at the invitation of Sandra Wall. She had withdrawn £10,000 from our partnership account to give to me."

"Why did you need that sum?"

"I didn't have a bank account available to me, due to my passport being taken by the court on a lesser matter. I owned a penthouse at Squirrels Chase, and I had arranged to have it furnished by an interior designer, and she needed paying."

"How do you think Sandra Wall ended up in the midden, trussed up in a builder's sack, and her car with your fingerprints on the wheel, parked in the wooden garage?"

"I have no idea Sir, it wasn't me."

"How do explain your fingerprints on the steering wheel?"

"Well Sir I had driven the Audi a few weeks earlier when Sandra and I had a fight and the police ran into the car preventing me from leaving Sandra's garage."

"Is there anything else you wish to say to the court?"

"Only that I am not guilty of any of the charges Sir."

"Thank you Mr McLeod, I think that will do for today," said the Judge, "we will continue tomorrow."

"Court adjourned," called out the clerk of the court.

Michael Fitzallen was escorted back to the cells.

*

"John, how's the case going?" enquired Sienna.

"It's going well. Michael was on the stand today, and lying through his teeth. I guess the prosecution will tear into him tomorrow."

"That's great. Darling the legacy from Sandra is

fantastic. It certainly sets James up for life. What happens if we have another child?"

"In that event we could apply to the court to have the legacy split between both children."

"Oh, I see. Well, Mr Lawyer, you'd better start drafting a document."

"Oh Sienna that is wonderful news."

"Rather than just phone the relatives why don't we ask them over for Sunday lunch. We could have some champagne – it's time everyone lightened up and looked forward."

"You are a one! What a great idea – you fix it."

Sienna didn't need asking twice. She did as she had planned – celebrations all round as the news was broken. Rhys and Francesca came over and the four of them had a champagne supper together, except Sienna drank water.

CHAPTER 33

Chester Crown Court was again packed to hear the details and outcome of the case against Michael Fitzallen, who was still in the witness box. The judge reminded him that he was still under oath. The prosecution were to cross examine him today.

"Mr Fitzallen, where did you go to school?"

"St Judes secondary school in Manchester."

"Did you leave with any qualifications?"

"Yes Sir - four O Levels at C to B in English, Maths, Geography and Art."

"Did you go to university?"

"No Sir."

"So when you left school what did you do?"

"I got a job in an Estate Agents, as a junior. I worked my way up to a negotiator."

"So it reasonable to assert that you are a good talker and negotiator?"

"I like to think so Sir. I have been able to build up a valuable business, Inside Property Investments, which made millions."

"That's good, so would you say you are a good businessman?"

"Yes Sir, thank you, I have received such comments before."

"So Fitzallen as a bright and successful businessman I find it hard to accept your evidence when you said you had no knowledge of the content of the drug parcels you were delivering."

"Well Sir, without knowing what was in the parcel, how was I to know?" He smirked and smiled at the jury.

"When you handed a parcel to Ali Hussain, what happened?"

"How do you mean what happened?"

"Well did he give you any money for instance?"

"Oh yes that was the deal."

"And how much did he give you?"

"Ten thousand pounds Sir."

"Quite a lot of money."

"Yes Sir."

"How was that calculated?"

"Two pounds a pill, oh errr..!"

"Exactly! So you did know that the parcel contained five thousand pills."

"You tricked me Sir, I can't say for sure what was in the package."

"Well Fitzallen we shall leave that to the jury to decide. High finance seems to have been your stock in trade with buying and selling property, what put you on the scent that the arrangement with Phelan was potentially unlawful."

"Oh I wasn't aware it was unlawful, it's just that he was taking half the money to Ireland every week. It didn't seem right somehow."

"Didn't both of you, Lamb and yourself, go and have it out with Phelan?"

"No we were scared to do that Sir."

"So why did you fly to Ireland in 2005 together? You surely didn't go for a holiday?"

"It's a long time ago Sir, I can't remember."

"Can't or won't Fitzallen?"

"No Sir I don't recall."

"Did you stay at Dunmore Hall? Did you meet Sarah Perlaki there?"

"Yes Sir."

"Did you have sex with her?"

Fitzallen went red in the face.

"Well did you?" pressed the prosecution barrister.

"Er, yes Sir."

"So you do recall the visit, I suggest you recall every detail of the visit?"

"Now you remind me Sir I do."

"Well I have an exhibit 'A'." The clerk of the court held up a laptop computer.

"This computer was recovered from your possessions when your apartment was searched in Spain by Sandra Wall. She couldn't open the machine as it was password protected but brought it back to the UK for examination. Forensic computer experts have interrogated this machine and found a document written by you which we think you intended to send to Wayne Lamb, either in Spain or let him read the text in Ireland. What happened to this machine Mr Fitzallen?"

"It was stolen from my room Sir."

"The text that has been recovered is reproduced in document 6B in the bundle my Lord."

The barrister held up the paper document.

"Have you seen this before Fitzallen?"

"Errrr, no Sir."

"Are you sure?"

"Yes Sir, someone else must have written it."

"For the benefit of the court, I have a statement from our computer expert. It is only short. May I read it out your honour?"

"Yes are you putting it in as an exhibit?"

"Yes Sir."

McLeod jumped up from his seat. "My Lord this document has not been disclosed to us. I object."

"My Lord this is simply a statement of fact as to how modern computers store information, there is nothing that changes the content of the document in the bundle."

"Very well proceed. If necessary we will have to call the computer expert so he may be cross examined."

"I understand Sir." The prosecution barrister read out the contents of the document.

Whereas cryptography is the practice of protecting the contents of a message alone, steganography is concerned with concealing the fact that a secret message is being sent as well as concealing the contents of the message. The document we recovered and subsequently printed out as Document 6B was protected using this system.

"This is effectively Sir from the secret side of the

computer. May I now read out document 6B for the benefit of the Jury Sir?"

"Yes please proceed," advised the judge.

Log of the day.

I met with Niall Phelan this morning who told me a story about how his wife and son had been killed by the British army for not stopping at a road block on their way to Belfast.

Niall's son was a roadie for an extreme pop group who had managed to get Niall's son high on drugs. He was always stoned. He looked like a vagrant. His mum and he were on the way to a gig when the event occurred.

Niall is of the opinion that his wife was at her wit's end with the boy and she decided to commit suicide and have the boy killed as well by ignoring the demand to stop on the motorway up to Belfast.

This incident was the catalyst for Niall to set up Drug Users Anonymous – DUA – which was designed to create drugs which were harmless yet gave something of a 'high', but would hopefully wean drug users off the hard stuff.

In the afternoon Niall took me to the laboratory where these new drugs were being synthesised. Quite a smart set up. It transpired that Sarah's brother worked here as well as the professor who had invented the compound.

Michael.

'That is all this document says, so Mr Fitzallen do you recall the visit now?"

"Oh yes I think I do."

"Do you recall writing this log?"

"No comment."

"I will ask you again did you write this log?"

"No comment."

"Well Mr Fitzallen the court will decide if you are suffering from a memory loss or that you don't wish to own up to something else you have done."

"Let us move on Mr Fitzallen, to the murder of Sandra Wall. We have a witness who can be called if necessary but her affidavit is in the bundle Sir, Daisy, a stable girl who saw you and Sandra on the day in question as she was leaving the stables at the end of a busy week for her home. Her statement says she rode her bicycle home to the far side of Tarporley. On arriving home she realised she had left her coat at the stables, so she returned. When questioned she says she did not see Sandra Wall drive past her on her way back to Long Acre farm. When Daisy arrived at the stables you were still there, she said you looked flustered. Daisy asked where Sandra was, you told her she had driven home. Daisy found that odd as she had not seen Sandra or her car drive past her on either the ride home or back to the stables. So Mr Fitzallen what had happened to Sandra Wall?"

"Search me I don't know."

"Let's go back a bit you met her to collect the large sum of £10,000. Did she have the money?"

"Yes Sir."

"What did you want it for?"

"I have told you to pay for the furnishing of my penthouse at Squirrels Chase."

"I see, who was the interior designer?"

"It was Pam of Pam's Pads in Chester."

"And you paid her all the money?"

"Yes Sir."

"Can you look at the bundle marked Pam's Pads and look at her statement of account. It shows that you paid her

£8,000 of the £25,000 you owed her. I have here an up to date statement as of yesterday which shows you still owe her £17,000. Why would that be if you had paid her the £10,000 you assert?"

"She is a bit batty. She can't add up properly."

"You paid her cash I assume?"

"Yes, there is no credit into her bank account of £10,000 from the day you were at the stables with Sandra, and last week."

"I can't answer that. She may have put the money under her mattress to avoid paying tax on it." Michael smirked again and smiled at the Jury, believing he had won a point with this barrister.

"Very well Michael, so assuming you did pay Pam the money, what did you use to buy the following: a ferry ticket from Liverpool to Dunlagoire, a hotel in Wicklow, an Allied Irish bank card worth 3,000 euros, an air ticket on Iberia to Lima and onto La Paz in Bolivia?"

"I don't know what you are talking about."

"Assuming you were going to travel to Bolivia, you would need money there, how did you ensure you had funds there?"

"I deny I was going to go there."

"Well your bank in Puerto Banus had an instruction from you to send one million euros to a bank in Bolivia. How do you explain that?"

"I can't except they may have me confused with someone else."

"Oh, someone like Wayne Lamb your dead business partner?"

"I don't see how they could do that?"

362

"Really, I have in the bundle for you to look at confirmation of a flight booking made by you in Paris at Iberia's office, that you booked a flight to Bolivia. Very difficult for you to deny that as it was the flight to Bolivia that we radioed to have you arrested on arrival, as Mr Wayne Lamb, your dead partner. You were using his passport. I put it to you Mr Fitzallen your flight to Bolivia was to try and avoid arrest in the UK. You were breaking your bail conditions weren't you?"

"I don't recall the bail conditions."

"Did you tell Sandra Wall that was what you were going to do?"

"No I did not."

"No because being a solicitor she would have told the police the minute you left the stables."

"No comment."

"You became angry, that she would upset your plans, so you decided on the spur of the moment as she bent into the car to get the money for you, you hit her hard on the back of the head. She bled slightly onto the car seat. You then trussed her up in a builder's bag. You moved her in the bag to the midden. You placed more bricks in the bag to weigh her down and pushed her in. She drowned in that awful mess of a tank. That's what you did Fitzallen isn't it?"

"No comment."

"I have no further questions your Honour," said the prosecution counsel.

"We shall have closing statements tomorrow morning before I send the jury out for a verdict.

The court is adjourned," said the Judge.

*

The following day the two barristers made their final submissions. The prosecution first, then the defence. They were to all intents and purpose a repeat of the opening remarks.

"Ladies and Gentlemen of the Jury. You have heard the prosecution and the defence arguments in these matters. It is for you to come to a unanimous verdict on all three counts. You are not to communicate with anyone else on mobile phones et cetera. Please advise the clerk when you have arrived at your decision."

Within an hour of being sent out the jury was back. The clerk requested that the foreman of the jury tell the court of their verdict on the following counts.

"What is your verdict on the money laundering charge?"

"Guilty."

"What is your verdict on the drug dealing charge?"

"Guilty."

"What is your verdict on the charge of the murder of Sandra Wall?"

"Guilty."

There was a gasp in the court.

"Michael Fitzallen, you have been found guilty on all three charges before you. You are a dangerous and manipulative man. I sentence you to five years in prison for the money laundering charge, I sentence you to ten years in prison on the drug dealing charge, and finally I sentence you to life imprisonment for the murder of Sandra Wall. You are to serve a minimum of twenty one years before parole is considered. All sentences are to be served concurrently. Take him down."

Michael Fitzallen was taken from the dock down the stairs straight to the cells to begin his life sentence.

"Kim, thank you for clearing up the Wall's murder. Pity we couldn't nail Goose - I guess we will one day. So you retire in a few days time and start your new consultancy for us and Greater Manchester Police. Are you looking forward to it?" said the Chief Constable.

"I am, Sir. It will be totally different but exciting and may give me some time to myself."

"Good luck, Jon, you will be hearing from us soon I'm sure."

Jon Kim left the employment of Cheshire Police at the end of the week to continue his semi-retirement. He was ready to accept the next challenge presented to him either by Cheshire Police or Greater Manchester Police.

*

Seven months later, Sienna England gave birth to a daughter – Sandra Ann. She was a beautiful little girl and the pride of her parents and grandparents. John England then applied to the court to split Sandra's bequest which was granted.

John England also applied to the court to have the partnership agreement between Michael Fitzallen and Wall's Holdings to be declared void, as a consequence of Fitzallen breaching the specific terms of the agreement. The court made an order to that effect.

CHAPTER 34

Ann Wall, having recovered from the torture of the trial into the murder of Sandra, decided the only way forward was to be positive. Positive to a fault. She took over the organisation of the wedding of Rhys and Francesca with gusto. This wasn't the first wedding she had organised, Sienna and John's wedding was some time ago now but she had the file, and the check list so she set about all the jobs to be done to organise such an event. It would be the highlight of the year.

Whilst Ann was busy, so too were John and Sienna arranging the final bits and pieces of the bequests set out in Sandra's will. The share splits were easy, as it was simply a matter of completing some forms for Company's House and re-registering the shareholders and their various interests. The Wall's holdings accounts took a sudden leap forward in strength. The company now owned in its entirety the whole of the block of apartments in Manchester. The even better news was that the block was fully let and the rents were increasing slowly. Sienna took it upon herself to be the main shareholder director of Wall's to run this business. It was all Wall's had, but valued now at ten million, with no borrowings, and fully let it was not a major issue. She visited Manchester and the agents about once a month, so she could keep on top of maintenance, cleaning, security and all those boring things that just have to be attended to.

"Is that John England?"

"It is, who is this?"

"It's Terry Pritchard, you may remember me Sir?"

"I do Terry, good to hear from you, how are things?"

"Well Mr England, I had some good fortune helping Mr Goose with his finances once he was released from prison. Because I helped him he made me a very handsome gift. I now have my own garage repair shop specialising in the Jaguar Range Rover range of cars and the odd classic car."

"Well Terry that is wonderful. Good luck to you."

"Mr England, I recall that you own a Range Rover, when you need a service or repair would you think of me?"

"Certainly Terry, but where are you based?"

"I have a garage in Baughton in Chester Sir. It doesn't matter where I am based, because we come and collect your vehicle, leaving you a very clean and tidy Volkswagen Golf, for the day. When we have finished with your car we bring it back to you washed and polished, and cleaned inside, fully serviced with the official stamp which will not invalidate your warranty, if you have any left."

"Well Terry that is an excellent service, I bet you get a lot of customers for that?"

"It's a matter of becoming known Sir, the business is growing slowly."

"Terry you deserve it to be a success. Can I book our car in next Wednesday?"

"You certainly can Sir, we will pick it up at eight thirty if that's okay?"

"Just fine, it's in the diary. Well done Terry. Bye."

At that moment Sienna came into the kitchen with James in tow.

"You will never guess who has just phoned?"

"No, I can't."

"It was Terry Pritchard, cutting a long story he has his own garage and I have booked the Range Rover in for service next Wednesday. He brings a courtesy car for us to use during the day whilst he services the Range Rover."

"John, I wish you would ask me first, I am booked in to go to Manchester that day."

"No worries, go in the Golf which he will lend us."

"Oh alright, I just wish you wouldn't interfere."

John decided not to reply and get on with his other jobs.

*

"Hello Mum, how are things?" enquired Sienna.

"Fine, I am just very busy. I have made arrangements for the marquee people to come and visit the farm and the field where it is to go, next Wednesday. I hope that's alright?"

"Not you too?"

"What do you mean?"

"Well John has just booked the Range Rover in for a service that day and now you have the marquee people coming, and I am booked to be in Manchester. No one ever thinks to ask me first."

"Oh I am sorry dear, I don't want to put them off because they are getting booked up."

"John is in his office over the yard now, can you ring him mum and sort it out I am afraid I can't help, bye."

Despite the minor irritations the England family and Ann Wall were getting on famously.

The wedding for Rhys and Francesca was in that hold phase. The big items all booked, and smaller contractors had the date in their diaries but it was too soon to press buttons on flowers, cars and the like.

"The farmhouse is coming on a treat Rhys, the builders say they will be finished in a month."

"Well we shall see, but it will be really exciting to move in. Daisy is thrilled that the flat she always thought was to be hers soon will be."

"Yes darling, I am going to Manchester with Sienna on Wednesday, do you think you could drop me off at the farm first thing, so we can go in the same car," said Francesca.

"Oh, that's a new one, what are you going to do in Manchester?" enquired Rhys.

"Well, I am actually going to look at wedding dresses."

"Ah so I hope you have your credit card with you."

"Yes that will be with me."

"Who is looking after James for the day?"

"I gather Dot is doing that."

"Okay that's all fine by me, have fun," said Rhys.

*

The month of June arrived as if by magic. Everyone had been so busy and caught up with the excitement of the big day. Daisy had moved into the flat over the barn at the stables. She had been made manager of the stables. Rhys and Francesca had moved into the farmhouse, once they had sorted out the carpets, curtains, and furniture. They had four bedrooms now and in view of the family coming over from Mallorca, some would be staying in the farmhouse, every room needed furnishing. Rhys decided that the cost of new stuff was far too much so he and Francesca went to the local sale rooms and bought very cheaply furniture for the bedrooms and dining room. They splashed out on beds and lounge furniture, the stone floor in the farmhouse kitchen was crying out for a large refectory table. They managed to find just what they wanted at a sale, and the eight chairs to go with it. The house was finished.

On June the 10th the farmyard at Long Acre Farm looked more like a parking lot for lorries. The marquee firm had brought three lorries loaded with flooring, tents, poles, tent lining and so on.

Once the bare bones of the encampment were laid the caterer's equipment appeared, more vehicles. By the end of the day all the tents were up. The floors were down the kitchen and bar area ready. The following day marquee linings were erected. Fridges were filled with food and a mobile cold room arrived. The bar was set up and there seemed to be enough booze to sink a ship.

The carpet was laid in the marquee, tables laid out as well as a dance floor and area for the band and disco. Electricians were all over the place with a stand by generator, for lighting of the buildings, the farmhouse and trees. The car parking area was illuminated. Then it rained.

"Oh my goodness, let's hope this is just a passing shower," implored Sienna.

Rhys and Francesca arrived. To their amazement what had been an empty field a few days before was now like a small village. The excitement was now at fever pitch. As Rhys and Francesca were there Ann arrived, as did John and Sienna with James by her side. Immediately Francesca picked up James and gave him a big hug.

"Well what do you think of it you two?" enquired Ann.

"It's just wonderful Ann, you have done a fantastic job. It is truly fantastic. I daren't think what all this will cost me," said a rather worried Rhys.

"You don't need to worry about that Rhys. All this is my wedding present to you both, I hope you have a wonderful day," said Ann.

"Oh Ann you can't do that."

"I can and I will and I have. Most of the contractors have been paid. It's some of the small things like photographs and the like that just need paying for."

"Goodness me," said Rhys. Francesca gave Ann a big hug with one arm the other still holding James.

"You have all been so incredibly kind to us I have no words to express it. Thank you Ann," said Rhys.

Saturday 12th June 2010 came and went in a flash. The farm was full of cars and people, relatives flown in from abroad. The whole place was like a carnival. Rhys and Francesca were married. Mr and Mrs Williams. Francesca's father's champagne disappeared like water in sand. The following day the happy couple left for a week's honeymoon in Paris. Ann returned to her cottage in Tarporley totally exhausted.

On the Monday morning the 14th June, the vicar's wife called to see how Ann was. She knocked on the door several times but there was no answer. She could hear Purdey inside, which was unusual because Ann took Purdey everywhere with her.

"Is that John England?"

"Yes it is. Who is this?"

"I am the vicar's wife, I don't seem to be able to rouse Ann today. Purdey is in the cottage, but no sign of Ann."

"Okay we will come over, we have a key."

In about half an hour John and Sienna arrived having

left James in the care of Dot. They gingerly unlocked the front door and Purdey gave them an excited welcome. She was hungry and thirsty.

"Mum, it's Sienna, can I come up?"

No response. John and Sienna made their way gingerly up the stairs, slowly opening the bedroom door. There was Ann, asleep. Having her last sleep. Her long lasting sleep.

"Oh John," cried Sienna, "she's gone." They hugged one another.

"She looks so peaceful."

They both went downstairs and called the doctor who came within the hour. He visited Ann, and said to John and Sienna that they were correct she was in fact dead. I knew it would not be long for her."

"Oh, how did you know that?" asked Sienna.

"She has had an acute cancer on the brain, I was surprised she lasted so long. It was possibly the relief that the wedding was over that let her die. The organising of the wedding I think kept her going until now."

"She never said a word of this," cried Sienna.

"No, she didn't want anyone to know, it was her secret, in fact she said it was a secret kept in her secret side."

THE END

AUTHOR'S NOTE

During the writing of the five books in this series I've been extremely fortunate to receive guidance, advice and knowledge from many people many of whom I've made specific reference to in the leaves of the five books which make up the series: Time's Up, England's Wall, Laundry, Cracks in the Wall, and Secret Side. Without their help I couldn't have managed to fulfil the task. The most important person who has typed the manuscripts, Sheila McEwan, gets extra special mention – thank you, Sheila.

My daughter in law has read and proofed the text, a job which is essential. She has made an excellent job, so thank you again Vanessa.

It's very strange how events in the books sometimes took on a life of their own. It's been a very unexpected experience and, for instance in England's Wall Roger Whiteside was found to have been hit on the head and thrown over the suspension footbridge into the River Dee in Chester. I went to that bridge to make sure that the deed could in fact be done. Imagine my surprise when I discovered a plaque on the bridge indicating that the bridge had been opened in 1917 by then Mayor of Chester, the Rt Hon Alfred Wall. I had no idea that the fictional Wall family I chose would have the same name as a dignitary in Chester. The fate of Jon Kim is now in the hands of two police forces and, of course, he is free to pursue any projects of his own. My next novel will be a standalone detective fiction featuring Jon Kim. Thank you for choosing to read my books. I hope you have enjoyed reading them as much as I have enjoyed writing them.

I am now working on my next novel featuring DCI Jon Kim in his rather unusual role for two police authorities. It is called *Match Day Murder*.

ABOUT THE AUTHOR

Robert Jordan has put together a pentalogy of novels following the fortunes of the Wall family. *Secret Side* is the final in the series.

Jordan has drawn on his life long experience as a Chartered Surveyor to inform the plot with business and property dealings and intrigue. Jordan started his own business in 1974 and has been heavily involved in property throughout his working life. His experience of writing professional articles and reports has informed his writing.

He is a keen sailor, classic car owner and sometime golfer. Married with two children and five grandchildren.

The author's website: www.rajordan.co.uk

Printed in Great Britain
by Amazon